Lady Derring Takes a Lover

She'd taken two steps when he said, his voice raised only a little, "Lady Derring . . . something puzzles me."

She halted.

Closed her eyes.

Took a shuddering breath for courage.

Turned back to him. From the relatively safe distance of three feet, she said, "Surely not. We've established you know everything."

His smile was small and patient. "You seem to excel at so very much here at The Grand Palace on the Thames. Yet you can't seem to disguise how much you want me."

By Julie Anne Long

Lady Derring Takes a Lover

The First Time at Firelight Falls
Dirty Dancing at Devil's Leap
Wild at Whiskey Creek
Hot in Hellcat Canyon

The Legend of Lyon Redmond
It Started with a Scandal
Between the Devil and Ian Eversea
It Happened One Midnight
A Notorious Countess Confesses
How the Marquess Was Won
What I Did for a Duke
I Kissed an Earl
Since the Surrender
Like No Other Lover
The Perils of Pleasure

Lady Derring Takes a Lover

THE PALACE OF ROGUES

JULIE ANNE LONG

AVONBOOKS

An Imprint of HarperCollins*Publishers*

This is a work of fiction. Names, characters, places, and incidents are products of the author's imagination or are used fictitiously and are not to be construed as real. Any resemblance to actual events, locales, organizations, or persons, living or dead, is entirely coincidental.

First Avon Books mass market printing: March 2019

Print Edition ISBN: 978-0-06-286746-9
Digital Edition ISBN: 978-0-06-286747-6

Cover design by Guido Caroti
Cover illustration by Juliana Kolesova
Cover photograph © Peter Dedeurwaerder/Shutterstock (stairs)

FIRST EDITION

19 20 21 22 23 QGM 10 9 8 7 6 5 4 3 2 1

Lady Derring Takes a Lover

Chapter One

LADY DERRING had been raised to believe breeding and manners were a bulwark against all of life's vicissitudes. So as she peered through her black veil at her husband's solicitor, her spine was straight, her chin was high, and her brow was as smooth as the curve of the Chinese porcelain urn she'd wrested from the hands of the man who had come to take it away this morning.

"But I've a list!" He'd thrust it at her. "And I've a crew what's been promised a day's pay!"

He did indeed have a list.

One could very nearly ruffle its pages like a book.

It read like a diary of every beautiful thing her husband had ever purchased.

With the possible exception of her, of course.

By the bottom of the first page (which ended with "statue, naked, stone, Leda and Swan") suspicion had crept in like a killing frost. Her heart felt like a foreign object she'd inadvertently swallowed. Lumpen, frozen, jaggedly lodged.

She took a breath.

And then another.

Only then was she able to look up at the man through her eyelashes. "I'll just have a more thorough look at this, shall I?" she said brightly and firmly, in her best, most imperious countess voice.

And then using the only weapons she had at her disposal—guilt, widow's weeds, and limpid brown eyes—she somehow managed to herd him back out the door.

She aimed a black look at the perfidious butler who'd accepted a bribe to let him in.

He had the grace to cast his eyes sideways.

Then she'd called for the carriage and paid her first unannounced visit upon her husband's solicitor four days after her husband's funeral and one day earlier than Tavistock, in a hushed, sympathetic voice, had arranged for her to visit him.

Mr. Tavistock, round, balding, and self-satisfied, had been startled to see her, but blunt. Doubtless he charged extra for blow cushioning.

"Oh, yes. Devil of a way to find out, so soon after the funeral," he mused. "But our Derring hadn't an honest sou to his name when he cocked up his toes. Was in debt up to his eyeballs. I daresay the whole of his estate was held together by credit."

Her heart was now thudding inside her like a trapped beast. It was the only thing she could feel. Her tightly folded hands, gloved in smooth black kid, felt oddly separate from her, like a creature that had crept into her lap looking for refuge.

This peculiar numbness was about to become a luxury, that much was clear. Her wits were going to need to get involved.

No one, particularly not her late husband, had ever valued her for wits.

Oh, but she possessed them.

"This is all that's left of his estate, if you'd like to have a look." He opened a drawer and grabbed a fistful of papers. "I'm sure it can be reconciled with the list of items you have in your hand."

She gingerly accepted them.

While Tavistock silently watched, she read through three of the bills.

The first was for "statue, naked, stone, Leda and Swan." From a mason in Sussex.

The third was from Madame Le Fleur. "Gloves, black kid."

The ones she was wearing.

That was when she stopped. She laid the bills carefully back down on Tavistock's spotless desk and returned her hands to the safety of her lap.

Tavistock didn't say a word. He began to fidget with a quill. He had the air of a man who was mightily struggling not to glance at a clock.

She cleared her throat. "But Derring was wealthy—"

"Was," Tavistock repeated laconically.

"Perhaps there is a more recent will, Mr. Tavistock, reflective of more current holdings." She heard her own voice as if through a pillow. "Perhaps you could ask the nice young clerk outside the door to have another look through—"

"There was but one will and one Earl of Derring, the one that you and I knew and loved well, rest his soul."

And then Mr. Tavistock had the nerve to bow his head.

Delilah stared at him, fascinated and repulsed. The

stink of sanctimony clung to him like the smoke from Derring's foul cigars—the ones that called to mind the meaty breath of a fanged carnivore, mingled with the things the gardener burned after a day of trimming the roses, with a top note of perhaps leather.

The only things Tavistock had "loved" were Derring's connections and those foul cigars.

And the most feverish emotion she'd felt for Derring was gratitude.

She had tried to love him. She'd wanted nothing more. She'd yearned for a house full of children and laughter and friends and musical evenings, a house of easiness and joy. She'd struggled to find a handhold—a hearthold?—some endearing habit, like humming when he read the newspaper, the way her father had for instance, some little *ember* of charm or vulnerability that she could somehow fan into love. Derring was fifteen years her senior. And by the time they'd met, his personality was as fixed and impermeable as those statues he loved to collect.

Her wedding night—a revelation composed of sweaty grappling, muttered instructions (*If you would be so good as to shift to the left, Delilah?*), and a grunted *sorry, sorry* and *thank you*—put paid to those notions. Clearly romantic love was a myth, like unicorns or leprechauns, used to lure young women into marriages in order to perpetuate the species and produce heirs so future generations could go on enjoying being aristocrats.

She had lavished Derring with kindness. She hoped he'd never known the difference. Perhaps the failing was, indeed, hers.

Tavistock cleared his throat. "You're still on the young side, if I may be so bold, and you could mar—" He stopped abruptly. "Well, perhaps you could marry a widower with children who need a mother, if you can find one."

She was glad of the veil. Shame and fury arrived in swift succession, nauseating and scorching. If she couldn't provide an heir in the six years she'd been married to Derring, what good was she to anyone, really?

And now she would be passed about among relatives, like the little carved stool from India that Derring had bought for no reason, and which was shunted from room to room, from house to house, always a little out of place, a little in the way. She'd last seen it in the library, where she'd barked her shin on it.

"Thank goodness I have you to advise me, Mr. Tavistock."

"It's no trouble at all, Lady Derring," he said, surrendering to a glance at the clock.

"Am I keeping you from another appointment?"

He looked surprised. "I'm about to set out on holiday with my wife and family. Long overdue. Long overdue. Nothing like the seashore, isn't that so?" he said brightly.

She merely stared at him.

Their heads turned in unison when voices suddenly rose in the little anteroom where Tavistock's young clerk sat—a woman's, dulcet and cajoling, determined; the young clerk's, polite and firm.

Delilah cleared her throat. "Mayhap some item has been overlooked in the accounting. If you would be so kind as to review it one final—"

"I assure you, Lady Derring, we do not make mistakes here at Tavistock, Urqhardt, Ramsey, and Donne."

Unctuous toad didn't think her sentences were worth finishing, apparently.

"Isn't it odd that I should find so little reassurance in assurances of your firm's infallibility, Mr. Tavistock?"

He blinked as if she'd flicked water into his eyes.

She could hear her mother's appalled voice now. *Irony will not catch a husband, Delilah.*

That had been the entire point of her, once it had become clear that she was going to be pretty: to catch a husband. They'd all been relieved, Delilah included. It meant she might be a savior, not a burden, to her family. Her father was a minor lord, but the guillotine of poverty had gleamed over her entire childhood such that they seemed to live in held breath, hushed tension, lest one wrong move bring it crashing down.

That the Earl of Derring had been smitten with Delilah was seen as both an act of providence and a triumph of her mother's careful training. Be sweet, be dutiful, be awestruck. Yield to his needs and moods. Flatter his vanity. *Lilt,* do not *declare.*

If only her mother had taught her the pitfalls of trusting a man completely.

Funny. Delilah never *lilted* in her private thoughts.

And in her fantasies, she never yielded.

"You ought not worry, Lady Derring. Women who look like you need never go hungry, if they prefer not to."

Tavistock would never have dared to use that melting, insinuating tone only a few days ago. Inside her unpaid-for gloves, her hands had gone clammy.

And now she understood that the only bulwark against vicissitudes was a husband.

She imagined Mr. Tavistock climbing aboard and rolling off his poor, unfortunate wife. Something of her thoughts must have radiated clear through the veil, because Mr. Tavistock's little smile vanished.

He cleared his throat. "As you are aware, the properties in Devonshire and Sussex will now go to the next male heir, a nephew, since there was no male issue of the marriage . . ."

Issue was a grotesque word.

"But—" He froze as some realization struck.

Suddenly Tavistock pulled out a drawer and slapped something that jingled on the desk between them. A great collection of keys on a ring.

"I'd nearly forgotten. Derring owned one building outright. Think he won it in a card game or some such. The one at 11 Lovell Street by the docks. It is now yours."

She looked down at the keys.

"The one on Lovell Street by the docks," she repeated slowly.

Derring had never mentioned it. She choked back a nearly hysterical laugh. But only scoundrels and rogues lingered by the docks. Countesses did not go by the docks.

"A right wreck of a building, I believe," Tavistock continued blithely. He cast an eye on the wall clock. Busy men like him could only apportion a certain amount of time to explaining the destruction of her life.

Delilah swept the keys toward her. Clutched them in her hand. "What kind of building is it?"

"Don't know, to be honest. All I know is you've a week to vacate the London townhouse, as Derring is in arrears."

The voices on the other side of the door rose suddenly to argument volumes.

The doorknob rattled.

The door was wrenched open a few inches.

It seemed to be yanked shut again.

Then was wrenched open a few more inches. Delilah could see a woman and the young clerk who manned a small desk outside were doing battle over the doorknob.

It was wrenched open another few inches.

"For heaven's sake, Mr. Mackintosh," the woman cajoled, "he'll see *me*, no need to fuss so. By the by, have you gone and had a new coat made? You look *dashing*. I think you're finally growing into your looks."

Paralyzed by the confusing compliment, the clerk turned pink and loosened his grip on the doorknob.

The woman's perfume—sultry, celebratory—preceded her, but the rest of her arrived in a swirl of the most dashing black silk widow's weeds Delilah had ever seen.

Mr. Tavistock shot to his feet so swiftly his chair staggered drunkenly.

"Angelique—er—Mrs. Breedlove—"

His head ricocheted between Delilah and the woman and back again like a pendulum on a clock.

"Tavvie, darling," the woman interjected crisply.

"I'll be brief. I've creditors knocking at my actual door. Not the metaphorical sort of knocking." She rapped her knuckles sharply on his desk. "This sort. You've not responded to the messages I've sent over, so I'll do you the credit of assuming you've been busy, rather than neglectful."

She tipped her head ever-so-slightly coquettishly, and the feather in her hat—no veil for *this* widow—bobbed. Delilah caught a glimpse of a pert nose and large wide-set light eyes. It was hard to know how old she was; her brisk confidence made Delilah feel, for an instant, childlike.

Also, the woman was frightened.

Women who go through life wearing masks learn to recognize the ones other women wear to get through their days. It was in how her voice was vivacious but pitched a bit too high, the tightness of her jaw and around her eyes, how her fingers gripped the edge of her pelisse.

Despite her own predicament, Delilah's heart squeezed in sympathy.

"Mrs. Breed—" Tavistock began. Sounding a little desperate.

She ignored him. "I know dear Derring, rest his soul, would not have cocked up his toes without making arrangements for my pension. He vowed that he would on several memorable occasions. The matter is now of some urgency. Perhaps you can be a dear and facilitate this for me?"

Tavistock's eyes darted toward Delilah.

Then he looked down at his desk and heaved a defeated sigh.

The ensuing brief silence rang like the moment after a gunshot.

Realization seeped in, the way blood seeped out of a wound.

Delilah gave a soft laugh.

It marked the first bitter sound she'd ever made.

Well, then. And so it seemed the awfulness of the past few days contained infinite strata and variety.

And to think she'd once or twice indulged in the luxury of feeling *bored*.

Mrs. Breedlove—if that was indeed her name—gave a start, a hand over her heart, and pivoted toward Delilah's chair. "I beg your pardon . . . I didn't see . . . I'm terribly sorry to intrude."

Delilah slowly, slowly pushed the veil up off her face. And stood.

All was so silent, and she felt so raw, the very air seemed to hurt as it pressed against her skin.

She wanted to see that woman clearly.

She wanted that woman to see her clearly, too.

Mr. Tavistock's face had gone gray. He'd frozen like a statue. He was probably three seconds away from wringing his hands.

And all of this confirmed the suspicion, which had gathered, like a bath of icy acid, in her gut.

"If I were you, I would never take up gambling, *Tavvie* darling," Delilah said. Apparently she had great, great stores of suppressed irony to call upon. She didn't take her eyes away from the woman's face. "You haven't a game face. Perhaps you ought to introduce us."

Mr. Tavistock sighed again. And then resolutely,

like a man charged with issuing a verdict in court, cleared his throat.

"Angelique," he said evenly, calmly to the woman. The woman glanced toward him, then back at Delilah. She'd sensed something was amiss, and her expression hovered somewhere between concern and wicked curiosity. She seemed perfectly willing to commit to either one. "I will speak to you after I conclude my business with the Countess of Derring."

He laid those last three words down slowly, evenly, like bricks.

Tavvie didn't have a game face.

But Angelique, it seemed, did.

She didn't flinch. She didn't blink. But nevertheless Delilah thought she could see the moment her heart stopped, for just one second. She'd gone motionless, frozen like one of Derring's statues, half turned toward Tavistock, half turned toward Delilah.

She met Delilah's stare.

Some emotion, very like pity but also like shame, scudded across Mrs. Breedlove's features.

Her chin went up ever so slightly.

"My apologies for the interruption, Lady Derring, and my condolences on your loss," she said quietly. "I shall speak with you another day, Mr. Tavistock."

She closed the door very, very gently behind her.

Chapter Two

MRS. BREEDLOVE'S perfume lingered, but the rest of her was gone when Delilah emerged into the anteroom five minutes later.

Young Mr. Mackintosh was behind his desk, the pink of his blush still fading from his skin. The poor dear was still a few years away from being old enough to savagely disappoint a woman.

How much he knew or understood about anything he'd just heard was a mystery, and she supposed, in the end, it didn't matter.

To his credit, he looked distressed.

"Thank you, and good day, Mr. Mackintosh," she said.

"Lady Derring, Mrs. Breedlove wanted me to give this to you."

He leaped to his feet and handed a sheet of folded foolscap to her.

Her hands, awkward with nerves, fumbled as she opened it, and read:

I recommend sewing your jewels into the hems of your dresses before you flee into the night.

It was unsigned. The handwriting was tidy and elegant, even a little prim. It might have been an invitation to tea from the Duchess of Brexford, whom Delilah despised and whose approval she had craved because her husband had wanted her to crave it and didn't every woman want what her husband wanted?

Delilah growled low in her throat and crunched the note in her fist.

The extraordinary . . . the unmitigated . . . the *gall!*

Hot, furious breaths shredded her lungs as she pulled them in and out.

To write to her as though they were equals!

But aren't you? said some unwelcome, bitterly rational voice in her head.

Two women impoverished by the same man?

And Delilah was *no one* without a man, wasn't that so? Her title meant not a thing when she hadn't inherited it and she was poor.

Vertigo swept in. The husband, the land, the manners, the clothes, the vases and rugs, the friends, the horses, the barouche, the jewels, her favorite chair by the solarium window. How odd that they formed the fabric of her life, and yet none of it was hers. Her very personality wasn't hers. It was something she'd donned like widow's weeds or a pantomime costume in order to play her role. Who was she? Did she even exist? Perhaps this was all a dream. But would that be better?

She held the crumpled note in her fist while Mackintosh eyed her warily, his shoulders hunched as though he was prepared to dive beneath his desk. Perhaps her expression suggested she intended to hurl it.

She stuffed it into her reticule instead, next to that jingling ring of keys.

Her life thus far: nearly two decades of fear and ceaseless tension of poverty, followed by six years of relief and luxury and boredom and tolerance.

And now, it seemed, hideous fear was having a turn again.

She thought these thoughts on the way back to a house that didn't belong to her, in the carriage that didn't belong to her, drawn by horses that didn't belong to her, driven by a driver whose expression was, as he handed her in, cagey—when days before it had been all warm deference. She knew that all the servants in London were part of a circulatory system and word would get out, quickly, that Derring's life was being dismantled because he owned none of it.

The shock. The shame.

She leaned her aching head against the cool carriage window.

She'd likely return to a townhouse of dead fires and unlit stoves and dark chandeliers.

The staff would, quite pragmatically, flee if they hadn't already with their satchels of belongings (but hopefully not the silver), confident of being absorbed into other fine households, because Delilah had a particular skill for hiring the very best staff.

With the exception of Dorothy. Delilah had taken on Dorothy as a lady's maid—such a sweet girl, all shy smiles and eagerness to please—in a fit of outraged mercy when she'd been dismissed without references by the Duchess of Brexford. But a few years with Dorothy had brought Delilah closer to an understanding of martyrdom. Dot burned, spilled, dropped, and broke things. Daily. She tried so very hard and meant so very well and yet she revealed a talent for nothing except cheerful devotion. Delilah hadn't the heart to let her go.

What would become of Dorothy?

Or of Mrs. Helga, the magically talented cook, warm of heart and loud of laugh, who was the heartbeat of the kitchen? Her apple tarts and lemon seed cakes and rich sauces were the stuff of heaven. Countesses and duchesses would wrestle in a pit of mud in the middle of Almack's for the services of a cook like that.

And what about me?

Thank God her parents were now dead, she thought mordantly. They would not have to witness this or experience poverty again.

Should she throw herself on the mercy of Derring's nephew, who would inherit the family estate? Should she write to her cousins in America to ask if they could use an additional relative to feed? Her mind recoiled from every option it touched on.

Perhaps this was why their circle of acquaintances, and even women she'd considered friends—like Lady Ragland and Lady Corvalle, women with whom she'd dined and shopped and gossiped—had seemed to subtly fan away from her after Derring's funeral, like fleas disembarking from a dead dog. They'd all known. A little debt was one thing. Penury was quite another, she supposed.

The scorching shame of it.

She shifted her reticule in her lap and the great wad of keys jingled.

She poured them out into her hand and as she did, the crumpled message tumbled out with it.

She'd forgotten she'd stuffed it in there.

After a hesitation, she smoothed it out and read it again in the carriage's dim light.

And now she understood why she'd kept it.

Because there was something indomitable about it. A sort of dry, worldly wit that wasn't without sympathy. It included Delilah in the joke. Inherent in it was the assumption that Delilah was that sort of woman, too: Strong. Mordant. Resilient.

Was she?

If she had loved her husband this revelation of—betrayal? Humiliation? Neither word truly fit, if she was being honest, and all she wanted, for the rest of her life, was to be honest, to be who she truly was—might have been the undoing of her.

How odd to regret that she wasn't undone by the knowledge of her husband's mistress.

Her pride was scorched. But scorched pride seemed the least of her concerns.

And it seemed she hadn't known her husband at all, because he hadn't seen fit to let himself be known.

Then again, he hadn't truly known her, either.

Which might very well be the only reason he'd ever married her at all.

WHEN THEY ARRIVED in Grosvenor Square, the door of their townhouse was propped open, and two snickering men were ferrying out a mostly nude statue. Daphne becoming a laurel tree to get away from Apollo.

Lucky Daphne, Delilah thought, to have such an appealing option. At least she knew how she'd be spending eternity.

"Jamesy, why is a woman made of stone better than a real woman?" One of the men was bellowing over his shoulder to his friend.

"Why, Jonesy?"

"Her nips are already—"

They saw her and clapped their mouths closed.

She gave them the icy, quelling look they deserved.

Derring had filled a gallery with those statues, many of them all but naked, all pectorals and penises and nipples and curving buttocks and aquiline noses, and quite expensive, so uncharacteristically sensual a collection for a man as rigid as Derring. Of some ordinary stone, not marble or alabaster, they ought to have been in a garden somewhere, she'd always thought.

And there they were, lined up to be loaded into carts like so many shamed orgy attendees.

In broad daylight.

She could practically feel the breeze created by her nosy neighbors abruptly dropping curtains when she'd appeared.

Delilah hiked her skirts in her hands and dashed up the stairs and through the broad double doors. And then she heaved them shut and threw the bolts behind her. She was halfway across the foyer when she stopped abruptly: her footsteps were echoing oddly, dizzyingly.

All at once she realized that it was because everything that had once genteelly cushioned her life—acres of plush, patterned Axminster, velvet curtains bound in tasseled golden ropes, the plump settees on their little bowed legs—was gone.

Her stomach was ice once again.

She stared down at the floor contemplatively, as if it were the sea she intended to cast herself into.

And then she ran, her footsteps eerily clattering as though there were an entire herd of Delilahs chasing her, and bounded up the stairs to her rooms. She lost a slipper (dyed black satin with a tiny heel, unpaid for) on the way.

She skidded to a panting stop at the doorway of her chambers.

Astonishingly, everything—the mirror, the wardrobe, the writing desk and chair, her bed with its fluffed pillows, the rose-and-cream carpet—was still precisely as she left it.

There sat Dorothy on her bed, holding a hatpin in one fist and a knitting needle in the other, like a Turk wielding two scimitars. Her big blue eyes were fierce.

"I wouldn't let them through, Lady Derring. They just laughed and said they'd be back on the morrow."

"Oh, Dorothy. How valiant. Lay those weapons down so that I may hug you."

Dot obeyed.

And Delilah gave her a quick, fierce squeeze.

"What is happening, Lady Derring?"

"Well, creditors are taking our possessions away. It seems Derring was in a bit of a financial bind. I've only just learned this myself from the solicitor. He didn't mean to leave us this way, but it cannot be helped. I didn't know it would happen, and I am in a bind, too." She kept her voice bright, for Dot's sake. "We will need to leave here within a week as the rent has not been paid. Now, I will write you a letter of reference so you can find another—"

"Oh, I would never dream of leaving you, Lady Derring." Her eyes were wide and earnest.

This was precisely what Delilah was afraid of.

"Who else would have me?" Dot added practically, showing an uncharacteristic sense of self-awareness that lacked self-pity. Or pity for anyone else who employed her, for that matter.

As this was all too true, Delilah said, "Oh, now."

All at once, she was pathetically glad to not be alone. Dorothy's loyalty was touching.

And suddenly, now that she was responsible for someone other than herself, she could think more clearly.

"What about Mrs. Blenkenship?" she said, furiously thinking. She was the head housekeeper, who had a ring of keys very similar to the ones now stuffed in Delilah's reticule.

"Went off to the Duchess of Brexford straight away. The duchess fired her own housekeeper to get her." Dot said this with some awe.

Perversely, Delilah was proud. Her staff was the best.

"And Mrs. Vogel? Helga?"

"The Duchess of Brexford," Dot confirmed.

"The Duchess of Brexford again? That . . ." She considered which word to use, then chose the one that fit best. "Bitch."

"Lady Derring!" Dot breathed, delightedly scandalized.

Odd that uttering the word gave her a little burst of

energy. She'd never before said such a thing out loud. So *that's* why people did it.

Not that she intended to make a habit of it.

Then again, she was apparently a woman who owned a building by the docks, so maybe it was appropriate.

"Oh, Lady Derring, what will we do?"

Delilah didn't answer. She stood slowly, and ventured toward Derring's room, adjoining hers.

It had been all but stripped of its furnishings and appointments.

A coat lay on the floor. She hesitated.

Then lifted and smelled it.

And dropped it immediately. It reeked of those cigars.

It ought to have been poignant. But it brought with it a sizzling fury.

And with fury came clarity.

"Come with me, Dot." She seized Dorothy by the arm and led her down the stairs, retrieving her shoe on the fourth step, then headed out the kitchen door.

"IT MIGHT BE helpful for you to know, Lord Kinbrook, that I haven't a soul. I found it an encumbrance in my line of work."

Captain Tristan Hardy explained this in a kindly tone to the aristocrat who sat across from him and was sweating nearly through his Weston-tailored coat.

White's was crowded tonight. Waiters bearing trays disappeared into and emerged from clouds of cigar smoke like genies coaxed from bottles. Spirits were high. Laughter loud.

Not at his table, of course.

Captain Hardy was not a member of White's, as he was not a gentleman in any sense of the word. His manners, though exquisite, were acquired, not innate; he wielded them, like his charm, the way he wielded a sword: strategically, only when necessary, and, if need be, ruthlessly. Nor was he likely to be invited here merely for the pleasure of his company. "Why, he's a right bastard, ain't he?" was often the delayed, rather surprised conclusion after a conversation with Captain Hardy. The surprise was because Captain Hardy was so charming and well-spoken and, indeed, a truly fine specimen of a man, the realization that he'd ruthlessly maneuvered them into a confession of some sort arrived with a delayed sort of shock.

From a distance, he didn't look very different from Lord Kinbrook. The buttons on his coat gleamed; they were silver. The toes of his boots mirrored the overhead chandeliers. They were made by Hoby. But after a second glance somehow it was clear that he was constructed of different material than the men surrounding him. Shaped by entirely different forces.

"You'd sooner want to walk about with a wolf on a lead, darling," wiser women told the women whose eyes inevitably hungrily followed him.

But heads invariably turned to follow him when he entered the room; gazes often settled upon him, unconsciously drawn. The way one's eyes would follow a mysterious ship sailing into port, uncertain of its provenance or the number of cannons it carried.

So if Lord Kinbrook thought Tristan would blink, he was in for a long wait.

"It's true," Lieutenant Massey said. "I witnessed the transaction meself. The devil, 'e says, I'll take your soul off ye, Tristan Jeremiah Hardy, if ye'd like to catch your man every time."

"A fair bargain," Tristan agreed placidly, in almost a drawl. "Because all I've ever wanted is to catch my man."

His middle name wasn't Jeremiah. As far as he knew, anyway.

Lord Kinbrook's antipathy radiated from him. His broad pale brow gleamed damply; the sweat threatened to bead and pour. That was the thing with gentlemen: they never expected to be caught, let alone punished. They thought they could do anything they wanted to do, so they never *practiced* subterfuge or deception. Tristan almost had more respect for the thieves in Newgate awaiting the noose or deportation, who at least applied some effort to lying. Survival of the wiliest. He ought to know.

One of the other things he knew was that all men and women were the same beneath the skin. Title or no title. He had no illusions about gentlemen or gentlewomen possessing more honor.

"Handkerchief?" Tristan asked politely. He produced one. Lawn. White. He hadn't any females in his life who would soften the sharp, plain corners of his life with things like embroidered initials. Women, like embroidery, were complications.

Lord Kinbrook stared at it as if Tristan had extended a handful of dog feces.

Then he looked back into Tristan's face resentfully.

"I don't know how I can help you, Captain Hardy."

Tristan leaned back in his chair and sighed at length. He gave a thoughtful drum of his fingers on the table.

He accepted a brandy from a passing waiter.

Kinbrook looked stubborn, yet wretched.

"Have you a favorite hunting dog, Lord Kinbrook?" Tristan asked lightly. "One who simply never gives up, and never disappoints you, and always finds its quarry?"

Kinbrook brightened cautiously at the change in topic. "Yes. Darby is his name. A spaniel. Raised him from a pup."

"I am the king's favorite hunting dog."

Kinbrook's face fell almost comically.

"No one but the king calls me to heel." He didn't add that the king hadn't called him to heel yet, and that there was no certainty he would obey if that should happen. The arrangement had suited both of them thus far. This time both the king and Tristan had a far more personal interest in hunting down their quarry, for slightly different reasons. "Answer my question and we'll be off. Clearly you know you're in possession of contraband. If you don't tell me how you happened to have those cigars, we'll only try another way, and another way, each increasingly uncomfortable for you. It's all I know how to do, and all I truly enjoy. I'm a simple man."

He shrugged with one shoulder.

This wasn't quite hyperbole. There wasn't much Tristan hadn't sampled or witnessed in his life, from violence to lust to humiliation to opium to triumph to heartbreak. It was all useful. It had all been distilled into a man singular, and perhaps deadly, of purpose.

Lord Kinbrook stared at him, loathing thinly veiled.

"Come," he cajoled with a sort of menacing tenderness. "Look into my eyes. Do you think I ever say anything I don't mean, Lord Kinbrook?"

Kinbrook looked.

Whatever he saw there made him quickly look away.

He swallowed.

Tristan heaved a sigh, and thunked his brandy glass down on the table.

"Derring," Kinbrook muttered tersely.

"Is that a compliment? An epithet?"

"The Earl of Derring. He snuffed it in that chair over there two weeks ago." He gestured with his chin. "Doubtless you've heard about it. Not every day an earl dies in public, surrounded by young loobies, without issue. I got the cigars from Derring. I don't know where he got them."

The chair in question was occupied now by a young man leaning forward and laughing, mouth wide open, hands on his knees, at another man who was pantomiming riding a horse, slapping his own arse and tossing his head.

Tristan stared at that. How on earth—*why* on earth—was that amusing? Tristan was thirty-six years old. He sometimes felt he'd lived a thousand years and a thousand lives. If one started out life in St. Giles, you either grew old quickly or didn't grow old at all. It would never occur to him to slap his own arse for any reason.

"Convenient to blame a dead man," he said idly to Kinbrook. "Wouldn't you say, Massey?"

"Seems a bit facile, guv," he said regretfully, to Lord Kinbrook.

Tristan spared a single arced brow for the word *facile*.

The grim line of Kinbrook's mouth suggested he did not like the word *guv.*

But both he and Massey knew that most roads led to Derring.

"Nevertheless. I got the cigars from Derring. If you're wondering what the Fourth Earl of Derring would be doing mixed up in such an affair, well, desperate men do desperate things."

"In what way was a man like the Earl of Derring desperate?"

"He liked fine things, didn't he? Rumor has it that he was up to his eyebrows in debt. I wasn't privy to all of this. I do know his property has been snaffled up by creditors. Thought I might have a run at his widow. I always rather envied him his young, beautiful wife. Mine is getting on, you see." He paused, as if waiting for some sign of approbation from either of the two men. "Derring's widow . . . penniless, pretty, quiet, pliant, used to a certain lifestyle . . . doubtless she's quite frightened right now." He smiled as if this was a charming thing for a woman to be. "She should be easy pickings."

Tristan stared at the man thoughtfully, idly imagining what it would be like to lean over and perhaps violently head butt Lord Kinbrook.

His own head was made of granite, both figuratively and literally.

But Tristan had not risen to Captain of the King's Blockade though superfluous applications of violence to members of parliament. He was not a legend in certain circles for impulse.

He was, however, usually one step ahead of anyone who thought they could get away from him and his men.

Not this time.

It maddened him.

"How thoughtful of you to consider Lady Derring's welfare."

"I am at heart a decent man," Kinbrook said. Piously. He laid down his cigar butt in a tray on the table. The smoke, vile yet somehow enthralling to aristocrats, curled from it.

"Well, certainly now that you've unburdened your conscience, you can resume believing so, Lord Kinbrook."

Kinbrook looked at him sharply.

Tristan wondered about Lady Derring, this pretty, frightened widow, and whether she would become a burden or a servant to some relative, or some man's desperate mistress, and how the weight of fate tended to displace people.

The way the cigar butt displaced Kinbrook's brandy when Tristan plucked it up and dropped it in.

The brandy seeped into the tablecloth as he and Massey took their leave of him, Kinbrook's oath ignored.

Chapter Three

THE WORLD turned in woozy circles for a second when Paul, Lady Derring's driver, helped her and Dot from the carriage outside of 11 Lovell Street.

Which is when she realized she hadn't eaten a thing all day, and Dot likely hadn't, either.

The darkness around them was alive. It, and its noises, was mysterious, but did not feel immediately menacing, any more than the woods at night did. It was interrupted by the glow of lanterns through windows of shops and pubs and presumably dwellings where humans lived, stacked upon each other in little flats. A hundred feet or so away from where they stood, hulking buildings rose; they were perhaps warehouses, or workshops. She had never been in this neighborhood before in her life.

Above those, into the fast-deepening mauve of the night sky, rose the spires of ships, looking almost churchly. And high above those was the glowing disk of a full moon.

Distantly, she heard voices raised in argument.

Raucous laughter floated toward them from another direction. It concluded in a violent coughing fit and an extravagantly, protractedly juicy spit.

She and Dorothy winced.

Somebody screamed off in the distance. It was a bit difficult to tell if it was due to murder or glee.

Dot jumped six inches and then nearly climbed Delilah like a frightened cat.

Delilah batted her down and set her firmly away.

"It was just someone expressing a powerful emotion, Dot. Nonetheless, it might be best to hold your hatpin in your hand."

"Very well, Lady Derring." Dot's voice was a little wobbly.

The scent of sea was layered like a complex perfume, wild and briny, a bit foul, a bit sweet, carrying with it a bit of everything it swept through on its way to where they stood: tar and salt and smoke, among other things. A wind whipped through and tried to steal her hat and she slapped her hand down upon it. Their skirts billowed and lashed their legs.

"Would you be so kind as to wait for us here, Paul?"

Paul was one of the servants who hadn't yet fled, but he'd told her he'd accepted new employment. And yet he'd been kind enough to drive her out to the docks without so much as a raised eyebrow. She wondered if he thought that, now that she was penniless, she was doing the practical thing and going straight away to join a brothel, because surely that's where the brothels were, down by the docks.

"Of course, Lady Derring."

He pragmatically yet surreptitiously laid his musket across his lap and retrieved a flask from his coat pocket.

Lovell Street barely qualified as a street; it was more

like a bit of fringe dangling at an angle from the main thoroughfare. As far as she could tell, three buildings occupied it.

Number 11 was the largest.

Her building was the largest.

She had never owned anything of such significance outright before. Hers, and hers alone.

Mine. She'd never realized what a powerful word it was.

Of course, two prone bodies were propped at odd angles against it. Drunk rather than dead, she hoped. Prayed.

One of them stirred and murmured, chuckling to himself.

Chuckling wasn't *terribly* sinister, was it?

The building was about the width of two and a half townhouses and filthy with coal smut. A battered sign creaked and swayed on rusty chains in front of it; whatever it had once said had worn away.

She shifted her gaze upward; were those gargoyles?

Suddenly something savory wafted out the door of what appeared to be a little pub adjacent. Her stomach, a crucible of terrible emotions all day and filled with nothing else, growled.

The pub's battered sign, rocking and dancing in the wind on its chains, read "The Wolf And." The final word was no longer legible.

Ladies did not frequent coffeehouses or pubs, she knew, unaccompanied or not. But what did she have to lose? If she was kidnapped and sold into slavery or murdered for the joy of it, it would at least be a dramatic denouement to her story.

She was hungry and thirsty and doubtless poor Dot was, too. They would enter *her* building fortified.

"Dot, we're going into this pub to have a meal and perhaps a coffee."

Dot hesitated. "Oh, Lady Derring, but ladies don't—"

"*Widows* may go wherever they choose. But widows ought not go alone, which is why I'm grateful for your company."

Dot looked relieved. "Is that so? I'm right famished, Lady Derring."

"Well, in we go then."

The Wolf And was snug and nearly dark as a cave and glowed like an ember thanks to a healthy fire at one end and a series of lanterns hooked across the smoke-dark beams.

A century of smells seemed to have soaked into the timbers of the place—smoke, ale, food—and she wouldn't be surprised if blood had found its way into the mix. It was pungent, but not oppressive.

A young woman with a resolute expression and dark hair scraped and pinned back away from her face was swishing a rag over the bar with one hand and pushing a sloshing tankard over to a man with the other. Next to the fire, another man in a chair snored like a tree branch cracking. Another two men were in the corner, heads together, speaking in murmurs.

The barmaid looked up. "Look what the wind blew in! Are ye lost, my dears?"

The unexpected kindness, and the smoke, made Delilah's eyes sting a little. "No, but we are famished. Have you anything that might make a good dinner?"

"I've meat pies. Not rancid yet, I shouldn't think. Bought from the pie man earlier today."

"That's quite an endorsement. What sort of meat?"

"Does it matter much if ye're hungry, lass?" Pragmatic. Unapologetic.

"I suppose not. We'll have two meat pies, please. Have you any tea or coffee?"

She studied them a moment. "I'll bring you coffee, bless your hearts, but it won't be the sort you're used to, I'd warrant. My name is Frances."

"Thank you, Frances."

She didn't offer her name in return.

She and Dot settled at a little battered table and Frances returned apace with two meat pies.

Delilah counted out a few coins and Frances beamed. She had all of her teeth, which was probably quite an accomplishment here at the docks.

And then Delilah and Dot tore into their meal like caged beasts.

The pie wasn't terrible—whatever the meat was, perhaps offal and a shred or two from some animal's flank, it was liberally spiced and churned up with potato. It filled the pit of her poor stomach and she felt immediately better.

The coffee arrived a moment later. Other than its color it bore little resemblance to the brew she'd become accustomed to. But it was hot and wet and she drank it.

It helped to have begun life in a certain genteel poverty. She had a feeling flexibility was going to figure largely in her future.

"Oh, Lady Derring," Dot said suddenly. "There's a lady sitting alone over there. Perhaps we ought to ask her to join us."

Delilah doubted the word *lady* applied, but she looked.

The woman in question was dressed all in black and sitting very, very still. Which could be why they hadn't noticed her at all.

"Dot, ladies sitting *alone* in pubs are usually looking for . . ."

Then she saw the hat resting on the chair opposite the woman.

A black one, with a jaunty feather.

Something about the cant of her head . . .

The color of her hair . . .

Delilah's heart lurched.

She stared.

"Please wait for me here, Dot."

She scarcely noted that she'd risen from her chair. But she was moving across the room, slowly, toward the woman as though some external force impelled her.

She stopped at the table where the lone woman sat staring at what appeared to be a small, nearly full glass of sherry.

A somewhat haunted, hunted expression fled from Mrs. Angelique Breedlove's face when she looked up. She looked as weary as Delilah felt. As though she were beyond surprise.

They stared at each other.

"Are you going to toss a drink into my face? Or do you have an absurd, tiny pistol in that tiny, absurd little reticule?"

Mrs. Breedlove said it lightly. But her eyes were cool and there was something of the coiled spring about her posture.

Delilah matched her tone. "What a waste of a drink that would be. And you appear to be wearing silk. Did my husband buy it for you?"

This was the person she was, apparently, when nobody was around to tell her who she was or who she ought to be. An ironic person. Someone who came out with questions just like that.

It was as liberating as loosening her stays.

"Yes," the other woman said.

They regarded each other with less hostility than one might imagine. More in the manner of two people who'd just discovered they're not alone on a previously deserted island, and who are uncertain as to whether this new person is a cannibal or not.

"May I sit down?" Delilah surprised herself by asking.

Surprise flared in the other woman's face.

After a hesitation, she gave a slow, wary nod.

Very, very gingerly, as if it was the very first thing she'd ever learned to do on her own, Delilah pulled out the chair.

And settled herself into it.

For a moment the silence was nearly ringing at their table, as if they were alone there beneath a dome.

Mrs. Breedlove's eyes were hazel, and her lashes were thick and gold. She was admittedly very pretty, but she didn't in the least resemble Delilah's notion of a fallen woman. Apart from perhaps the dashing hat. She'd always assumed fallen women were daring dressers.

"We haven't actually been formally introduced, Tavistock's amusing performance notwithstanding," Delilah began. "My name is Delilah Swanpoole. Countess of Derring."

The other woman smiled faintly. "Ah, yes. Formality. We mustn't abandon that even in the face of penury. I would rise and curtsy, but once I sat down I felt as though I may never stand again. My name is Mrs. Angelique Breedlove."

"Is that your real name?"

"Good heavens, no." Her face lit with amusement, and for a moment Mrs. Breedlove looked five years younger than the haunted soul she'd seemed an unguarded few minutes ago. "What decent English mother names her daughter Angelique? And my mother was decent, I assure you. I was born Anne Breedlove, in Devonshire. The 'Mrs.' is an honorific I bestowed upon myself. It makes me more respectable, you see."

Mrs. Breedlove was winning the irony competition.

They resumed the stares. Angelique's chin was up ever so slightly, the only hint that she perhaps had a good deal to be defensive about. Her posture suggested it had gotten that way through repeatedly walking across a room balancing a stack of books as a child, the way Delilah's own mother had trained her. Mrs. Breedlove's pride was evident.

"May I ask you another question?" Delilah said finally.

Mrs. Breedlove nodded slowly.

"Were you my husband's mistress?"

Chapter Four

Mrs. Breedlove's little smile was weary and taut. "Do you often ask questions you already know the answer to?"

"A simple yes or no will suffice, Mrs. Breedlove."

"Yes, for the last three years. Which I'm certain would be your next question."

Delilah took in this information wordlessly.

She knew what she ought to feel. Or rather, what she was expected to feel. But she was beginning to understand how filtering her true self through a screen of *oughts* and *shoulds* had diluted her essence little by little, like water added to whiskey. If she wasn't careful, there would be nothing left of her, whoever she once was, before Derring.

And God help her, she could not find it in herself to regret that Derring had mostly neglected the marital bed for the last two years, regardless of the reason.

Her next question required her to reach into a heretofore untapped reservoir of nerve. It was just that she needed to know the depth and breadth of the lies that had apparently formed the foundation of her life before she could free herself from them. She took in a subtle sustaining breath.

"Were you . . . were you in love with Derring? Was he in love with you?"

Angelique's eyes flared in astonishment and something like jaded amusement, which she quickly squelched.

She regarded Delilah with something like sympathy, tinged with perhaps a little condescension.

But she was silent for a moment.

"Forgive me, I'm trying to decide which answer will be both accurate and sparing of your feelings."

"I no longer have feelings, so you needn't worry on my account."

The corner of Angelique's mouth quirked. "Ah, yes. The numbness. Don't worry, all of your feelings will return with a vengeance at an inconvenient time."

"You're a sage as well as a mistress, then, Mrs. Breedlove?" The woman's jaded worldliness was beginning to abrade her nerves. And, to be perfectly honest, her pride. She was accustomed to being a *countess*: to issuing orders, albeit pleasantly. To commanding a certain respect and deference, without, of course, having done much of anything to deserve them apart from marrying an earl.

Perhaps this was why she perversely admired Mrs. Breedlove's worldliness, too. It seemed borne of an earned confidence. The sort gained from experience.

"I believe I do have a specific sort of wisdom to impart," Angelique said coolly. "And no. I didn't love him, Lady Derring. Nor did he love me. I've come to believe that romantic love is a fallacy. I think life is cobbled together by business arrangements and compromises, and it's this fact—the pure business of it all—that I hoped you wouldn't find hurtful. It suited him to have a mistress, I believe, because all of his friends had one, even that odious little Tavistock. The way it suited him to buy sculptures and urns and whatnot. I feel as though I was collected, and as my straits were dire when we met, I was grateful. I did spare a thought or two for you, but not many, I confess. Under certain circumstances moral cringing becomes a luxury."

Delilah absorbed this silently. She didn't know whether it was a relief to know or not. It certainly rather bleakly echoed her own conclusions about life and "love," which interestingly wasn't entirely pleasant to hear. It confirmed her own instincts about Derring. She supposed there was a bit of satisfaction in that.

And yet something about the unadorned directness of this answer was exhilarating. Refreshingly lacking in self-pity, illusions, delusions, or obfuscation, and sprinkled liberally with multisyllabic words. She did enjoy intelligence. Frankly, it was like breathing clean air, which was in short supply in London. When one literally has nothing left to lose, communication probably got more efficient.

But the cool, dry recitation had cost Mrs. Breedlove, somewhat: her chin had hiked, her face was taut and pale.

How had such a woman come to such a pass?

"Certain circumstances?" She tried to sound cool, but sympathy had crept into her voice.

Angelique's hazel eyes were fixed searchingly on Delilah's. Something she saw there made her suddenly pivot toward the bar.

"Frances, love, would you bring my friend a sherry? A large one?"

"No, thank you," Delilah said firmly. "I seldom drink. I'm not even in the habit of taking sherry after dinner."

"You will tonight," Angelique said. "I think you need it, and besides, that way we can be certain you'll ask all of the questions you wish to ask and you shall be honest with me and I shall be honest with you."

Delilah considered this. "Very well. I've nothing to steal, so there's very little risk in getting so drunk that you're able to rob me. And if you attempt to sell me to a brothel, my ferocious lady's maid, Dot, will stab you with a hatpin."

It was rather dark, as jests went. And it *was* a jest.

Mostly.

Dot, hearing her name if not the context, yawned, smiled shyly, and gave a little wave with the hand wielding the hatpin, then tucked her chin into her chest again and continued dozing.

Mrs. Breedlove glanced at Dot then back at Delilah, eyebrows raised.

Her eyes flashed genuine, nearly mischievous amusement.

Delilah was dangerously close to rather liking Mrs. Breedlove.

It seemed unlikely that this little pub would stock something so native to fine drawing rooms as sherry, but Frances rummaged beneath her bar, produced an appropriate little glass, glugged the sherry into it, and brought it over.

"Now we'll drink to dear, dull, dead Derring," Angelique said.

Frances thunked it down on the table in front of Delilah. "Oh, Derring!" Fran crowed. "Annie, wasn't he the one what asked whether you'd be willing to get down on all fours and crow like a—"

"Finish that sentence, and it will be your last," Angelique said with deadly calm.

Frances froze in shock. Then she raised her hands as if in surrender. "My apologies. No harm meant, Mrs. Breedlove."

She backed away on her tiptoes, arms raised in the air.

Delilah's jaw had swung open.

There transpired an exceedingly awkward moment, during which Delilah said aloud only one of the dozens of things she was thinking. As it so happened, it was the one thing guaranteed to appall her mother.

"I wish I could get away with saying that sort of thing. What you just said to Fran."

Mrs. Breedlove looked a trifle ruffled, however. Perhaps embarrassed. "You are better off not knowing about that sort of thing, Lady Derring. And no. She was mistaken. Derring had no imagination at all."

Delilah had no real idea what any of this meant, though she suspected it was appallingly sexual. No amount of sherry would persuade her to ask Angelique to expound on that. Perversely, she was both resentful of and grateful for her own naivete, and a trifle irritated by Mrs. Breedlove's assumption of it.

"I will take your word for it, now, Mrs. Breedlove. I

expect you are uncomfortable expounding. But I think *I* shall decide what I'm better off not knowing."

Mrs. Breedlove tipped her head and studied Delilah as if she were a cunning little jewel box and she'd just noticed she had a hidden compartment.

"Drink it," Mrs. Breedlove advised firmly, but gently. "The sherry."

Delilah sighed. They raised their glasses simultaneously and ironically clinked them together. Delilah threw hers back like she'd seen men do, and swallowed.

She gasped. Her eyelashes whirred as water flooded her eyes.

Then a lovely warmth spread from her diaphragm out in little tributaries in her body. Simultaneously reviving and anesthetizing. Magical, really.

"Well," she said. Intrigued.

"Smooths the edges a bit, yes?" Angelique was amused. She'd sipped hers. Even though only a tiny amount remained.

"Rather." As she had earlier with cursing, she understood, suddenly, the point of a little alcohol.

They sat in silence a moment.

"You didn't love Derring, either," Mrs. Breedlove said. It sounded oddly sympathetic.

Delilah's jaw dropped. "Of *course* I . . ."

Hell's teeth. She hadn't the strength to continue to prop up her own facade.

She lowered her voice. "What makes you say that?"

"You're a woman of feeling, clearly, but none of your feelings seem to be shredding grief for your late husband."

Delilah breathed in and released the breath slowly. Behind her, both the fire and the man snoring next to it crackled.

"I tried." Her voice was hoarse. He'd frowned in discomfort when she was playful or laughed too loud. And yet he always, always expected her to smile.

And suddenly the regret for *years* she'd lost in that loveless stasis was lacerating. To what end? She had ensured the last years of her parents' lives were comfortable. Was safety worth it?

"I was grateful to him." Her voice was frayed. "I truly was. He wanted an heir. And I felt as though I failed him. I wanted children, and a house full of music, of—"

"Guilt is ballast," Angelique said startlingly firmly. "Release it. It won't serve you in your—our—current circumstances."

Ah, yes. The *current* circumstances.

Delilah fell silent again, as the current circumstances asserted themselves through remembering where they were: a pub by the docks, because she was penniless.

"He held you in the utmost esteem, you know," Angelique said gently, ironically. "Derring did."

She didn't know what to say to that. It seemed impossible that you could truly care for someone and leave them ignorant of living on the knife-edge of disaster.

"If only one could pay the landlord with esteem," Delilah mused.

Angelique gave another slow smile, as if everything about Delilah was both unexpected and a little entertaining.

"Haven't you family, Lady Derring? A place to live?"

Delilah slowly shook her head. "I was an only child. I haven't family on this continent, anyhow. I have Dot." They looked over at Dot, her petite frame slumped in the chair, mouth open, snoring softly. "She's the only one who didn't flee. And . . . I haven't decided yet where I might go. My options are limited and unattractive and involve begging for charity."

Angelique quirked the corner of her mouth. "I had two servants who abandoned me with alacrity when they sussed out the state of things. And no place to go."

She tapped her fingers against her sherry glass. "Imagine a world in which someone can buy an entire life—and two entire women—on credit propped up by virtue of a *title*. An accident of birth. Though of course some of them think their titles are ordained by God. The world is ridiculous."

She said this last word with surprising venom.

Which made Delilah realize that Mrs. Breedlove was not so much cool as very, very controlled. That beneath her facade was, as she put it, a woman of feeling, and those feelings were as seething and complex as her own.

"How did you come to be here, in this pub, tonight, Mrs. Breedlove?"

Angelique sighed. "Oddly, it was where I met Derring. That's the briefest answer."

"You met Derring here? But how did . . ."

"I should like to briefly outline the events that led to our meeting. I will omit unnecessary details for the sake of brevity."

Delilah nodded. "Very well. Carry on."

"My mother died when I was young. My brother died in the war. My father was a surgeon and believed in educating girls, so I had excellent tutors. I can speak and write in several languages," she said with a flash of faintly defensive pride. "But then my father fell gravely ill and to support us I became a governess for a wealthy family who had two young daughters."

"Ah!" Delilah inadvertently said aloud. She could easily imagine Angelique as a governess. Bossy and certain of herself.

"The father of this family . . . took a fancy to me." She cleared her throat. "He was handsome and persistent. I was flattered and naive and a little frightened. And then I was quite ruined. Dismissed from my position and turned out by the lady of the house just after my father died."

She relayed this as steadily as a governess conducting a grammar lesson, but her hand had closed around her sherry glass as if it were the one thing anchoring her to the earth. Her knuckles were as white as little skulls. She didn't wait for a response, and Delilah didn't say a word. The muscles of her stomach had contracted.

"Without references, I could no longer work as a governess. None of my relatives—I've an uncle in Scotland, and an aunt and some cousins in Devonshire—were willing to take me in after that debacle. Eventually I found work in a tailor's shop down the road from this pub. My needlework is fine and I'm unafraid of hard work." Her chin went up a little. "Customers hailed from all walks of life and I found the variety refreshing, oddly. A young lord, very handsome, visited the shop often. He persuaded me he was in love with me and convinced me to go away with him to Scotland. I thought we were headed for Gretna Green."

Suddenly she stopped as though she'd encountered an iceberg and wasn't quite certain how to navigate around it.

She looked down at the table a moment, as though her composure could be found there.

Delilah's stomach contracted in fear of what was to come.

Angelique lifted her head. "In Scotland, in a room above an inn, he explained that, since I seemed so worldly, he thought I understood that I wasn't the sort of girl he could ever marry. He thought I'd understood we were just having a bit of fun. Though of course at no point had he ever said such a thing. He was, in fact, about to become engaged to an appropriate young woman. He hoped I would wish him well."

It was on that last word that her nearly rote recitation finally cracked.

For a second, Delilah couldn't breathe.

The whole of Angelique's history churned in the pit of Delilah's stomach. This. *This* is what men did. They did things that led to two women being penniless, frightened, and alone in a tiny pub by the docks, cast there like much-churned earth flying in the wake of a plow. Just that consequential.

She knew not all men were monsters. But they could chart whatever course they pleased. They didn't have to care about consequences if it didn't suit them.

She hadn't words. She honored Angelique's story with silence.

And even as she ached with furious sympathy, some all-too-human part of her envied the sheer sweep of Angelique's life—the illicit attractions, the thrill of hope, the budding of love, though Angelique hadn't said as much. Whereas Delilah had been transferred from her father's household to her husband's like crated porcelain.

Behind the bar, Frances had, of all things, retrieved a book and was reading it. Dot and the man by the fire snored in counterpoint.

"Is this particular lord still alive?" Delilah asked finally.

"Yes."

"That *is* a pity."

Angelique's eyes flared in surprise. And then a smile began at one corner of her mouth and spread slowly to the other.

Then she sighed. "And here we are. After that debacle, I stopped in to the tailor shop to see if they would have me back, and of course they wouldn't, as I'd run out on them quite unceremoniously. So I came in here to visit Frances and have a meat pie and a good cry. Which was when Derring walked in, looking like what he was, an earl in his later years. Full of his own importance but not insufferably so. He inquired as to why I was weeping. I don't weep anymore, mind you."

Delilah imagined it: Dear Dull Derring, an aging wolf chancing upon a wounded doe.

She suppressed a shudder. She didn't need to know more details.

"The one building Derring owns outright is the building next to this pub—Number 11 Lovell Street.

Tavistock surmised he won it in a card game. Apparently it's mine now. Perhaps that was why he was here, in this pub, the day you met him."

"Interesting. He never said a word about the building. Congratulations on . . . having a possession."

Delilah quirked the corner of her mouth. "I am sorry for your misfortunes," she said gently.

Angelique gave a short nod. "And I yours."

The silence that followed marked an unusual mutual sympathy and détente.

"What you said about working at the tailor . . . it reminds of how I felt when we stayed in a coaching inn once when I was a little girl—we were quite poor and trying to disguise it—but I never forgot it. People who had unusual accents, spoke different languages, from all different walks of life, all convening in this one place, in bonhomie or temper . . . I thought how lovely it would be to live there."

"Variety. Just the sort of thing Derring would hate," Angelique mused.

Delilah quirked the corner of her mouth.

Angelique cleared her throat. "You should know that despite our arrangement, I didn't see Derring often. Once or twice a month I'd host a dinner for his friends and their mistresses in my flat. He liked me to sparkle and flatter and flirt."

Never had three such lively words sounded so acid.

"Interestingly, those were my duties as well," Delilah said, abstractedly. Which made Angelique smile again. "Were these titled friends, or . . ."

"Mostly titled. Some, like Tavistock, were not."

"Any dukes?"

"No dukes."

"I could imagine the Duke of Brexford would have a mistress, given the wife he's saddled with."

"The duchess? Saw her once at the theater and her eyes were so cold it near froze my liver to look into them."

Delilah gave a little laugh. "She hadn't the time of day for a little bumpkin like me, the daughter of *such* a minor lord. She never missed an opportunity to make me feel that way, whenever our paths crossed. But she did finally succeed in stealing my cook, the envy of all the households in London."

A snore crackled through the air. It was Dot, whose head was tipped back, her mouth open wide. The hat-pin remained still gripped in her fist. Her cap was sliding off the back of her head.

"Now, Lady Derring, I wish to ask you a question," Mrs. Breedlove said.

"Very well."

She was quiet so long that Delilah thought perhaps she'd forgotten what she intended to say.

When she took a breath, it became clear that Angelique was mustering nerve.

"Do you hate me?" She said it quietly and evenly. Her chin had gone up ever so slightly.

Delilah drew in a sharp breath.

She knew what she ought to say. *Ought.* It was a bully, the oppressor, the weight, that word. What need of it did she have?

"No." Her voice was low and nearly wondering. "I know you're asking because it's the sort of thing one might expect. Granted, at first I was furious to learn about . . . well, *you* . . . and my pride was rather wounded . . . but none of those feelings lasted terribly long. Maybe it's the sherry, but I can think of more reasons to like you than to hate you. Though you are a trifle bossy."

That last bit was definitely the sherry talking.

Angelique's face illuminated in bemused relief. She leaned back in her chair and Delilah saw her release a breath she seemed to have been holding.

"Perhaps you are a saint," Angelique mused after a moment, critically. She sounded like a dressmaker eyeing a client who'd been wearing the wrong kind of sleeve, one that didn't suit her. And she had in mind the perfect alternative.

Delilah leaned forward. "Oh, I wish that I were, but I fear I am not. I have simply resolved to be real and truthful when I speak and to live a real and truthful life since so much of my life has apparently been something of a mirage. And being truthful is a bit like forgoing my stays. It's *lovely.*"

Angelique gave a startled laugh.

"Can I tell you a shecret? I mean secret." All at once, the sherry had gotten control of her consonants.

"I wouldn't dream of stopping you."

"It's this: I'm not an entirely pleasant person all the time."

"Oh, I can tell. You are as vicious as a little chipmunk. *Grrrowr.*"

"Stop that right now." Delilah clapped her hand down on the table. Both Dot and the snoring man jumped a little, opened their eyes, shut them again. "I won't have it."

Angelique's eyes widened.

"See what I mean?" Delilah said this in a sort of gleeful wonderment. She didn't apologize. It was just so exhilarating not to lilt.

"I do see." Angelique sounded as though someone had just explained a tricky mathematical equation to her, to her delight.

"My thoughts are sometimes unkind and even, daresay, shar . . . that is, sarcastic."

"Never sarcastic! I believe they hung witches at Tyburn for sarcasm."

Delilah surprised herself by laughing.

And Angelique laughed, too, a merry, genuine sound.

Dot's head jerked up off her chest and she laughed, too—"ha ha ha!"—sleepily, before nodding off again.

Of all the peculiar things that had happened in the last several days, laughing with her late husband's mistress scarcely a week after his funeral might have been the oddest.

"Derring never laughed at my jokes. But I laughed at all of his, even though I didn't find him amusing. He sulked if I didn't," Delilah said.

"It's a small but killing thing, isn't it?"

"It is."

"He wasn't funny at all."

"He really wasn't." Delilah felt only a twinge of disloyalty. It was the truth. She was beginning to like the truth, though, like sherry and cursing, she suspected it was probably best to be judicious in the partaking and delivery of it.

A lull fell.

"So what will you do now, Mrs. Breedlove?"

"Well," Angelique said, "I intend to finish this sherry, fill my pockets with rocks, and wade into the Thames. Oh, and do call me Angelique."

Delilah's breath left her in a gust. "You don't mean it!"

"Oh, I'm quite serious," Angelique said almost blithely. "I've had enough. I have played all of the modest hand that I've been dealt in life and I have played it badly, and I have lost again and again, and I am out. I am weary of the perfidy or sheer tedium of men, and I see no way to prosperity or comfort without saddling myself with one of those creatures, and I haven't the fortitude to begin again, or the imagination to become a flower peddler, for instance, and dream of being rescued by a prince. Princes do not exist, and if they did, they certainly wouldn't exert the effort to rescue me. Dreams are pointless. I am done. But cheers to you, Lady Derring. I wish you the best."

"But . . . your jewels! You can sell your jewels and live on the proceeds!"

Was she was actually campaigning for her husband's former mistress to sell the jewels he'd bought her?

"If I sell them, I shall have enough to live in relative comfort for a year, perhaps two. I aspire to more than mere survival."

And with that, she reached for her glass of sherry.

Delilah seized Angelique's wrist and held it fast.

And suddenly Delilah knew, without a doubt, that she was stronger when someone needed her. Stronger, perhaps, than this woman, who might be sophisticated and clever and jaded but who had acquired her polish the way gems in a tumbler do. Angelique might know infinitely more than Delilah did about all manner of things. But she suspected one could only be tumbled and jostled so many times before saying *enough*.

Delilah had been a countess for six years, after all. She'd gotten accustomed to controlling one or two things.

Angelique wasn't the only bossy one.

"It's a shame," she said, her tone light, her grip firm. "I am here tonight because I came to look inside my inheritance, the building adjacent. But I'm not certain Dot and I should venture into it on our own. Since I am a bit naive and unfamiliar with the hazards that may await in this part of town. And do call me Delilah."

Angelique narrowed her eyes.

She clearly suspected Delilah of a tactic.

The reason Delilah was so very good at hiring the best staff (with, perhaps, the exception of Dot, and the traitorous butler, her husband's choice) was because she understood that everyone, to some extent, needed to be needed and appreciated for the things they liked best about themselves, and for fine qualities they might not even realize they possessed.

"Well, then," Angelique finally said, "do you care to pull one of your hatpins, Delilah, so that we have a fighting chance against rats?"

Chapter Five

ON HIS first day as blockade commander, Tristan had ordered the burning of every single sailing vessel in Hackbury.

He'd stood there, cold-eyed and stone-faced, on a gray morning in Sussex, staring down the villagers through the flames as his men torched the boats, one by one. And there had been defiance in some of the villagers' eyes, but not one of them dared say a word. They knew their days of lending horses for late-night smuggling runs in exchange for a cask of contraband rum, of ferrying contraband tea along secret cart tracks toward London, of rowing out to reel in casks of goods sunk near shore brought in by boats painted black, of piloting their own black boats, were over. Every last sailing vessel in Hackbury had been used in smuggling somehow. They were, in fact, getting off lightly.

Next time they would not.

Hardy is ruthless. Word spread quickly: he was a different sort of blockade commander. He taught his men to be relentless. Organized. Thorough. And tactically, skillfully violent. They slashed open coiled ropes on ships to find the tobacco hidden within. They found the false bottoms in barrels where illicit liquor was stored; they once even hacked apart the mast of a cutter to find it hollow and stuffed with silks. They were everywhere, day and night, haunting the country and coastal byways on horseback and watching it in towers. They could not be bribed, like blockade runners of yore. They were zealots and they were heroes. Because while some villagers were willing participants, more of them were terrorized into silence or participation by increasingly murderous gangs. Smuggling had held them captive, and Hardy's men were setting them free.

He was born for the job. Tristan understood smugglers. How they thought, and how they survived. Like cockroaches, when dispersed, they ran for the baseboards, the cracks of England: the tunnels, the byroads, the tributaries, the caves. And recongregated.

But they were no match for a commander who'd survived his first ten years in St. Giles slums. He was fueled by a cold hatred for those who preyed on the defenseless. In St. Giles he'd known terror and ugliness; withstanding them was the foundation of his own courage. He'd learned to fight, to hide, to steal, to strategize. And while he'd never known his father and he'd been orphaned when he was eight, from one or both parents he'd inherited a conscience and a wily intelligence and perhaps, after a fashion, luck: he'd stumbled into a position as a naval captain's assistant when he was ten years old. He rose ceaselessly in the ranks from that point on. The navy knew what they had in him.

Hardy had nearly broken the back of smuggling gangs in England.

All save one.

He stared out at the water now, black and oily smooth, at the ship he'd arranged to buy before Lord and Lady Millcoke's house had burned to the ground, killing them and their young children. All because Millcoke had refused to allow the Blue Rock gang to conscript their horses to transport contraband cigars.

He'd sent Massey back to the Stevens Hotel to get some sleep and to await further orders from him.

"I'll have a word with Derring's solicitor. And we might as well try to track down his widow, too," he'd told him.

Massey had told him he was going to stay up for a few more hours trying his hand at writing a poem about his sweetheart.

Tristan had furrowed his brow. "What is your sweetheart's name?"

"Emily, sir," Massey had told him tolerantly.

Tristan knew her name, of course. Emily Emily Emily Emily Emily Emily Emily. For God's sake. That was the whole of Massey's conversation when they weren't catching smugglers.

He did like to tease his very patient and literal lieutenant.

"Sometimes it's too much, sir, the feelings, and you just have to try to write a poem," Massey said earnestly.

Whatever on earth that meant. Sticky sentiment was a foreign language to Tristan. His own carnal education had taken place at the hands of generous whores and willing widows, and his one foray into actual courtship had been an illuminating lesson in how one's heart, loins, and social status could conspire to hand him a rare and shocking defeat. He was, he understood now, much better off. And much wiser.

"Do not inflict that poem upon me if you do write it," he warned Massey.

"Of course not, sir," Massey soothed. He'd tried that once before. He'd learned his lesson.

Massey was a brutally talented soldier and a loyal right-hand man and, after a fashion, a friend.

But he, too, dreamed of the next part of his life.

Which is what Tristan was doing here at the East India docks, staring at the *Zephyr*, the ship he intended to purchase. Staring into the abyss—or rather, the Thames—helped him think.

He quirked the corner of his mouth humorlessly. And to think, he'd decided last year that by this time in his life he'd be a dull, respectable merchant, running respectable cargo—silks and spices—with his own ship. It hadn't seemed unreasonable. After all, hadn't he nearly ground the smuggling trade into dust?

Instead he was tracking cigars.

One. By. Bloody. One.

He would do it as long as it took. But it was making him, and all his men, restive. They were designed for a different sort of action.

It was a wonder the water below him didn't begin a slow boil, such was his focus.

Of all the fatal mistakes the Blue Rock gang had finally made—the fire set in a barn meant to intimidate an aristocratic family into allowing them the use of their horses but which had gone horribly wrong; incurring the rage of the king, who had a soft spot for Lady Millcoke, an old lover; and igniting a cold, vengeful wrath in a certain Captain Tristan Hardy—the cigars were probably the biggest.

Because they were singular. Staggeringly expensive. A unique sop to the vanity and boredom of wealthy men, and wildly profitable for the smugglers. They arrived already rolled and needed to be transported quickly. Typical smuggled cargos—tea, tobacco, spirits—were so undistinguished as to be difficult to trace, if they got past the blockade men at all. And since Tristan had become commander, they simply didn't get past the blockade.

But those cigars—created somewhere in France, by God knows who—were as distinctive as animal scat, and just as trackable.

And Tristan and his men knew the Blue Rock gang was smuggling those particular cigars.

But they didn't know how the gang was getting them to London from the Sussex coast. Which maddened them, because they had all but choked off the flow of any contraband along that route.

And despite watching all the docks along the Thames, they'd been unable to discover how the cigars were being distributed in London, or how they wound up in the hands of the likes of Lord Kinbrook, in White's.

Which probably meant someone considered untouchable, who could move outside the usual confines of a smuggler's world, was funding or abetting them.

In short: some aristocratic bastard.

They'd located a few merchants who sold them in Piccadilly. Both claimed they hadn't had any new ones in at least a fortnight.

At least three of the smug, entitled, aristocratic bastards he'd had the displeasure of charming, cajoling, threatening, or coercing revealed that Lord Kinbrook always had more than one on hand.

And they'd finally learned that Kinbrook had purchased his cigars from Derring.

Only to learn that Derring was dead.

Bloody.

Fecking.

Hell.

But it made sense, somehow: the flow of cigars seemed to have stopped right about when Derring died. Which could be coincidental. Except that he didn't believe in coincidences.

He also wasn't accustomed to grasping at such wispy, ephemeral evidence.

Then again, he'd learned to trust his instincts.

It was just that so many people were trusting his instincts at this very moment.

The king was on his neck. And the king behaving in a kingly way was unusual, but when his stomach and his penis were involved, he took matters quite seriously. In fact, he was, Tristan understood, a man of feeling and intelligence in the wrongest possible job for him.

But he represented a country Tristan loved and believed in.

And the king had offered Tristan a reward if he could bring those bastards in.

He didn't really need the reward. He'd bring those bastards in, no matter what.

But in a future he could read as clearly as he

could read the murky ocean below, money—earned honorably—of course couldn't hurt.

For either him or his men, who would get their share—who were counting on him to lead them to this victory, too.

Tristan's pride and his legacy were at stake. Not to mention the future in which he hoped to be . . . ordinary? Was that what he wanted? What would life be like without fighting, strategy, and maneuvering? Who would he be?

Alive, *that's* what he'd be.

And a life like Massey's, a house in the country, a doting wife, a brat or two who looked like him—not even using the reliable Thames for scrying could Tristan conjure a home or life like that. He'd never known one; likely he wasn't cut out for that sort of thing, anyway, a man of action like him.

Then again, he'd probably never had a prayer of being ordinary, anyway.

And that, at least, was bad news for the Blue Rock gang.

IT TOOK ALL three of them to shoulder open the studded oak door of Number 11 Lovell Street once she got the key to turn, and its hinges screeched like a murder victim.

Which probably wouldn't attract much attention in this area.

It thunked shut behind them in a permanent-sounding way. Delilah felt for an instant as if they'd pulled up a drawbridge against marauders. Or were perhaps trapped inside a castle keep.

They all stood in silence for a moment, borrowed (from Frances the barmaid) lanterns held aloft. The hush was so thorough one could nearly grab handfuls of it. The building was solidly built, which was a fine thing.

Distantly they heard a thunk, as though a dragon was kept in the basement.

Doubtless it was one of the mysterious noises from outside.

"The floor is unnervingly rather soft," Delilah finally said, carefully.

"Probably mouse pelts," Angelique said.

Dot gave a guttural shriek and performed a sort of revolted high kick, which sent the beam from her lantern swinging in long, woozy arcs.

Delilah seized her elbow, her heart in her throat. "Oh, for heaven's sake, Dot, it's just dust. You need to be brave if . . ."

Dot's swaying lamp beam had skipped across something dazzling.

Delilah looked up and her breath snagged.

The dust Dot had kicked skyward was sifting down, down, down in lazy, amber, lamplit spirals through the tiers of an improbably fine chandelier twinkling in the middle of the high foyer ceiling like a little constellation. The lamplight made the faceted crystals wink in rainbow colors—red, blue, green.

Dot might as well have flung fairy dust.

Their silence, for a moment, was wholly mesmerized.

It felt, somehow, like a sign, this hidden, shambly, fine beauty. *And it's* mine, Delilah thought, with wondering exultation. *That beautiful thing is mine. The filthy floor we stand upon, that staircase in front of us, all the rooms we have yet to see*—mine.

Dot sneezed like a wolf trying to blow down a pig's house of straw.

Angelique tugged her gently out from beneath the chandelier. "One sneeze too mighty and that thing might crash down."

The spell was broken. "You're quite right," Delilah concurred. "And no more shrieking unless we see a murderer, Dot. No, do not faint," she said, as Dot's eyes seemed about to roll back in her head. "You're sturdier than that and we both know it and seeing a murderer is unlikely." She wished she was more confident of this. "Have you your hatpin?"

"Sorry, Lady Derring. Yes, Lady Derring."

"She probably frightened the vermin good and proper with the shrieking," Angelique said. "Well done, Dot."

"Thank you, Mrs. Breedlove." Dot beamed.

"But the vermin are very determined here by the East India docks," Angelique added, wickedly.

"*Brave*," Delilah growled, cutting Dot off mid-whimper. "Angelique, you're not helping."

"*I* feel braver when I can make light of something."

Delilah cast her a baleful sidelong look. A sardonic Angelique was at least better than the one who wanted to wade into the Thames. "Let's see what we have on this level."

They aimed their lamps in various directions—east, west, up, down. They soon determined they were in a foyer, in front of a staircase, flanked by what appeared to be two sitting rooms.

Everything was so blurred with dust and laced with cobwebs it was like seeing everything through a haze of laudanum.

The banister and balustrade of the handsome staircase before them seemed to be carved in bulbous shapes and vines, but it was impossible to know quite what those shapes were. Delilah toed the floor to clear some dust; it *felt* like marble.

"Looks just like a townhouse like ours, Lady Derring, don't it? Only bigger." Poor Dot sounded infinitely relieved, as if she'd fully anticipated that the studded oak door opened onto the Gates of Hell. And yet she'd followed Delilah through anyway. What had Delilah done to deserve that kind of loyalty?

"I do believe that's precisely what this is," Delilah said brightly. "How very interesting. Let's have a look, shall we?"

She led the way to the right, where they found a modest sitting room. The fireplace was blacked with soot, and its corniced mantel and carved pilasters had been in vogue around the time King George III was still sound of mind; likewise, the balding rug—it was Savonnerie, if she had to guess—the peeling wallpaper, and the two deteriorating settees on spindly legs—Chippendale, or copies. All seemed to be in various shades of red. They'd probably been home to generations of mice. Cobweb bunting swung from the windows and corners.

It was snug—the shuttered windows let in no drafts—and had once been gracious.

Who or what had occupied it? Why was it empty now? Why on earth had *Derring* owned it?

They moved across the foyer and discovered the room opposite was twice the size, dominated by a fine fireplace of the same vintage. It was bald of rug and bare of furniture.

Except for a pianoforte.

"Ohhhh," Delilah breathed.

She moved toward it slowly, almost on her toes, like a hungry leopard stalking an antelope.

No sarcophagus creaking open had ever sounded quite so eerie as the dusty, closed lid when she lifted it.

Dot muttered something that sounded like a string of prayers.

Delilah touched a dirty key. A G note echoed, like a ghost of long-ago parties.

Behind her, Dot visibly shuddered.

"Do you play?" Delilah asked Angelique, her voice dreamy.

"Yes," Angelique confirmed. Sounding as mesmerized as Delilah.

And maybe it was weariness, maybe it was the spell cast by the chandelier, maybe it was the sherry, but Delilah could have sworn she could *hear* very faint voices raised in song and laughter, as if from a parade approaching from miles and miles away.

Something stirred in her. She could not have put it into words if asked; it was more a feeling than an actual idea. But the feeling glinted like one of those chandelier crystals. An idea was forming.

"Let's go upstairs," she said.

The fourth stair creaked, but no one vanished through any of the steps with a scream and cloud of dust. Their lanterns threw giant shadows of the three of them on the wall opposite, which made Delilah feel as though they were going up with reinforcements. Oddly, this made it just a little easier to go down strange hallways when they could light only a few feet ahead at a time.

Which she supposed was rather a metaphor for life.

Some of the fourteen doors on the two floors opened with a twist of the knob; most of the locks, however, needed oiling and required finesse and fussing, except for the one for the largest suite on the first floor, which seemed to have been recently oiled. The rugs and wallpaper in the rooms and halls were shredded ghosts of their original selves. The rooms were empty save for a few toppled pitchers, a wash-basin, and several surprisingly decent wardrobes in the larger suites.

Each sealed-up room released a stale gust of air but no other untoward smells or entities. Until the last room, which released something sporting a long, skinny tail and tiny, shiny eyes.

It vanished with such startling speed no one had time to scream, but they all certainly wanted to.

"Well. That wasn't as bad as I thought it would be," Dot announced in a voice that wobbled up and down the scale.

"I'm very proud of you," said Delilah. Her voice was none too steady.

Angelique shimmied her shoulders as though the creature had crawled right down the back of her dress.

Rat or no rat, by the time they reached the kitchen the feeling that had begun next to the pianoforte had crystallized into an idea, and Delilah's heart picked up a beat.

The centerpiece of the kitchen was an enormous heavy work table, furred with dust. She stopped short, so vividly could she imagine Helga cheerfully shouting orders to the kitchen staff while they sat here and chopped and stirred. She could almost smell simmering onions and fresh bread and—had she just caught a whiff of one of Derring's cigars? Perhaps she'd dredged it from her imagination? Or had he stood in this dusty kitchen, for some reason?

It was empty of everything apart from the table and dust, and it could easily become the bustling heart of a house again.

The light in here was gray now, squeezing in through the chinks in the shutters.

All at once Delilah's heart was pounding. Hope was painful, but it was also like exposing a wound to the light it needed to heal. She hadn't realized how little hope her comfortable, stultifying life had contained. She'd been sealed and locked up, in some ways the same as this house.

"I think this building has potential," she began idly, offhandedly. She traced a *D* in the dust on the table.

"The potential to be a whorehouse, which I suspect it was some time ago. Or a truly fine and dangerous gaming hell, given its location," Angelique agreed, on a yawn.

Delilah cleared her throat.

"Actually . . . I think it has the potential to be a very fine boardinghouse."

She'd said it.

"Do you think you may still be a little drunk?" Angelique tipped her head, suggesting gently.

"On *hope*," Delilah said, beatifically. Though she was, in fact, still a little drunk. "But think about it. The rooms could be made very comfortable and charming. The whole *house* can be made very comfortable and charming. It's filthy, not decrepit. Look around you at this kitchen . . . imagine it filled with cheerful staff, making apple tarts . . ."

"Ohhhh, apple tarts," Dot breathed, caught up in the vision. "I do like apple tarts!"

"And if the roof leaked, it would smell like mildew, and it doesn't, does it?" Delilah demanded.

"It doesn't," Dot agreed.

Angelique was staring at her oddly.

"And we'll get a cat or two for rats and mice," Delilah said firmly.

"Oh, I do like cats!" Dot enthused.

There was a little silence as her words, her idea, her vision, hung and sparkled in the air like that listing chandelier.

"*We'll* get a cat?" Angelique said quietly.

It was a fair question. Delilah hardly knew this woman. Their only bond was that a certain feckless earl had kept both of them alive, bored them silly, rolled on top of them and rolled off, and then left them terrified and flailing and penniless. At this moment they might be cleaving to each other the way shipwreck victims will cleave to the first available flotsam. Her judgment might be colored by terror, sherry, hope, hunger, and fury. But her instincts about people—save, perhaps, Derring—had always been good.

"Why not?" she said on a sort of bemused, gleeful hush. She hiked and dropped her shoulders.

Something like hope flickered in Angelique's expression, as fleeting as one of those rainbow colors winking in the chandelier. Her mouth twitched, and she almost smiled.

She visibly, ruthlessly tamped it down again.

"But Delilah . . . here near the docks . . . the people who want to stay in an inn might be a little . . . well, they might not be the sort a countess is accustomed—"

Delilah waved a breezy hand. "Oh, we'll have mixed company, of a certainty. But it could be so lively! I would *love* it. Just imagine! You might be able to use all of your languages."

Angelique began to laugh, then she bit her lip to stop it.

But now Delilah was slowly rotating, as if filling all the shelves with food and imagining a cook before the stove.

She pressed on, her words rushing together now. "At first I thought I might be mad, too. But the more I think about it, the less outlandish it seems. Between us we've enough experience to run a large home. We need only allow people we *like* to stay, and we'll charge them handsomely for excellent service. And—" She allowed the fantasy to bloom fully, drumming her fingers on her chin. "*And* we'll require guests to eat dinner together at least four nights per week and sit in the drawing room with other guests most nights out of the week. So we'll all come to know one another and feel like family. Oh, we can even have *musicales*."

It was very nearly everything she'd ever wanted.

She clasped her hands beneath her chin in something like entreaty.

Dot was lit up with reflected zeal and hope.

Angelique had gone very still. Her hazel eyes were abstracted as if she were calculating something on an internal abacus.

And hope was a bit like that pallid light forcing its way through the chinks in the shutters. It would find a way, given the slightest bit of an opening.

"But you own the building, Delilah. Which puts me in a position I never want to be in again—beholden to someone. How would we make my participation official?"

It was the perfect sort of shrewd question that convinced Delilah she was absolutely right to put this proposition to her.

"Presumably you know where to sell the jewels we own outright. We'll pool our funds and draw up papers."

And after a moment, during which Delilah held her breath, Angelique gave a slow nod, as if Delilah the pupil had just given a correct answer.

"I *do* know where to sell them, as it so happens. And to find people willing to do the dirtiest of the heavy work for reasonable pay."

"Splendid! And as for the location, well, we will make this place so appealing that people will go well out of their way to stay here, and won't want to leave. And we'll call it something very enigmatic and exclusive, like . . . like . . ." Delilah waved one hand like a sorceress with a wand. "The Grand Palace on the Thames!"

"Ohhhhhhhh, Lady Derring . . ." Dot breathed. "That's tray magnefeek."

Angelique gave a little snort. But her posture suggested that some sort of internal knot had finally loosened.

"Can you picture it?" Delilah demanded on nearly a whisper.

"I *can* picture it," Angelique conceded. "And it's not only *not* mad, we might never have to be at the mercy of another man again."

"*Precisely* my thought." Delilah took a breath. "Shall we shake hands on it?" Her voice was shaking.

Angelique drew in a long, long breath.

And then with a certain ironic flair, extended the hand Delilah had lately stopped from taking that last sip of sherry.

They shook briskly.

"To The Grand Palace on the Thames!"

"To The Grand Palace on the Thames!" Dot and Angelique echoed.

And they all raised their lanterns and toasted each other with light.

Chapter Six

Six weeks later . . .

THE FACADE of Number 11 Lovell Street had been washed, and recently. This was either optimism or folly; Tristan knew it would be coated in a fine layer of coal smut apace, like everything and everyone else in London, particularly here by the docks.

Still, this clean white box of a building seemed to him as improbable as Avalon emerging from the mists. Seldom did dens of iniquity call attention to themselves thusly, but iniquity came in many disguises, he knew.

Ironically, it was a fifteen-minute brisk walk from where the *Zephyr* was docked.

He was here because bloody Tavistock had finally returned from his holiday and had revealed—after skillful, charming yet vaguely threatening, coercion—four fascinating things: Derring had indeed died in great mounds of debt; he'd kept a mistress; he'd owned one building outright; and Tavistock had given the Countess of Derring keys to it. Weeks ago.

Just when Tristan had begun to believe she'd vanished into thin air.

In the intervening weeks, he'd learned the St. James

townhouse they'd lately occupied had been vacated and emptied of belongings. Neither Derring's acquaintances nor his heir—they had traveled to the countryside to meet the supercilious new earl, who didn't even pretend to be grieving—had an inkling about where she'd gotten to. Or they were unwilling to tell him. As for her character, words like *sweet,* and *devoted,* and *pretty thing* were employed.

Which rather contrasted with Tavistock's description of her, which was, "More sting than fuzz, if she were a bee. If you take my meaning."

Doubtless, like Lord Kinbrook, Tavistock preferred his women frightened.

The Derring servants had apparently scattered to the four winds. They could not be found for even the mildest of queries.

While it was possible that she'd been kidnapped or had hurled herself into the Thames out of an excess of grief and devotion, it was tempting to conclude that Lady Derring did not want to be found. Possibly for cigar-related reasons.

And a building by the docks was the ideal place from which to distribute contraband.

No informants had come forward in the maddening interval of Tavistock's absence; clearly they were all terrified of seeing their own homes and families go up in flames, and not even the promise of reward and protection could sway them.

No smugglers had dared try to get anything out of Sussex; Tristan's men would have stomped them.

Tristan stood back and peered up.

Small, irritable-looking gargoyles crouched above

the dormer windows at the roofline. A row of corniced windows faced the street.

The sign swinging on shining chains across the facade read The Grand Palace on the Thames.

He wondered if the object was to startle a laugh from anyone looking up at it.

He peered at it closely. He could just about make out the letters *RO* and possibly a *G* etched faintly behind the newly painted letters. They had made use of what was already there. Something about Rogues?

He advanced to the door, which had recently been painted red and was flush with the street.

A sign hung from it, too. Welcome! it said. Complete with exclamation point.

He studied this bit of exuberance skeptically.

"They dinna mean it, guv," said a voice from down around his feet.

He glanced down. A man was sitting on the ground, torso up against the wall. "They willna let ye in, if you've no the blunt or if ye dinna look like bloody prinny."

"Is that so?" Tristan said sympathetically. "And how does bloody prinny look?"

"Fat rich bloke."

"Ah. Who is this 'they' you reference, if you wouldn't mind telling me, sir?"

"Women. Women are cruel, guv. Cruel."

"Aye, don't I know it. Do you see many people going in or coming out of The Grand Palace on the Thames?"

"Nay, sir."

This meant very little, given the man's condition.

"Not since the last fat rich bloke, that is, nigh on some months ago. Gold tip on his walking stick. Gold watch. I've a view from down here, I see. I can see shiny things when I look up. Like stars in the sky, so they are."

"I can imagine." Tristan was alert now.

"Brought 'is friends, now and again so 'e did, in a cart. They was half-naked and couldna walk on their own, I s'pose, and he had to drag them in."

This was colorful, indeed. Then again, rumor had it this place had been a brothel some decades earlier.

"Half-naked, you say? Did you ever speak with this man?"

"Nay. His lordship poked me with his walking stick and asked me to do the impossible."

"And what would that be?"

"Stand up."

Tristan sighed. Well, he'd asked. "Have you seen the Earl of Derring or the Countess of Derring enter this building?"

The man gave a shocked guffaw. "Do I look like I consort with the likes of them, guv?"

Tristan laid his ear against the door. It smelled of new paint and was so thick it would probably muffle cannon fire.

"One never knows. I've learned to never leap to conclusions, sir." Tristan took the brass knocker between his fingers. Above it was a tiny shuttered window that could be opened so that the people inside could inspect the people outside.

Something made him stealthily try the doorknob instead.

To his surprise, it turned easily in his hand. Ah, instincts.

The door hinges didn't creak and the door glided nicely open. He found himself approving. Combatting rust near the ocean was a Herculean task requiring vigilance, and it had been one of his jobs as he rose steadily through the ranks.

He took one step gingerly inside.

He closed the door very, very gently behind him.

It might be a den of iniquity, but it smelled a bit like a church: of dust aggressively vanquished by lemon and linseed oil rubbed into good old wood. Under it all was the faint—surprisingly faint, given that this was a building near the docks after all—hint of mildew. It did tend to creep into all old buildings. He didn't mind it; it was a bit like seasoning, and reminded him of the sea.

He dragged his toe experimentally across one of the checkerboard marble tiles beneath his feet; every square had been cleaned to a gloss. In the black ones he could see his reflection, dark and distorted. He imagined, mordantly, he might just appear to his enemies like that.

The banister of the rather handsome staircase before him was carved in mysterious bulbous fruit and leaves, through which peered the occasional cherub or nymph. A window on the first landing aimed a rectangle of light down at his feet. Something overhead flicked little bits of light off the toes of his boots; he tipped his head back to study a surprisingly fine chandelier. One would have to look very closely to notice the two or three gaps where crystals were missing from its tiers, rather like some of the denizens of the docks who had more gaps than teeth. Tristan always looked very closely at everything and everyone.

Nary a cobweb trailed from its branches, and the candles in its sconces appeared to be wax, rather than tallow. Not an insignificant expense, and a building of this size would require a ceaseless supply.

How would a boardinghouse that allegedly had no customers afford such an extravagance? Not to mention the sort of staff that apparently cleaned to his own standards, rigorously honed from years of swabbing decks and the like.

A loud pop alerted him to the fire leaping cheerfully in the room to the right of him. Two rose brocade settees sat opposite each other before it, and a bouquet of flowers was stuffed into an urn on the mantel. He didn't see any stacked boxes of contraband cigars. Nor did he smell cigar smoke.

He was about to venture deeper in when he heard, of all things, someone merrily singing.

He halted and craned his head to peer up the stairs.

A maid was standing on a ladder on the second landing in front of a window, her body stretched as high as she could reach. One half of the window glittered; pallid London light peeked through. The top half was dusty.

She was singing a song in waltz time.

The windows are dusty la la la la la
The door hinge is rusty! Ta ra ta ra ra!
The hallway is musty la la la la
But my rag is trusty

Let's give them a polish let's give them a shine
We'll make the old place look just divine

It was perversely the most entertained he'd been in some time. It would simply never occur to him to narrate his own duties in song.

LATER DELILAH COULD not have said what made her turn so suddenly. It was as though the air in the room had shifted to accommodate something significant. She could feel it as surely as if a finger had touched the back of her neck.

She pivoted on the ladder swiftly and looked down.

Right into a pair of eyes as hard and bright as polished shillings.

She at once understood how a target must feel when an arrow pierces its red center. The jolt thrummed her from her scalp down to her ankles.

Her hand flew to her heart in a protective, slightly admonishing, gesture: the damned thing had skipped. It wasn't entirely due to fright.

The man below was tall enough to reach the sconces without scaling a ladder, and after weeks here at The Grand Palace on the Thames, this was likely going to be the first thing she noted about anyone for the rest of her life. The light flattered yet exposed him: he wasn't precisely young. The ruthlessly cropped hair and severe, elegant planes of his face implied he was humorless and unyielding.

The sensual swoop of his lower lip and the lines raying from the corners of his eyes tempted one to believe he occasionally laughed. Maybe even occasionally yielded.

His posture, however, was a warning against getting comfortable with that particular notion. Vast of shoulder, erect, he seemed singular of purpose and sleekly constructed for maximum devastation, just like an arrow.

Odd. She had not once in her life thought of a pair of lips as "sensual."

He was holding a beaver hat between two hands, his coat was black and crisply tailored, and his buttons and boots were tended and glowing. He was every inch respectable.

And yet there was nothing about him suggesting the indolence of most of the gentlemen she'd met.

She'd warrant this man had needed to *try* in life.

And that he had quite conquered it.

"My apologies for startling you. I would have announced myself, but I was captivated by your song."

His voice was grave and low, his delivery courtly. As if he was accustomed to soothing plebeians he'd frightened with his stern majesty.

She was both charmed and irritated.

"Oh, surely you jest, sir. I can hardly carry a tune. It's one of my failings."

"Is it? Have you many?" He sounded genuinely curious.

"I count them at night, instead of sheep."

"I should think that would keep you awake. Perhaps you ought to have a brandy, instead."

She wasn't certain he'd meant it to be funny, but she fought and lost the battle to not smile.

FOR TRISTAN, WHAT followed was like the moment of blindness that comes after inadvertently looking into the sun. It dazzled him mute.

He frowned, as if she'd been insubordinate.

A speculative furrow appeared between her own straight dark eyebrows.

"Can *you* sing?"

"Yes," he replied, surprised and wary.

"As it so happens, we've planned monthly musicales at The Grand Palace on the Thames. It's just we haven't anyone to sing the masculine parts. Something to keep in mind if you're musically minded."

Oh, Christ. This was alarming. In his experience, when women wanted something they had a tendency to maneuvers rather than direct requests. He'd once had to extricate himself from the musical machinations of the wife of a superior officer, and it had been like fighting his way out of a fishing net. He'd prevailed, but not without injury: to his pride and her feelings.

Besides, he had the unflattering sense this maid asked every able-bodied man that question.

"I was actually looking for a pub," he said. "And I thought I would inquire here, as the facade is so charming and respectable."

She brought her hands together in a delighted little clasp. "Oh, did you think it was charming?"

Her face had gone radiant as the moon. And he should know: he and the moon were on intimate terms; how many nights had he navigated by it? Countless. It wasn't a fanciful observation. It couldn't be. He was not a fanciful man.

He gave a short, cautious nod. It occurred to him then that her diction had more in common with a duchess than with a maid, and that she was, in fact, almost alarmingly pretty.

He decided it was best not to ask her about Lady Derring directly. If indeed the building was the seat of a smuggling ring, subtlety would be key to learning what he needed to know. And if the drunk fellow outside was correct, no one had come in or gone out of this place. A sudden, blunt inquiry might sound alarms and send her fleeing.

"How lovely to know The Grand Palace on the Thames's excellence is apparent from the street." She pronounced the name of the place like a governess correcting the French pronunciation of a young charge. "The little pub adjacent will give you a decent hot meal and treat you kindly."

"I suppose I'll go then."

And for the instant between the time he said that and the moment she answered, he wanted her to say, "Not just yet," and go on saying surprising things.

"I hope you have a lovely day, sir, and thank you for visiting The Grand Palace on the Thames."

Well, then. He'd been briskly dismissed.

Was there a reason this maid wanted him to leave so quickly?

But because it amused him to do so, he turned to obey her.

He paused in the doorway. "Perhaps a rag affixed to a pole or a mop would help with the top of the window. And perhaps it would be wise to lock the door behind me."

She cast a glance over her shoulder again. "Thank you, sir. I should never have worked any of that out on my own. Thank goodness a man came along."

He closed the door gently behind him.

If he was not mistaken, she'd just taken the piss out of him.

He stood motionless a moment, staring down the street. He realized he was smiling. Albeit faintly.

"They sent you on your way, did they not?" said the man near his feet. "What did I tell you, guv? Cruel."

"Aye. Cruel, indeed."

As Tristan jammed his hat back on, he heard the door lock behind him.

Chapter Seven

THE PUB adjacent—which seemed to be called The Wolf And, Tristan noted—was composed of four tables and eight chairs, all crammed chummily together in a place as snug as any animal den. The fire burned hot but not too smokily. Likely the place had been squatting on that corner of Lovell Street for at least a century.

Two men were having what appeared to be a profound, conspiratorial conversation over tankards of ale. Although he was aware that nearly anything seemed profound when one was drunk enough.

Behind the plain oak bar, the barmaid was, of all things, reading a book.

She looked up and smiled warmly.

"Well, good morning, sir."

"Good morning. A half pint, if you would. How's the light?"

"It's piss, I fear. We'll do better with the next batch. You'd be better off with the dark."

"Thank you for your honesty."

He took a seat in a battered chair that wobbled a bit.

The table before him looked pocked with knife stabs.

"Do you get much of a crowd in here?" he asked when she brought the ale over.

"I'm Frances, sir, but you can call me Fran. And oh, nay. I own the place outright—once belonged to me da, and his da before him—so I don't need much of a crowd to keep it going and it suits me. Perhaps because there's not much room to fight in here, sir. They wind up in the street straight away. More satisfying to crash about when you can knock things over and get other blokes involved, I expect."

It was a hilarious summary and indictment of his gender.

"I suppose that's true. One would think you'd get customers from the boardinghouse next door, however."

She hesitated.

"One would think," she said.

Cagily, he thought. And, oddly, a little wistfully.

"It *is* a boardinghouse, isn't it?" He furrowed his brow innocently. "It isn't immediately apparent from its name."

One of the men at the table looked over at him alertly. "Oh, ye dinna want to go in there, guv."

"Oh. Why is that?"

"It's just the word out on the street, like. To keep clear of The Palace of Rogues." He waved an arm, indicating the street, apparently. "Not a place you want to go into."

"It's called The Grand Palace on the Thames," the barmaid said stoutly, and Captain Hardy said somewhat reflexively. After all, he'd been told the name three times, and he was not a slow learner.

One of the men at the tables snorted. "A sheep doesna change its spots."

So: drunk, then, judging by that scrambled metaphor.

"Any particular reason I ought to avoid it?" he asked them. "How long has it been open?"

"Just heard it said, is all. You can ask nearly anyone." He swept an arm vaguely to indicate everyone, Tristan supposed. "Was a brothel nigh on a few decades ago, or so I've heard. Could be anything now, could it not? They hung that sign a fortnight ago, is all I know."

"But it seems . . . benign."

Tristan thought about the leaping fire, the lemon and linseed oil, a face illuminated with a pure and unguarded pleasure. All at once he found he didn't want to drink his ale. He felt oddly as though he'd already drunk something pleasant and a little intoxicating, and he wanted the feeling to linger.

"It's a *lovely* place," Fran the barmaid insisted. "Was a right disaster before. Boarded up for years. Hasn't been anything at all for over a decade, and I ought to know."

"Looks deceive, guv," the man who'd mixed his metaphors about sheep and spots said morosely.

"I suppose they sometimes do."

Tristan knew better than to instigate a frivolous debate here at the docks.

But when he thought of the maid singing about her duties, he thought there was a person who was exactly who she was. He could not imagine her deceiving anyone. He slapped that thought dead as if it was a mosquito out for blood. He moved through life in a constant state of objective suspicion, of necessity.

"A friend of mine mentioned this pub, Frances," he called to her. "Said it had a certain quiet charm."

Her face lit up and he was glad he'd embellished his lie a little. "A friend of yours, guv?"

"Happened into it by accident. Derring."

"The . . . Earl of Derring?"

He would have called her expression *studied neutrality*. He had the sense that she was judging him ever so slightly for calling the earl his friend.

"Rest his soul," he said somberly.

"Rest his soul," she echoed rotely.

"Did he introduce himself to you?"

She looked caught.

"No," she admitted, after a hesitation. "But he spoke to a friend of mine. A woman. Sitting alone. A good sort of woman," she said hurriedly. "He introduced himself to *her.* And she told me who he was. That's how I know who he was."

"Do you know the proprietresses of the boardinghouse, Frances? Ought I take a room there?"

"Lady Derring and Mrs. Breedlove are all that is good and kind."

So Lady Derring *was* there.

"Thank you for your opinion, Frances," he said gravely.

What on earth would make a countess undertake the running of a boardinghouse? If that *was* indeed what she was doing?

"I knew I was right to stop in here today, Frances."

He drank his dark and left a gratuity large enough to put high color in Frances's cheeks.

AFTER SHE LOCKED it, Delilah touched the door—only half-whimsically—to see if it was hot, the way it might be if a flame had licked all the way up to the entrance. Because the backs of her arms had furred with an odd heat and her heart was beating as though she were competing for a prize.

Or running from something.

She could not recall ever before meeting a man who *reverberated* after he was gone. She wasn't certain it was entirely pleasant; she did not like the realization that her senses could be so easily overcome without her permission, because she didn't like being reminded of vulnerabilities. But she was also oddly regretful, as if a stirring piece of music had been interrupted.

She whipped off her cap and apron and dashed up the stairs, her bunch of keys jingling all the way. She was musical nearly every time she moved now, and she didn't mind in the least. She'd sung quite a bit for no reason at all in the past few weeks.

She found Dot hemming a curtain in the upstairs sitting room. Gordon, their striped cat, whose head was as big as a small pumpkin and body as plump as a cushion, was lounging in a basket next to Dot.

"Dot, you need to remember to lock the door after you open it! A gentleman just strolled in and there I was on the stairs, singing like a looby in my cap and apron."

"Oh, my apologies, Lady Derring! But you sing very nicely, not like a looby! Was he indeed a gentleman? Did he want to stay?"

Dot sounded wistful. They were all getting to be

wistful for the days when gentlemen—people with money and manners—were thick on the ground. They had no illusions about the wonderfulness of gentlemen.

However, they *did* like—and need—money.

Because they'd been open for business for a fortnight.

And until today, not one person had knocked on the door.

Though, more precisely, the man with the silver eyes had simply strolled in.

"He meant to go to the pub."

Dot looked crestfallen. And Dot's blue eyes were enormous and worried like those of a forest creature at the best of times.

"Don't worry, Dot, it will just take a little time for word of our establishment to spread. And then you'll see."

"A little time" was all they had, if time was measured in pounds and shillings.

FOR THE REST of the day those few minutes the man had stood in their foyer kept returning to Delilah, much like an itch she couldn't reach. She told Angelique about him briefly that night in the small sitting room at the top of the stairs. They'd gotten into the habit of gathering there in the evenings, talking and laughing; sometimes Delilah or Angelique read aloud—they were working their way through the Greek myths, and had just gotten to poor Persephone, who was presently still stuck in Hades.

Angelique absorbed this news silently. There were a good deal more wordless stretches between all of them as the weeks wore on and no one came to stay.

"Perhaps if we place an advertisement in *The Times*," Delilah finally said, into the silence.

"Perhaps if we sent Dot out into the street with a bell like a town cryer," Angelique countered tautly. "That wouldn't cost a thing."

Dot's head shot up.

"I do like bells," she allowed, somewhat worriedly.

Delilah sighed. "We won't be sending you into the street with a bell, Dot."

Dot began to smile.

"Yet," Delilah muttered, a moment later. She was only half joking.

It was just that the fortnight of stillness was a shock after weeks of ceaseless and, quite frankly, exhilarating and triumphant activity. Together Angelique and Delilah made decisions about expenditures and aesthetics shrewdly and effortlessly; they'd done clever things with the curtains and carpets and counterpanes and so forth left in Derring's townhouse that hadn't been taken away by creditors. The Grand Palace sparkled.

Such was Delilah's confident pride and zeal in their endeavor she'd even managed to lure Helga, her old cook, away from the Countess of Brexford with the promise of absolute autonomy in the kitchen and the potential for renown far and wide, given that they expected an exotic variety of guests.

"It'll be so much fun, Helga! Imagine!" Delilah coaxed. The way she had coaxed Angelique.

"The duchess pays me well, but I'm right miserable, so's I am," Helga admitted. "And I miss you, Lady Derring. I'll do it!"

And she'd given her notice and moved in at once.

On the day they'd hung the sign (painted artfully over the old one, which said something about rogues) and dispatched Dot and the two newly hired scullery maids-of-all-work with notices to post in all the businesses nearby, they waited in breathless delight.

Absolutely no one appeared.

It was baffling. London fairly teemed with people coming and going. Ships and mail coaches disgorged them every day. Surely one or two of them would find their way to The Grand Palace on the Thames, if only accidentally?

But no.

And in the gathering tension of the quiet days, the gears of Delilah and Angelique's partnership began to slip and scrape. Every now and then a spark would shoot—a quip emerged perhaps a little too pointed, a tone a trifle too irritable. They laughed less together as the weight of worry began to settle heavily in, the way Gordon settled into his basket. Only infinitely less cozy.

By the time the clock struck eight they'd fallen so broodingly silent that the sudden knock at the door resounded through the house like a gong clash.

They all froze like thieves caught in the act.

Delilah cleared her throat. "Would you go and see who it is, Dot?" Delilah said, as though this happened every day.

But Dot was already a blur, scrambling down the stairs.

She and Angelique remained silently, almost comically frozen in position.

Dot returned moments later, panting.

"Lady Derring Mrs. Breedlove Lady Derring Mrs. Breedlove Lady Derring Mrs. Breedlove! There's a chap downstairs! Looks full of himself and . . ." She paused, and then said on a hush, "He wants to let a room!"

Angelique and Delilah exchanged glances. Well, then. Perhaps that silver-eyed man had been an augury of the guests to come. The first drop in a refreshing rainstorm.

Perhaps it *was* him? The description certainly fit.

At the notion, Delilah's heart lurched in a way that stunned her.

"Dot, will you make some tea?" Angelique said coolly.

Delilah and Angelique shook out their skirts, removed their aprons, reviewed the mirror for any hairs that might have escaped from their pins, then followed Dot downstairs.

In the reception room they found a man of modest scale and scrupulous neatness and plainness. His features were tidy: a short straight nose, a small thin mouth. His black hair was clipped so severely and flawlessly, surely a ruler of some sort had been employed. And his clothes were exquisitely, precisely tailored. He was a man who could fit in or disappear into the wallpaper nearly anywhere.

He rose when they entered.

"We would like to reserve your finest, largest suite," he said without preamble.

They surreptitiously, out of the corners of their eyes, cast glances about the room.

It was Delilah who asked it, very gently. "We?"

In case he was merely a convincing lunatic who had wandered in off the street.

"I represent a man who would like to remain anonymous for the time being. He is a man of some means who, for his convenience, keeps a number of suites available at all times for his use in the ton. I am his man of affairs. We will pay handsomely."

Of all the practical and whimsical things they had discussed regarding the running of The Grand Palace on the Thames (*What if the king should stop in? Should they one day plan to keep a horse?* That sort of thing.), letting a room to an invisible man had not once come up.

A silence fell.

Delilah began, carefully, "Well, you see, Mr. . . ."

"You may call me Mr. X."

There was a protracted silence during which Delilah and Angelique carefully did not look at each other, such was the temptation to roll their eyes.

"One would think your employer would have reserved such a splendidly mysterious name for his own use," Angelique suggested.

Delilah bit the inside of her lip to keep from laughing.

"Nevertheless," was all Mr. X said.

"Nevertheless" was neither an explanation nor a sentence. It was, however, arrogant.

"Perhaps his employer prefers to be called Mr. . . . E," Delilah suggested politely.

Angelique pressed her lips together to keep from laughing.

"Amusing," said Mr. X, clearly not meaning it.

Mr. X, whoever he was, was growing impatient. "All we ask is that you keep the room in a state of preparation should he choose to use it." That *we* again! "The room should remain locked and comfortably clean as though he is, in fact, occupying it, and should he wish to use it, you will be informed so that you can make other preparations accordingly."

"But Mr. . . ."

Delilah couldn't bring herself to say it.

"X," he prompted patiently.

"It's our goal to make The Grand Palace on the Thames feel like home for all of our guests, a safe and secure haven, and that means knowing who is coming and going and who is in residence. We like to conduct interviews before welcoming someone new. It's difficult to interview an invisible guest for suitability."

He regarded them sympathetically for a tick or so, head at a slight tilt.

"Guests?" he queried, gently.

For the second time today, Delilah's cheeks heated. Part temper, part mortification.

She held his gaze.

"For two months," said Mr. X. "At which point we would like to either renew or release our claim. You have our assurances that my employer knows how to behave properly."

There was an unusual emphasis on the word *knows.* As though he knew how but considered proper behavior optional.

The man reached into his coat and opened his wallet.

Then he clinked two sovereigns on the table. As indolently as if they were bread crumbs.

She'd seldom hated a person more. How she longed to be able to say no and send him on his way.

"Is your employer indeed a gentleman, sir?"

He seemed to consider this.

When he smiled, it was small, weary, long-suffering, and ironic.

They waited.

But he didn't deign to answer the question.

"We'd like a moment to discuss this generous but unorthodox arrangement, Mr. X," Angelique said smoothly. Dot had just arrived with the tea. "If you would enjoy your tea we'll rejoin you shortly."

"By all means," he said. Like a judge or a king.

Their guest took a sip of tea and raised his eyebrows in approval.

Delilah and Angelique moved across their shiny foyer into the opposite drawing room, the one with the as-yet-unused pianoforte. It was a little chilly, because they had decided not to light a fire in this room, in order to conserve money.

And this fact suddenly infuriated her. Once again, a supercilious man was assuming they would do whatever he wanted them to do simply because they could not say no. Because he had the money. And the money meant he had the power.

They spoke in whispers.

"I hate him," Delilah said simply.

"Me, too," Angelique agreed.

"It feels like a trap of some kind, but I cannot see how. What if we'll be harboring a criminal?"

"I don't know. Mr. X"—Angelique rolled her eyes extravagantly—"certainly dresses with a severe splendor for a mere assistant of a criminal. I would warrant it's someone notorious, however, which could be thrilling."

"First of all, we don't want thrilling. And it can't be thrilling if the actual Mr. E isn't here and might never be. But what if . . ."

Delilah didn't finish the sentence.

She was going to ask the questions that had no answers: *What if no one else ever comes? What if we fail? What if we starve?*

"I so longed to make all of our decisions out of hope and discretion, not fear," she said instead.

"Well, one day we will, perhaps. I'm not certain we have a choice at the moment." It was Angelique's dryness that helped sober Delilah.

"Then I suppose *that's* our choice, and that makes all the difference, if we are choosing it. We'll be equal to what comes. We've been equal to everything in our lives so far. And it could be an adventure."

"I certainly hope not," Angelique said.

"Then we are decided."

"We are decided."

They conveyed the good news to Mr. X, who didn't so much as waste a muscle twitch on surprise or celebration.

He'd left the sovereigns sitting on the table.

Delilah would rather die than leap upon them before he took his leave of them.

"You will know him when and if he presents the other half of this to you."

He extended to Delilah something the size of a sovereign, forged of metal. It appeared to be half a crest of some sort. Perhaps the leg of a lion, or a unicorn? It was difficult to tell.

Honestly.

"Do you dole these tokens out about the ton, Mr. . . ."

"X," he repeated, patiently.

He ignored her question, patted on his hat, collected his coat, and disappeared into the night without another word.

THE STEVENS HOTEL'S dining room was brimful of men who were wearing, or had worn, or would wear when they were back on duty, the uniform of an English soldier. All attempting to eat a breakfast somehow striking in its flavorlessness.

"Number 11 Lovell Street appears to be a boardinghouse," Tristan told Massey.

"A boardinghouse by the docks?" Massey repeated. Puzzled. "Is that another way of saying brothel?"

"If I meant brothel, Massey, I would have said brothel. I suspect it is nothing quite so interesting anymore, even if it might have been in days of yore. Save your envy."

"What is it like?"

"It appears to be very clean and it smells like a church. I saw a healthy fire in a grate in one room and there's a little pub adjacent."

He looked wistful. "Sounds lovely. Just like me mum's house."

Captain Hardy eyed him balefully. "Did your mum live in a former whorehouse near the docks?"

"I hail from Dover, Captain. Me mum's a saint."

A saint with eight children and a mouth on her like a sailor, Hardy knew, but did not repeat.

"And Derring's widow is apparently one of the proprietresses. I spoke to the barmaid at the pub adjacent."

Massey gave a long, low whistle. "That is interesting. A countess come down in the world of a certainty. Is she pretty?"

Tristan regarded him quellingly. "How on earth does that signify?"

"Pretty women can get a man to do just about anything."

"Not this man."

He had an errant thought: how pleasant it would have been if the maid on the ladder had needed him to do something for her. He feared he might have scrambled to do it.

"No," Massey agreed. Long experience and observation had shown him that no one could persuade Captain Hardy to do anything he didn't want to do.

"I did not meet the countess yesterday, Massey, nor the other proprietress, a Mrs. Angelique Breedlove. I held a brief conversation with a maid."

It felt somehow untruthful to summarize that encounter thusly. In the same way saying "I saw a rainbow" excluded a good deal about the actual experience. "I intend to attempt to let a room. My instincts tell me there's something going on in that building. Wait for orders from me. I'll tell you if and when I'm settled in there."

Massey stifled a sigh. He missed action. "Very well, sir. I'll use the time to write to my sweetheart."

"You have a sweetheart, Massey?" he said idly.

"Yes," Massey told him patiently. "Her name is Emily, sir."

Chapter Eight

AND WITH Mr. X, the floodgates, such as they were, seemed to open the very next day.

"Margaret is very shy, you see, so I do most of the speaking for both of us. She tends to whistle when she talks and it's quite hurtful when people make fun." Miss Jane Gardner's watery pale eyes were pinkish at the rims.

Margaret Gardner glanced up from between her eyelashes. She smiled, swiftly and sadly, then looked down at her lap again.

Based on that glimpse, Margaret's mouth was equal parts teeth and gaps.

Delilah, sitting alongside Angelique on the opposite settee, ached for her. Miss Margaret Gardner's eyes were small and she had a blunt nose and what appeared to be a scar beneath her ear, as though someone had lunged at her with a knife with murderous intent.

Life had not been benign to the Gardner sisters.

Dot had admitted the two of them into the reception room at half past nine, ten minutes ago, then roared up the stairs to the little drawing room in a pitch of excitement.

"We've a pair of sisters what be lookin' for a room! They look somewhat decent!"

While this was not a triumphant endorsement, hope surged painfully.

Delilah and Angelique removed their aprons, smoothed their hair and skirts—their version of donning battle armor—and headed downstairs.

They found two women sitting side by side on the blue settee, looking about the room with bemused expressions.

It was a bit difficult to quite get a sense of how old they were, but if their clothing was any indication, they'd been sealed up in a room for a decade or more, much like The Grand Palace on the Thames itself. They were swathed in shawls, probably two apiece. They were, in fact, dressed as modestly as nuns, in dark brown and dark red wool respectively, with high-rucked collars and long sleeves fitted at the wrists. They each wore a mobcap. A few gray ringlets traced Jane's temples. Her face was long and tapered to a pointed chin.

They didn't resemble sisters so much as a fox and a bear in dresses.

Delilah felt protective of them almost at once.

"We saw your leaflet, you see, advertising your boardinghouse. We lost our previous rooms in London, you see, to a fire. We've a small income and wish to spend it comfortably, near the sea air and the liveliness of London, and this place sounded hospitable and comfortable. And it seems so."

It was like listening to a frail, whispery woodwind. As though Jane Gardner had been shouted at all of her life to stay quiet.

"Oh, it is indeed." Delilah found herself accidentally

speaking loudly to compensate. She cleared her throat and adjusted her volume. "Particularly for women. Our guests are family here. We, in fact, ask all of our tenants to join us in the drawing room at least four nights a week, so that we all might come to know one another better. And gentlemen will be required to put a pence in a jar if they curse. We feel it is a playful way to keep things civilized. It's one of the requirements for staying here. We've rules, you see."

They had indeed. They had printed them on little cards, which were stacked on the table behind them. "We've even printed them, if you'd like to review them."

Margaret and Jane exchanged a swift look.

Margaret looked disconsolately down at her hands, which were squeezed into gloves that looked a little too small, and which were folded in her lap tightly.

"Oh, we trust that your rules are fair. But Margaret is so very shy, you see, it would be a bit of a torment for her to be surrounded by . . . er, gaiety. Where she might be expected to speak."

"Very shy," Margaret confided in a sad whisper. To her lap.

"How do *you* feel about gaiety, Miss Jane?" Angelique asked.

"Oh, I don't suppose I remember, it's been so long now." She laughed timidly behind her knuckles.

"Well, perhaps she can just sit quietly with all of us in the drawing room and we can enjoy her presence," Delilah suggested. "And *you* may yet rediscover an appreciation for gaiety, when you hear the pianoforte played well. We are planning to hold musicales."

She ignored the dry look sent her way by Angelique.

Margaret's head shot up briefly and Delilah got a glimpse of the whites of her eyes, flared in alarm.

"Perhaps she'll feel free to come out of her shell when she sees that we are all friends here, and we will not tolerate anyone making fun of her whistle. We will all be patient," Delilah continued. Sweetly but firmly.

"You've come to a welcoming place for women to live," Angelique soothed. "We will have male guests, too, but they will be held to a strict and gentlemanly code of conduct. And that also means no sneaking gentleman callers up to your rooms."

Delilah shot Angelique a reproving look.

But Miss Margaret giggled softly behind her fingers. Her gloves were kid, and fine. It was rather touching to see that she had indulged herself in at least one elegant thing.

"It all sounds lovely. We should like to share your largest room, on a low floor."

"Oh, I'm sorry to disappoint you, but our largest room suitable for two people has *just* been let."

The sisters went absolutely still.

They appeared paralyzed by disappointment.

The mutual faint creaking of stays signaled the resumption of their ribcages moving in and out with breathing.

"We're so sorry to disappoint you," Delilah said warmly. "We'd be happy to show you our second-largest room, which we will make just as comfortable for you. You will be nice and snug. It's on the floor above."

The silence was oddly protracted.

"Very well." Jane sounded a bit martyred.

"We'll do everything possible to make sure you're happy here at The Grand Palace on the Thames," Delilah soothed.

"Oh, we're certain you will, dear." She smiled.

DELILAH AND ANGELIQUE decided that since they had three guests now—one invisible, two visible—serving something fancy involving beef would be a splendid way to celebrate. Helga and Angelique set out to see if they could get a roast, happily squabbling about the price of it and the inventive ways they could stretch the meat throughout the week.

Delilah fondly saw them off.

In the spare moment here and there it occurred to her how odd it was that they'd all easily slipped into this unique way of life, when in typical circumstances their lives—hers and Angelique's and Dot's and Helga's—would have been stringently partitioned from one another. What would her mother have said if she'd caught her chatting cheerily with Helga in the kitchen about her cousin in Dublin this morning? She could even now hear her hissing, *One doesn't exchange girlish confidences with the* servants, *Delilah!*

She was still a countess, at least in name. And it wasn't as though a part of her didn't feel a bit of a tug toward everything she'd been taught. But it was the sort of tug a rose must feel when trained up a trellis. The trellis had crumbled. She could grow how she pleased.

She felt as though she was both weaving, and already woven into, this life here at The Grand Palace on the Thames. It was hers, and *of* her, in the way nothing else had felt in her twenty-six years. She hadn't time to miss the luxury and leisure. *Maybe* one day it would seem like a sacrifice.

Until then, she would happily sing while she did the dusting.

Dot took the Gardner sisters up to get them settled into their room. Delilah decided she'd dust the large drawing room, paying special attention to the pianoforte just in case musically inclined guests began to pour through the door. Then she took a cup of tea to the drawing room to ostensibly finish some mending, but in truth mostly because she wished to scratch Gordon beneath the chin.

Both she and the cat sprang apart like startled lovers when she heard Dot's feet thundering up the stairs, all three flights. Dot was quite fit.

"Lady Derring Lady Derring Lady Derring Lady Derring Lady Derr—"

She leaped to her feet. "Good heavens, Dot, what is the trouble?"

"There's a man downstairs what wants to let a room, and . . ."

Dot paused and pressed her lips together.

Her face was lit up with a blend of wonderment and a sort of delicious fear, the kind engendered by horrid novels.

"What sort of man?"

"Very tall, not a spare ounce nor frill on 'im. His clothes fit like a skin, they're so perfect and I could see me own face in his boots. I could not decide between Lucifer or the chap what holds up the world—"

"Atlas?" They'd been reading that particular myth aloud to each other in the upstairs drawing room at night.

"Aye, but summat about him is like both. I would and wouldn't like to meet him in an alley alone, if you ken what I mean."

"Good heavens."

She most certainly did not ken what Dot meant, but she was going to have to go downstairs and face this remarkable person alone, with just Dot for reinforcements.

She untied her apron, shook out her skirts, reviewed her reflection for respectability. Huge, too-hopeful brown eyes gazed back at her. She was growing weary of mauve half mourning but at least the color suited her. She tried on a cooler expression, something like welcoming hauteur, and followed Dot downstairs to the reception room.

The man turned slowly at the sound of her footsteps across the foyer.

But even before she saw his face she knew. Because she *felt* him. His very presence was as distinct a sensation as velvet, or flame. And her heart lurched in both alarming untoward exultation and fear.

She stopped short on the threshold of the room as though the carefully chosen and trimmed carpet was instead lava.

He lifted his head.

His abrupt stillness thrilled her. As though he'd braced for impact, too.

"I noticed the windows are very clean," he said

gravely. Finally. And after a long moment during which no one said a thing.

He hadn't yet blinked.

"La la la la," he added. As solemnly as one might deliver a speech in parliament.

Her usual responses to things were in a snarl, as bound tightly together as Margaret Gardner's shy, folded hands. She was suddenly acutely aware of how her shift felt against her skin. *All* of her senses, in fact, were suddenly, painfully alert. As if they'd finally found something truly worthy of their attention and had been lying down on the job for the first two decades of her life.

"Is Lady Derring indisposed then?" he said gently. As though he was both resigned to her being witless and quite accustomed to being gawked at. "Shall I speak with you instead?"

"I am Lady Derring." Her voice was even, if thready.

Instantly a cool, hard screen of a sort moved over his expression.

She could see at once that he was making an internal adjustment, a reassessment of some sort, and it wasn't a flattering one.

It occurred to her all at once that she would not want to play cards with this man.

He bowed, gracefully as any courtier.

"Well, then. A pleasure to meet you, Lady Derring. I am Captain Tristan Hardy."

The name was a bit of a surprise. But it fit him, all of it. Tristan, with its air of implied heroism and tragedy, and Hardy, because anything with "hard" in it would suit. As Dot had said, not a spare anything on the man. One got the sense bullets would bounce right off.

The *captain* part probably explained that air of implacable, insufferable authority. As though he moved through the world with ease in part because he knew destiny wouldn't dare countermand his orders.

"What brings you back to The Grand Palace on the Thames, Captain Hardy?"

His small, intimate smile removed the bones from her knees.

"So you do remember me, Lady Derring."

She ignored the smile and remembered that her blood was blue, even if keys jingled at her hips now.

"My maid, Dorothy, informs me that you are seeking a room to let, Captain Hardy. Would you care to have a seat to discuss it?" She gestured at the settee.

"There's to be a discussion? I thought these sorts of things were usually dispensed with a yes or a no."

He said it almost lightly. But he sat down. Immediately his presence elevated the settee, with its small burn carefully patched and the nick in one of its legs, to something like a throne.

"We like to be certain all of our treasured guests are comfortable here and that new guests are a proper fit and willing to abide by the rules, so we ask a few questions."

"Treasured, are they?" he said smoothly. "I've long aspired to be treasured."

"All guests who pay their bills, follow the rules, and do not disrupt the other guests are indeed treasured."

He regarded her with those eyes which were all that was polite and yet she couldn't shake the sensation that he could see right through her dress to her stays.

"There are rules?" he said with idle interest.

"Indeed. It's hardly anarchy here at The Grand Palace on the Thames."

"And how much does it cost to be treasured?"

"Twelve pounds per week."

She decided this was his rate, no matter whether he took a small or a large room. The two extra pounds were a surcharge for arrogance.

"And what benefits do your guests receive in exchange for their princely twelve pounds?"

"Two truly fine meals a day, a libation in the morning or evening brought to your room if you should request one, a warm, tidy room, and mending of smaller items. For a small additional fee, we will engage a laundress if you need one, and we will bring a bath up to your room no more than once per week. We feel, all in all, it is a splendid value."

"And of course the occasional musicale. One can't put a price on that."

"I'm so glad you agree."

He smiled with vanishing swiftness, as though she'd said something charming.

She couldn't imagine what.

"And guests with money to burn flock to your establishment, do they, Lady Derring? I could scarcely move through your foyer without brushing against a skirt or a greatcoat."

Her breath caught. *Why, the basta . . . !*

It took her a moment to recover.

"Naturally our guests do not mill about the foyer,

Captain. From this location our guests can go about their employment or enjoy all that London has to offer, such as . . . the theater."

"Is *the theater* a euphemism for brothels?"

In the silence that followed, the fire gave a violent pop, as if in indignation.

Neither one of them blinked.

Well.

No man had ever said the word *brothel* to her in her twenty-six years of life—that, at least, was one of the advantages of being a countess. It just didn't come up in polite conversation.

Captain Hardy was either trying to disconcert her, or he was trying to find out whether she indeed was running a brothel. To what end, she could not have guessed.

Still, it was only a word. And she was hardly a fragile flower. Flaming cheeks notwithstanding.

"I'm afraid I can't provide you with a list of brothels, Captain," she decided to say carefully. "If that's your aim, and you're attempting to speak in code. We aren't that kind of establishment. Perhaps you ought to seek a different boardinghouse? Or are you in an indirect way attempting to ascertain the quality of our clientele?"

And damned if Tristan didn't admire her response.

"It's just that to get to all the other things that London has to offer, your guests must navigate a gauntlet of what Lovell Street near the docks has to offer, including robbery, pub brawls, and the occasional murder. It's an unusual location for an exclusive boardinghouse with rules regarding propriety."

She didn't even blink. Up close, Lady Derring's eyes were as velvety and alluring as a settee in an opium den. Yet he would warrant she'd just inventoried his eyelashes.

"Isn't it lovely that The Grand Palace on the Thames is an oasis of comfort and safety in the midst of a chaotic world?"

That was deft, he'd hand that much to her.

"By the way, how did you come to open a boardinghouse?"

She cleared her throat. "Well, I am lately a widow, Captain Hardy—"

"My condolences."

She acknowledged this with the rote nod it deserved. "—and it seemed to my business partner, Mrs. Angelique Breedlove, and me the perfect opportunity to meet people from all walks of life." She sounded proud.

"Ah." He took pains to sound faintly puzzled. "I was curious. I've heard your establishment referred to as The Palace of Rogues. A place for rogues, one would assume."

She went still. Then a hurt that seemed genuine flickered across her features.

He knew a startling—a rogue, even—and tearing sense of regret that he may have been the source of it.

"Scurrilous," she maintained stoutly. "That's what that assertion is, if that's what you heard. If you hear it again, I should be obliged if you'd correct them and tell them it's a fine establishment, as you can see for yourself. I'm sorry if this disappoints you."

"I'll do that," he said gently. "And it hardly smells

of mildew at all, which is a remarkable feat for a building so close to the docks."

She narrowed her eyes ever so slightly.

"Are you attempting to negotiate the price of your room, sir?"

"That depends. To my original question: *Have* you a room to let, Lady Derring?"

Intriguingly, she paused.

"Based on our discussion, I do wonder if this is the sort of place you'd feel at ease, Captain. And our prices are not negotiable. We feel our guests are given great value for their money."

"Ease," he repeated thoughtfully, after a moment. As if it were a word only plebeians found use for.

She seemed to take this as an invitation to tip her head and study him critically with those soft eyes.

He could feel the jagged old glacier of his heart creak as if exposed to a violent sunbeam.

He thought perhaps he should look away.

And then he thought: *what a waste of a moment it would be, if I should look away when I could be looking at her.*

A pretty woman can get a man to do anything, Massey had said to him.

But he was a man willing to do just about anything to get *his* man.

Easier still if the man he needed to get was instead a woman.

He lowered his voice to one of confiding sympathy. "Would you like to inspect beneath my chin, Lady Derring? I might have missed a hair or two whilst shaving, though I'm not inclined to miss any detail at all. About anything. Ever."

A little silence.

"It's difficult to shave the day after a liquor-soaked evening, I should imagine," she said smoothly.

She was very, very good.

"While I'll allow that this is true, that wasn't the circumstance this morning, nor will it be during my stay here at the Ro—"

"Grand Palace on the Thames."

"Ah, yes, of course. Very well, then. Now that I know a bit more about what sort of establishment this is—and it does sound like a fine establishment—would you mind telling me a bit more about the rules?"

She looked relieved. "They're very simple, really. We expect our male guests to behave like gentlemen in the presence of ladies. Drinking, spitting, or smoking will not be tolerated in the drawing room when ladies are present, and rough language will be fined one pence per word. We've a jar, you see."

"A jar." He said this with every evidence of fascination.

"But we also have a withdrawing room for gentlemen, in which they can unleash their baser impulses in case the effort of restraint becomes too much to bear."

Lady Derring was very dry.

"What a relief to hear. Tethering instincts wears a devil out."

He was rewarded with a smile, one of delightful, slow, crooked affairs, as if she just couldn't help herself, and he, for a moment, could not have formed words for admiring it.

"Suitable guests don't find the rules a challenge at all, and if you're of sound character, you've scarcely need to try to behave. You will simply enjoy the camaraderie of our drawing room evenings."

"I assure you my character is both sound and unassailable."

"Apart, perhaps, from a slight issue with modesty?"

Perhaps an example of the "more sting than fuzz" the solicitor had mentioned.

Odd. He found it rather bracing.

"Do you keep a jar for braggarts? Perhaps you ought to have a jar for every sin or character flaw. Gluttony. Loquaciousness. Untoward musical tendencies."

"If you feel it would be helpful in terms of modifying any of your impulses, we'll certainly consider implementing a system of jars. We don't anticipate a wide variety of sin, here at The Grand Palace on the Thames. Nor, by the way, do we encourage the indiscriminate inviting of guests to one's rooms."

He nodded thoughtfully. "Very good, very good. I do wonder how you manage to keep your establishment so apparently civilized and comfortable, Lady Derring. It must require significant expenditure and loyal staff. Who like to be paid, I imagine. As well as a steady supply of guests. And yet it is so wondrously quiet here."

Another slightest pause, during which she studied him as if he were a mysterious corridor and she was deciding which door she ought to open.

"It's simple, Captain Hardy. We do not let our rooms to uncivilized people, and should our judgment prove in error, we request that they leave. They will find their belongings neatly packed and placed by the front door."

Notably, she didn't take up the issue of expenditure. "St. Peter has less rigorous standards."

"He'd do well to follow our example."

"Why, that's very nearly heretical, Lady Derring."

"What a shame it would be if heresy deterred you from taking a room at The Grand Palace on the Thames, Captain Hardy. May I ask, why *do* you find you have need of a room here?"

"I'm in the process of purchasing a ship which will make merchant runs to China and India, and as this establishment is nearest the harbor, I feel it will be a convenient place from which to conduct my business."

It wasn't untrue.

"And then you'll sail away for good?"

Her tone was interesting. It straddled something between hope and regret. With just a dash of yearning. For what? Sailing to faraway places? For him to leave?

"I shall certainly be away from English soil for great swaths of time, yes. One can only be shot at so many times, you see, before retiring begins to make sense."

She regarded him with those eyes and he could have sworn something like grave concern flickered there. "Where *is* your home?"

"Due to the nature of my work, I haven't a permanent home." Oddly, he felt as though he were confessing a flaw to her.

She blinked. Then took a breath, as though she intended to say something, then changed her mind. "Well. Our intent is to welcome a variety of people here and to make all of them feel as though it is home. We feel it makes life more pleasurable and interesting."

She stood and moved to a little table upon which sat a stack of cards. She was small and graceful and there was an elemental pleasure in simply watching her move.

She handed one of the cards to him.

All guests will eat dinner together at least four times per week.

All guests must gather in the drawing room after dinner for at least an hour at least four times per week. We feel it fosters a sense of friendship and the warm, familial, congenial atmosphere we strive to create here at The Grand Palace on the Thames.

All guests should be quietly respectful and courteous of other guests at all times, though spirited discourse is welcome.

Guests may entertain other guests in the drawing room.

Curfew is at 11:00 p.m. The front door will be securely locked then. You will need to wait until morning to be admitted if you miss curfew.

If the proprietresses collectively decide that a transgression or series of transgressions warrants your eviction from The Grand Palace on the Thames, you will find your belongings neatly packed and placed near the front door. You will not be refunded the balance of your rent.

"Curfew?" He was bemused.

"Is there a gaming hell that will miss your presence after eleven o'clock, Captain Hardy? We feel our guests will be more comfortable if they can be assured of who is coming and going."

This actually made very good sense.

"No, no. I was just admiring it. Rules. Regimentation. Perhaps you ought to have considered the military, Lady Derring."

"I assume you mean to flatter me, Captain Hardy, given that was the choice you made for yourself. If only my options had been quite so diverse. Would you like to take a moment to reassure yourself that you can abide by the rules?"

"If there's anything at all I've learned in the navy, it's to abide by rules . . . and to enforce them. My nature isn't anarchic. It is, however, indomitable."

She regarded him with a certain quizzical sympathy. "We might be able to pay for an additional maid with the contents of your braggart jar."

He gave her a little smile. And then he reached into his coat, and from his wallet he laid down twelve one-pound notes. One at a time. As if placing a wager.

She eyed them, a flare of undeniable hunger in her eyes, quickly disguised.

It wasn't greed, he'd warrant. It was need.

Interesting.

"I should like your largest, most comfortable suite of rooms, please."

"I fear we've already let Suite Three, which is our largest. We've also let the next largest, Captain Hardy.

But all of our rooms are comfortable and I'm sure you'll not want for a thing."

"I shall be content in whatever room you choose."

"We shall make certain you are. And you'll have a chance to meet your fellow guests this evening."

To Tristan, it sounded like both a promise and a warning.

"INSUFFERABLE," WAS HOW she described him to Angelique when they were in the kitchen discussing the menu for the week with Helga, who had triumphantly returned with a cut of beef that pleased her. "Naval captain. Well-spoken. Thinks very highly of himself. I could see myself in his buttons and boot toes. Not a speck of lint on his coat. Also, this man is *very* tall."

They were all wistful about the word *tall*. All the window cleaning and trimming of the candles in sconces made them covetous of long legs and arms.

A few hours later, Angelique met Captain Hardy in the reception room just before he left for a previous dinner engagement. He was charming and brief and then was out of the door in a flash.

She stared at the door after he departed.

Then turned toward Delilah abruptly.

Delilah was studying the urn full of flowers as if it had suddenly become fascinating, and pretended not to notice that Angelique was staring at her.

"Funny," Angelique said finally. "I pictured a bluff, red-faced, gray-haired sea dog. Find it very interesting that you didn't mention that Captain Hardy is, shall we say . . . compelling."

There it was. It was absolutely the perfect word for

him. Equal parts enigmatic and magnetic. But it didn't encompass the temperature changes she experienced in his company.

"Did you find him so?" she said idly.

But Angelique's incredulous stare threatened to singe a hole in her forehead.

"Oh, for heaven's sake, Delilah. He is gorgeous." It didn't sound like a compliment. It sounded like a warning.

She looked up at Angelique finally and bit her lip, almost apologetically. "If you like that sort of thing."

Angelique sighed. "There's something about him," she said thoughtfully, after a moment. "I cannot shake the sense that we've let a room in the henhouse to the fox, though I can't for certain say why. I don't think Captain Hardy is the sort who does anything without a reason. Which makes me wonder why he's here, at The Grand Palace on the Thames."

A tiny part of Delilah, where her vanity lived, longed to believe that Captain Hardy had returned to The Grand Palace on the Thames because he'd hoped to see her again. Beyond this sop to her vanity she didn't want to think. The male of the species was not to be trusted in the way wild animals quite simply could not be trusted, even years after they'd been domesticated. One just didn't know what they would get up to.

"Do you think his presence has to do with Mr., er, X and his employer?"

They both still felt ridiculous saying "Mr. X."

"Well . . . I have no idea. But we are blameless, in that regard."

"And we've Captain Hardy's twelve pounds, anyway."

"You charged him two additional pounds?"

"It was an arrogance surcharge."

"So far our business is based on somewhat extorting two men. One for invisibility, one for arrogance," Angelique mused.

"I cannot find it in my heart to regret that."

This made both of them smile.

Chapter Nine

A MERE TWO and a half hours later she and Angelique sat side by side in the reception room again.

"I don't know *what* he is, but he's quite nice," was how Dot had described the newest potential guest when she'd raced up the stairs to fetch them. "And loud."

Dot was a savant, as it turned out, when it came to describing their arrivals. She was absolutely correct on all counts.

"I know I'm an unprepossessing sort."

"Nonsense, Mr. Delacorte," they lied prettily, in unison.

Perched on the settee, his feet just barely touched the floor. His black-and-gray hair was unevenly trimmed, and tufted out about his ears, which made him look incongruously like a baby bird. The toes of his boots were well creased, but they'd been polished, and the buttons on his waistcoat were nearly audibly straining. Delilah imagined the threads holding on to them groaning like tree branches stressed by a windstorm. One in particular looked moments away from launching.

She canted ever so slightly to his left, lest it take out her eye.

But the tailoring was good and his hat was brushed

and tended and his greatcoat was new. Dot had taken them from him and laid them over a chair.

His clothes clearly had not kept up with his appetite.

His smile was vast, genuine, and rueful.

His eyebrows were bushy affairs.

His blue eyes were twinkly.

And his speaking volume suggested he was standing on shore shouting a farewell to travelers sailing away in a ship rather than sitting across from two ladies on the settee.

They quickly established that he wasn't hard of hearing. Though demonstrating proper volume hadn't yet encouraged him to calibrate his own.

"I like my food, you see." His stomach gave a resonant thud when he smacked it.

Delilah kept a weather eye on the waistcoat button.

"We've an excellent cook," Angelique told him. "And nothing makes her happier than watching someone enjoy her food."

"I saw your advertisement in the apothecary and I thought, well, that's the place for me! I like rules. I want a bit of civilizing, as you can see."

"We could all use a little help now and again," Delilah soothed.

"And I wanted a place what feels like home. Until I have a home of my own."

"Well, that's precisely what we offer our guests, Mr. Delacorte," Angelique told him warmly. "And we feel the ten pounds per week is worth every penny."

He didn't blink, which meant he'd passed that particular financial test.

"I've longed for a bit of looking after, but it's hard

to find a wife, you see, when I travel so much for my work. A fine, sturdy woman who wouldn't mind coming along with me sometimes, but who keeps a home waiting for me. I'd like a bit of domesticating, perhaps." He sounded wistful.

"It sounds like a lovely dream, Mr. Delacorte. May we ask what line of business you are in?"

"I import cures for ailments and I sell them to surgeons and apothecaries up and down the coast of England. Chinese herbs and bits and bobs from India with unpronounceable names, ground-up horns and testicles of exotic animals and the like," he said cheerily. "Make a fair penny, or two."

Delilah and Angelique were startled rigid.

Mr. Delacorte twinkled at them.

His smile began to dim as the silence grew by seconds.

"If we may make a suggestion?" Delilah said gently.

"It was *testicles*, wasn't it?" he said disconsolately. "It's just that all I ever talk to is men, surgeons and apothecaries and the like, and one begins to forget how to speak to women."

"Well, here at The Grand Palace on the Thames we've a jar in the drawing room, and we ask gentlemen to put a pence in when they slip up and say a word that might be a bit rough in the presence of the ladies. We know how difficult it is, sometimes."

"Oh, aren't you clever! You see, a little bit of help now and again to knock off my rough corners, if you know what I mean. I don't mind a bit of nagging at all, if I'm to win over the right sort of wife for me one day."

Despite themselves, they were charmed.

"Why don't you enjoy your tea, Mr. Delacorte, while Mrs. Breedlove and I have a quick word about the availability of accommodations."

Angelique and Delilah stood in tandem and walked together to the opposite drawing room.

They stood in thoughtful silence.

They could hear Mr. Delacorte slurping his tea.

"Ahh!" he said, with great satisfaction.

"I think I would enjoy," Delilah said slowly, finally, "seeing Mr. Delacorte and Captain Hardy in the same room."

Angelique smiled slowly.

They returned to Mr. Delacorte, who looked up hopefully.

"Welcome to The Grand Palace on the Thames, Mr. Delacorte."

BACK AT THE Stevens Hotel, where probably every man—and they were all men—surrounding him in the restaurant was in the army or navy, Tristan had no compunction about abandoning his attempt to saw off a slice of chicken with the sad, dull utensil provided, and reaching into his boot for his knife.

It was clean and sharp. Tristan took excellent care of his weapons.

He handed the knife across to Massey, who grunted his thanks and sawed his own chicken.

He knew better than to do that at a *formal* dinner table. When in Rome, however.

"Lady Derring is one of the proprietresses of The Grand Palace on the Thames," he told Massey. "Which is indeed a boardinghouse."

Massey gave a low whistle. "That is interesting, indeed."

The next challenge was chewing the chicken. They took a moment to accomplish this.

Tristan sincerely hoped Lady Derring's cook was as good as she claimed.

"Is she pretty? Lady Derring."

Tristan stopped to stare at him.

"That's quite a vehement stare, Captain Hardy."

"Oh, *forgive* me. Have I hurt your feelings, Massey?"

"I'm only noting it," Massey said easily. "Because if she is pretty," he continued, when Tristan didn't take up the subject, "one wonders why a pretty, penniless widow would choose to run a derelict boardinghouse rather than marry again. After proper mourning is observed, of course. Or one would think a relative would take her in."

"I wondered the same thing."

"So she *is* pretty."

Tristan paused to choose a word.

"She is tolerable." He was darkly amused at himself for this assessment.

Massey stared at him, with a furrow of suspicion in his forehead.

"And before you ask, Massey. Yes, Mrs. Breedlove is pretty, too. And the boardinghouse, as such, can no longer be considered derelict. It's very well kept. Which leads up to the questions of where said penniless widow found the money to repair and furnish the boardinghouse. And print *rules*," he said grimly.

"There are rules?"

"Oh, yes."

There was a silence as they both determinedly chewed. They'd masticated hardtack and biscuits. This chicken hadn't a prayer of defeating them. Torturing them, perhaps, when they attempted to digest it later.

The clink of silverware and male laughter filled the silence.

"What does she look like?" It was as if Massey couldn't help himself. "Lady Derring."

Tristan sighed heavily and laid down his fork. "Honestly, Massey."

"Humor a man who misses his sweetheart, sir."

"What's your sweetheart's name, again?" Tristan said, devilishly.

"Emily," Massey said patiently.

Tristan chewed his chicken. Then said, "Petite. Black hair. Brown eyes."

For the first time it occurred to him what a disservice those descriptors did people. These were the ones always trotted out, along with the occasional "and she has a hump" or "his legs are uncommonly long" or that sort of thing. The table was "brown." Lady Derring's eyes had a rare luster like the stock of his pistol, polished to a gleam. And a depth that called to mind calm seas, with all the potential of storms to pull a ship under.

He doubted any woman would want to hear such a thing. Gun stocks and that rot. But his notions of beauty were singular.

"Mrs. Breedlove is fair with light eyes," he added.

Mrs. Breedlove was also a very different woman

than Lady Derring. He could see it at a glance. Oddly, he was glad someone more cynical was in partnership with Lady Derring.

"How did you establish that it is indeed a boardinghouse, Captain Hardy?"

"After a fairly rigorous interview, I was led to a room that seems comfortable. While I haven't been able to look into every room or every part of the house—though I intend to do that—I have no reason not to believe that the other rooms are similar."

"Oh, she interviewed you rigorously, did she?"

"I command you stop leering right now."

When Tristan spoke like that even the people nearest gave a little shudder and wondered why the temperature had just dropped several degrees.

Massey got control of his expression.

"In addition to the rules, there is a curfew, and a jar in which to place a pence if you curse in front of a lady. The interview took place because apparently she needed to ascertain whether I was suitable."

"Sounds precisely like the type of boardinghouse a fine lady would run, sir."

"It does, at that."

"What is your room like?"

"The counterpane is quilted and blue. The bed could fit two people the size of me. There is an adequate wardrobe, a chest of drawers, and a writing table."

"Are the pillows soft?" Massey said wistfully.

Tristan had indeed punched the pillows. They'd billowed like clouds. One of the advantages of being a soldier was that one never took for granted creature comforts.

He'd in fact stood in that room arrested in a moment of unguarded, absolute wonder. That little flower in a vase on the writing desk, the braided rug next to the bed, the clean, smooth counterpane of a vivid, lovely blue—these were the sort of touches women thought to do to a house—and it was a bit of a trap. One could get to like and need softness and comfort and clean things. One struggled to fight one's way out of them as though they'd indeed fallen into a deep pillow.

But because Massey knew him and would half expect it, he rolled his eyes. "By definition, pillows are soft, Massey. And before you ask, the chamber pot has blue periwinkles on it."

Massey's eyes crinkled. "Me brother has a chamber pot that makes it look as though you're pissing in the king's mou—"

"We serve at the pleasure of the crown."

It was a sharp, coldly worded warning.

The king was wildly unpopular, but he was the representative of the country Tristan would fight and die for, and of all English citizens, and as such, Tristan was loyal to the bone.

He had his own opinions about the king and Massey likely knew them. The king was more complicated, and less happy, than anyone understood. He hadn't been born to rule. Not everyone had the luxury of a destiny that fit them like a suit of clothes. But he would die for that king.

"Yes, sir. Sorry, sir."

Tristan allowed a little moment of silence for the admonishment to sink in.

And another moment to scoop into his mouth a few peas.

"Keep in mind that many a man has been murdered in a comfortable room."

"Have they, sir?"

Tristan sighed. "Oh, probably."

Massey grinned at this.

"I won't be that man, Massey. I will talk to the guests and have a look around once I'm inside the building. I should like you, Morgan, Halligan, Roberts, and Besson to make a note of who exits and enters the building at all hours, so take it in shifts and assign extra men as you see fit. I'm to meet the three other guests tonight because apparently there's a mandatory gathering in the drawing room four nights per week."

Massey's eyes had gone misty. "A gathering in a drawing room sounds rather nice. I can't wait until Emily and I have our own drawing room."

Tristan rolled his eyes.

TRISTAN WAS UNACCUSTOMED to aimlessness or leisure for the sake of leisure. His life had been composed of taking action, planning action, or waiting for action. Attacking, defending, fleeing. Shouting orders or taking them. Aiming a gun, wielding a mop. That sort of thing.

Nothing in his experience to date had involved sitting—just sitting!—quietly at a little table in a firelit room while two maiden aunts stared at him in apparent horror from a dark corner.

"He's not quite as fearsome as he looks," he heard Lady Derring whisper to them.

Although in truth it was more of a stage whisper.

He quirked the corner of his mouth dryly and lowered his head to his book. He'd brought to the boardinghouse a satchel of belongings, including a change of clothes, tooth powder, shaving soap and brushes, and a book. He'd been attempting to read *Robinson Crusoe* for some time now. He'd gotten to page five over the past three months or so. Something *always* interrupted.

"How do you do," he'd said gravely, earlier, when he'd been introduced to the Gardner sisters.

The one called Miss Margaret had uttered a sort of squeak and ducked her head. Which was massive, he noted. He'd seen the whites of her eyes before she did that.

She hadn't lifted her head since, that he'd noticed.

She was a strapping woman. Perhaps a retired laundress.

The other, Miss Jane, had said, "How do you do," so quietly he could easily have imagined it. She had the sort of voice a bird would use if a bird could speak.

Where on earth had Lady Derring and Mrs. Breedlove found these two?

"Miss Margaret is shy," Mrs. Breedlove had explained on a whisper a moment later, though this was a secret to no one, least of all Margaret.

Despite the fact that he felt as though he was quite literally in Purgatory—the place beyond which he was not allowed to move—doubtless the sentimental Massey would find it pleasant.

An old brown-and-cream brocade settee nearly the size of a barouche was arrayed at an angle across the room. An assortment of mismatched little tables—he'd chosen one for himself at a gentlemanly distance from the fire, along with a wooden-backed chair—were studded with little lamps. The leaping fire threw a flattering light upon all the ladies present except for the Gardner sisters, because they had chosen the corner farthest from the fire, apparently seeking the quiet and the dark. Lady Derring and Mrs. Breedlove were glowing like lovely candles in their chairs. Lady Derring's head was bent over an embroidery hoop.

Perhaps the embroidery was destined for a pillow. Perhaps it was an image of a man putting a gun to his head because he was forced to sit quietly in a drawing room.

He supposed it was "cozy."

Dot, the maid, was mending something. "Ouch," she said softly.

A second later: "Ouch," she muttered again.

He'd noted the pianoforte against the wall and amused himself by imagining what it would be like to glue it shut, and to watch them struggle to get it up to no avail.

He had no objections to music. It was just that he had a weakness for music played well, and it so seldom was in drawing rooms such as these.

"I count only two guests, Lady Derring. Where is your third? Did this person pay an additional fee to escape the drawing room? If so, I must shake his hand to congratulate him on his bargaining skills."

She regarded him coolly a moment. Then her head swiveled.

"Ah, here's Mr. Delacorte! Why don't you go and have a smoke and a chat with him in the gentlemen's room, Captain Hardy?"

It sounded like an order. So he went.

Chapter Ten

THE ROOM set aside for gentlemen to smoke and curse in was set off the drawing room. Some pains had been taken to make it pleasant. Three large brown upholstered chairs with winged backs were arranged about a low table upon which a man could heave his booted feet, if he so chose. The carpet featured a black-and-brown scrolled pattern. Presumably the sorts of colors that could disguise smoke and any other unspeakable thing a man might take it into his head to do.

He and Delacorte stood about for a wordless moment, like two dogs tied up outside while their owners have tea in a shop.

"You missed a truly splendid dinner," Delacorte began. "It was remarkable, in fact. The things the cook can do with a *sauce*. Was all I could do not to lick my plate. Even *I* know enough not to do that! Ha ha ha!"

Tristan smiled tensely.

Mr. Delacorte was hearty. He didn't speak so much as boom, like a man shouting over a crowd at a race track, cheering on a horse.

"But I've *nothing* on Miss Margaret Gardner's enthusiasm. Shoveled it in with both hands as though she thought it might be snatched away any moment! Never saw a woman with an appetite like that."

Tristan stifled a sigh. Now he had something to look forward to at dinner the next day.

"So you're a captain, eh? Career naval officer?"

"Aye."

"Did you know Admiral Nelson?"

"Served under him."

Nelson, like God, needed no further exposition.

"WELL." Delacorte stood back and planted his hands on his hips. "I'd warrant that makes you a hero, too, you old sea dog!"

"No," Tristan said.

That wasn't entirely true—a street rat from St. Giles doesn't rise to be an infamously effective, ruthless naval captain without someone bandying about the word *hero*. The king himself had used it. Once. In a private conversation, granted.

It was just that the heartier Delacorte became, the more air he expended, the less air Tristan felt inclined to expend in the form of words, as if to maintain the balance of air in the universe.

Delacorte was silently contributing other things to the atmosphere, too. His enthusiasm for the food at dinner had begun expressing itself in other ways.

Tristan was hardly delicate. He'd spent a few years crammed on ships with hundreds of men and was well aware of how cheerfully disgusting they could be. It was just that he hadn't had to do it in recent years. One of the privileges of being a captain was having his own quarters, in which he didn't have to listen to snoring, gastric eruptions, weeping, night terrors, or surreptitious masturbation.

"Oh, I suspect you're being modest, Hardy."

"No one who knows me would ever suggest that."

While this was true, Delacorte laughed heartily for no reason Tristan could surmise.

There was a lull, during which Tristan thought he could begin making inquiries, though it was difficult to imagine Delacorte as a smuggler, roaring away about cigars in a black boat slinking up the coast, or nimbly leaping ashore with purloined goods. There was nothing of subtlety in the man. He'd be hung with alacrity in no time if he were a smuggler.

"Hardy!" Delacorte whisper-barked behind his hand, pantomiming secrecy, even though they were completely alone. "Have one of these."

He slipped his hand into his coat and withdrew, of all things . . .

. . . two cigars.

He wagged his eyebrows at Tristan by way of encouragement.

Tristan stared at them.

Slowly, wordlessly, Tristan accepted one.

Ran it beneath his nose.

The little hairs on the back of his neck prickled.

"You'll love it, Hardy," Delacorte enthused. "They taste like . . . a damp house made of chocolate and perhaps parsley or sage, in which two zebras have been fucking on a dirt floor."

Tristan stared at him.

It might be the most profane thing he'd ever heard.

And he'd been a *sailor.*

But Delacorte had lit it and he was studying it pensively, even beatifically, as smoke wreathed him, his brow wrinkled a bit.

"No—*lions* fucking," he amended, cheerfully. Satisfied with that conclusion, he sucked until the tip glowed. "And yet, it's delicious, somehow. Most interesting thing I've ever smoked."

This was why women wanted to segregate the men for a time. One just never knew what they were going to say or do. For the same reasons one oughtn't to keep an ocelot for a pet. He'd heard of a French aristocrat who had tried that once. It had humped the family dog and eaten the cat.

And they were bound to talk about all the things they'd smoked, eventually, because men had those kinds of conversations.

"I must regretfully decline at the moment, Delacorte, but thank you. Where did you get these singular cigars?"

"Bought them at the apothecary up the road on Courtland Street a month ago. Said they'd get more in but never did. Now they're selling them for ten pounds each. Ten pounds! I ask you." He shook his head mournfully. "Who has that sort of money to spend on cigars?"

"Did the apothecary say from whom they'd purchased the cigars?"

"Didn't ask, my good man. Was selling him exotic concoctions and I didn't want to remind him of another vendor at that delicate juncture."

"I understand." He made a note to tell Massey to pay a visit to that apothecary.

"So what else have you smoked, Delacorte?"

"Oh, opium, just the once, just to see. I like my head clear, you see. All manner of herbs. As one does in my line of business. Testing the wares. I smoke nothing with any regularity, mind you, and thank goodness for that. Weakens the mind. And other things, too, if you take my meaning!" He winked heartily.

"I take it." At no point in the history of the world would someone be unable to take Delacorte's meaning.

"What manner of business *are* you in, Delacorte?"

"I sell bits and medicinal bobs of herbs and treatments imported from all over the world to apothecaries and surgeons. Crushed test—er, parts of various exotic animals, some very potent herbs. Was me own idea, you see. Took a treatment in China once, worked a charm!"

It was just inside of legal, barely, Delacorte's profession, but doctors and surgeons, as far as Tristan was concerned, often operated on a wing and a prayer half the time, anyhow, and he knew from experience that some Chinese herbs and the like were quite effective in healing or easing pain.

"Make a good living?"

Men could ask this sort of thing of other men, casually, over cigars.

"Oh, fair bit. Fair bit. I can afford the rates here at The Grand Palace on the Thames, and so far I believe I've made a good choice. The company is fine," he said gallantly.

"I suppose it's fortunate there's no cursing jar in this particular room."

"Ha ha oh ho, the *jar*!" He gave Tristan a friendly whump on the back and Tristan clamped his top and bottom molars together to keep from reflexively clipping Delacorte about the ears. "You see, Hardy, I don't mind a rule or two. Keeps a man civilized, wouldn't you say? They know we're all heathens at heart, even Brummell, I'd warrant. I'd love a woman of my own to bellow at me 'Stanton, knock the mud off your boots before you come in the house or I'll take a rolling pin to ye!' Wouldn't you?"

"I can't say that I've ever yearned for a woman to bellow at me, no."

"Used to being the one giving the orders, eh?" Delacorte winked.

After a moment he said, "Yes."

The tone and nature of this *yes* caused a little stutter in Delacorte's determined bonhomie.

He smiled at him a little uncertainly.

Tristan stifled a sigh. Part of the difficulty, Tristan realized, was that he for the most part was exposed to one kind of man, who treated him one kind of way: as though he were the ultimate authority. All he did was give orders.

He didn't need anything from Delacorte, unless it was information. And what did that say about him as a person if he couldn't speak to someone unless they were of use to him?

"May I keep this?" he said, more pleasantly. Gesturing with the cigar.

"Certainly, certainly. Enjoy it later when the mood for vice is upon you." Another wink.

Ten pounds, this foul, exotic cigar. Tristan contemplated again the value people placed on things. That smugglers would be willing to risk their lives and the lives of others to avoid paying taxes on something like a cigar, or silk, or tea. That such things acquired arbitrary value. That someone's entire family had died, perhaps accidentally, but nevertheless, an ugly death, so that some aristocrat or adventure seeker somewhere could say he spent ten pounds on a disgusting cigar.

"So what brings you to The Palace of . . . The Grand Palace on the Thames, Mr. Delacorte?"

"I found an advertisement at the apothecary. It sounded like a lovely, orderly feminine sort of place."

"And yet you came here anyway."

"Ha ha!" Delacorte was surprised and delighted by the joke.

"Do you like your room? I asked for the largest suite, and was told it was taken."

"I was told it was taken, too. I believe the Gardner sisters have the second largest."

"I gather we haven't yet met the person fortunate enough to have let the largest suite."

"I suppose not," Delacorte said with equanimity, entirely untroubled by this.

Tristan kept the obvious question to himself, which was: If we're all required to gather in the drawing room, why is the tenant of the large suite exempt? He would find out soon enough.

A little silence fell.

"So. Got a sweetheart, Hardy? A wife? Perhaps on a distant shore?"

"I am unmarried."

"I'll wager it's difficult for an old sea dog like you to settle down. You ought to get yourself one. A woman. Fine respectable bloke like yourself."

"I shall give your advice due consideration, thank you."

"Harder for a chap like me to find just the right one, you see."

He didn't expound, but neither did Tristan disagree.

Nor did he tell him what he thought: that it was equally hard for a chap like him, who didn't fit precisely into any defined social strata. A chap whose ways had perhaps calcified. A chap who had learned to trust no one completely, because he'd learned that people would do just about anything, and when someone did not precisely fit a niche people became uneasy. It had, in part, been the downfall of his very first courtship.

"What do you think of our fair proprietresses, Hardy? Brownie and Goldy?"

He half hoped he'd get to see their faces when Delacorte trotted out those nicknames in mixed company, which seemed inevitable.

"They seem to have created a comfortable place here," he allowed, cautiously.

"Well, just between you and me . . ."

He lowered his voice, and Tristan braced himself for another startling profane assessment, or perhaps a thrilling revelation.

"I think they're ladies through and through. Too good for the likes of you and me! Ha ha ha!"

Tristan leaned back a little too late to avoid getting a moist "Ha!" in his ear.

"Just look at what they did! Sewed my buttons on as good as if they were stitched on there with steel."

He gave a mighty tug on his waistcoat buttons, which were indeed taxed, and his face was luminous with the miracle of it. "Didn't come off in my hand!" he marveled, with awed sincerity. He strummed a hand down them, as though they were an accordion. "They said they'd help give me hair a trim, too. I can sew a button, mind you, but there's just something about a woman's touch."

Tristan was oddly, ever-so-slightly, very surprisingly, moved. And pleased for him.

"Congratulations, Delacorte. That's a fine thing."

He supposed it sometimes was the small things like buttons that would keep your waistcoat closed that made the world feel secure and like a gentler place, a place in which people cared enough about you to make sure you weren't bursting through your clothes. Just as the smallest tasks on a ship—ensuring bolts were tightened and wood was cleaned and waxed and oiled and sails were neatly mended—were the ones that made it possible for him to bring criminals to justice in the name of the English empire.

It was the first time he'd considered that strength was only allowed to exist by virtue of something like gentleness.

Vividly now, he suddenly recalled Lady Derring's face as he'd left the room with Delacorte: a sense of mischief—which he now understood more thoroughly—and a sort of hope. He suspected she was trying to create something in particular here at The Grand Palace on the Thames.

But why?

And at what cost, if she *were* abetting a smuggler?

If she *was* a smuggler? It was very difficult to imagine

a woman who had those soft eyes, and whose emotions moved across her face so easily, engaging in something so nefarious and sordid.

She had an epithet jar, for God's sake.

But desperate people do desperate things.

He recalled, with a pang, that flare of hunger in her eyes when she'd seen those twelve pounds.

"Hasn't been easy for me to find a wife or a sweetheart," Delacorte said. "I'm an old-fashioned sort. I know I'm a bit much to take. Got loud from having only meself to talk to when I'm on the road, I suppose. Drown out the silence. I expect you got a bit quiet from the noise of sailors, eh?"

It wasn't an insight he expected from a loud, gassy salesman of dubious medicines. No one accused him of being quiet, which he doubtless was; no one troubled to wonder why he'd gotten that way, not even himself, not really.

It was a little irritating to be inspected thusly.

But he liked it, too, perversely. It was a bit like looking out of a heretofore undiscovered window in a room. A different angle on a familiar view.

"I suspect I've gotten more economical in speech as the years have gone by. You learn what's worth commenting on."

"I might have gotten a bit more loquacious from years of being alone, but if I'd a wife to sit by the fire with, perhaps we'd be cozy and quiet together."

"Bit hard to picture you quiet, Delacorte." He said it lightly.

"Ha ha ha!" Delacorte was delighted to be teased.

Tristan, in spite of himself, smiled.

And made a note to have Lieutenant Massey speak to the apothecary to check out Delacorte's story.

WHEN HE EMERGED from the smoking den for air, he'd found that the ladies had all exited the drawing room for the evening. The fire had burned low, the lamps were doused. In this soft light, the furniture didn't look worn or tawdry; it was easy to imagine that the sag and fray of the settee had been put there by generations of shifting bums of a reading, sewing, laughing, cuddling family.

And it reflected the current occupants of The Grand Palace on the Thames: nothing quite matched. And yet, because of that, it did match.

A paradox of sorts.

An errant, unwelcome thought flitted through his mind: if he ever had a home of his own . . . he wouldn't mind if it looked like this.

He would *never* say this out loud to sentimental Massey.

But why had Derring owned this building?

And if his widow was wallowing in contraband cigar money, shouldn't there be a little gilt or ormolu about?

Maybe it was all upstairs, where the proprietresses kept their rooms.

He could hear the maids at work down below in the kitchen still, laughing and calling to each other.

Unhappy employees, especially scullery maids, don't laugh while they work.

But it meant he couldn't "accidentally" meander down there and wander about freely exploring. Not just yet.

And as he climbed the stairs to his room, he thought he could hear feminine laughter above, like distant birdsong. Something about it tugged at him nostalgically, though it wasn't a part of any memories he'd had of his life.

As he scaled the stairs he tested each one for squeaks and groans, and made a note of it. Because he'd be coming back down this way in a few hours, after everyone was asleep.

In his room, he got his boots off, hung up his coat in the little wardrobe, stuffed a tiny wad of cotton batting in his keyhole, stretched out on his blue counterpane, and listened to the house.

There were light, swift footsteps overhead; the floor creaking and sighing as women moved across it, rocked in chairs, perhaps.

Something landed on the floor with a small thump. A book perhaps.

There was a muffled shout of feminine laughter.

At last the creaking and moving about ceased.

It was odd how different a sleeping house felt from a wakeful one. Houses were as alive as people, in some ways.

He heard the tiny thunder of an animal of some kind racing down the hallway. Probably a cat. Or a terrifyingly enormous rat.

He frowned, puzzled, when he became aware of a low rumble, like a crouched animal nearby, growling. He gripped his counterpane in shock as the sound swelled and swelled into what sounded like the slow, painful rending in two of a giant tree.

It dropped abruptly.

It was followed by a lengthy, mighty snort, like some creature inhaling the contents of a room.

Dear God above.

It was Delacorte.

Snoring.

Right below his room.

Well, at least he'd have the cover of noise when he did what he was about to do.

At half past midnight he pulled on his black coat, pocketed a flint and a candle, and slipped out of his room.

HE KNEW WHERE and how to place his feet on the stairs to keep them from creaking to get from one landing to the next.

All the sconces had been snuffed and curtains drawn in the halls. There was a half-moon behind clouds out there, shining through an exposed alcove window, but it did little more than turn the shadows a slightly lighter shade of black. He felt his way along the wall toward the mysterious room number three.

He froze.

Something disturbed the dark. At first he could feel it more than hear it.

But then he did hear it: breathing. Audible, but only just.

Accompanied by footsteps. Slow, deliberate. Someone was attempting to be stealthy. They were only partly succeeding.

It was Miss Margaret Gardner, who hadn't a prayer of being unobtrusive, even under cover of shadow.

Had she been in *Delacorte's* room?

But Delacorte was already snoring.

And then Miss Margaret scaled the stairs, doing a fairly decent job of avoiding squeaks.

If she was on an innocent journey through the house, she would have brought a candle with her, he thought. As it was, she was just a bulky shadow disappearing around the corner.

He paused and waited. What on earth was she doing?

And what if she chose to return to this floor?

He didn't want to be caught on his knees peering through a keyhole in the dark. So a few moments later, he returned to his room up the stairs as stealthily as he'd gone down them.

Chapter Eleven

THE FOLLOWING evening at The Grand Palace on the Thames was quiet. Delacorte had gone happily to a boxing match, the notion of which made the ladies wince; Captain Hardy had offered no explanation about where he was heading in the rain when he bid them good evening after dinner, crammed on his hat, and departed on a swift, long-legged stride. "A bit of business to take care of," he'd told them.

Dinner was delicious, of course—a lovely stew of beef and vegetables, some potatoes, good bread, a tart—but the scattered attempts at niceties dwindled as one by one, everyone paused to watch, riveted, Margaret Gardner's evident enjoyment of her food. She plunged in like a retriever offered a bowl of meat. Her fork and knife a blur as she used them more like spades than utensils.

Her sister seemed better able to calibrate her eating. She calmly, and with evident pleasure, ate her stew, mopped it with bread, dabbed her lips with a napkin. And appeared not to notice anything amiss.

Delilah stifled a sigh. The Gardner sisters were not everything she'd dreamed when she envisioned a houseful of guests, gathered in warm camaraderie around the dinner table. Then again, they were only at the beginning of things here. Perhaps they needed to be nurtured, guided a little, like Delacorte. Certainly between her and Angelique they could refine the devil out of them, if given an opportunity.

But she remained wistful when she retreated to the upstairs drawing room with Angelique, leaving the cleaning up to the maids and to Dot. She listened to the rain fall hard as she knitted another row of what would be a nice warm blanket that she hoped, one day, would wrap a guest.

They went still when they heard Dot's light footsteps coming toward them at a trot.

"We've a *new arrival*!"

The tone of her voice said a good deal, but by way of expounding Dot merely rolled her eyes and fanned her bodice.

Which prepared Delilah and Angelique for the golden-haired, long-legged, strapping young vision standing before the fireplace in the reception room. The beaver hat he clutched in his gloved hand poured rain out on the carpet.

"Good evening, sir. I am Lady Derring and this is Mrs. Breedlove. Have you come looking for accommodation?"

"Accommodation?" He had snapping dark eyes and ruddy cheeks, and he seemed fair bursting with nervous, suppressed excitement. "Certainly, if that's what you call it. Do you suppose you can, er . . . accommodate me?" He flicked his eyes between Delilah and Angelique and they lit with delight and surprise.

They hesitated.

"Perhaps," Angelique allowed, cautiously.

"Oh, wait! I've got it now. I am here to request a room in the . . ." He bent toward them and whispered conspiratorially, "Rogues' . . . Palace."

Then he stood back and waited as if he'd uttered the password that would swing wide a magic second door and allow him admittance.

They gazed back at him. Puzzled.

"Sir, this establishment is called The Grand Palace on the Thames. Perhaps you saw the enormous sign indicating as much hanging from the building?" Delilah said this gently.

He looked puzzled but undaunted. "Well, it's very dismal weather, you see, but I gave the hack driver the address and he brought me right to your door. Is this not Number 11 Lovell Street?"

"It is," Delilah allowed, darting a glance at Angelique.

He seemed increasingly puzzled. But he still radiated suppressed delight, even an air of mischief. He was young enough, and perhaps innocent enough, that he'd never seen a need to hold his features still. "Oh, I think I see. Is this a test?"

"Of . . . sorts?" Angelique tried.

He pressed his lips together thoughtfully. "Hmm . . . oh, wait . . . wait."

He reached into his coat and fished out a sheet of foolscap, folded into squares. He carefully unfolded it and consulted whatever was written upon it.

"I've come to sample the"—he lowered his voice to a whisper—"the Vicar's . . . Hobby."

He waited.

His breath seemed held.

He was destined to hold it for a good long while, until Delilah said, "I'm afraid, sir, that we aren't quite certain what you mean by that."

He became brisk again. "Well, blast and damn, don't you offer that anymore? Well, that's a shame. Very well, then. Let's see . . ."

He consulted the paper for a tick.

Delilah and Angelique exchanged another baffled, increasingly concerned, glance.

"If not the Vicar's Hobby, I think I might enjoy the . . . Scoundrel's . . . Wheelbarrow. A bit pricier, but still. You see. Sounds delightful."

He said it on a hush. His cheeks pinkened, as if in a bit of embarrassment. Then he peered up at them, hopeful as a child on its birthday.

Angelique and Delilah were motionless as realization began to seep in.

"Sir, if we may have a look at your . . ."

"Certainly." He surrendered the foolscap to Delilah's extended hand.

Angelique peered over her shoulder as they reviewed what appeared to be a detailed menu.

"Oh!" Angelique said in amused recognition just as Delilah said, "Oh!" in horror.

Angelique caught hold of Delilah's arm just in time to prevent her from hurling the thing upon the fire.

The young man understood their horror. At least he had the grace to scorch red.

He'd been had, and was just beginning to realize this.

"Where did you get this, er, menu, Mr. . . ."

"Farraday. Andrew Farraday. My friend Roddie

gave it to me. Bloody Roderick! He's the one who told me to come here."

"I'm afraid if you're going to use that language you'll need to put a pence in the jar, and another for the previous expostulation beginning with the word *blast*. We shall not charge you this one time, but this is a warning," Delilah said gently.

He blinked at her, astonished. Mouth dropped open. As if he'd been having a lovely dream about angels, who turned out to have fangs.

"Mr. Farraday, would you like to sit down by the fire? You'll take a chill. We'll bring you something hot to drink."

Like every young man, he was helpless against warm motherliness.

He sank down next to the fire on one settee and seemed prepared to be doted and waited upon. Clearly he was accustomed to it.

"I'm afraid, Mr. Farraday, that your friend Roderick has pulled a prank. We are a respectable boarding establishment. We are *not* what your friend Roderick has suggested to you we are."

It seemed no one quite had the nerve to say *bordello* or *whorehouse*.

"You're not a . . ." he said to Angelique.

She shook her head.

He turned to Delilah. "And you're not a . . ."

Delilah shook her head, too.

He looked shattered.

"So neither of you are . . . and this isn't a . . ."

It was rather sweet that this clearly well-bred young man couldn't bring himself to use the word *whore* in front of two women who, only seconds earlier, he fervently hoped would be administering the Scoundrel's Wheelbarrow.

"Breedlove?" he repeated. "Lady Derring," he emphasized meaningfully. "But surely, with names like those . . ."

They both shook their heads.

"Forgive me. Well, I'm terribly embarrassed."

"And you should be," Delilah said almost tenderly.

Angelique stifled a laugh.

"I don't get up to that sort of thing, ever, you know." He beseeched them with big dark eyes.

"We can tell," Angelique assured him.

He looked crestfallen and a little anxious. "I daresay. Well, that leaves me in a bit of a bind. I've no place to stay for the night."

"Well, what brings you to London, Mr. Farraday, besides those, er, pastimes?" Angelique asked.

He blushed again. Then fidgeted a little.

At last he sighed. "I bolted, you see," he said earnestly.

They didn't see.

"Bolted?" Delilah prompted, gently.

"I bolted because I don't want to marry her!" he blurted, in frustrated anguish. "I was meant to propose—everyone expected it of me—and I couldn't bring myself to do it and so . . . well, I bolted. Was days away from a house party where it was supposed to happen to much rejoicing, and in my bed at the coaching inn, and I thought, sod it, I can't, I just can't. And I left. I suppose that makes me sound heartless and callow."

They contemplated the responses that were most

honest and truthful: a swift boxing of the ears or a *why, yes, you great oaf, you're a cad of the first water.*

"We think you sound just like a man," Delilah decided upon finally, sweetly.

Also truthful.

"Thank you." He beamed.

They both fought powerful urges not to roll their eyes.

"I am not proud of myself, mind you, but I'm too young to be leg shackled and I'm not in love with her. She's my friend! How tremendously odd would it be to marry someone who has been your lifelong friend?"

"It actually sounds quite tolerable, even preferable," Delilah said.

"I'd like a chance to be in love, you see. A little passion. A little excitement! A little adventure! Some worldly experience!" He blushed a little again.

They both could volunteer to him that worldly experience wasn't precisely what it was cracked up to be.

Though Delilah, when he'd said that, was surprised to realize she might like a little more of that as well.

She thought of Captain Hardy's long-legged stride as he disappeared out the door this evening. Where did he go?

Why had the tiniest part of her gone with him?

"Before we permit you to stay, we'll need to learn a little more about you," Angelique told him.

"You're going to interview me for suitability. But . . ." He looked bewildered. "This is a building by the *docks*."

"By the River Thames, London's glorious lifeblood. A place where travelers from all over the world first lay foot on British soil. It is the very beating heart of London. By the docks!"

She made *docks* sound like Fields of Gold.

"But you've a man sleeping across your entrance. He said you were coldhearted."

"It's adorable that you think he's sleeping," Angelique said at the same time Delilah said with great delight, "Only one man?"

Mr. Farraday's eyes darted toward the door. Then back to them.

He jounced his leg uneasily.

They smiled upon him warmly.

His frown disappeared. He appeared to be basking in their pretty smiles.

Delilah smoothly continued, "It's just that the poor man outside was refused entrance to The Grand Palace on the Thames on the grounds that he's a bit of a rogue and he has been drinking away his sorrows ever since."

This wasn't entirely untrue.

Mr. Farraday might be country gentry, but he wasn't a fool. He took this in with an eyebrow dive.

And then he began a surreptitious and more thorough inspection of the premises. Perhaps beginning to become more resigned to the reality of things, his eyes flicked up to the ceiling, took in the chandelier, scanned the floors, the stairs.

She imagined he lived in a manor house in the country, built a century ago to withstand anything from marauders to visits from wandering royalty.

His expression suggested he was satisfied, if not ecstatic.

"But I've no other place to stay tonight," he fretted. "Nobody knows I've bolted to London and I don't want anyone to know."

"Fortunately, we have a marvelous room just come available. And while you certainly look like a gentleman and we have sympathy for your plight, there's no guarantee you shall have a place to sleep tonight, either, until we learn a bit more about you."

Flattery, vague threats, a faint air of menace, a certain risk—her mother would have been appalled to find all of these things in Delilah's conversational repertoire, and moreover, that she found them rather invigorating.

"I'm certain I can pass your interview. I think I'd like to stay at least a fortnight."

"Have you twenty pounds upon your person? You'll need to pay in advance of your stay, you see."

"Twenty pounds!"

"Mr. Farraday," Angelique interjected, her voice all velvety sympathy. "It's a filthy night, and there's no guarantee of getting a hack or, if you manage to get to Mayfair, room at the inn. Or at any other inn. And it will cost you considerably more. I assure you, ten pounds is a bargain for what we have to offer."

"Your morning and evening meals are included, and we have a fine cook. Our staff will launder, press, and mend your clothing during your stay. We will bring up to two libations to your room on a given day before nine in the evening, and our cook has a collection of simples and tisanes should you feel your health is in need of bolstering. We've mandatory nightly gatherings in our drawing room and we're certain you'll find it comfortable and amusing. Our aim is to make it feel like home."

"But at the moment home is what I'm trying to leave!" he said wildly.

"A different *kind* of home. With more liberty. With delightful new friends."

"But no freedom to curse or stagger about drunkenly or entertain dubious lady friends in your room," Delilah added.

His lower lip began to extend a trifle glumly.

"There is an ale room and coffeehouse adjacent. And you may take cigars and brandy in a separate room after dinner with our male guests."

His face reflected some cautious cheer.

"And we've planned to have musi—"

Angelique shook her head so vigorously a bit of a breeze was created.

"And we've a list of rules," Delilah amended smoothly.

There would be time to broach the subject of musicales later.

"Rules?" It was a cry of melodramatic anguish.

"All the finest, most sophisticated establishments have them," Delilah improvised. "Why don't you review them, Mr. Farraday? We'll have a fire built in your room and your pillows fluffed. Would you like us to prepare chocolate or perhaps a coffee, and send someone to help you off with your boots so you can warm your feet at the fire?"

These words—*fire* and *fluffed* and *chocolate* and *boots* and *feet*—were chosen just for Mr. Farraday, who, they were both convinced, was indeed not ready to be leg shackled and would make a woman miserable, but could be lulled into complacency with the comforts of home.

His gaze swung between Delilah and Angelique and he was partially melted, partially worn down, in the face of their feminine determination and pretty solicitousness.

"Chocolate would be lovely," he admitted.

"Read the rules first, Mr. Farraday. And if you would be so kind as to show us your ten pounds?" she said gently.

Chapter Twelve

"SORRY, GUV. Sold two, and at ten pounds each. I've none left." Mr. Wilkie, the apothecary, peered up at them through wire spectacles. His blue eyes were both shrewd and sympathetic.

Massey feigned crushing disappointment as Tristan sighed and tucked the cigar back into his pocket as if it were a gold doubloon. He gave it a pat, which seemed to release the scent of smoke from his coat. It was pungent from the evening he and Massey had spent jostled in filthy, crowded local pubs striking up casual conversations and slipping into them questions about The Grand Palace on the Thames.

"Oh, you don't want to go there, guv," he'd been told more than once. "Not the kind of place a body wants to be." Which was funny, given that Tristan and Massey had just been compelled to break up a knife fight and counsel the two involved into shaking hands.

No one could tell them why they shouldn't go there, instead of to a pub that had bloodstains on the floor, for example. It was a mystery. Especially since the entire time he was there he couldn't help imagining the fluffy pillows, the blue counterpane, the warm drawing room filled with people who weren't trying to get drunk or murder one another.

He was relieved to return—before curfew, of course—even if it felt as though he'd accomplished nearly nothing.

Last night he'd dreamed of Lady Derring, sitting across from him, her big brown eyes enigmatic, smoking one of those foul cigars, and was appalled to have awakened still in his smoky clothes when he'd meant to try to peer into the keyhole of Suite Three. The damn bed was simply too comfortable.

He'd punished himself by walking past the breakfast aroma of eggs and sausages gloriously wafting from the kitchen and met Massey to visit Mr. Wilkie, the apothecary. He'd sent a half dozen other men to question other merchants.

"That's a shame about the cigars, Mr. Wilkie. A friend of mine said he bought his here some time ago. Perhaps you remember him? A Mr. Delacorte—"

"Ah, Delacorte!" The apothecary brightened. "Good fellow, that one. Sold me an impotency cure quite popular with my customers. I don't suppose either of you need—"

"No," Tristan and Massey said simultaneously.

"Oh, well, of course not," Mr. Wilkie soothed. "But should there come a day . . ."

He trailed off at Tristan's blackly incredulous expression.

"Mr. Wilkie, do you know if or when you'll get more of these marvelous cigars in?"

"Well, I expected a few going on a month ago, in fact, but haven't yet seen them. Good thing I didn't pay in advance, like I do with some of my orders. I would not be pleased."

Interesting timing. Tristan felt a tiny pinprick of hope.

"I've an acquaintance, the Earl of Derring, who was able to get some, but I don't know where."

Wilkie's expression showed nary a flicker of recognition. "He's lucky then," said Mr. Wilkie earnestly. "Perhaps he'd be inclined to share them with you."

Massey pushed a pound note toward him.

"Would you be willing to tell me where *you* got them?"

Wilkie eyed it speculatively, then sighed, and pushed the pound note back. "Oh, now, gentlemen, what manner of businessman would I be if I revealed my supplier? I don't know his name. Just a bloke, you see."

He gazed evenly up at Tristan and Massey. His shop might be stocked with expensive ointments and unguents whose ingredients were murky and mysterious things in jars, but his conscience was apparently clear. After a fashion.

Hell's teeth.

Massey waited for a cue from Tristan.

Tristan weighed barking something about being on the king's business, because frankly this painstaking business was maddening. But that might sound an alarm among area merchants. Which might get back to the smugglers.

They would have to maintain their painstaking approach.

"Thank you, Mr. Wilkie. If you could recommend a local merchant who might have a few—"

"Oh, any of them might." He waved an airy hand. "I don't rightly know."

The bell jangled on the door as a customer entered, and he and Massey took their leave.

He imagined tonight he would dream of needles and haystacks.

His mood was dark indeed by the time he made an appearance in the drawing room of The Grand Palace on the Thames that evening, and wasn't improved when he saw, sitting on one of the settees, a strapping young man whose blond hair swooped over his brow à la Byron, posture alertly erect, arms crossed tightly across his chest and hands tucked into his armpits, as though he feared someone would reach in and pluck out his heart. He was jouncing one knee. His expression was decidedly bemused, uncertain, a trifle mutinous. The face of one who wasn't certain whether or not he was dreaming and rather hoped he was.

The Misses Gardner were in the corner settee, naturally, taking to the shadows. They did not look up when he entered. They apparently found their laps endlessly fascinating. He stared at them, troubled by something he couldn't quite articulate. Mrs. Breedlove was examining something Dot the maid appeared to be embroidering. She was wearing a puzzled frown.

His restless eye finally found Delilah sitting in a chair near a lamp, something soft, blue, and woolly unfurling from her knitting needles.

He went still. That image bypassed a place in his mind where cynicism lived. In fact, it thrust a soft pillow under the cynicism and bade it take its shoes off and have a nap.

"Captain Hardy! Good evening." Delilah looked up, and in that unguarded instant he thought perhaps the expression on her face alone was worth the twelve pounds he'd paid to stay here.

Even if she was a nefarious smuggler, or aiding and abetting one.

It was such an inconvenient and yet quite educational realization that he, somehow resistantly, refused to cross the threshold into the room just yet.

"We've a new guest, as you can see." She said this somewhat triumphantly. *See, we have guests, Captain Hardy!*

He glanced at the big young blond man. "Do you mean guest or captive?"

"Ha!" The young man brightened and his arms loosened a bit. He flicked a gaze over at Tristan, taking in the Hoby boots, the well-cut coat, the demeanor, making the kinds of judgments and drawing the kinds of conclusions that people all over England did.

"Oh, Captain Hardy, you are a card." Delilah managed to make the entire sentence sound sweet, but the word *card* emerged through slightly gritted teeth. "I'd like to introduce Mr. Andrew Farraday, of Sussex, in London for a visit."

Mr. Farraday sprang to his feet, radiating the sort of self-satisfaction and bonhomie that made Tristan feel about a thousand years old. He had a Grecian nose and a chin with corners like a box, and doubtless, whatever part of the country he was from, young ladies suffered scorching blushes whenever he was near.

He wondered if he'd been lured in right off the street by Mrs. Breedlove and Lady Derring and their pretty smiles.

Tristan accepted the large outstretched paw and shook it.

"Captain, is it? Don't your sort, military blokes, usually stay at the Stevens Hotel? I've heard as such from a friend at White's."

It was a friendly, completely reasonable question.

Delilah swung her head toward Captain Hardy, her entire face a question. He wondered if it was hopeful: *yes, do, Captain Hardy, go and join your own kind.*

Mrs. Breedlove looked immensely curious, too.

"I like to be near the ship I'm intending to buy as I make preparations for travel, and I find the accommodations here to be tolerable."

"Oh, *tolerable,*" Delilah repeated. "You'll come to know, Mr. Farraday, that this is Captain Hardy's way of gushing."

"And the evenings in the drawing room are not to be missed," Captain Hardy added. And after a beat added, "Literally."

Having thoroughly confused young Mr. Farraday for no good reason, he settled in with his book.

A glass of brandy had already been poured for him. He had to admit, there was little to complain about so far concerning the accommodations at The Grand Palace on the Thames.

"I found my room quite comfortable and the view of the Thames stirring, Captain Hardy," Farraday said, clearly gamely attempting to follow the rules regarding socializing. "The pillow was fluffy and the fire *most* warm."

"I've little use for fires that aren't warm, myself," Tristan said.

"Ha," Mr. Farraday replied uncertainly.

"We're so pleased you were comfortable, Mr. Farraday," Angelique soothed.

Tristan opened his book.

"A captain, eh! That sounds very interesting. Have you seen battle?" Mr. Farraday tried.

Tristan looked up. He waited a beat, then gave a faint, patient smile. "Yes."

He returned to his book.

"Have you ever been wounded?" Farraday continued, a moment later.

Tristan looked up. "Yes."

He returned to his book.

Another moment of silence.

"Shot?"

Captain Hardy slowly, slowly lifted his head.

"Yes." He leveled upon young Farraday a lengthy, quelling look. "You?"

Delilah raised her knuckles to her lips to stifle shocked, completely inappropriate laughter.

"No," Farraday said faintly after a moment. Crestfallen.

It was a little like watching an affectionate, panting spaniel given a rude nudge by a booted foot.

"Perhaps something about hunting," she suggested, just shy of desperately. "Or . . . dogs. Or horses? Perhaps Captain Hardy would prefer not to relive the glories of battle in our sitting room."

There was a little silence.

"Glories," Captain Hardy muttered, sounding mordantly amused.

He ducked his head to his book, looking like a turtle stubbornly ducking its head into its shell.

The man was insufferable.

And yet whenever she looked at him something happened to her breathing. As if she'd been snatched up and transported to the top of a mountain.

"Who wants to play chess?" Mr. Delacorte boomed, and everyone jumped a bit. He swept into the room like a refreshing storm system.

"Mr. Farraday does," Angelique said instantly.

"Who is . . . where is . . . ah! I'm Mr. Stanton Delacorte." He planted himself before Mr. Farraday. "And *you* must be Mr. Farraday. Deuced good to meet you. Captain Hardy won't play me because he's afraid to lose, something he's not accustomed to doing."

He winked broadly.

"The very notion makes me quake in my boots, Delacorte," Captain Hardy intoned, without looking up.

Delacorte laughed delightedly.

"He's never quaked a day," Delacorte told the room at large. "Damned hero!"

Captain Hardy glanced up balefully and returned his gaze to the page.

Mr. Farraday, proving he was indeed like a spaniel, immediately glowed at the sound of a friendly voice and proffered his hand to be vigorously pumped by Delacorte.

"I sell exotic treatments to apothecaries," Delacorte said. Who, resigned, moved over and put a pence in the jar for his *damned*.

"Oh!" Mr. Farraday said, in complete confusion, but cheerfully enough, because what else could one say? "I'm a fair hand at chess."

"Well, then, shall we?"

Angelique had poured a sherry for the two of them and a cordial for the Gardner sisters as they attended to their mending, and Delilah had taken two sips when she said, offhandedly, softly, "I wonder if it's just that Captain Hardy is a bit shy?"

Angelique turned her head slowly and regarded Delilah with incredulity.

"Words like *shy* do not apply to men like Captain Hardy any more than they apply to a rock or a trebuchet."

"I see. And you know this because you've cataloged all the varieties of men, then?" Angelique's tendency to adopt sagacity—about, well, nearly everything—was lately shaving curls off Delilah's nerves. "Or have you been privy to a menu?"

Angelique was not rattleable. "I'm not saying that I have. I'm also not saying that I haven't."

"A field guide would be useful. Perhaps a set of books like those Mr. Miles Redmond wrote. If one showed up at the door, we could identify him straight away. I suppose we'd call him the Silent Bronze-Visaged Taciturnicus."

Angelique's face lit up with wicked amusement and a little surprise.

Why were people always surprised to find Delilah was amusing? Why did people persist in thinking she was sweetness and light?

"I think we ought to bring him out of his shell,"

Delilah mused. "Perhaps with a little more encouragement he would be more charming."

"He's *all* shell, Delilah. As in *musket* shell. If you bring him out of his shell, you'll get naught for your trouble but a little smoke and a powder burn."

And yet Captain Hardy looked benign enough at the moment, legs outstretched at the little table, book propped in his hand, a scarcely touched glass of brandy next to it. The firelight was burnishing his already golden skin, and the tips of his eyelashes had gone a sort of apricot shade. They were thick, and she wondered, absurdly, what he'd looked like as a boy. They seemed a vulnerability in a man who was elegantly spare and whose presence was weighty.

"His thighs are very good," Angelique allowed, as though assessing the lamb chops.

"I don't suppose I've ever thought about a man solely in terms of body parts before."

"Don't start, darling. You haven't the constitution."

Delilah clamped down on her back teeth. The success or failure of The Grand Palace on the Thames hinged on its proprietresses maintaining a congenial relationship, but it seemed increasingly unfair that she was the one who so often had to bite her tongue.

"Mrs. Breedlove, would you care to be our third in Whist?" Mrs. Jane Gardner said very shyly.

"I'd love nothing more," Angelique lied prettily and went to join them.

But once Angelique got started in Whist, Delilah had learned, she was a ruthless, gleeful player. And this was why, Delilah was certain, Angelique would never have truly filled her pockets with rocks and waded into the Thames even if Delilah hadn't come along, and this was why, no matter what, their endeavor would be a success. Neither one of them liked to lose.

The room, if not precisely unified in social activities, was pleasant and easy and she exhaled a little. Surely they could make this a success.

Perhaps it was the sherry.

Or Angelique's condescension. She laid her knitting aside and picked up her glass of sherry and made her way across the carpet to the captain, feeling like a sailor navigating to the Rock of Gibraltar.

Chapter Thirteen

"PLEASE DON'T get up, Captain. I've just come to see if everything is to your liking."

"'Everything' seldom is. But this evening and my accommodations are tolerable. Won't you please sit down?"

Delilah pulled out a chair and settled in across from him.

"Tolerable," she repeated thoughtfully, as if rolling a fine cognac about in her mouth. "I don't suppose you're familiar with the word *hyperbole,* Captain? It doesn't always go amiss."

He smiled faintly. "The very fact that a word like *hyperbole* is even necessary is what is wrong with the world."

She smiled. "What an unusual mind you have, Captain Hardy."

"I expect it's quite an ordinary mind, perhaps extraordinarily focused."

"On things like war, rather than, for instance, musicales."

"I do not focus on war when I'm not fighting a battle," he explained with a certain maddening, condescending patience.

And then he was silent.

And waited for her to say something.

"What do you focus on?" she tried.

"At present, I am struggling to focus on page six of *Robinson Crusoe.*"

"I've always wondered what war would be like."

"Women wouldn't understand or be able to endure the physical rigors of combat, Lady Derring. I see no point in describing them to you."

"Yes. While having a baby is as easy as a game of Whist."

This made him go absolutely motionless.

His eyes actually widened.

She'd managed to shock him.

Then again, she'd also shocked herself. Why on earth had she said that?

"Have you . . . had a child, Lady Derring?"

But he was certain he knew the answer—Derring had no heir—and for some reason Tristan regretted asking it instantly, because her eyes were briefly stricken.

"No," she said softly. Sounding ever-so-slightly defeated.

He hadn't the faintest idea what to say next. Absolutely none. And this seldom happened to him. He wanted to apologize, but he wasn't about to presume her childlessness was a source of regret for her. Or imply that she had somehow failed. He supposed the information was useful.

He did not enjoy her obvious discomfiture, however, even though she'd quite brought it on herself.

Bloody hell. No good could come from aimless social occasions, he thought grimly.

"I have never felt as though . . . sometimes I wonder at the point of having a body," she said softly.

"I *beg* your pardon?"

"Did that sound odd? I'm sorry. I have had too much sherry, I fear."

He looked at her glass, which was full, minus perhaps three sips.

"If we're to discuss bodies, I'm going to need another brandy. Perhaps you must have another sherry, too."

She gave a little laugh. "I think not. No, that is, I *will* not. You see, one of the luxuries of being a widow is that I can now say no when I want to. Until now, there has never seemed to be a point to me, other than as a commodity for someone. And now I can do as I please."

She'd said it lightly and with some satisfaction.

And yet it was perhaps the most devastating thing someone had said aloud to him.

He wasn't quite certain why. But he felt the weight of it land on his chest. Along with a peculiar irritation. Something not quite anger, but more like helplessness, as though he ought to be able to save her from that. Not something he'd had occasion to feel before.

"I'm not certain I understand what you mean," he said carefully.

"You see, I went from my parents' home straight to my husband's. I was the savior of the family. Or rather, the Earl of Derring was, and I was the means by which he rescued us from poverty. After my husband died, there were a few moments where I couldn't quite feel my limbs, as though nothing about myself had ever actually belonged to me. Perhaps it was shock. It wasn't because of sherry or laudanum, certainly, for I'd had none. I'm rather new to sherry. Angelique's influence. The earl liked a brandy. I liked chocolate in the morning. I am rambling now, you see, you must stop me—you've quite a bemused expression."

He'd been listening, his stomach contracting in what he recognized as a response to something like injustice. As if he ought to have been there to prevent her from feeling that way, which made no sense at all.

But also, strangely, he listened because he liked hearing the lilt of her voice, and how she was flustered now, when everything about her was usually so brisk and competent.

"My expression, I hope, is thoughtful, and forgive me if it seems bemused," he said carefully. "I was a soldier, you see. As an enlisted man, I was primarily cannon fodder. Cannon fodder is necessary and expendable, so I suppose I felt useful in that regard. And part of something. And yet. And so . . . I think I understand to a small degree."

He'd never expressed such a thought to anyone before. Let alone a woman.

"Expendable," she repeated on an exhale. "What a horrible word."

She was watching him as though the idea of his being slaughtered in battle was distressing. Perhaps it was simply in the way of hospitality here at The Palace of Rogues. Limpid-eyed sympathy dispensed with the after-dinner brandy and the smuggled cigars.

But it was admittedly not unpleasant to be looked at in that fashion by those soft eyes of hers.

"I was there to kill or be killed. I understood that. I

had orders and I obeyed them. But there are moments in the mass of men in battle where you forget you are a separate being . . . and so . . . I do believe I know what you mean. It's humbling to realize that one's importance in the scheme of things is, in fact, quite small. While it can be devastating, in some ways it becomes a source of strength."

And he was amazed, in fact, that he did understand her.

"Beautifully put, Captain Hardy. I believe I'm coming to realize that."

He had never thought about it in such terms. And what it might do to a person's will or soul, to be seen as expendable.

They sat in a moment of silence.

"But you rose in the ranks."

"I rose in the ranks."

"And you are no longer expendable."

"Arguably." He smiled faintly.

She smiled, too, as though she was pleased to make him smile.

"But if you were an enlisted man, not there on an officer's commission, there must have been a compelling reason for them to promote—"

"Valor," he said shortly.

She blinked.

"Valor," she repeated. Her voice lowered to a baritone.

She was taking the piss out of him!

The effrontery!

He stared at her. He had no idea what to feel in the moment, so astonished was he.

He was amazed to discover that he liked it quite a bit.

"Did they teach you how to answer questions with one word, Captain Hardy? You're a miser with your history." She was teasing.

"I'm not terribly interesting."

"I doubt that sincerely."

He lowered his book completely and stared at her. "Are you flirting with me, Lady Derring?"

Her jaw dropped. Then she clapped her mouth closed again. "Good heavens . . . I . . . what on? . . . *No.*"

She seemed so shocked and appalled his internal pendulum swung wildly between insulted and amused.

But her cheeks were glowing pink.

Which is why that pendulum came to rest on *fascinated.*

Lady Derring was *lying.*

And she was bad at it.

"I'm accusing you of disingenuousness, Captain Hardy."

"Disingenuousness? I've called men out for less."

When she smiled, a painfully charming crescent moon of a dimple appeared at the corner of her lush mouth. Her top lip rose into two little rosy peaks in the middle.

He imagined tracing them the way he would draw his finger along a route on a map.

His breath was briefly, shockingly, and violently stopped by a surge of lust.

As if it had been lying in wait for him for days now, like the blockade runners on the road lying in wait for smugglers. Just waiting for him to notice.

"What is the point of you?" she asked.

"Duty." He was still reeling a bit.

He lifted his gaze from her mouth.

He didn't mind if she noticed he'd been staring.

Knowing Lady Derring, he was certain that she had.

"My goodness. You didn't even have to think about it. And it's hardly a lighthearted philosophical question."

"It is entirely the thing that gives order and meaning to my life. That, and your list of rules here at The Grand Palace on the Thames, of course."

"Ha. And do you think life is so anarchic as to require the ceaseless imposition of order and meaning?"

"Yes."

Oh, hell's teeth. Now her eyes were full of questions. The sort he didn't want to answer.

The questioning light evolved into a sort of troubled thoughtfulness.

Oh, God. She was imagining things about him, no doubt, because that's what women did. They embroidered. In their minds and on their pillows.

But she didn't ask those questions.

"Perhaps the point of me is to be kind." She said it almost to herself. As though she'd been waiting for him to ask, and she'd given up.

He sighed and lowered his book again. "Lady Derring," he said, with grave, ironic pity that made her expression immediately alter to one that suggested she'd like to do him a small violence. Perhaps just a little jab with a knitting needle. "Such naivete will be the ruin of The Palace of Rogues. I think perhaps being jaded will afford more protection in this part of London."

Her eyes sparked outrage. "Don't you think I might be all too clearheaded about the world? I am a widow, after all. It isn't every day a countess runs a boardinghouse. Consider that I might have been buffeted a bit."

"No. I don't believe you are all too clearheaded. Nor do I believe you have been particularly buffeted. I suspect you view the world through a very particular lens, which makes it easy for you to be beneficent in your new circumstances."

She didn't splutter.

She didn't even blink.

But she did go still. And fixed him with a thoughtful, rather penetrating gaze.

If he'd been at all a fanciful man, and he most certainly was not, he would have thought perhaps she was rifling through the contents of his soul.

"Well. I stand corrected. You certainly know everything, Captain Hardy."

"Well, very nearly," he amended, modestly. Only a little ironically.

She smiled tautly.

"I must say, however, Lady Derring . . . that I'm intrigued and impressed by how you've managed to engage such a fine cook and such committed servants and keep the rooms so comfortable if you've experienced an adjustment, shall we say, in means. Wax instead of tallow candles in the sconces, crystal at the table. It must be some manner of sorcery."

She went still. Their eyes met across the little lamp.

Then she leaned forward confidingly. "Captain Hardy . . ." She'd lowered her voice to a hush. With her came the faint scent of flowers, no doubt released by the warmth of her body, perhaps thanks to his presence. *Lady Derring,* he imagined saying for the pleasure of seeing her blush, *I have admired your lovely body since you were on the ladder, reaching up to places that were too difficult for you to reach.*

"Yes?" He matched her confiding tone.

And thought: perhaps he would know for certain in moments whether she was a smuggler. But some errant impulse in him wanted this moment to last forever, this moment where he could see and feel and be near her and not know such a thing.

"Perhaps because you are not, strictly speaking, a gentleman, Captain Hardy, you're unaware that it's a bit gauche to ask your hostess questions about such matters."

He sat back again a little too abruptly.

She continued gazing at him. He could have sworn he'd seen a glint of triumph? Challenge? Maybe even a little sympathy in her eyes. Or was that pity? For what? he wondered. Not his station. For some reason he was certain that was not the case.

In all likelihood it was pity for the male arrogance that made him assume she was just that simple.

"Ah. I see. Well, thank you for the enlightenment, Lady Derring."

"My pleasure. I believe Mr. Delacorte and perhaps Mr. Farraday would be pleased to have your company in the smoking parlor. Mrs. Breedlove is prepared to offer you a cigar. She's presiding over the humidor at present."

"As Mr. Delacorte silently expresses himself gastrointestinally after the rich meals prepared by your clearly excellent cook, I am disinclined to be enclosed with him in a small room ever again."

She took this in with the slightest of brow furrows and a little head tilt. As if he were a peculiar phenomenon, rather than a boor.

"Well, cigar smoke ought to disguise that nicely, Captain Hardy. Something tells me hot air is a familiar environment for you."

She rose, graceful as a flower blooming, and took herself off, having just given him a lesson in what it was to be a lady.

He watched her walk all the way across the room because, for some reason, it was difficult not to and he could see no reason to deprive himself of that pleasure.

"Gauche?" he repeated softly to himself. After a moment. Still watching her.

He realized he was smiling.

He put a stop to that right away.

SHE SAT DOWN next to Angelique, who had returned to her sewing when the Gardner sisters had retired for the evening, having completed their stint in the parlor.

"Well, did it work? Did Captain Hardy emerge from his shell like a vulnerable, fluffy baby chicken?"

Delilah was reeling as if she'd run headlong into a wall.

"I mentioned childbirth," she said dazedly. "Quite irritably. And I don't quite remember why."

Angelique's mouth dropped open. Then closed. "Well, that ought to get him to erect a stone fortification around his shell. Not to mention a moat."

"And then he mentioned flatulence."

This stunned Angelique into silence.

"Not his own," Delilah added.

As if this was somehow better.

". . . yours?" Angelique ventured, in hushed horror.

"No. Delacorte's."

"Oh. Yes. Well. I can see that."

Delilah looked over at Captain Hardy now with a sort of shaken, awestruck resentment, as if he were an unseen rock her ship had foundered on.

He sipped his brandy.

He turned a page of his book.

He wasn't looking her way.

"Perhaps we shouldn't let you drink more than a sip or two of sherry in the evening," Angelique said finally.

"I think that would be wisest," Delilah agreed, somewhat glumly.

She reached for her embroidery.

She held it in her lap for a moment, staring at it as if it were a crystal ball.

"It's just that he's so very irritating," she said rather vehemently, in a low voice. "One wants to combat his certainty."

"*You* do. *I* don't. I know better. And by *irritating* I think you mean *desirable in a frightening way.*"

"Nonsense."

It was exactly what she meant.

She rather resented that Angelique knew what she meant better than she did.

But then Angelique apparently knew the costs, too, of that sort of thing.

And yet she wanted to know what Angelique knew.

And what Captain Hardy likely knew.

But as her ruffled feathers settled and her dazed thoughts coalesced into reason once more, her thoughts were pulled, as if by a magnet, to that moment he'd gone utterly still in the drawing room the day he'd come to stay. The moment he'd seen her.

As if he'd finally found due north.

Captain Hardy referred to his watch, closed his book, stood, and politely, dispassionately, bid them all good-night.

His eyes brushed hers as he left the room.

She would warrant that Captain Hardy found her desirable, too.

Possibly even frighteningly so.

Chapter Fourteen

FOR SEVERAL weeks now, Delilah had been in the habit of dropping off to sleep nearly immediately after days of rigorous household work. Tonight she was watching her ceiling. Her body was humming as though each of her cells harbored a little choir singer.

Are you flirting with me, Lady Derring?

She'd promised herself she'd be truthful in all things from now on, but as it turned out, she was a rank coward when tested.

Because she feared the real answer was, in fact, yes.

She tossed and turned and cast off her blankets as if her skin was too sensitive for their weight.

Well. So this was desire, she thought, none too pleased. It wasn't entirely convenient, given the maddening object of it.

Even in the midst of Derring's . . . attentions . . . something in her had stirred, somewhat hopeful, not entirely disinterested. She did know it had a vague resemblance to pleasure.

She had long suspected there had to be more to all that nonsense, otherwise men and women wouldn't behave like such fools about it.

And now, thanks to what Angelique had said—*Derring had no imagination at all*—she knew both that she was not at fault and that imagination, such as it was, seemed to be important.

Did she *want* to know what he knew, and what Angelique knew? When she knew full well how easy it was to come to grief, or to be used or savagely hurt? Did she want to know simply to have the experience, for the reason one visited Kew Gardens and the like?

Did Captain Hardy have an . . . imagination?

Why should *this* difficult, arrogant, taciturn, dryly funny, condescending man so occupy hers? Apart from the fact that all of these qualities came so thrillingly packaged in a tall, hard body. Handsome, well-formed men abounded in London. It wasn't as though they were an entirely new species to her. Not one of them had made her breath hitch with a single glance. Obviously, it was because she was perverse and ironic and complicated, precisely the sort of person her mother had feared she'd grow up to be.

Somehow, this realization didn't bother Delilah.

So. He was not a gentleman. He'd been shot. He seemed well-nigh implacable.

But tonight he had spoken to her, one human to another, about feeling expendable. It was the sort of conversation she'd never had with a man. Or another human, for that matter. It was the sort of thing that one didn't typically discuss with anyone, any more than one whipped off one's stays because they were confining, or went into battle without armor.

All exchanges between men and women tended to amount to transactions in the end. They seemed to be means to ends. And how weary she was of being an object in any fashion, and how luxurious it had been to just be a person here among other women at The Grand Palace on the Thames.

But she'd also seen the look in his eyes when he'd stood on the threshold of that room tonight. As if he wasn't certain he was welcome. Until his eyes met hers.

Did he know how his pupils flared hotly? Even now she could make her breath come short picturing it. Did he care whether she noticed?

And his face had gone undeniably soft, just for an instant, when she'd told him she didn't have a child.

Captain Hardy was neither rock nor trebuchet.

But one moment of softness didn't mean he wasn't hard.

Whether or not it was wise, it was this soft expression—surprised, careful, vulnerable, human—not his thighs, that lingered like a lullaby before she drifted to a restless sleep.

HIS PLANS TO pick the lock on the first floor were daunted by a full moon and a cloudless sky. The door was lit up like a stage. He woke at dawn and decided that charming his way into the Mysterious Room via one of the maids-of-all-work who crept into the rooms, built fires, and ferried away chamber pots, was his best option for getting into it.

But when he arrived on that floor, a woman was already backing out of the room.

"Captain Hardy!"

"Lady Derring. And now that we've identified each other, good morning."

"Good morning."

And then, for an awkward instant, during which they both missed the appropriate window for bidding each other good-day and getting on with their business, they merely looked at each other as though they'd each happened upon an interesting, somewhat puzzling view.

It was increasingly apparent that the laws of gravity were suspended when she was near. Which perhaps accounted for his reluctance to leave her, or to watch her leave. In her presence, whatever force pressed him down to earth, or settled the weight of responsibility onto his shoulders, relented. Stepping away from her was increasingly similar to stepping back into a cage.

"Perhaps you've forgotten," she said gently, after a moment, "but *your* room is on the second floor, right above Mr. Delacorte's."

"How could I forget, Lady Derring? Were you aware that Delacorte snores like a dragon with a head cold when you put me in that room?"

"You know, I truly wasn't aware," she said, with wide-eyed mystification. "I suppose it's just serendipity."

He tried, and failed, not to smile at that.

A soft pink flush moved into her cheeks. She looked down, and her hands absently fussed with the keys at her hip.

He savored knowing he could disconcert her with a smile. He could throw smiles like kindling onto whatever was simmering here between them.

She looked up again swiftly. "We can move you to any other available room at a moment's notice, if it truly does prevent you from sleeping," she added hurriedly. Remembering she was meant to be hospitable, no doubt.

Speaking of serendipity. He seized upon her offer as an opportunity and a bit of a test.

"Well, that could be a solution. May I see all the other available rooms before I decide?"

She looked delighted. "Oh, what a fine idea! They're all a bit different, you know," she said proudly. "But all equally comfortable. I'll send Dot to give you a tour if you like."

One got the sense that she'd been dying to show her rooms to guests who had yet to appear. She didn't sound the least bit as though she was attempting to hide heaps of contraband cigars.

"Thank you. It would be most appreciated. I'm amazed that you *can't* hear Delacorte snoring from where you sleep at the very top of the house."

"We can, at that, hear it a bit, sometimes. It sounds a bit like Gordon, from that distance."

A rogue wave of shocking jealousy stopped his breath. Who the devil was—

"Gordon is our tiger cat," she expounded, "who rumbles when he's purring, or when the cook has given him a nice bit of liver. He snores, too, when he sleeps."

He did not one bit like the relief that swept in; he did not one bit like the sense that his emotions seemed to be attached to a pendulum. He was usually compared to a rock, and he'd always found the comparison flattering.

"I haven't yet had the pleasure of meeting him, but I believe I heard him galloping down the hall. The building shifts and creaks a good deal in the middle of the night, doesn't it?"

"Isn't it lovely?" she said in all seriousness. "So cozy, those sounds."

He was charmed. "It's a bit like listening to someone attempting to digest a rich meal. I've heard a particular muffled thunk. As if the building swallowed something that won't go down properly."

She laughed. "Oh, we've heard that, too. Once before we all moved in. Once after. We haven't been able to discover what it is. Perhaps a large r—"

She stopped. Pressed her lips together.

"You were going to say *rat*," he said.

"We haven't any rats, thanks to Gordon."

He could have sworn she was surreptitiously crossing her fingers in the folds of her skirt.

He gave her a slow, crooked, intimate smile. Amused.

She smiled, too. Suddenly, acutely, he saw her as curves and textures, all as alluring as a crooked finger. Her lips. Her long throat. The skin that glowed like a pearl in this light and probably felt like petals beneath one's fingertips. The dark hair spiraling against her temple, and her lashes. The swell of her breasts, which looked precisely designed to fit into each of his hands, neatly.

The bands of muscles across his stomach tightened as if they were struggling to contain that sudden surge of lust.

The notion of seducing her made him breathless, because he thought it was both possible and inadvisable for a dozen reasons. If he applied himself, he could rationalize those reasons out of existence.

"What *are* you doing on this floor, Captain Hardy? Oh! Were you going to visit Mr. Delacorte?" All at once she was radiant with hope. "Did the two of you become friends? I know he likes to play chess. He's loud but he's clever and quite a nice fellow all in all, I think. But he's already gone down to breakfast, I'm afraid."

She sounded like a mother who *so* hoped someone found her slow son likable. And he remembered her expression—the fleeting bleakness—when he'd asked her if she had a child. Lady Derring was trying to create a family of sorts here, he was fairly certain.

He was hopelessly charmed. "My chess skills are moderate at best and if I'm going to lose at something I'd rather put up a more respectable fight."

"I don't suppose you often lose at anything, Captain Hardy."

"Not since that one time, lo these many years ago."

He allowed himself a moment of basking in her smile. Like the fluffy pillows here at the boardinghouse, pleasures like her smile were so rare in his life as to qualify as luxuries.

"But if you're not looking for Mr. Delacorte, then, Captain Hardy, what brings you to this floor? I should think you'd have mastered navigation by now."

She was dogged.

"I must have inadvertently headed out one flight too soon in my eagerness to get to my comfortable blue room."

He'd said that to make her face glow, and it did, even if she was a trifle skeptical of the flattery.

"Speaking of winning . . . by the way, who *is* the

lucky bas—who is the person who managed to reserve this suite before I could? And when will we meet him or her?"

She hesitated. Interesting that she was taking care with the words she chose.

"Oh, one day, perhaps, you will meet this guest, depending upon how long you stay, Captain Hardy. Until then we keep the room tidy and comfortable, the same way we keep yours tidy and comfortable."

He wasn't certain she was being *unreasonably* discreet, but it did sound rather like circumspection.

He would find out, one way or the other, because he always did.

And if he found out while he was lying in bed next to her, naked, so much the better. Whatever sacrifice had to be made.

He lowered his voice conspiratorially. "Do you know, on my way up to my rooms late last night I saw Miss Gardner coming down this very hall. Away from the room."

"Miss Gardner?" She was confused. "But she's . . . but they're . . . which Miss Gardner?"

"The . . . big one." He felt a right fool for saying that.

"You don't think . . . Mr. Delacorte . . . and Miss Gardner . . . were . . ." She was pink again, and her hands went up to her face then came down.

She was picturing it, and no one ought to do that for sanity-preserving reasons.

"But there are rules here at The Grand Palace on the Thames about entertaining strange women in one's room!"

He gave a short laugh. "If rules alone would keep

people in line, the way a harness keeps a team of horses neatly trotting along, England would have no need for a navy, Lady Derring."

Her face was a picture. "I think life has been unkind to Miss Jane and Miss Margaret," she said, hesitantly. "I'm glad they are here so we can treat them gently and kindly and make them feel safe."

He felt he was hearing a list of things that Lady Derring wanted from life.

Why did it feel like he was hearing his own true purpose delineated for the first time ever?

"I'm certain Miss Gardner simply took a wrong turn," he said gently. But he wanted to take the worried, conflicted expression from her face.

He wasn't at all certain this was the case, but he'd find out.

She looked relieved, and as though, suddenly, his emotions were a mirror of hers, he was relieved, too.

Which troubled him. He frowned faintly, as if desiring her was something uncomfortable she'd compelled him to against his wishes, like sitting in their drawing room at night.

He ought to go. Massey would be awaiting orders.

She noticed his silence and his frown. "Is there anything *I* can help you with, Captain Hardy?"

"Perhaps," he said tersely. "Delacorte offered me the most vile yet interesting cigar. You wouldn't happen to know where I might find such a thing?"

She sighed. "Did it smell like . . . something that had perhaps died inside the walls of a house, then was buried in a variety of herbs and spices in a kitchen garden watered by the contents of a slops jar?"

He struggled not to smile. "It wasn't quite how Delacorte put it. But your description is equally apt."

"Derring used to be fond of cigars that were precisely . . . that unusual. I don't know where he purchased them, however. I never did see a bill or receipt for them."

"Did you *often* see his bills and receipts?" He said it lightly, and with some surprise, as though receipts were a comical thing to inflict upon a countess.

She hesitated. "For the running of the household, of course. Not for Derring's purchases." She searched his face curiously, as something was clearly troubling her about the question. "If you're wondering how it is I came to acquire the expertise to run a grand boarding establishment, Captain, I tracked those expenses very carefully, and I am very good at budgeting and managing a staff," she said proudly. "Derring wasn't, of course," she added shortly, dryly.

He believed her. Surely someone who was intelligent, and blushed so very easily, wouldn't lie as smoothly as that, or volunteer that sort of information.

Then again: one never knew anything about anyone, as he'd told the drunk man lying in front of The Grand Palace on the Thames.

"Your spotless facilities and my comfortable room are a testament to your household management skills, Lady Derring."

Her crooked smile once again indicated she was skeptical of flattery, particularly from him, but nevertheless, he could see she was leaning into it the way a flower leans into a cool spring rain.

Which was precisely how he was leaning into that smile.

The realization made him frown again. "I expect you should want to get on with your duties. Am I keeping you from them?"

"I was just about to trim the candles in the sconces." She looked up at them somewhat ruefully.

He recalled her body stretched to reach the top of the window. The compulsion to help her with something was like an itch needing scratching.

"Why don't I do . . ." He gestured to the sconces. "It's easier for me to reach."

She looked up at him, dark eyes thoughtful, a little reluctant.

"That's very kind of you." She said it somewhat stiffly, a little shyly. As if it were a sort of surrender.

She handed him a candle.

He effortlessly reached up.

First one sconce.

And then the next.

Conversation had been safer than this silence, or as safe as anything could feel in Captain Hardy's presence; he was, she realized, precisely as Dot had described him: part Lucifer, part Atlas. Trouble. And, quite frankly, Desire on Legs.

The silence made her both acutely aware that they were alone, and that as she handed up the candles, she was so close that her next breath took in a tantalizing hint of smoke and soap and musk, clean but heady. Immediately she understood how Derring had felt about those cigars. She wished for a blanket that smelled just like this. She would wrap herself in it every night. She would never sleep again.

She handed him another candle.

And when he reached up, she leaned forward a little more and inhaled, quite sneakily, near his elbow.

Her head went light. Her eyes closed.

When she opened them, he was staring down at her. His face was absolutely motionless. His face a study in amazement.

"Did you just . . . sniff . . . me, Lady Derring?"

His voice was amused. And very, very soft. Like a voice from the pillow next to hers.

After a long and shameful delay, during which he did not blink once, and during which her face rose several degrees in temperature, she finally whispered, "Perhaps inadvertently?"

The trouble was, he was still very close, and she could still smell him. She knew a terrible, frightening urge to rest her head against his arm.

And all at once something he saw in her face made his go closed and unreadable.

He silently turned, leaving her simmering in mortification.

He moved on to the next sconce.

She handed him the candle, and he reached up. "Lavender," he said. His voice was gruff.

"I beg your pardon?"

He turned and met her eyes and said, very clearly, very steadily, his voice confiding and quiet, "Last night, when you leaned forward to tell me I was gauche, you smelled of lavender and spice. Like fine-milled soap."

His silvery eyes were suddenly pins, and she was a butterfly.

She could not possibly have spoken if she tried. She merely stared. Her breath lost.

He did not release her gaze. "I thought about it a good deal last night, when I was stretched out on my comfortable blue counterpane." He delivered that like a spy offering a password to a sentry.

She said nothing.

He turned away.

She watched the slow insertion of the last candle.

And when he was done he went still and turned to her.

The silence now was as alive as the night and hummed a good deal of unspoken things. *Are you flirting with me, Lady Derring?*

"Do *you* snore, Captain Hardy?" she said softly.

She saw the breath leave him. His gray eyes flared to black.

It was the most thrilling, vixenish thing she'd ever done, that subtle question, which was born of real curiosity. But she knew immediately that she was quite in over her head.

She pivoted to leave, and swiftly.

She'd taken two steps when he said, his voice raised only a little, "Lady Derring . . . something puzzles me."

She halted.

Closed her eyes.

Took a shuddering breath for courage.

Turned back to him. From the relatively safe distance of three feet, she said, "Surely not. We've established you know everything."

His smile was small and patient. "You seem to excel at so very much here at The Grand Palace on the Thames. Yet you can't seem to disguise how much you want me."

One of the things *Tristan* excelled at was ambush.

Her eyes grew enormous as his words sank in.

She looked both stricken and resigned, like a thief nabbed in the act.

Finally she drew in a breath and resettled her shoulders, as though she'd been ruffled by a stiff wind.

"Well, Captain Hardy, I must take issue with your assessment, on the grounds that I'm not trying to disguise it at all."

Holy—!

His breath left him in a gust.

And as she turned again to walk away his hand shot out.

It was a primal reflex, but not the about-to-fall-off-a-cliff sort. It was somewhere in between a cat with prey or a miser with gold.

He got hold of her forearm.

He held her like that long enough to feel brutish. Three seconds all told, though something had gone wrong with time—it seemed to have stopped—so it was difficult to know.

She ought to slap him.

He ought to let go.

Unless one counted lungs moving in and out, color flooding into cheeks, pupils flaring to shilling size, neither of them moved.

And then he slid his hand down, down, down along her arm to bracelet her wrist.

He felt her heart drumming against his fingertips. At least as hard as his was beating.

It was what he needed to know.

He tugged her up against his body.

It was nearly as much a collision as a kiss, at first, fierce and hard, as if they were both intent on punishing themselves and each other for wanting this.

This was a mistake. He'd known it was, and he could not stop himself from making it.

He fanned one hand against the small of her back; with the other he cradled her head, threaded his fingers up through her hair. And tugged her head back to take that kiss mercilessly, greedily, carnally, deeper.

She moaned softly. And opened to him with a sweetness and hunger that stunned him, then made him nearly savage. Her hands rose to grip his shirt and she pulled him hard up against her. He slid his hands down beneath the curve of her arse and scooped her up hard against the swell of his cock and he felt her ribcage jump against him as her breath snagged.

And then she shifted to fit him more snugly between her legs and pulled him closer and lust threatened to tear the top from his head.

It was already out of hand.

The hallway spun, as if he'd staggered from an opium den.

Her finger remained curled into his shirt. Her body was still crushed to his, and he could feel her heart beating against his body, in counterpoint to his.

He could rest his cheek on the top of her head if he wanted to. It was as seductive as those pillows in his room, a moment of infinite weakness.

God, how he wanted to.

Which was why he didn't.

"I'm not a gentleman," he said gruffly. Finally.

He didn't know why these should be the first words he said after he surfaced from the kiss. A warning, perhaps. Or an explanation. Not an apology.

He would never apologize for something that could not be helped.

She finally stepped back from him and drew in a breath that shuddered.

Her hands rose, and he thought for a moment she meant to cover her face. But she dropped them again. And she stared at him. Not censorious. Assessing, perhaps. Amazed, certainly. Her eyes were hazy and soft.

"No. You certainly aren't," she said finally.

He said nothing.

She adjusted her shoulders, as though realigning herself with propriety.

And then she turned and went down the stairs without another word.

Albeit carefully, and a little more slowly, as though she were finding her footing in a world that was still shifting beneath her feet.

Chapter Fifteen

"I've missed you, sir," Massey said. "Your snorts, your grunts, your frowns, your growling commands."

Tristan obliged Massey by scowling. He carved his sausage. Stabbed a segment and lifted it toward his mouth.

It had been two days since they'd convened.

They were in a pub opposite the livery stables that angled The Grand Palace on the Thames. Tristan told Massey what he'd discovered, which was nothing, essentially, though he supposed it was a discovery after a fashion.

It was noisy with an equal balance of honest workmen and ne'er-do-wells in varying stages of inebriation, and he and Massey had thrown back ales—or pretended to throw them back—and bought ales for other men while they casually slipped questions about The Grand Palace on the Thames into conversation.

"Oh, you don't want to go *there*, guv," several men told him.

Yet no one seemed able to tell them why.

"Everybody knows it," he was told. This was accompanied by shrugs.

He had the increasing suspicion that someone had, in fact, put the word out that people were not to go there. But *why*?

He'd sent word for his men to watch the building, and to follow everyone who entered and left The Grand Palace on the Thames.

He'd assigned four others to questioning, as casually and surreptitiously as possible, the locals about the building. Did they know Derring? Had they seen him about? Did they know where they could buy a particularly foul cigar?

He glanced out the window. Carts and carriages and fine glossy horses moved in and out of the livery stable in a satisfying, steady stream. The streets were teeming and busy and loud.

"Are you taking the waters at that boardinghouse, sir? Are they perhaps feeding you a tonic?" Massey asked suddenly.

"Of course not."

"You look . . . better."

Tristan stared at him. "I always look well."

"No, you have a sort of . . . glow."

"I always glow with health."

"Yes, sir. Of course, sir. What was I thinking, sir."

What did Massey see? Tristan knew how he felt. There was something about his nerves of a dropped brass bowl. Ever since that kiss, they continued to jangle and hum. Sounds and sensations landed on him a little too hard. He ought not to have kissed her; he had not planned to kiss her; he could not have stopped himself; it had happened almost without his realizing it. These four utterly disparate facts disturbed him, along with the notion that he wanted, very much, to do much, much more than kiss her.

He suspected she wanted it, too.

Though he had no true idea what Lady Derring was thinking.

And perhaps he could justify it, in the name of duty. Rather than in the name of desperation. He'd thought he'd transmuted desperation into cold determination long ago. But it wasn't cold determination causing him to stare at his ceiling nights, listening to Delacorte snore.

For the past two nights he'd sat at his table with his book and his brandy in the drawing room while the women did things to fabric with needles and whatnot and murmured pleasantly amongst themselves. He hadn't been shunned. No one so much as looked at him askance. He suspected Lady Derring had been discreet; she hadn't told a soul.

So he'd read to page eight of his book until the suspense, such as it was, regarding whether his belongings would show up packed next to the front door was enough to drive him to stand with Farraday and Delacorte in the smoking room.

Whereupon he seized the opportunity to find out how Farraday had come to be at The Grand Palace on the Thames.

He heard the entire sorry version, including the part about the Vicar's Hobby.

"A bit craven to run off like that, wouldn't you say, Farraday?" he'd said.

Not without sympathy, however. Still, he wanted scolding.

"Yes," Farraday said glumly. "That's the word. I had to, you see. Not sure how I'm going to fix it now, but I'm glad to be going to a boxing match tomorrow with Delacorte," he said, brightening.

"Delacorte is a good influence," he'd said quite dryly.

Delacorte and Farraday both beamed at him, pleased with the compliment.

He asked the room at large a question that had been troubling him. He could not quite say why yet.

"What do you think of the Gardner sisters?"

Both Delacorte and Farraday were silent. They were decent sorts at heart, clearly, because the first things that came to mind were ungentlemanly and obviously could not be said.

"I've an herbal concoction in my case of medicines," Delacorte began thoughtfully. "From the deepest heart of China. One makes an infusion of it to cure a variety of ailments. And if you take too much of it, inadvertently, you'll have fascinating hallucinations. I once took too much of it. The Gardner sisters could have stepped out of one of those hallucinations."

It was so eloquent both he and Farraday gave him their tribute of awed silence.

"Quite like it here," Farraday had said finally, with great cheerful satisfaction, downing the rest of his brandy. "Good company."

Oddly, Tristan found that he did not precisely disagree.

"Learn anything else while you were milling about the pub?" he asked Massey, who was silently watching him brood.

"Nay. Either they know nothing at all about the place, or they know to stay away, but no one can say why."

"It occurs to me, Massey, that someone might have a reason for attempting to ward people away from The Grand Palace on the Thames."

"I had the same thought, sir."

Tristan took another bite of sausage. "I got a tour of the rooms from one of the staff—an incurious innocent named Dot. I looked thoroughly in wardrobes and under beds and behind curtains and saw nothing untoward or even curiosity piquing. None of them smelled like cigars. All the rooms are a bit different and looked quite pleasant and comfortable."

They did, in fact. Evidence of that womanly care that Delacorte had so cherished was in every one of them. One featured a colorful quilt; another was hung with a sampler that said Bless Our Home. There were braided rugs and little vases and those cloud-like pillows.

"I haven't been able to pick the lock of the first floor suite and I haven't been able to talk my way into it yet. It's surprisingly easy to be interrupted in the midst of things at The Grand Palace . . ."

He was remembering the last time he'd been interrupted at The Grand Palace.

"Sir?" Massey looked concerned.

Tristan cleared his throat. "However . . . I think it's possible another of the guests has taken an interest in it. One who hasn't a room on that floor."

"Which one?"

"Miss Margaret Gardner. Woman the size of a bear, who eats dinner like one."

Massey tapped his fork against his chin. "That one. I've meant to tell you that Morgan followed her out of the boardinghouse yesterday. She went into the livery stables."

"The *livery* stables?"

"Yes, sir. Pity the horse what has to carry that—"

"Yes, Massey, that's enough," he interrupted sharply. He suddenly recalled Delilah's face, stricken and soft, when she talked about the Gardner sisters.

"Sorry, sir. He didn't see her leave the stable on a horse. She walked out again after a few minutes."

"She was alone?"

"Aye, sir."

"Interesting that she would go to such a place alone. Miss Gardner seems terrified of men. She won't talk to me. She sits with her sister in the darkest corner of the drawing room at nights, away from the fire, and when she glances up it's as though she's certain I will bite."

"Then she must be a good judge of character, sir."

"Very amusing, Massey. The other sister scarcely talks at all, but she forms complete sentences."

They sat back, puzzling over this. Tristan drummed his fingers against the side of his ale and looked out the window at the boarding stables. He missed a good ride. He missed action. One didn't wind up passionately kissing widows when one was galloping down Sussex roads in pursuit of smugglers. Perhaps it was all the enforced proximity.

"What is the drawing room like, sir?"

Massey sounded equal parts inquisitor and child who wishes to hear a bedtime story.

"It is filled with comfortable, slightly mismatched

furniture. It is warm and well lit from well-placed lamps and candles. Somewhat ominously, there is a pianoforte in it." *And if you sit close to a certain woman, it smells like lavender.*

"And guests are required to make appearances in the drawing room?"

"It's one of the rules, in fact. And if I wish to stay, I abide by the rules. Rather like the navy."

Massey had a faraway look in his eyes again. "Are they very strict, these rules?"

"No, rather practical. And . . . kind. It's meant to foster camaraderie."

"Camaraderie?" Massey was as bemused as Tristan about that. "Has it worked?"

Tristan hesitated, and absently flexed his hand, and remembered threading those fingers up through Lady Derring's soft hair to tug it back, and how her lips had felt beneath his, and the bands of muscle across his stomach tightened.

He looked up. "After a fashion," he said finally.

HE TOLD MASSEY to keep watching the boardinghouse and following the guests, and to keep up the questioning.

That evening, as usual, he settled in at a little round table with a brandy and *Robinson Crusoe* in the drawing room, gallantly at a distance from the fire. He thought of poor Massey at the Stevens Hotel, surrounded by men instead, with no jar to keep their heathen impulses in check.

As irrational a thought as he'd ever had. Who *wouldn't* prefer the company of soldiers?

Delacorte and Dot were chuckling aloud over something Mrs. Breedlove was reading, and the Gardner sisters were huddled in the corner, as if this drawing room was instead a dungeon. And there was Lady Derring, swathed in a shawl, working some more soothing words into a sampler, no doubt.

All theories about enforced proximity banking lust rather vaporized in her presence. No: he would want her no matter where, or when.

She stood. He watched as she moved across the room to him, quite casually, pulled out the chair across from him, and sat down.

He gazed at her steadily.

It occurred to him that he'd love to see her in a color, any color, other than half mourning. Red, or gold, or green. The mourning reminded him that she had once been Derring's. It was yet another irrational thought in an increasingly troubling series of them.

"I've been looking for my belongings next to the door every day this week, Lady Derring. Are you going to ask me to leave The Grand Palace on the Thames?"

"No. Nor have I told Mrs. Breedlove or any other members of the staff about it, and I won't. But . . . you shouldn't take this decision as encouragement to take liberties again."

He studied her.

"Take," he repeated slowly, musingly, "liberties." As though she'd introduced a sophisticated philosophical concept requiring some rumination.

"What would you call it?"

"If I instigated a liberty seizure, I daresay you voluntarily gave one up."

She mulled this. She gave a short nod. "Fair enough."

He smiled faintly. It occurred to him that he had not expected to like her as much as he did.

"But that . . . sort of thing . . . should not happen again," she added hurriedly, firmly. "The Grand Palace on the Thames is a fine establishment and its reputation means everything to me. I can't behave heedlessly, and I fully don't intend to."

He thought of a dozen things to say. He wondered if she knew that "word" on the street had it that one ought not go into The Grand Palace on the Thames. He decided not to tell her, because he didn't want to see the hurt flash across her features.

He'd heard the words *should not*. There was a world of difference between *should* and *will*, and they both knew it.

What he said was, "Fair enough."

He didn't mourn. In negotiations—and this was a negotiation, he was certain—as in investigations and campaigns, patience was the greatest weapon.

She didn't get up to leave.

She also didn't look particularly relieved at his acquiescence.

Then laughter rose up from the room behind her. Dot and Delacorte and Farraday.

Her face at once reflected warmth and genuine delight that this strange blend of people were enjoying themselves in her parlor; she seemed poised to leap up to participate.

She didn't.

He realized he'd been holding his breath. And when she turned back toward him, he knew the tiniest frisson of delight and relief.

He wondered if he would see something new in her face every time. Because so far, that's precisely how it felt.

The room was filled with cozy ambient sounds: a page turning, a quill scratching along foolscap, the fire crackling, a chirp from Gordon, the cat.

"Captain Hardy . . ." Delilah had folded her hands before her and was lacing and unlacing her fingers.

"Yes?"

"I know that I am pretty . . ."

He smiled faintly. "I will offer you no argument."

"It isn't a precisely burdensome quality."

"I should think not," he said agreeably.

"And yet I feel as though I had nothing at all to do with it. It is like being congratulated for an archery prize when I haven't even shot an arrow."

He was tempted to say, *I have perhaps seen more beautiful women, but the difference between them and you is like the difference between the grimy window and one rubbed clean, one through which the sun shines. It is about a certain quality of light.*

"Do you excel at archery?" he said instead.

"This isn't about *archery,*" she said, with such impatience he bit back a smile. "That is . . . I suppose I was wondering . . ." She cleared her throat. Then she drew in what sounded like a fortifying breath and released it slowly. ". . . why you 'want' *me*?"

She stumbled a little over the word *want.*

He watched her cheeks slowly flush rosy.

He went motionless.

Once again, he was absolutely flummoxed by the question.

He nearly felt a blush coming on, and he could not recall the last time he'd done that.

A woman no doubt had been involved, because that was the kind of creature they were.

But her expression was earnest, and a trifle tortured. The issue was clearly of some importance to her. He'd best wade in very, very gingerly.

"Is the emphasis on the *want* or the *me* in that question?"

"I wouldn't mind at all if you addressed both."

"Because, Lady Derring," he said carefully, "if you are seeking flattery or persuasion, I'm afraid I can't oblige. Not only do I not know how to do that, but my objective with regard to you is specific."

This was an example of why he was often referred to as a "right bastard."

Perverse female that she was, she just shook her head with a little "how you do run on, Hardy" eye roll. As if it was entirely what she'd expected him to say.

"And if you were hoping for flowers, or"—he cleared his throat—"I suppose poetry is also done, I'm afraid I . . ."

"Oh, dear heavens, no." She brought her hand down on the table with an emphatic smack and was startlingly firm. "Imagine *you* bearing a bouquet of flowers!"

He frowned.

"I mean"—she leaned forward earnestly—"they're

meaningless, aren't they? Flowers, poetry? So much ritual nonsense." She gave her fingers a flick, as if releasing something she'd crumbled into dust.

He blinked.

He rather agreed—he'd learned that the hard way, long ago—but hearing her say that out loud was strangely less pleasant than he'd thought it would be.

"They do serve to signal intent," he said cautiously. "They give poor hapless bast—er, men—a sort of language. Because communicating the finer feelings is often a struggle for our gender."

"Signaling intent?" she repeated. Amused and bemused, all at once. "I suppose they do serve as offerings. Of a sort. That is, all manner of things certainly preceded my wedding to Derring. Bouquets of hothouse flowers. So expensive to grow and maintain for such fleeting beauty. They say more about money, don't they? They say, look at all my money! Little books of poems, Byron and the like, though I was certain Derring had never so much as entertained a metaphor in his life. They were flattering, and I was grateful, and at no point was his intent, as you say, ambiguous. A man as conventional as Derring doesn't lightly publicly woo the daughter of a lord, no matter how minor. But they don't signify *affection*, do they? Not really. They do not make a person feel *known*."

He listened to this, absolutely fascinated by something he'd failed before to consider and by a deeper glimpse into *her*.

"Perhaps they don't always."

"Forgive me. I am trying, I suppose, to be truthful in all things. To say the things I wish to say and ask the things I wish to ask, and not try merely to please someone else."

Once again, he knew a swift stab of loathing for Derring, who had clearly not known, or cared, who she was.

"Do you like flowers?" he asked a moment later.

"I love flowers," she said wistfully. "Daisies, especially."

"Daisies?"

"They grow where they want to, don't they? Often in surprising little places. Seldom in a hothouse. They're not confined, bought, and sold like more exotic blooms. I've always liked daisies best."

She made it sound as though she might never see another daisy again.

Why did he have an impulse to shower her in them suddenly?

"On that point, it's not what I want. I do not intend to ever marry again." She gave a little illustrative shudder. "I am now my own woman *entirely* and it suits me."

"Excellent, Lady Derring. We are agreed on that point of courtship and matrimony. If you would be so kind as to help me understand your question?"

She drew in a breath, fortifying her nerve.

"Do you 'want' every pretty woman you see?"

He stared at her, once again astounded and nonplussed.

And then his head went back a little in comprehension.

Then a tiny flame of fury flared inside him at the people who had treated this uniquely lovely woman as someone who was merely a sort of bargaining chip or an ornament or as a means of continuing a line. This singular *person.*

If she were any other woman in any other circumstance he might say, *I've never wanted anyone like this! I must have you!* or something equally impassioned and florid in a low sultry voice. He was reasonably confident he could weaken the knees of a nun if he ever wanted to do that—he had, in fact, done that, once, an aspiring nun, rather—and have her knickers off and legs in the air with alacrity.

He wasn't certain this was true, however. The never wanting someone quite so much.

He'd certainly known lust, some of it fierce.

He *was* certain he'd never met a woman like Lady Derring.

Somehow he knew this had something to do with the wanting of her.

Perhaps it was as simple as that: she was unique. Who *didn't* enjoy a little variety?

Shimmering around the edges of that realization was, in fact, a unique sort of danger, one that he couldn't quite bring into focus, one that he couldn't quite name.

Certainly he'd never had a conversation like this one.

"No. I don't want every woman I see. When I was younger it sometimes felt that way. It's quite harrowing to be a man at times, for that reason, you know. The sway of a fishmonger's hips beneath her skirt, a stray breeze. Honestly, anything can set us off. As I got older, I suppose I gained, er, discernment and discretion. And so. No."

Her eyes were full of wicked, laughing lights. "I'm so very flattered to have survived the winnowing."

"Well, you ought to be."

She laughed. She was a maddening woman who laughed when he didn't expect her to. At times when she probably shouldn't. He didn't think of himself as particularly witty, but her laugh made him feel like he did on the deck of a ship on a glorious day, wind snapping in the sails. As though his mind, singular as it was, was a delightful place.

He realized that was another of the reasons he wanted her.

At this, caution and a sort of alarm slammed down.

"You're frowning at me," she said suddenly.

"It's my usual resting expression."

"It isn't, you know. And the lines on your face tell another story."

He turned his head away a little, toward the fire, nonplussed. He didn't particularly want anyone to notice, let alone read, the lines on his face.

He didn't want her to know that.

"Ah ha ha, I *have* you now!" Mr. Delacorte chortled. Mr. Farraday moaned in dismay, and Delilah cast a glance over her shoulder, her smile pleased that two such mismatched souls were enjoying each other in part because of her.

Something about her posture suggested she was about to get up to join them, to bestow a smile or some hospitality.

"Because you've a spark about you," he said swiftly. "In a room full of people you seem like the one visible star in a night sky."

He said it because saying it suddenly seemed better than watching her leave.

And because those were the things he knew: The moon. The stars. The wind. The sea. It wasn't poetry. It *wasn't*.

She turned slowly to face him.

Her eyes had gone enormous.

She said nothing.

"And the way you move, it's . . ."

What he wanted to say: like witnessing something fine and natural. It was simply an indefinable pleasure, like watching a well-built schooner, or a fast horse, or a wave beating on the shore, but he knew enough not to say these things aloud. She moved as though life was a pleasure and her body was wings.

"Like the fishmonger?" she prompted gently, teasing.

"No."

A fraught, rather soft silence, not entirely comfortable for Tristan, stretched between them.

He knew she wouldn't linger much longer.

"Because you are surprisingly prickly and clever while also being beautiful and I find that erotic. And the top of your head comes to my collarbone. Which I like."

She gave him one of her slow, slow, crooked smiles, as if the sheer mirth, were it to burst forth, would send tables toppling and objects flying about the room. "There's no accounting for taste, I suppose, Captain Hardy."

He smiled at her.

Her cheeks went pinker, which he didn't mind a bit.

But his smile faded as he realized there was a reason he'd only skirted around her question.

His answers would reveal as much, or more, about himself as they did about her.

Because I kissed you for all of fifteen seconds and even now I think I can feel the imprint of your body against mine, as if you'd stamped me like a coin.

Because suddenly I am nearly as afraid of having you as I am of the prospect of never having you.

That was ridiculous.

Afraid couldn't possibly be the word.

He'd run out of things to fear. He was never afraid anymore.

Unless it was of musicales.

He lowered his voice to reasonable, conversational tones. "Because it's fundamental, the desire between a man and a woman. It's an intangible thing, not something one can or ought to measure or dissect. It needn't be anything more than desire and one need not feel guilty about satisfying it. And I think you are curious enough to let me do all the wicked things to you that I want to do."

Her swift, sharp, secret intake of breath was perhaps the most erotic thing to happen to him to date.

It conjured an image of her, eyes half-closed, head thrown back, hair spilled across a pillow. He curled one hand into a tight fist, as if could contain all his lust there.

"CHECK. And MATE."

"You *bastard*!" Mr. Farraday breathed in good-humored amazement.

Mr. Delacorte was celebrating with little gleeful hops in his chair, hands thrust upward in triumph.

But all the feminine heads had whipped toward them, uniformly reproachful.

"Begging your pardon, mesdames, sorry. The heat of competition, you see."

"Congratulations, Mr. Delacorte, on your win. But I'm afraid you'll need to put a pence in the jar, Mr. Farraday," Angelique said.

"A pence, not a *bean*, as you did the other day," Delilah added. "Don't think we aren't paying attention."

He glared at her incredulously.

He slowly swiveled that glare about the room, as if, once again, he was wondering how he'd gotten there at The Grand Palace on the Thames in the first place, or perhaps searching for someone to take his side.

He just met limpid-eyed reproach from the women.

And a "what can you do, mate?" one-shouldered shrug from Tristan, who followed rules, and didn't mind at all seeing the handsome squire called to task by two women.

He sighed heavily, pushed himself away from the table. Everyone watched Mr. Farraday trudge across the room. His pence clinked into the jar.

He returned to his chair.

They all smiled warmly at him.

And after what was clearly a valiant struggle not to smile, he smiled, too.

And all at once Tristan felt an errant little knife twist of resentment that her attention should be fixed elsewhere.

"Lady Derring . . ."

She turned back to him, her smile still in place.

"Why do you want me?"

She went still. She studied him, lamplight turning her eyes into enigmatic pools.

And then she just curved her lips in a little smile.

And then she pushed back her chair and stood to leave.

As she passed him, she bent slightly and whispered in his ear, "Because you want *me*."

Chapter Sixteen

It was a negotiation now. Of that, Tristan was certain.

Should not happen again, she'd said. *Ought not* was also true.

Will not had not been said by either of them, and this was the lever he would use.

She would not *behave heedlessly*. She was a grown woman, and hardly a virgin. And it wasn't heedless, if one deliberately made a choice to take a lover.

He suspected she knew that well.

She wasn't to know that he was a ruthlessly subtle negotiator and he knew how to identify an opportunity and take the advantage.

Which was what he did the very next morning. He'd just turned the key in the lock of his room and was about to run downstairs to meet Massey when he saw her.

Arms full of folded linens.

She'd paused in a rectangle of wan light thrown in from the windows in the alcove on his floor. She was staring down at the street wearing a complicated expression. Wry, wistful. Pale shadows beneath her eyes.

"Tolerable day, isn't it, Lady Derring?"

It was the best one could say about London weather at most times.

She gave a start. Her face lit, then went uncertain, then turned swiftly back toward the window, cheeks a little pink.

"The gentleman who relieved himself against the building certainly thought so."

"If only he'd had a chamber pot painted in periwinkles, it might have been more picturesque."

She gave a short laugh. But her expression remained wistful. Her posture was a trifle tense. It was both his presence, he suspected, and the fact that Lady Derring wanted the world to be one way, and it wasn't. A list of rules notwithstanding.

"Have you plans for the day, Captain Hardy?" Her voice had gone lulled and soft. This was what his presence did to her now.

"Oh, yes. Various bits of business about town. I'm to meet a friend for a meal."

How did it happen that the distance between them all but dissolved in a few seconds? He hadn't moved and neither had she, not perceptibly. But suddenly he could feel the heat of her body against his. Like water sinking into earth.

But he closed his eyes briefly, and breathed her in.

A strand of hair had slipped from her cap to lie against her cheek. And his fingers, as if of their own accord, went up to delicately lift it away, tucking it behind her ear, then trailing down her throat. Which was as precisely as satiny as he'd dreamed.

Her eyes fluttered closed; her lashes shuddered on her cheeks.

And her breath was coming short.

"Imagine," he whispered close to her ear, as his finger delicately traced the whorls of it, then skimmed to where her heart swiftly thumped. He watched the gooseflesh rise along her throat. "That my fingers are my tongue, and my lips. Imagine that there is nothing at all between you and me, not nankeen, not muslin. Just my skin against yours. My hands and mouth discovering every part of your body. Imagine me taking you here . . . now . . . where anyone may come upon us."

She swallowed. Her head had tipped back. Her lips had parted, and now her breathing was ragged.

His fingers traced the pulse in her throat.

He let his breath play over her skin as he whispered, "Imagine how you feel now . . . and multiply it by a thousand. That's how it would be."

He stepped back.

"Because you'll *have* to imagine, you see, as we agreed we shouldn't do anything about it."

He left her.

THAT BASTARD!

Delilah was *very* impressed. It was quite a tactic. And it certainly conveniently answered her question about whether Captain Hardy possessed an imagination.

She couldn't move a hair from that window for a full minute, her body was in such an uproar of pleasure. She wanted to savor every hot, shivering, yearning feeling that he had started up until it faded completely.

Her breathing did not recover for another minute after that.

And then thinking about him *thinking* about her—

because clearly that's what he'd been doing—brought with it a fresh wave of that delicious, unnerving heat.

And it was not so much that she'd thought about nothing else for days since he'd kissed—very well, since *they'd* kissed—in the hallway. It was just that lust now formed the very emotional weather of her days. Every single thing she did occurred against a languorous, thrilling backdrop of it.

And her sleep—though she did sleep—was fitful. It was fair to say she was *just* a little irritable.

She thought about *oughts,* and how she'd vowed to never again let them dictate her decisions.

She *ought* not do a thing with him.

And then there were the *wants.*

My God, did she have wants.

But if it was merely an affair—and surely widows had them all the time—well, why shouldn't she be *that* sort of widow?

The problem lay in the other things he'd said. The things that stole her breath for other reasons entirely.

The one visible star in a night sky.

Any fanciful notions about romance she'd consigned, like her childhood ribbons and christening spoon, to a locked keepsake box. There was no point in taking them out to revisit. But even if she could choose only one perfect thing for a man to say to her in her lifetime, she would not have arrived at something quite as romantic as that.

He was not the sort to resort to words in order to effect seduction. He was stating something he saw as a fact.

And while Captain Hardy claimed his intentions

were specific—the satisfaction of an appetite, nothing more—the thing that worried her was that inherent in it, no matter their intentions, was the possibility—even the probability—of hurt.

For both of them.

And could she do it? Could she be someone who partook of pleasure for pleasure's sake, without feeling like an object again, like a man's means to an end? It was not so long ago she'd reclaimed her true self. It was still a little fragile, fresh out of the cocoon, as it were.

Would the hurt be worth the pleasure?

Oh, how she wanted to know about the pleasure.

When she could move again from the window, she went downstairs to the kitchen.

And as she'd anticipated, the kitchen was so bustling—Angelique and the two maids-of-all-work and Helga were all chatting, chopping, and peeling—it was temporarily easy to forget that while the rest of the building was emptier than she preferred it to be, one particular man seemed to take up an undue amount of space and air.

Delilah sat down and took up a paring knife and set into the apples.

"They eat like horses, men do!" Helga said happily. She was in her element stuffing hungry people full of food. "Girls, the scullery needs attention. Off wi' ye now! Dot, would you be a good lass and go and fetch a bit of butter?"

The scullery maids and Dot scurried off.

Delilah lowered her voice. "May I ask you ladies a question? I must warn you it's of a rather personal nature."

"Of course, Lady Derring. There is very little what can surprise me now at me age," Helga said briskly.

"Perhaps you'd like to put the pan down first, Helga?"

Angelique had already fixed Delilah with a wary look. Almost as though she knew precisely what she was about to ask.

"Well, now, I'm just about to put these apple tarts on to bake, Lady Derring. I've not a moment to spare, if we're to have them with dinner, and I assure you my constitution is sturdier than even this." She gave the bottom of the cast iron pan an affectionate pat.

"Very well." She cleared her throat. Her face was already scorching. "My question is . . . my question is this: Does . . . having . . . er, relations with a man ever feel . . . well, pleasant?"

They all clapped their hands over their ears when the pan hit the floor.

They really had no choice but to wait it out as it wobbled to a stop.

"Is it *really* that shocking of a question?" she asked, weakly, when it did, finally.

"From *you*," Angelique and Helga said at once.

"Sorry," Helga had the grace to add hurriedly. "It's just you're so sweet and proper, Lady Derring, one doesn't imagine you . . . wondering those sorts of things. Or doing those sorts of things."

Delilah was scorching with a blush now, but she was determined to soldier through. "Because proper women don't do them?" she said dryly. "Or because proper women don't enjoy them?"

Helga and Angelique didn't answer this question.

"Delilah . . ." Angelique began. "Whatever you're thinking or considering, you ought to stop it straight away. You do not have the experience or the constitution to handle the consequences."

To her astonishment a red haze of fury moved over Delilah's eyes.

"Angelique."

Her tone made Helga and Angelique go motionless in shock. It dripped icicles.

Angelique's eyes went huge.

"I understand that life has been unfair to you and that your acerbic nature is something of a defense," Delilah said. "I enjoy your humor more often than not. But I've grown weary of the condescension and I will thank you not to treat me like a child. Please remember how and through whom we came to be acquainted if you think to lord your experience over me."

She was an aristocrat speaking to an underling. Even as the words left her mouth she was aware that she'd said too much, in the wrong tone, and in the wrong place, and the wrong time, and it was thanks to her nerves being abraded by want and the lack of sleep due to lustful imaginings.

And yet. The words and the sentiments had been simmering there all along.

Angelique's face had blanked utterly.

Her eyes fixed on Delilah, unblinking.

Then she slowly pushed her chair back.

Stood motionless for a millisecond, while everyone watched her breathlessly.

And walked out of the room with the grace and dignity of an empress.

She didn't look back once.

The room was silent after that.

"Shall I begin looking for other employment?" Helga sounded resigned. She'd worked in a number of households and circumstances, was accustomed to thinking three steps ahead. "Will it all go to pieces now?"

"No. Forgive me, Helga. We are adults. I shall fix this."

But not right away, she wouldn't.

Angelique needed to marinate in those words a bit, too.

Still. Delilah felt like that dropped pan. Miserable and ringing and raw. She sighed and resumed peeling apples.

It seemed they had found yet another of the problems with men.

"Lady Derring . . ." Helga said. "In answer to your earlier question . . ."

Delilah looked up alertly. "Yes?"

She lowered her voice to a whisper. "Oh, my lord, *yes*." She fanned a big hand across her bosom. "It bloody well can be *pleasant*. Pleasant isn't the half of it."

Delilah smiled slowly. And took a deep breath and sighed it out.

It didn't help much. And yet it did.

"Thank you, Helga. I appreciate the benefit of your expertise."

"Always happy to be of assistance, Lady Derring."

A FEW HOURS later Delilah found Angelique in the upstairs drawing room hemming a petticoat with swift, meticulous little stabs of a needle. She'd brought up tea on a tray.

Angelique didn't look up when Delilah entered, even when Delilah deliberately gave the tray a little shake to make the teapot rattle.

She settled it on the table with a clink.

Angelique did look up then. "Well, it seems you were right, Lady Derring. You're not an entirely pleasant person."

"I did try to warn you."

Angelique regarded her with a taut little smile.

Then ducked her head and resumed the stitches. Delilah dropped in a sugar and poured two cups of tea. She passed the sugared tea over to Angelique. How odd that she should know how her husband's former mistress liked to take her tea, but there it was.

They sat in silence for a time.

"If we were men," Angelique said thoughtfully, "I probably would have called you out, and we would have met over pistols at dawn, and one of us would now be laid out in the parlor, freshly dead."

"Which parlor do you envision for funerals, should that unhappy occasion arise?"

"Perhaps the other downstairs parlor. The smoking room. More gloom. Enough room."

They both flashed little smiles at the dark humor. Because they *both* had thought of this, which was why this partnership was going to be a success.

If Delilah hadn't ruined it.

"If your sense of honor is offended, perhaps we can instead have a contest to see who can mend a petticoat faster," Delilah suggested.

"Just *imagine* the bloodshed."

A little more of the tension seeped away. They would in future be able to disagree, or even fight, no doubt, and survive it. Hopefully.

But it had begun, indirectly, because of a man.

She had a suspicion Angelique knew which man.

The fact that she hadn't said anything outright meant she probably trusted Delilah more than she let on.

"Oh, I think men have their merits," Angelique said. "But they are invariably stupid about pride, and honor, and that rot. And thoughtlessly cruel. And selfish. All to varying degrees, but it seems to be built into their gender."

The second hand swung away a few more moments of awkward silence.

"I should not have spoken to you in that tone of voice in front of the staff, Angelique. It was wrong and I apologize and I won't do it again. But I don't apologize for the spirit of my message."

Angelique blew out a breath and laid aside her mending. She folded her hands in her lap.

Then cleared her throat.

"You're also right that I have a tendency to talk to you as though you are a child. And for that, Delilah . . ." She inhaled again, releasing her breath at length. "I apologize."

The hot spots of color on her cheeks suggested this apology was a good deal more difficult than it sounded.

"Has it something to do with Derring? Your . . . condescension?" Delilah hesitated to ask the question, but she needed to know.

Angelique winced. At which word, *Derring* or *condescension,* Delilah was uncertain.

She thought for a moment before speaking. "Less directly with Derring . . . than perhaps the circumstances of your birth and your position. I suppose I am not as immune to"—she cleared her throat—"envy as I thought. I hadn't realized it until I just kept doing it. Talking to you as though you are a child. And you are quite brave to call me out."

This moment certainly felt perilous and delicate and important.

"Well, those I cannot help. My birth. My marriage. Any more than you can help yours. And I respect you no less."

"I know. Of course I know. I shall attempt not to direct any of my lingering uneasiness about that at you. If you can refrain from speaking to me as though you're the Duchess of Brexford."

"I loathe the Duchess of Brexford! Did I sound like her?"

"I'm assuming. I loathe her, too. But if she should ever wish to stay here . . ."

"We'd charge her double the rate."

They laughed at this.

"Derring never would laugh at my jokes," Delilah said. "But I laughed at all of his."

"Puns," Angelique said blackly. "How I hated his puns."

Delilah wanted to say, but didn't: *Captain Hardy smiles at me when I say things, and nearly every one of his smiles contains something of surprise and delight, like I've handed him a gift. His laugh is wonderful, and rare. He is far more thoughtful than one would think. He has on occasion made me laugh. He is dry, and a deeper thinker than one would suspect.*

But if a woman were to take a lover solely for the sake of taking a lover, none of these things ought to matter. She ought not to consider them at all. His magnificent thighs, on the other hand . . .

A wave of weakness passed through her at the thought.

Angelique said, somewhat haltingly, "I have found that desire . . . doesn't care whether a man is good or not. It doesn't distinguish. It sometimes fixes itself to an inexplicable object. It seems grotesquely unfair that women should be burdened with such a thing when it's infinitely more dangerous for us, in many ways, than for men. And yet, there we have it. And the first time your heart is broken is by far the worst. The second time is not much fun, either. And finally you consign the thing to a scrap heap because it rattles about in your chest like dropped china."

Delilah's own heart hurt terribly, hearing this. How she wished Angelique hadn't learned these things the hard way.

"Or so I've heard," Angelique added. "I never had one to begin with, you know."

Delilah snorted.

Chapter Seventeen

"Mr. Brinker? I'm Lady Derring, one of the proprietresses of The Grand Palace on the Thames."

Dot had gone and let a strange man into the house after curfew. "I'm so sorry, but I did it without thinking, Lady Derring." She'd wrung her hands. "It's so very wet and cold out, you know how the wind gets, and it's so warm in here, and he looks like a gentleman, and I thought, what would Lady Derring want me to do? She would want me to be kind."

Lovely. Delilah had apparently been imparting lessons to Dot and perhaps hadn't let on that those lessons contained nuances.

Angelique had already gone to bed. Their other guests, Captain Hardy included, were safely in, Dot had told her. She'd in fact left him with a pot of tea an hour ago.

The man in question turned at the sound of her voice. He was tall and thickset, almost perfectly rectangular. His elegant, many-caped coat swung in flawlessly cut elegance from his shoulders to his ankles. He appeared to be holding their list of rules.

Dot was right. She could almost trace the provenances of his clothes to Hoby, to Weston, or to Guthrie.

He looked at her rather . . . longer . . . than she preferred before he finally bowed.

And when he was upright, his gaze remained a trifle too familiar. His dark eyes were sheltered by straight, bushy brows and his face was heavy, pale, and very English. She fought the impulse to smooth her hair or her apron, to fidget.

Familiar. A word that belonged to her past, she realized, because she might have a title, but her station couldn't really shield her from a gaze like that.

A man would, however, she thought rather bitterly. Damn it.

She thought of Captain Hardy snug in his bed, hopefully sleeplessly watching his ceiling and revisiting, again and again, that kiss. In other words, precisely what she'd been doing for the past two nights. But she'd also avoided being alone with him. She rather hoped, given distance, sense would settle in, because the decision seemed too momentous and too fraught, the outcome too uncertain, and part of her thought that everything would be easier if she didn't have to make it.

She resented that she wished he was standing here right now. Lucifer and Atlas, indeed.

"My horse threw a shoe and I cannot get it seen to until tomorrow morning, I fear, Lady Derring," Mr. Brinker told her. "I've stabled him at Cox's Livery and I wondered if I could prevail upon you for a room for the night."

His delivery was gracious and his voice was low and pleasant.

And yet something prevented her from inviting him to sit.

"Ah, that is misfortunate, Mr. Brinker."

"I thought the women who ran boardinghouses were built like houses themselves, and brandished rolling pins and sported chin hairs. You sound like . . . an actual lady."

She gave a short, polite laugh, the kind that reminded her uncomfortably of how she used to laugh for Derring to salve his ego and keep the peace. "I *am* a lady, Mr. Brinker. A widow."

Though she thought, at that moment, it might be more useful to be the built-like-a-house, chin-hair sort of proprietress.

"Ah," he said. After a moment, "I see."

Why did everything he said sound so puzzled?

"I should tell you, Mr. Brinker," she said pleasantly enough, "that our guests typically stay a little longer than one night, for the security and comfort of our other guests, so that we can all come to know and trust one another."

This was his opportunity to apologize and leave.

He took this in with a little frown. "Here at the . . . docks?"

"It's a convenient location for people from all walks of life. Why, even you yourself are here." An acerbic quality was creeping into her tone.

"Of course. Who knows? It might be the next St. James Square."

She disliked his tone, for reasons she couldn't quite put a finger on. "Perhaps."

Perhaps he was merely weary and wet and inconvenienced and uneasy being away from his usual haunts. Perhaps if she made him feel at home, if he was treated well, he might tell other people with money about The Grand Palace on the Thames.

"What sort of business brings you to Lovell Street, Mr. Brinker?"

"I'm a merchant—I deal in silks, typically. My father owns a textile mill in Kent and I am involved in the investment end of it."

"How interesting." It sounded respectable enough.

"In some ways, yes, I suppose it is." His little smile was odd. Nearly insinuating.

And then he very swiftly, almost imperceptibly, swept the length of her with a look.

And perhaps he wondered if she was the sort to rob him in the night, and was trying to ascertain whether she was hiding a little pistol or a sharp little knife.

But it didn't feel like that sort of look, because it made her want to shudder as if an insect had crawled across her arm. Her heart picked up a beat or two.

"As I said, Mr. Brinker, it isn't our usual policy to let rooms for one night only. I'm certain you can imagine why." She said it more firmly.

"I'm willing to pay handsomely for it." Suddenly, in his hand, were several sovereigns.

She went still. Her breath snagged.

And for a moment she merely stared at them.

Damn men and their money.

Damn life and the choices it presented daily.

He didn't, on the surface of things, seem dangerous. One never knew. Appearances never told the whole story. She ought to know. And the things they could do with three sovereigns . . .

She crossed her fingers beneath her apron. Said a silent prayer.

"Follow me, Mr. Brinker. Ring the bell if you'd like tea brought up to you. We'll leave it outside of your door."

HE'D BEEN IN for the evening for a half hour when Dot appeared, clinked and clanked her way about his room, fluffing a pillow, building the fire, leaving him with a cup of tea he'd requested earlier in the day—whimsically ringing for tea in the middle of the night struck him as the worst sort of laziness and selfishness, even though the rules allowed it—and a quiet little good-night.

These were all things he could in all likelihood do more competently for himself.

But it did, in fact, make him feel cared for.

He let the tea sit for a bit and poured himself a brandy instead, and sipped.

He wondered if he'd overplayed his hand with that bit in the window.

He'd spent the past two days out with Massey and the rest of his men, questioning merchants. A pattern was beginning to emerge, of sorts.

And yet whoever had allegedly let the mysterious suite had yet to appear in the boardinghouse. In all likelihood there was a benign reason for it. Perhaps it was the only messy room in the entire house; they wanted to keep it hidden.

He didn't think so, however.

At half past twelve, he thrust his arms back into his coat. His pockets stuffed with lock picks and candles and flint, he quietly closed his door behind him.

"THREE SOVEREIGNS, THREE sovereigns, three sovereigns, three whole sovereigns," Delilah muttered all the way down the stairs to the kitchen, and all the way through the heating of the water and the dispensing of the tea. Most guests were considerate enough not to ring for tea late in the evening, even though their rules generously allowed for one nightly libation.

But not Mr. Brinker. Which didn't surprise her in the least.

Before she drifted off to sleep tonight perhaps she ought to count the kinds of things they could buy with those three sovereigns. Enough staff so that neither she nor Angelique would need to rise in the middle of the night to see to a guest—so she would never need to do it again, for instance. Or perhaps a pair of footmen. Though the cost of feeding a footman was almost equivalent to the cost of feeding a horse.

She settled the tea on the tray and balanced it carefully up the stairs. She'd reached the foyer when a voice called softly from the larger drawing room.

"I'm in here, Lady Derring. Would you please bring the tea in?"

She froze. Hell's teeth.

She was trapped there, in her night rail and slippers, braided hair spilling out of her cap.

"Oh . . . Mr. Brinker. I thought I told you I'd leave the tea outside your door."

"I would rather take my tea in this comfortable

drawing room. Would you please bring it in and leave it before it gets cold?"

It sounded much less like an invitation than an order.

Her heart instantly stuttered. Damn damn damn. Then set up a pounding that sickened her.

Her arms were now trembling, and not just from the weight of the tea. Which would crash to the floor in seconds if she didn't set it down.

Quickly, she stepped into the drawing room, lowered the tray to the nearest table, and pivoted to bolt.

She choked on a gasp.

Mr. Brinker was standing right behind her. Between her and the door of the room.

He said nothing. She couldn't see his expression in the dark. His breathing, however, was heavy.

"Perhaps, Mr. Brinker, because you're only staying the evening you weren't aware of our rules. Our guests are usually in their rooms at this hour." She'd raised her voice in the futile hope that someone might hear.

"Rules," he snorted, softly. Genuinely amused. "Come, now, Lady Derring. I gave you *three* sovereigns. Surely you didn't think it was just for lodging and tea?"

"I did indeed think that you were simply generous."

He snorted.

And she understood why he'd done what he'd done: down here, in the parlor, if he wished to assault her, it was possible that no one could hear her scream.

That was when terror set in in earnest.

"Come with me over here to the settee, please," he said offhandedly.

"I think not."

"If you'd *like* to put up a bit of a struggle I won't complain, as sometimes it can be a bit exciting, am I right?"

"Not in the least," Delilah said brightly.

She took two steps sideways to the next little table, where a pewter candlestick stood next to a book.

She reached behind her. She succeeded only in tipping the candlestick over just out of reach.

The lowering fire threw shuddering shadows of her and Mr. Brinker against the wall. She was uncomfortably aware that in all likelihood he could see more or less clearly through her night rail.

She tried bravado and reason. "Well, Mr. Brinker, I've explained how things are. I should be happy to return a sovereign to you if you object to the amount you paid, because you will be enjoying no other services apart from the ones listed in our rules. Now, if you would be so kind as to step aside to let me pass?"

She'd just given him an opening to claim this was all in jest. An opportunity to change his mind.

"But I also won't pay more for it, if you'd like to put up a struggle," Mr. Brinker added, as if continuing a conversation. As if she hadn't said a thing. "I do expect to get my money's worth, however. Just come with me, lie back here on the settee, and we'll get it done swiftly."

And he reached for his trouser buttons. She feinted quickly to the left. She managed to get around him.

She was wrenched back. He'd seized her forearm. His hand was a heavy clamp of a thing.

Her scream was soundless, a raw rasp, shredded and frayed by terror. Useless.

He yanked her up hard next to his body and walked the two of them toward the settee.

"Please unhand me." How fiercely she hated that it was nearly a whimper. A desperate plea.

"This will be over before you know it. So quickly, in fact, we can do it twice."

Horribly, he laid one hand over her breast, and just as his muscles tensed to push her backward, the sound of a pistol cocking echoed behind them.

More primal, more frightening, in some ways than an actual gunshot.

Because it contained within it anticipation of death for the victim.

Brinker froze.

Delilah's eyes closed, and her heart lurched, and she thought perhaps her very consciousness winked on and then off, like the guttering flame of a candle.

"The pistol now pointed at the base of your skull is for show. Still, I shouldn't move if I were you."

Oh, dear God, it was Tristan. Delilah imagined the guardians of the Gates of Hell probably spoke just that laconically.

Mr. Brinker's complexion was now as white as her nightdress. She could feel the dampness of his terror sweat where his palm gripped her wrist.

Mr. Brinker was mouthing what appeared to be prayers, of all things.

Then again, they could also be curses upon Captain Hardy's soul.

"I can certainly put an end to you in a dozen other

ways involving hands, feet, and strategy without firing so much as a shot," Tristan said thoughtfully. "I'd sooner do that than subject the staff to cleaning your brains from the spotless furniture. But rest assured, if you so much as ruffle Lady Derring's hair with an untoward breath . . ." And now Delilah heard the cold, black rage in the words, how they were emerging through ground teeth. ". . . I will do one or the other. And after that, no one will ever hear from you again, and they'll never know what happened. So take your hands from her. *Now.*"

Brinker's hands went up immediately.

Delilah stifled a whimper of relief.

"Now take one step back away from her. One small step, lest your cranium meet the barrel of my pistol."

Brinker stepped back.

Delilah half stumbled, half ran at a crouch across the room.

Belatedly she snatched up the candlestick. Just so she could.

"Captain Hardy, his name is Brinker," she hissed. As if cursing him for all time.

"Thank you, Lady Derring." Tristan didn't look at her. "Now raise your hands, Brinker. But do it very, very slowly, as I've been known to be a bit jumpy when I haven't shot a man in a day or two."

All these terrifying theatrics from a man who was a miser with words.

But Brinker, proving there was no end to the idiocy of men, twisted swiftly and swiped for Tristan's pistol.

After that he was a blur.

Because Tristan had seized him by the shoulders,

spun him around, and hurled his head down—BAM—on the edge of the table as though he were a sack of flour.

Brinker crumpled to his knees then tipped over backward and lay flat like a ninepin on the floor.

And didn't move at all.

"Oh God oh God oh God, oh God, oh God." Delilah's voice was a hoarse whisper.

Was he dead?

They both peered down at him.

She half hoped he was. They could throw him in the Thames.

She'd never had such a bloodthirsty thought in her life.

A second later, blood oozed from his nose.

Her first thought—God help her—was that it would be remarkably difficult to get blood out of the carpet.

Brinker moaned, and his hand twitched.

"Oh, you're *that* Captain Hardy," he murmured.

Delilah stared at Tristan. What on earth did *that* mean?

But Tristan was a blur again. He caught hold of the big rectangular Brinker by his arm and yanked all thousand stone of him to his feet. The man slumped like a marionette from Tristan's grip before he somewhat found his footing.

"Wait here for me, Delilah," he commanded her.

They disappeared from view.

She heard the door open and close.

She wouldn't think of countermanding his order to wait. She sank down onto the settee. She wrapped her arms around her torso as if they were chains that could protect her, but she couldn't seem to stop the sudden, violent shaking.

The blindingly swift, preternaturally confident, skillful violence: she could hardly believe this man was the same one who read every night, an island of calm.

What did Brinker mean . . . *that* Captain Hardy?

Chapter Eighteen

TRISTAN STEPPED outside with his sagging, moaning, bleeding cargo and whistled softly.

A moment later, Morgan and Halligan, who happened to be watching The Grand Palace on the Thames at the moment, emerged from the shadows. He gave them hurried instructions to get Brinker as far away from the building as quickly as possible without killing him.

His heart in his throat, he returned moments later and sat down next to Delilah on the settee.

She didn't lift her face from her hands. She was visibly trembling.

He laid his locked pistol carefully on the table. He shook out of his coat.

Then very gently settled it over her shoulders.

She didn't look up then, either. But she took a long breath and sighed.

The trembling eased.

And something eased in him, too, to the point of being exulting.

"Delilah . . ." he said softly. Neither of them noticed he'd used the name he called when he was alone in bed, watching the ceiling, but never aloud to her. "Are you unharmed?"

She nodded without lifting her head.

"Would you like some brandy, some sherry, some tea, some—"

She shook her head vigorously. "What did you do with him?"

"I put him in a hack and paid them to drive him to the opposite side of London." It was a slight adulteration of the truth.

She didn't acknowledge this information with so much as a sound.

"It isn't fair," she said finally. The words were somewhat muffled, as she'd yet to take her face from her hands, as if to blot out the scene of assault and violence.

"What isn't fair?"

"Dot hasn't any skills at all. Or rather, she does, but she's terrible at all of them. But Dot is just a lovely person who wants to help and I suppose the world needs more lovely people. And she let that man in after curfew. Out of the kindness of her heart."

"Because you are kind and she admires you and wants to be like you, no doubt."

She gave a short laugh. "I suppose I am. You're right again, Captain Hardy. No, it's not enough to be kind. Not here. Not near the docks. I'm foolish. Feel free to gloat."

"I wouldn't dream of doing anything so frivolous as gloating."

He could have sworn that somewhere in her buried hands she was smiling.

There passed a little silence.

"Delilah . . ." His voice was tender. He heard the

faint, desperate ache in it. He could stop a man from hurting her, but he could not stop the fear from reverberating. And in this, he suffered.

"I am *not* weeping, you've no need to use that tone. I'm *furious*, is what I am."

"And you feel alone."

She went motionless. She slowly lifted her head from her hands and peered at him from across the tops of her fingertips.

"I suppose I do," she agreed crossly, surprised. Two eyebrows at slants. Eyes brilliant.

He liked anger better than despair.

Her eyes were actually a little red around the edges, however, and her lashes were clinging together in damp spikes. But those hot high spots on her cheeks were more representative of fury and frustration than devastation.

She was, in fact, tougher than he'd credited her for. He realized, all at once, that it took a certain steely courage to commit to kindness.

"Why did you say that? Do you feel alone, Captain Hardy? After all, there's probably only one of your particular species. Then again, I don't suppose you feel much of anything."

It was like taking a face full of tiny pebbles. The sting was negligible but shocking.

He knew she was lashing out. The men under his command did, too. Men, he knew how to manage.

But he was out of practice with this sort of thing. Things delicate and intricate. His impulse was to take her in his arms. Would she find this comforting, or would he be just one more man presuming what she wanted, and imposing himself upon her? Would he be doing it to comfort himself, or her?

And what would happen next? The inevitable, no doubt. They wanted each other as much as they didn't want to want each other.

She gave a short, bitter laugh into his silence. "Oh, the stoic, brave Captain Hardy. For once he doesn't have to answer a question. Doesn't feel the need to expound. What turns a man into . . ." She waved a hand at him. "So hard, so brave, so cold, so *dutiful*—"

"Enough."

He said it quietly. But it was a command. And underneath it was something raw and hurt.

Hearing her punishingly recite a list of things he'd always thought of as his best qualities as though they were the very things that made him worth loathing.

Something about his tone broke through her prickly shield.

She studied him, curiously. Her expression had softened, just a little.

"What I do have is this. I usually keep it next to my pistol in my coat pocket."

Cautiously he dipped a hand into the coat she was wearing.

Then he extended his hand, handkerchief dangling from it.

Her hand crept out. And she quirked the corner of her mouth and accepted it.

She dabbed at the corners of her eyes. Then folded it neatly. She did have her standards. They weren't going to begin being slovenly at The Grand Palace on the Thames.

He was relieved to be of some service to her.

"I'm sorry I was unkind to you just now," she said.

"I shall doubtless live through it, given that I'm hard, and cold, and dutiful."

For some reason this made her give a short, albeit bleak, laugh.

The laugh was good, but the bleakness alarmed him.

Silence settled like dust.

He didn't move, and neither did she.

How had it never occurred to him the peril in which women walked every day, even the most pampered of them? How valiant the simple act of being a woman was in so many ways.

"Do you know how we financed this place, Captain Hardy?" she said suddenly. "Angelique and I sold our jewelry to a man named Reeves on Bond Street so we could turn this building into a home. It seemed so tawdry. But it was so we wouldn't need anyone else. *Particularly* any other men."

He was breathless. He'd longed to hear the truth about this, but he was shocked by the piercing regret that she was telling him now, because she was vulnerable, and she'd come to trust him.

"It's just . . . I want so very much not to *need* anyone." Her voice cracked on that last word.

He quirked the corner of his mouth. "That's my very definition of Paradise."

She looked up at him. And gave another of those little ironic laughs. "Oh, you are a funny man, Captain Hardy. How did you get the way you are? I don't suppose you'll tell me, as doubtless it can't be summed up in one word."

She sounded as though she were asking herself as much as him.

Her new bitterness shortened his breath. She was innocent enough about people to share of herself openly. He partook of this generosity the way he would a breeze through an open window.

And he gave her back nothing.

She might not, of course, be entirely innocent. She might, in fact, still be abetting a smuggler. Still he could not stop himself from giving her what she needed, right now, in this moment. Something raw and true, and of himself.

"My origins," he began carefully, "are not the sort of story you should hear before you attempt to sleep."

That was as much as he'd admitted to anyone. He had never supposed his story had any value to anyone apart from himself, until now.

She went still. He could feel the change in her as surely as if she were indeed the weather.

But she ought not look at him that way. As if his words made her ache. As if she could read the story of his life in the lines of his face. As if he'd just opened a door a mere inch and she could now peer in and see everything.

And this was in part why he never said a word about it. He didn't need or want *comforting* from anyone. It was as easy to extricate one's self from comforting as it was to free a carriage wheel from a muddy rut. He didn't need to be known. He liked moving through the world without the ballast of sympathy or judgment.

No, she ought not look at him that way.

And he ought not like it.

What he needed—wanted—even in her moment of need—was to peel her night rail from her lithe body and bury his face in her throat, so he could feel her moan vibrate against his lips when his hands traveled lower and filled with her breasts.

Even now. Men were basically animals.

Doubtless she knew this all too well.

She cleared her throat. "Well, then." Her voice had gone a little thready. "Thank you, Captain Hardy, for the rescue. I suppose it's off to sleep."

That was certainly the wisest thing that either of them could do.

"Go on up, Lady Derring. No other unwelcome guests will enter tonight. I'll stand guard for the evening, if you think that would be helpful."

Delilah looked into his face, soft yet still implacable, his eyes hot but enigmatic, and loathed herself for how something in her immediately eased at the words. As though he alone had the answers. As though nothing could possibly go wrong while he was standing guard.

She'd meant it: she didn't want to need anyone. Let alone *want* anyone.

The first step was the difficult task of taking herself out of his presence. Sitting there like a beautiful rugged wall she wanted nothing more than to climb all over.

A wall that had let through a chink of light and she wanted to go toward it the way any moth goes toward light.

She'd probably dash herself to pieces.

Her words emerged in a rush. "I don't think standing guard all night is necessary, but thank you. Good night."

She turned so swiftly her braid whistled through the air toward him like a cat-o'-nine-tails.

He caught it in his fist like a striking snake.

They froze that way, absurdly for a moment, like one of Derring's statues. The way Hardy moved took her breath away. The speed and precision. As if he was prepared for every single eventuality because he'd already encountered them in some form or another. She gave herself permission to be awed.

He was, in fact, remarkable.

His mouth was turned up at the corner. "However frustrating you find me, Lady Derring, I don't believe I deserve the lash." He whispered it.

She gave a nervous little laugh. She opened her mouth to apologize.

But something about his expression stopped her voice.

Because now he was looking down at her braid with something very like wonder, maybe confusion. As if he'd stumbled across an exotic creature in a trap he'd set and he wasn't certain whether he ought to free it or name it. As if he hadn't the right to touch it at all.

Her heart, for some reason, was beating exultantly.

He gently drew the braid between his thumb and forefinger. "I don't think I'll return this," he teased, softly. "It might be useful. I could use this to lower myself out of a castle, like Rapunzel. Or raise the mainsail."

He raised his eyes to hers. She felt the heat in them.

"I'm not certain you've been telling the truth, Captain Hardy, about your facility for poetry."

She was whispering, too.

He frowned faintly. "Not a bit of what I just said rhymed."

She realized she'd been leaning ever closer to him all this time.

Tentatively, she laid her hand against his jaw. She wasn't certain why. Except that she wanted to touch his face after seeing that raw, amazed expression. It had pulled her like gravity.

His cheek was a little gritty with the start of his whiskers. Hard. Warm. She was close enough to see his scar, his lines, map the stern geometry of his face, his cheekbones, his chin.

Yet she couldn't quite read his eyes in the twilight of the parlor. Maybe that was all for the best. It made what she was about to do a little easier.

She kissed him.

Softly.

Chastely.

Fleetingly.

And she raised her lips from his; she drew in a shuddering breath.

He'd gone so motionless she'd warrant the blood had momentarily stopped moving in his veins.

The pleasure of shocking him was almost as good as the kiss.

She lifted her eyes to his face.

His eyes were all pupil now.

For a moment, it was hard to know who was breathing in and who was breathing out. It was a small storm contained between them.

"I'm not certain you're in your right mind at the moment, Lady Derring." His voice lulled, nearly hoarse.

"I'm not using my mind at all. You ought to take advantage of that."

The next two breaths he took and released were audible.

"Delilah . . . don't tease."

Ah. Stern Captain Hardy, issuing an order.

But the words were ever-so-slightly frayed. She recognized that he was in truth asking for mercy, this man who had probably never begged for a thing.

And they both knew the torment of wanting something out of reach.

She was disinclined to torture him. One man had tried to take her against her will tonight.

It was her glorious right to give herself to another.

So she kissed him again.

This time he captured her face with his hands as her lips touched his. He tipped her head back into the cradle of them with such deliberate grace she fleetingly wondered how many times he'd done precisely that.

And he plundered.

But from that moment on there was no question about who was in command or what was about to happen. Anticipation and uncertainty and fear and joy were all distinct feelings, all at once, and nearly physical pleasures. She knew nearly nothing. She suspected he did indeed know everything.

And everything was what she wanted.

He drugged her with the heat and dark sweetness

of his lips, his tongue, stroking and twining with hers, in so doing uncovering strata after strata of subtle pleasure that shivered through her bloodstream, lava, quicksilver, setting up camp between her legs, throbbing. She took hungrily, mesmerized, trembling, her hands clinging to his shirt hot from his skin.

And then she began to give, and to demand, and she could feel his need ramping in tandem with hers, in the hoarse oath he whispered, the low moan of triumph. Their breath sawed, hot and sweet; their tongues dueled, and their lips clung and released and went for more. And when the air slipped into her night rail she realized that somehow, sneakily, in the midst of this, he'd eased her night robe away from her shoulders.

He dragged his hands down over her throat, then with a tweak skillfully loosened the ribbon at its bodice so that the lawn confection collapsed like a scandalized maiden. And this, too, was eased from her shoulders, from her breasts, as she was in thrall to the things he was doing to her ear with his tongue. He filled his hands with her breasts, chafing his thumbs over her nipples, stroking. The shock of pleasure snagged the breath in her throat, and she choked an oath of her own as her head tipped backward. He buried his face in her throat, kissing the place where her heart was thundering. His lips, his tongue, his breath, laid a new trail of pleasure along her shoulder, a sensual Vasco da Gama, as his hands savored her breasts. She hadn't known her own skin, her own senses, contained such magic, such potential for furious bliss.

Desire was like claws sunk into her.

"I need . . ." She choked. "I want . . ."

She didn't know what she was asking for precisely.

"Anything," he said, low and fiercely. "Name it."

If only she knew what to call the thing he'd done to the hollow beneath her ear that sent rivulets of quicksilver pleasure through her veins. She'd name that.

"More," is what she said.

He knew. His grin was white in the gloomy light of the parlor.

She hadn't realized he'd already, through the magic of drugging her senses, levered her backward until she looked up and there was the water spot and the plaster rose on the chandelier. She'd lost a sense of where her body began and ended; she was a creature who accepted pleasure.

And then Tristan caught hold of the hem of her night rail and tugged, and it became a caress as it slid down her legs. She felt like a caterpillar shedding its cocoon. A naked butterfly on a sagging velvet settee, which, when she shifted, caressed her bum. Everything in the entire world was making love to her.

Egad, she was naked. She'd never been entirely naked in front of a man. The awareness burned a little of the sensual haze away, she nearly crossed her arms and legs out of nerves until Tristan made a sound, half sigh, half groan, like a man who beheld a feast, and then stretched alongside her and wrapped her with his arms, clothing her in heat and his singular smell, man and sweat and tobacco and the musk of desire. Maybe it was the smell of valor.

She slid her hands beneath his shirt. He was indeed a wall. A hot, smooth one, satin stretched over stone. A little fuzzy with hair.

He sighed something that sounded like "God, yes."

How lovely and erotic to make someone make those sounds.

So she did it again, marveling at the warmth and strength of him.

He shifted his body lower, ducked his head, and closed his mouth over her nipple. And sucked. Traced it with his tongue and sucked again. How extraordinary. How wicked.

His lips reclaimed hers again and she sank into the refuge of long sultry kisses while his hands dropped below, and his fingertips like delicate marauders lit fires everywhere they touched as they traveled the curving road of her waist, her hip, her thigh. She was rippling with waves of pleasure by the time his fingers crested the curve of her buttocks and slid between her thighs, which, she realized when they arrived, was exactly where she wanted them to be all along.

"I didn't know . . . oh God."

Her body was wiser than she was, and her legs dropped open even wider.

"Tell me what you want," he murmured, his fingers circling, stroking, until her lungs labored with hot ragged breaths and she was wantonly undulating against his hand. She'd had no idea.

"This . . . oh God, this . . ." Her voice was a rasp.

"This?" And he stroked, hard, between her legs, where she was satiny and wet.

She bucked upward into his hand, gasping a few words she was fairly certain she'd never said aloud before in her life.

He did it again, and again, hard, deliberately.

What was happening to her?

She dragged her hand over the hard swell in his trousers and watched his breath hiss in, the tendons of his throat go taut.

"Unfasten the buttons." It was a rasped command, all urgency and need. And it was hopelessly erotic, but then everything suddenly was.

Her fingers trembled, and it was all she could do not to use her teeth to tear the placket open, but even then she thought about the mending and freed each button in its own time.

His cock sprang forth.

He grasped one of her hands and closed it around the shaft, dragged it down. Clearly a demonstration of what she ought to do.

She obeyed.

"Holy mother of . . . sweet . . . oh God, Delilah . . . I can't . . . I want . . ."

Making this man utter hoarse, begging fragments of sentences would forever rank among the most thrilling things she'd done in her life.

She did it again.

And his pleasure was hers, and she wanted to do more to him.

Quick as an acrobat he lowered himself again to face her. His cock was hard, thrilling, enormous against her thigh and for the first time in her life she wanted what she knew he intended to do with it.

And as her thighs were so wantonly open they might as well have sported a Welcome! sign, it was easy for him to take up that stroking again. This time it was rhythmic, insistent, swift. He knew where she was going; she didn't. She was hurtling toward something, or something was hurtling toward her. She was terrified but desperate: never before had she so badly wanted something she couldn't even name. She was mostly afraid that it wouldn't live up to this fanfare.

"Tristan . . . please tell me . . . please . . . don't stop . . ."

They were gasps, raw pleas, and she heard them as if she were already somewhere outside of her own body. It was extraordinary.

"Trust me."

His voice came from beneath the low roar of her breath, a sound somehow everywhere and nowhere and far from her. His relentless, brilliant fingers sent bolt after bolt of breath-shredding pleasure raying through her until all at once what felt like a coat of feather-soft cinders rushed over her skin.

And just like that, an unimaginable bliss broke over her. It whipped her body upward and she screamed, soundlessly. Shattered her into fragments of pleasure, like the winking crystals in the chandelier. She was stardust.

Wave after wave of bliss shook her.

"Dear God . . . oh, my dear God . . . what was . . ." Her imagination was limber enough but never would she ever have imagined such a thing.

He flashed a piratical grin. "Not God. That was all me. And all you."

He was already deftly arranging her body for more sensual plunder. He'd risen up over her and tucked her legs on either side of his torso.

"Hold on to me, Delilah," he whispered.

She wouldn't *think* of disobeying, given how she'd essentially just been launched from her body into the stratosphere by unforeseen pleasure. Perhaps more of that was in store now.

And then he thrust into her. She locked him in with her legs round his back and her arms around his shoulders, took him as deeply as she could.

He moved slowly, at first. Sank into her slowly, withdrew, sighing, swearing softly his own pleasure and wonder. His face was shadowy. She kept her eyes fixed on it anyway.

His hips moved, postponing the pleasure for himself.

"I fear I must . . . this will be quick . . . I need you, Delilah . . ."

She laid her hands against the scoops made by muscle in his buttocks and arched up against him, absolving him of the need for control. "I want what you want."

Which was all the permission their bodies needed to collide and part amid a conversation composed of hoarse, ragged breathing: the odd "oh God, so good" and soft whimpering moans. The velvet settee rocked and thumped like a goat in a stall. And as his hips drummed ever more swiftly, driving himself into her again and again, the beginnings of that glorious thing once more began to build in her, as if inside her was a normally placid sea that could be boiled and churned by this storm and rush its banks. Until she was nearly sobbing with pleasure, clawing his shoulders, bowing to meet him. She buried her exultant cry in his shoulder.

And then he went still, with a stifled roar, and

swiftly rolled away from her. She knew why when his release felt sticky on her thigh. And she clung to him as his body shook hard, at the mercy of his release.

And they shifted so that they lay facing the ceiling, sweatily entwined. Her head rested on his chest.

"Was I wrong?" he whispered finally.

"No. Of course not. When are you ever wrong?"

He gave a short breathless laugh. He was breathing as if he'd swum across the Thames to get to the settee and exuding satisfaction.

"It was indeed very good. But was it wicked? I *felt* wicked."

There was a little silence. "You felt sublime." He said it softly. The word landed like poetry and made her feel shy.

"Something tells me you don't use that word very often, Captain."

He didn't reply. His chest rose and fell beneath her head.

Sometimes she thought that was entirely his strategy: every word acquired profundity when he issued fewer of them. Like a shot of whiskey, they were more potent for being distilled.

Instead he drew his thumb along her lower lip. Softly, back and forth. Like a mapmaker planning territory to conquer.

"I should have liked you to be more naked," she murmured.

She could feel his mouth curve against her shoulder. "Next time I shall be the nakedest man that ever was born."

"There cannot be a next time."

She hadn't realized she'd said that aloud until his chest stopped moving.

She realized she'd stopped breathing, as well, waiting to hear what he'd say.

"Very well."

His tone was indecipherable.

She didn't want to explain now, when her body was still humming like the final notes ringing in a symphony. She didn't want to explain at all, in fact. The idea of another time meant there would be still more times, as it was inconceivable at the moment not to want that again and again. And now that she knew precisely the kind of wizardry involved, how the race toward release dissolved one into the purest, most vulnerable self, she could imagine losing just a little of herself every time. Until she was all his.

And therein, alas, lay the potential for destruction.

It was easier to end it now.

"Thank you for . . . this time."

"No trouble at all." He sounded amused.

The sweat was cooling on her body and the official start of their morning was hours away. The cook's heart would give out if she walked into the parlor and found this.

"If I'm to be wanted for only one thing," she mused, "I am glad there's such pleasure to be had in it."

Once again, every muscle in his body went so rigid she nearly bounced from him as though he were a carriage seat.

Then he drew in a long, long breath. Released it at length.

It was wrong, but she loved the feel of his chest rising and falling beneath her when he did. His control was formidable. Unleashed, he was.

"And they say *I'm* a brute," he muttered.

"*Who* says you're a brute?"

He didn't answer the question. Which almost made her smile dryly. Exasperating man. The arrogance of him! He chose what to answer and when, as if he were the sole arbiter of what was important in the world.

"Your husband, he . . ." he began carefully. She waited. "Delilah, he ought to have been more considerate."

And even though they'd been groaning and begging and bouncing away on each other like wild animals a moment ago, her face went hot. It wasn't shame. Not precisely. It was for having a vulnerability exposed. It was for the care with which he chose those words. It bordered on tenderness.

But surely not. Surely it was mere accuracy from him.

She suspected whatever it was he felt was considerably stronger, and her own ferocious protectiveness unnerved her.

For a moment she couldn't speak.

"I thought it was me," she whispered. "That maybe I should have known, or—"

"No. He ought to have . . . you are . . . you are marvelous at this."

Funny. In another time, another place, when she was another person, that might be one of the most appalling things she'd ever heard about herself: that she was marvelous at boisterous sex on a velvet settee in a boardinghouse by the docks. With someone who *patently* wasn't a gentleman.

She certainly wouldn't feel exultant. Yet she was. Whatever brutal forces had shaped this man into this taciturn, unyielding person, she was glad to take and give comfort and surcease.

I need you, Delilah.

She wondered if he'd realized he'd said that.

Then again, the things *she'd* said shocked her.

She stirred to rise.

He shifted to allow her.

But first he laced his hands through the mussed wreckage of her braid and kissed her, so slowly, so softly, that delicious, wicked pooling of heat started up between her legs and she was amazed to realize that, given the slightest encouragement, she'd do it all over again on this settee, which likely wouldn't be able to stand the strain.

Perhaps it had something to do with being naked.

She found her night dress on the floor, and hurriedly clutched it to her.

"Delilah . . ." he said softly, suddenly. And her name almost sounded like a song.

She turned to him. It sounded portentous, and it alarmed her how her heart leaped with anticipation. Of what, she didn't know.

"The *things* you said . . . well, I reckon you need to put at least a pound in the jar."

Chapter Nineteen

THE NEXT morning, sitting at the work table in the kitchen just as Helga was beginning the day by beating eggs and shouting orders to the scullery maids, Delilah succinctly and in a low voice told Angelique about Mr. Brinker, touching upon just the salient points—well dressed, wealthy, supercilious toad, squeezed her breast, was hell-bent on rape until Captain Hardy pulled a pistol on him and put a dent in the little table with his head.

She didn't embellish with emotion. She didn't really need to.

Angelique was pale and silent.

"But at least we still have his three sovereigns," Delilah concluded.

They both smiled blackly.

Similar senses of humor certainly helped get them through their days.

"Are you all right, Delilah?" Angelique touched her knee. "It's a terribly shocking thing, and I'm just . . . I'm so very sorry that happened to you."

"I'm surprisingly very good. Not a nick on me."

Angelique tipped her head and studied her. Then narrowed her eyes. "You *do* look unusually radiant."

"Mmm," Delilah said.

She felt radiant, and a little sore in a marvelous way, but she wasn't about to say that. It was as though life had acquired an entirely new dimension. One where all the colors and feelings were kept.

Angelique continued her perusal of her, seemed to be considering saying something, thought better of it. "Did you tell Dot?"

"We can't tell Dot. It will destroy her."

"She likes opening the door, however. She finds it fun to discover who's out there. I think you need to tell her a very little, enough to genuinely scare her into not opening the door after a certain hour, but not enough to inspire her to don a hair shirt over it."

"Very well." Delilah sighed. "We need to hire footmen, perhaps. Or carry little knives in our bodices."

"I believe you are right. I think we need at least one footman," Angelique said, fretfully. "Blast it. Men eat so much and they'll want to be paid."

They both smiled at this.

Though with the new sovereigns Mr. Brinker had left behind, hiring a footman was now a possibility. Quite the irony.

Would any footman *want* to work in a household brimful of females?

Helga was now singing a little song in German.

"Delilah . . . what on earth was Captain Hardy doing in the drawing room at midnight?" Angelique said suddenly.

Delilah went still. She hadn't considered this. It was, in fact, a good question.

"Perhaps he couldn't sleep and heard voices? Went in search of a late-night libation?"

"He heard voices over the sound of Delacorte snoring?"

It was, in fact, a very good question.

"Do you know what Brinker said when he was flat on his back, blood oozing from his nose? 'Oh, you're *that* Captain Hardy.' What do you suppose he meant?"

Angelique looked thoughtful.

Then shook her head. "I couldn't begin to guess. Maybe Brinker was simply dazed from the blow to the head."

"That must be it," Delilah said blithely. "Helga, do you think we can have extra sausage for breakfast? I am *starving*."

A NIGHT OF unforgettable lovemaking put Tristan in a downright sprightly mood. He was bounding out through the foyer to have a look at his ship and to meet Massey for breakfast when a dulcet female voice called from the drawing room.

"Good morning, Captain Hardy."

He stopped.

Mrs. Breedlove was alone, sitting on the settee, fetching in a gray morning gown with the light behind her.

"Good day, Mrs. Breedlove. Tolerable weather we're having."

She was as different from Lady Derring as diamonds from daisies. They were both beautiful women in their ways, shaped, he suspected, by entirely different circumstances.

"I've a little tea left in the pot, Captain Hardy, if you'd like it before you leave. I thought I'd drink it quietly before we feed the family, as it were."

All at once he was certain Mrs. Breedlove had something she wished to speak to him about. It was also an opportunity to ask a few pressing questions of his own.

"That's a kind offer. Thank you."

He sat in the chair opposite her. "You and Lady Derring have created such a comfortable, welcoming place here. How did the two of you come to meet?"

"I was her husband's mistress."

Whatever he'd been expecting—circumspection? A delicate use of euphemism?—it wasn't that. He had the sense that she'd intended to shock him. Or to discover whether he was, in fact, shocked.

"You don't say," he said neutrally.

Which made her smile. "We discovered, awkwardly and quite accidentally, that Derring had left the two of us penniless. We found we had a good deal in common in addition to the feckless Earl of Derring. The only thing Delilah had left was this building, and she was kind enough to include me in her mad scheme. We rub along together quite well."

"Lady Derring is kind. As are you," he added, gallantly. Though he was less certain such a gentle word applied to Angelique.

She didn't thank him. Angelique merely tipped her head. "You and I are very alike, I think, Captain Hardy."

"Ah. Does your beard begin to darken at about five o'clock, too?"

She smiled politely. "Nothing makes a dent. Not anymore. But that's all to the good, isn't it?"

Tristan stared at her, instantly cautious.

"I find it so," he said shortly.

"I've concluded people are more or less the same beneath the surface. Saints, sinners, the differences are a matter of semantics and rather superficial."

"Then we are agreed. I can't help but suspect, Mrs. Breedlove, that you are taking the long way round to make a point. And in this approach, we differ. Hence the following direct question: What are you getting at?"

"When you are done with her, whatever your reasons, she will be in smithereens. And you won't even sport a nick."

For a moment he didn't breathe.

Tristan betrayed nothing of what he was thinking, which was, in fact, that she may be right.

And yet.

Mrs. Breedlove's eyes were hazel, which seemed a much too-soft, nearly dreamy color for a woman like her to have. There wasn't a thing soft or dreamy about Mrs. Breedlove, at least not anymore.

Yes, they were alike.

He wondered about the first man to compliment her eyes, for surely someone had been the first. He was sincerely sorry if life had been unkind to her; doubtless, to wind up as Derring's mistress, things had not gone the way she would have preferred. He had the sense that one took refuge from life in The Grand Palace on the Thames.

"Mrs. Breedlove, do you think I'm a man of whim?"

"No. Hence my concern. I suspect you are quite purposeful. But I'm not quite certain of your purpose here, at The Grand Palace on the Thames."

"Why, for the accommodations, of course. And for

the pleasure of being required to sit reading comfortably in your sitting room while the Gardner sisters stare at me."

"Then I shall be clear. On the off chance a scrap of heart remains in the iron confines of your chest, perhaps you ought to leave her alone."

He took a sip of his tea, now cold, and a little too strong.

Had he been obvious? This seemed inconceivable.

Or had Delilah—?

"No, she hasn't said a word," Mrs. Breedlove said, in answer to his unspoken question.

He wasn't going to obfuscate. He would not admit a thing. Nor would he deny.

He merely studied her.

"I think the very fact of your advice suggests you've not only been dented, Mrs. Breedlove. I believe you actually care very much about her."

For a fleeting instant her cool features registered surprise and vulnerability. She did not like being sassed out.

He thought perhaps she was reassessing him.

He almost smiled. Clearly she thought astute men were anomalies.

Perhaps they were.

"Or I'm looking out for the best interests of all of us, and I've grown weary of cleaning this drafty box and the nature of smithereens is that one must pick them out of the carpet or curtains *forever.*"

With an insouciant wave of her hand, she departed the room, leaving it somehow ten degrees colder than it had been.

"LADY DERRING SAYS that she and Mrs. Breedlove financed their boardinghouse with the proceeds of the sale of their jewelry to a pawnbroker called Reeves. We'll need to verify this. It doesn't yet definitively clear her of cigar smuggling. But my instincts say neither she nor her partner are involved. I had an opportunity to speak to Mrs. Breedlove this morning."

Tristan was more and more certain that Delilah and Mrs. Breedlove were innocent of any wrongdoing. But more to the point, he hoped that they were.

Which meant he had taken a side. And he made an internal adjustment to remind himself that he was here to try to track down the source of those cigars. Not prove Delilah and Mrs. Breedlove's innocence.

"Very well. We'll verify it, sir. But why did they open a boardinghouse, of all things?"

"Because . . . their options for survival and thriving were limited. Most of their options involved relying on men, which they preferred not to do. Apparently men aren't as wonderful as we think we are, or so they believe."

Massey pressed his lips together, considering this.

He knew about Brinker. About how he'd been taken to the opposite side of London by Tristan's men and grilled the entire way about his presence at The Grand Palace on the Thames.

That was how they'd ascertained that Brinker was a brute, not a smuggler. He'd in fact, when he was more lucid, conveyed his thanks to the famous Captain Hardy for stopping the smuggling in Kent, which was cutting into his own family's business.

He was assured his horse would be returned to

him in Kent. Which it would be. They were efficient, the blockade men. They also threatened to hand him his bollocks on a plate if Brinker ever returned to The Grand Palace on the Thames.

"Is Lady Derring right about men, guv?" Massey had clearly never considered this before. He looked troubled.

Tristan was mordantly amused.

"You're a good man, Massey. Rest yourself."

Massey looked relieved. Captain Hardy wasn't one to fling compliments about lightly.

Tristan was less certain about his own relative goodness, however. He'd gotten information he needed from Lady Derring—about her jewelry—when she was most vulnerable and trusting. She'd become vulnerable and trusting in part because they had been building a certain intimacy for days. He hadn't exactly set out to do it this way but now it all seemed knotted together—the desire and the investigation—and there was no way to undo it.

He'd always thought of himself as a man of decency and rectitude, upstanding in the pursuit of justice. He adhered to a personal code. But would a good man do that to a woman?

He now more fully understood the nature of the peril of this attraction. Inherent in it, from the beginning, was betrayal.

He knew it wouldn't stop him from making love to her again.

Because men were just that wonderful.

And rejecting a pleasure like that—a once-in-a-lifetime gift—somehow seemed the greater sin.

"Are we on the right track, sir?" Massey asked, into the silence. "The investigation?"

Massey was tentative. As though he hardly dared ask the question.

They were both men of action. All of his men were. And the action here—the interviews, the following of guests—was beginning to feel both painstaking and aimless.

"Yes, I think so. I think we have a few pieces of the puzzle, but we cannot yet see how they fit. We just need to be thorough."

This was enough for Massey, because there had not yet been a time when Tristan was on the wrong track. He looked somewhat relieved.

But there also had not been a time when he'd been requested to send a letter to the king to let him know of his progress, such as it was. He was due to write that letter.

"Well, if the Widow Derring is pretty, sir, perhaps to speed things up you ought to seduce her to make her tell you . . ."

Tristan's cold stare shocked Massey speechless.

He supposed it was his own guilt that made the idea of hearing that entire sentence unbearable.

"What if someone wanted to seduce Emily to those ends?" Tristan said finally. Quietly.

Massey remained silent and still, studying Tristan. And suddenly he thought he understood.

"You remembered her name, sir," he said gently.

DELILAH SPENT THE day sailing the choppy seas of her emotions, euphoric one moment (she'd had *ex-*

traordinary sex on a settee with a gorgeous captain she scarcely knew!), appalled the next (she'd had extraordinary sex on a settee with a gorgeous captain she *barely knew*). She could not and did not regret it. But was this the sort of person she wanted to be? She had been gently bred, whatever that, in fact, meant, and though she'd been triumphantly shedding *shoulds* and *oughts* for some time now, shedding her night rail in the middle of the drawing room was something else altogether. Try as she might, she could not get her thoughts to congregate and mull the problem of it. Her body was still echoing from the pleasure visited upon it. It drowned out reason.

She kept hearing his voice: *I need you.*

She had done her chores in a feverish, abstracted state and joined Angelique for tea in the upstairs drawing room.

They both gave a start when they heard Dot dashing up the stairs. She tripped on the last one, nearly arriving on her hands and knees in the little drawing room.

"Lady Derring, Mrs. Breedlove, we've a very young lady what wants a place to stay. She is rather, er, fancy and frantic and demanding." She crawled a few paces then righted herself.

It was apparent Dot's nerves had been a bit worked by this young lady, who had probably been under their roof for a few minutes.

"By all means let's rush to see her then," Angelique said, her eyes cast heavenward.

Delilah shot Angelique a wry look and laid her mending aside. "Of course we'll see a frantic young lady. Will you bring in the tea, Dot?"

On the reception room settee sat a girl who, they could see in an instant, came from a family of some means. Her turkey-red wool dress and matching pelisse were enviably smart and current, and a darling felt bonnet trimmed in darling cherries and leaves sat next to her on the settee.

She'd made herself quite at home, so it seemed.

"I can't go through with it. I can't! I can't, I tell you. I'd rather *die*," was how she greeted the two of them when they appeared.

Delilah suspected she'd been saying this to herself since Dot left the room.

"Of course you wouldn't rather die, darling," Angelique said firmly. "Whatever the 'it' in question is. You could always open a boardinghouse instead."

Delilah shot her a dry look.

"You don't *know*!" the girl wailed.

"I expect a man is involved," Delilah said.

This brought the girl up short.

"How did you know that?" she asked suspiciously. "Is it true what my mother says, with age comes wisdom?"

She was wide-eyed and disingenuous.

There was a little silence.

"I say we throw her outside to the wolves," Angelique said.

The girl flicked her uncertain blue gaze between Angelique and Delilah. She was pleasingly round, with charming little pale freckles across her nose that she probably hated, and her honey-colored hair, neatly curled and pinned, was surprisingly unmussed for one so frantic.

Delilah sat down next to her and touched her arm gently.

"Why don't you take a breath and tell us how you've come to grace our establishment, Miss . . ."

"Bevan-Clark. Lucinda Bevan-Clark."

"Miss Bevan-Clark, I am Lady Derring and this is Mrs. Angelique Breedlove." Angelique sat down opposite them. "We are the proprietors here at The Grand Palace on the Thames. Why don't you tell us what brings you here and what has you so upset?"

Miss Bevan-Clark took a breath. "Are either of you married?"

After a little hesitation, Delilah answered for both of them. "We are widows."

"It's the most awkward thing," Miss Bevan-Clark said fervently. "He's been my friend my entire life. But I am not in *love* with him. The very notion of *marrying* him!" She gave a shudder. "But my parents got it into their minds that we should make a match because our families are rich, you see, and well, our families would only get richer should we marry, and wouldn't that be lovely for everyone." She said this with great snideness. "I'm terribly afraid he'll be so awfully disappointed because I think he's in love with me, otherwise why *would* he propose? I got word from a mutual friend of ours that he intended to propose at a house party we were both meant to attend and I took it upon myself to run away from the coaching inn. I asked to be brought to the nearest boardinghouse and this is where the driver took me."

She looked proud of this, and she really ought not be.

"Rich, you say?" Angelique said just as Delilah said, "Are you in love with someone else?"

"Well, I'd certainly like the opportunity to find out if I'm in love with someone else!" she said indignantly. "Wouldn't you? I know you're both a bit on in years but I daresay even now you wouldn't turn away from the possibility of a grand romance."

Delilah and Angelique very, very carefully did not look at each other. Neither of them was yet thirty.

They were both tempted to give her ears a slight boxing.

They could tell her a lot about the myth of romance. Delilah, in particular, could now tell her that a disappointing marriage could be stifling but magnificent sex on a boardinghouse settee with a man she hardly knew and who was not a gentleman could be in her distant future by way of compensation. The delicious soreness between her legs and a hint of whisker burn against her cheek conspired to remind her of that all day.

But it seemed impossible to say that to such an open, indignant, hopeful face.

And something about that open, hopeful face made Delilah feel just a little bit sordid. A little bit nostalgic for a time when she didn't know all the things she knew. A little wistful that Miss Bevan-Clark could marry a friend, who knew her so well.

It wouldn't matter, regardless. Miss Bevan-Clark would *never* believe them if they told her there was no such thing as romance.

"To marry a friend! I ask you. I daresay we crawled about in nappies together! Not romantic at all!"

"There are worse things than marrying a friend, Miss Bevan-Clark."

"Is that what we should aspire to? Seizing upon something because it isn't the 'worst thing'?"

"Absolutely," Angelique said as Delilah was saying, "It's a bit more complicated than that."

But it wasn't as though Miss Bevan-Clark didn't have a point.

"I have money with me! A lot of it. I can pay you whatever you like. If you let me stay for a time."

Oh, the idiot child.

Delilah sighed. She and Angelique didn't even have a decade on Miss Bevan-Clark, she suspected, but she suddenly felt as old as Westminster Abbey.

"Miss Bevan-Clark, how old are you?" Angelique asked.

"I shall be eighteen next April."

"Very well," Angelique said. "First of all, do not *ever* tell strangers in London that you have a lot of money. You're fortunate that you've stumbled into The Grand Palace on the Thames, where we will charge you dearly but not more than what our accommodations are worth. We are quite respectable and you are safe and welcome here." She paused. "At the moment."

The faintest hint of a threat of eviction was a good way to keep unruly guests in line.

"All right," Miss Bevan-Clark begrudgingly allowed. "Thank you," she added, though the last two words sounded like a question.

"Second of all, you're the veriest twit."

Miss Bevan-Clark's mouth dropped open. "Well, I *never*!"

"What she means is . . ." Delilah leaned forward soothingly, placatingly. Then she sat back again. "No, Mrs. Breedlove had it right the first time," she said cheerfully. "You are indeed the veriest twit."

Miss Bevan-Clark clapped her jaw shut. Her eyes were enormous with amazement.

"You shall be respectful if we allow you to stay with us," Delilah said firmly. "You will speak to us with the respect in which you hold your mother, though we're scarcely much older than you." The word *scarcely* was all a matter of interpretation, of course. "We've experience of the world and you would do well to listen. I suspect you've been rather indulged until now, and now this—your parents' insistence on marrying your friend—is the first time you've been challenged. And so you've gone to pieces like a little baby."

There was a stunned silence.

"Well, that's very unkind." Miss Bevan-Clark seemed more surprised than incensed. Doubtless people had never been unkind to her before. She seemed a little pleased at the novelty of it.

"It is true, however. Buck up. Learning how to accept criticism without throwing a tantrum is how you become an adult. I don't suppose you're stupid. You don't seem so, anyhow."

Miss Bevan-Clark was clearly torn between pitching a dramatic little fit or basking a little in the compliment.

"I'm *not* stupid."

Her choice of words suggested she might be speaking truth.

"I thought not." Delilah beamed at her encouragingly, and Miss Bevan-Clark beamed in return, like a prized pupil.

"Are you here alone?" Angelique said suddenly. "This area by the docks is quite dang—" Delilah shot her a warning glare. "—erously appealing."

"My maid, Miss Wright, is waiting outside in the hack. She thinks I've gone quite mad. She refused to come in."

"Well, at least one of you is sensible," Angelique said.

"Thank you." Miss Bevan-Clark had Mr. Farraday's willingness to assume that all compliments were meant for them.

"Dot, go and bring her maid in. Miss Bevan-Clark, give Dot some money to pay the hack."

She looked startled, but she dipped into her reticule without question and pressed a handful of coins into Dot's hand.

"Miss Bevan-Clark, have some bracing tea. Why don't you take a moment to look over our rules and conditions?" Delilah leaned over and handed the rules to the girl. "We are not at all unsympathetic to your position, but we do not allow just *anyone* to stay at length at The Grand Palace on the Thames. We prefer our guests to behave like adults."

Now Miss Bevan-Clark looked worried.

"If we do admit you as a guest, we shall make you as comfortable as you would be in your own home and treat you as family," Angelique added.

The word *family* caused something like guilt and the faintest hint of yearning to flicker across Miss Bevan-Clark's features.

Delilah and Angelique stepped outside of the room and into the opposite drawing room, and spoke in whispers.

"I don't think we ought to mention Mr. Farraday, though the coincidence is delicious," Delilah said. "Could there be *two* such twits in the world?"

"I've come to believe nearly anything is possible. I suppose we shall find out later this evening—I'm given to understand Mr. Farraday will be out all day, and will miss dinner, but not chess with Delacorte. But what shall we do? We could have angry parents and Bow Street Runners convene upon us if someone sensible, like Miss Wright, sends a message to them from here."

"How much do Bow Street Runners make? Do you think they would like to stay here?" Delilah said.

Angelique stifled a laugh.

"And if we allow her to stay here and her parents discover that young Farraday is in the same place, they'll assume they ran off together," Delilah mused. "*She'll* be ruined, while he'll go on to make another match unscathed. Or he'll marry her out of honor and they shall both be miserable."

"Perhaps. But the odds of having a miserable life are about the same for nearly everyone. One just never knows. They like each other, or so she says, and many marriages begin under worse circumstances. We can address complications as they arise. We cannot pitch her out onto the street tonight. More to the point, we will make ten pounds if she stays."

"You make an excellent point, Angelique."

"We must compel her to send a message to her parents informing them of her safety."

"Perhaps they're meant for each other," Delilah surmised. "And they don't realize it."

"Is *anyone* meant for each other? Or are we all just rationalizing accidents of fate?"

It was a very good question, and one she ought to keep in mind should she be tempted to fall again into Captain Hardy's arms.

Chapter Twenty

CAPTAIN HARDY was, as usual, an island of calm in the little sea of gaiety in the drawing room after dinner, which had been a splendid lamb with mint that had the guests rhapsodizing and Helga blushing and curtsying.

Delilah noticed he'd reached page ten of *Robinson Crusoe* when she pulled out the chair to sit opposite him at the table.

"Good evening again, Captain Hardy."

"Good evening, Lady Derring."

The mere act of meeting his eyes had become an act of sensual daring. She was rewarded with a jolt of heat between her legs.

"Could we perhaps interest you in joining a game of Faro?" She gestured behind her to Angelique and Miss Bevan-Clark, and Dot and Mr. Delacorte.

"Faro," Tristan repeated thoughtfully. "Next you'll tell me you're opening a gaming hell."

She smiled at him.

He smiled, too.

"I grant you it's a bit *daring* for our cozy parlor, but given that we have younger guests at The Grand Palace on the Thames Angelique and I thought it might be invigorating for them."

"I am content listening to the ambient sounds of other guests as they go about their mandatory enjoyment. A bit like listening to birds in the cages in the Gallerie."

But she merely smiled at that, more broadly. It was clear the guests were enjoying themselves and each other. Captain Hardy included.

She'd done that. She'd helped create a place where disparate people could feel cared for, comfortable, safe, and amused.

"Speaking of the sounds of the other guests, I'm given to understand that our new guest, Miss Bevan-Clark, plays the pianoforte rather well."

He heaved a great sigh.

Miss Bevan-Clark had been gazing at Tristan with fascination, silently, since their introduction at the evening meal. Occasionally dropping her eyelashes to shield her admittedly pretty eyes. Then raising them up again. Obviously this had worked to bewitch men in some fashion previously.

Captain Hardy seemed more bemused than anything.

"Have you yet seen her blink?" he asked resignedly.

"Perhaps she's never seen a soldier before."

"Doubtless her parents wisely kept her far, far away from them."

"Perhaps you ought to tell her about the time you were shot. She might keel over into a swoon."

"By all means send her over here so that I may get the swoon underway. Anything to prevent her from playing the pianoforte."

"You're truly not a music lover, Captain Hardy?"

"I like music well enough." He sounded surprised by the notion that she might think otherwise. "Good music, well played. It's just that I'm haunted by one particular sound and I don't want anything to interfere with my memory of it."

"The wind snapping in the sails? The ringing sound that bullets make when they glance off your iron hide?"

He'd lowered his voice. "That sound you made when I moved inside you for the first time. It has quite ruined all other sounds for me."

It was as if he'd given the entire room a mighty spin, like a roulette wheel. Heat rushed across her limbs and convened in a pulsing pool between her legs.

He smiled, slowly, wickedly, with a certain sympathetic satisfaction. She imagined him smiling rather like that after he'd run a pirate through. Satisfaction at finding just the right vulnerability and promptly exploiting it.

She would not be surprised to hear the thunk of Miss Bevan-Clark's maidenly body toppling from the settee onto the floor.

As for Delilah, she looked down at the table.

Her breath, not to mention her composure, was lost.

He didn't say another word.

"The reason that *I* won't play Faro is that I'm not much of a gambler," she said. "The opening of perhaps The Grand Palace on the Thames notwithstanding. It was less an act of risk than desperation, which has, as you can see, become a triumph."

He smiled at that, too. "Where is young Farraday this evening? Certainly Miss Bevan-Clark would transfer her pretty gaze to him the moment he arrives."

"Is her gaze pretty, then?"

Out this came, unbidden. She was appalled that she sounded as much a twit as Miss Bevan-Clark.

He let her stew in mortification for a second or so, before he said, "Certainly. But it's not your gaze."

He said these things so matter-of-factly. As though he'd experienced everything in the world, sifted through the dross, and was confident that he emerged with the only things of truth and value.

It was thrilling.

And a bit irritating.

And, in a way, a bit overwhelming, in truth. She hadn't experienced any of this. Of affairs and flirtation and innuendos.

She caught Angelique's weather eye from across the room and forced a mild little solicitous smile onto her face, and cast a glance over at the maiden aunts.

"Captain Hardy . . . while I am far from unmoved . . ."

He waited. No prompts, no interruptions, no changes in topic. He waited. As he always did.

And despite the demands of his presence and personality, this waiting felt luxurious. He allowed her space in which to be herself. He did not assume that what she had to say could possibly have no merit, because she was a woman.

He did glance down at her hands. Which were knitted together.

He noticed things, Captain Hardy did.

She put a stop to the knitting.

"I have never before taken a lover," she said in a low voice. "And in your presence . . . reservations about that begin to seem frivolous."

"Excellent."

The little smile and the timbre of his voice and the way his skin took the firelight made it seem absurd that his long-fingered hands were resting against his ritualistic brandy instead of, perhaps, her breasts.

"But away from you . . . when I watch my ceiling at night . . . and perhaps it's the way I was raised, which seems to have more of a hold over me than I anticipated . . . I begin to wonder at the difference between a woman who takes a lover she knows scarcely a thing about . . . and a woman who works in a brothel earning her living from men she knows nothing about."

He went utterly still, his face stunned blank.

She saw the words sink in as he slowly leaned back in his chair.

His expression settled in and became troubled.

He, who so excelled at inscrutability.

Well. It seemed she possessed the power to shock, too.

"And while I understand I currently have a choice about such . . . such things . . . whereas other women may not . . . and I will never judge such a thing again . . . I confess it troubles me a little."

He rubbed his brow. It occurred to her that she'd never seen him indulge in a fidget. Unlike Delacorte, who probably didn't realize it, but fingered one of the silver buttons on his waistcoat when he had a good hand in Whist, or Mr. Farraday, who was *all* fidgets. Women could not be said to be fidgeting when their hands were nearly always busy with work.

"Clearly the solution lies in not watching your ceiling at night."

She smiled. "And they say you're not amusing."

"They say so many things about me."

His expression remained abstracted, however.

Odd to think that he might not have the answers to everything.

And then he took a sip of brandy.

"*Good* evening, friends." Farraday strode into the drawing room, bringing the scent of rain and tar and cigar smoke with him. He'd already whipped off his gloves and was making straight for the fire as though he'd lived there all his life and was perfectly at home. Then again, in all likelihood, he felt at home in the world, at home anywhere, really, because the world had been kind to him.

"Devil of an evening!" he declared. "Delacorte, break out the chessboard, I know precisely how to beat—AHHHHHHHH!"

It was a cry of horror worthy of any musicale. And it was quite genuine.

He'd fixed his eyes upon Lucinda Bevan-Clark.

"Andrew!" she gasped with a hand clapped to her clavicle.

She leaped to her feet and her head pivoted wildly to and fro. She darted a few feet to the left and a few feet to the right and then came to a stop right where she'd begun, in front of the settee.

Her maid, Miss Wright, sighed and rolled her eyes.

All of which rather answered lingering questions regarding coincidences.

The rest of the room was frozen in absolute fascination.

"What are you *doing* here?" they said at once, unanimously accusatory.

"Did my mother send you?" they said next, simultaneously.

Andrew took a breath. "Lucinda, why don't you tell me why you're here, when you were meant to be at a house party, just as I was."

"I'm here quite on my own, thank you very much."

"Without Miss Wright?"

"Of course with Miss Wright! She's right over there!" As if Miss Wright were an accessory akin to a muff or a pelisse and it would be unthinkable to make a move without her.

"Ho there, Miss Wright," he said.

"Good evening, Mr. Farraday," she said, with great irony.

"But that must mean . . ." Mr. Farraday was working things out.

"We were on our way to the house party, which is where I expected you to be, but I decided to escape from the coaching inn on the South Road in the dead of night and paid a driver to take us to a boardinghouse and this was the first place we came to."

"You could have come to harm, Lucinda!" He seemed genuinely distressed. "You ought not to have gone by yourself, even if Miss Wright was with you." It was rather sweet that he thought of her welfare before questioning why on earth she should want to escape.

"That's *precisely* what Miss Wright told her," Miss Wright muttered.

"Oh, Andrew, you're a dear to care." It was all desperate warmth mingled with agitation. Andrew's face visibly brightened. "That is, you're not like Captain

Hardy, you're still young and inexperienced in the ways of the world, but you're dear in your way."

Poor dear had no idea that flattery beaded up and rolled right off Captain Hardy.

Andrew cast a startled glance at Captain Hardy, as if it had never occurred to him that someone so elderly could hold any appeal for Lucinda.

"But . . . you're a very good sort." She bit her lip. "Oh, Andrew. It's just that I . . . I don't want to . . . I don't think . . ."

Every breath in the room was held.

But she didn't say the words.

"Lucinda, you're a *topping* girl," he said urgently, hardly poetry, but he said it so fervently and sincerely every older person in the room melted ever so slightly. "A bit prone to speaking before you've given it any thought, which can be a bit wounding," he said, looking a trifle wounded himself. "But you're so . . . funny and game, as well." He said this with a sort of tender exasperation.

She beamed at him, not the least offended. "You know me so well, Andrew. It *is* rather nice to see you. You're looking well. But . . ." Her pretty brow furrowed. "Why are *you* here?"

"But I don't want to . . . that is . . ."

He stopped.

He'd gone white about the mouth with the sheer terror of honesty.

"*Say* it," Miss Jane Gardner urged in a gleeful hiss from the corner.

Delilah darted a shocked, quelling look her way.

The silence was suddenly painfully suspenseful.

Miss Bevan-Clark bit her lip and clasped her hands tightly together.

Mr. Farraday twisted his kid gloves in his hands.

And then Dot dropped one of her knitting needles with a clink and everyone gave a start.

And yet no one spoke. The fire cracked and popped. Apart from a tiny squeaking sound which might have been one of the Gardner sisters' stays as she exhaled, the silence was so fraught it was very nearly like another guest in the sitting room. It would challenge Mr. Farraday to chess any minute.

When a voice finally came, the impact was like the voice of God.

"I've heard that you excel at playing the pianoforte, Miss Bevan-Clark. I would be happy to turn the pages for you if you would favor us with a song."

Everyone pivoted in shock.

Captain Hardy rose slowly, gracefully to his feet, and he was smiling—nay, beaming—at Miss Bevan-Clark.

Delilah stared at him. Her mouth was open. She could not be more stunned if the clock on the mantel had come to life and said the same thing.

Miss Bevan-Clark's mouth had dropped open. She'd slumped in her seat a little, amazed.

And then pink washed her charming, speckled cheeks.

"At this rate we can pay the bills by selling tickets to our quiet evenings in the drawing room," Angelique murmured.

Trepidation began to simmer in Delilah's gut.

What was he playing at?

But he wasn't looking at her and he gave her no clues at all.

He'd fixed his silver gaze on Miss Bevan-Clark as though she were due north. He probably had her freckles counted by now.

Mr. Farraday was staring at Captain Hardy with grave uncertainty.

She gave her head a frisky toss. "Certainly, Captain Hardy," she said, her voice a-tremble. "I should be happy to."

The girl rose with great dignity and, amidst a gauntlet of fascinated eyes, sauntered through the dense silence to the pianoforte and sat down on the bench.

And Captain Hardy joined her there, peering solicitously over her shoulder as she leafed through a variety of selections.

"She plays very well, indeed," Mr. Farraday said, suddenly. Ever-so-faintly belligerently. "I've heard her play *dozens* of times. At my family's home and at assemblies. And we've danced dozens of times, too."

Captain Hardy regarded him expressionlessly. "How fortunate you are."

Mr. Farraday flushed.

He sat down hard on the settee in the place vacated by Miss Bevan-Clark.

A moment later he'd crossed his arms about his torso protectively again, the way a cat will tuck its tail about its feet when it feels uncertain.

He, like everyone else, was riveted.

"Do you know 'The Soldier's Adieu'?" Miss Bevan-Clark asked.

"What manner of officer would I be if I didn't know 'The Soldier's Adieu'?"

She twinkled up at him as if it were the most enchanting thing anyone had ever uttered.

"But if you could perhaps play it in a key suitable to a baritone?" he said, so kindly Delilah's stomach knotted.

Of course he was a baritone.

She remembered the rumble of his voice in her ear. *I need you, Delilah.*

She was struggling with a sensation new to her. Rather like she'd swallowed a horse chestnut and it was pulsing spikily in her gut.

Somehow she'd failed to consider that taking a lover might entail jealousy. She was not attached; why should she be jealous?

So unnerved was she that she jumped when Miss Bevan-Clark pounced upon the keys with passionate vigor, swaying into the lilting ballad.

She played competently if not artistically.

Suddenly everyone was leaning forward just the littlest bit, on pins and needles waiting for Captain Hardy to open his mouth.

(In Dot's case, perhaps quite literally on pins and needles, given that she was mending. She was feeling in vain beneath her bum for a dropped pin.)

And when the first note emerged—rich, confident, soaring, and absolutely lovely—everyone sighed.

Delilah's heart literally squeezed like a little fist, a sort of sweet pain. She could not have said why.

And if he didn't land *precisely* on every note—sometimes just a hair north or south—he sang with matter-of-fact ease and imbued the sentimental song with a certain martial resonance, and for some reason her throat began to knot.

And then he finally—finally—glanced her way. It was just a flash of silver.

Rueful, though, that flash.

Even, perhaps, a bit . . . mischievous.

She loved and hated the relief that swooped through her like the winds off the sea. She understood what he was about now.

And it told her more than she wished she knew about how she felt about Captain Hardy.

She knew what to do next.

She moved from the little table, past Mr. Delacorte, who was patting his great thigh and humming along, past Angelique, who was looking reluctantly transfixed, as if it had been too long since she had heard music and was absorbing it like a flower absorbs rain, across to where Mr. Farraday was sitting in silence, reluctantly enjoying the performance, arms crossed tightly, and jouncing a leg.

She sat down next to him.

"It's remarkable," she confided to Mr. Farraday as Captain Hardy and Miss Bevan-Clark rounded on the second verse. "It's been such a challenge to bring Captain Hardy out of his shell, and Miss Bevan-Clark seems to have done it within minutes. She must be a truly singular girl. One of a kind."

"Yes," he said tersely, after a delay. He was watching the singular girl and Captain Hardy, and his face was a battleground of subtle conflicts.

At last the song came to an end.

Everyone applauded with great enthusiasm.

Captain Hardy even took a bow.

"Hardy, I suspected you had hidden talents, you old sea dog!" Mr. Delacorte boomed.

Captain Hardy manfully suppressed a wince. "Not hidden, Delacorte. Simply rationed."

Miss Bevan-Clark was gazing up at Captain Hardy as if he was responsible for the moon hanging in the sky.

Andrew Farraday was gazing at Captain Hardy as though he'd robbed him at knifepoint.

But then Miss Bevan-Clark's head pivoted to seek Andrew Farraday's gaze. And what she saw there made her blush pink again.

And duck her head.

Oh, the days when one blushed at everything.

Then she peeked up between her lashes.

Andrew was staring at her, with a faint frown, rather arrested, as if perhaps he hadn't seen her in this light before.

"Perhaps now we can all *dance*!" Delacorte enthused.

Captain Hardy froze. "Optionally, perhaps we ought not get carried away, Delacorte."

It was too late. Delacorte was carried away. He was already shoving furniture aside.

"Nonsense, nonsense," he said happily. "If you can sing then you can dance, Captain. I dance a fair reel and we've enough people here for a quadrille. A waltz wouldn't even go amiss if some of the ladies wouldn't mind dancing with each other. Oh! Shall we waltz? No one is about to care whether we do it well. We needn't stand on ceremony among friends."

"A bit daring, isn't it?" Angelique said. "But then, we did play Faro."

Very dryly said.

"It's all between family here," Mr. Delacorte said, which were such uncommonly sweet words to Delilah's ears she was tempted to kiss him on the cheek. "We'll make a lark of it. What say you all? Can you play a waltz, Miss Bevan-Clark?"

Miss Bevan-Clark opened her mouth.

Then closed it again.

Her expression revealed that she very much wanted to dance, rather than play the pianoforte.

"*I* can play a waltz," Angelique volunteered. Just a tad slyly.

"Well, *that* is splendid!" Delacorte could not be more thrilled.

Angelique stood and smoothed her skirts. "And perhaps Mr. Farraday would like to show Lady Derring how once dances the waltz in Sussex," she suggested.

Mr. Farraday's eyes went wide.

But he could not, of course, refuse this suggestion and still be a gentleman.

Captain Hardy may have started it, but they were all colluding now.

"I should be honored if you would dance with me, Lady Derring," Mr. Farraday said, because he possessed excellent manners and because Delilah was smiling sweetly at him and he was as putty in her hands. But then, in the hands of the right woman, Mr. Farraday was the sort who would be putty for the rest of his days.

Unlike the man who'd instigated this whole thing.

But a hunted look skittered across Miss Bevan-Clark's

face when he leaped to his feet and held his hand out to Delilah, who allowed the young man to pull her to her feet.

She stared at Delilah the way Farraday had stared at Captain Hardy. As if surely a grown woman—a widow, no less—no matter how pretty, couldn't possibly appeal. She was practically a different species, in Miss Bevan-Clark's mind.

"And I should be honored if you'd dance the waltz with me, Miss Bevan-Clark," Captain Hardy said.

"I should be delighted, Captain Hardy," Miss Bevan-Clark said as defiantly as if she was making a closing argument in court.

"I should be pleased to dance with Dot," Mr. Delacorte said.

He would until he tried it, thought Delilah.

Dot performed a witty little curtsy and managed not to tip over, and Delacorte extended his arm.

"Miss Gardner and Miss Gardner?" Captain Hardy surprised everyone by aiming a determinedly inviting expression toward the sisters in the corner.

"Oh, we cannot dance," Jane Gardner said very, very meekly.

"But I insist," Captain Hardy said. Kindly. Very gently. "I shall be happy to show you how to waltz if you're unfamiliar with it. Every woman ought to know it."

There was a brief silence as they stared at him, eyes enormous, before Margaret looked down at her lap again.

"You must," Captain Hardy repeated. Coaxingly.

"Oh, no one wants us to trod upon their feet." Jane

gave a soft laugh. "We shall dance with each other. It's how we learned, after all."

There were token protests and demurrals, but finally the Gardner sisters were persuaded to stand up together. They would need to run a gauntlet of furniture and dancers to escape from the room, anyway.

That left Miss Wright to turn the pages of the music for Angelique.

Angelique laid her fingers on the keys and leaned into a sprightly, competent version of the "Sussex Waltz."

And the unlikely troop of strangers rotated about the room in a rather constrained oval.

Mr. Farraday's version of a waltz approximated a lope, and it was a bit like hanging on to a large dog by a lead. Not unpleasant, but it required all of her skill and focus.

It was undeniably a surprising pleasure to dance again. Derring had done the minimum required of him at the three balls they'd attended while they were married. It had seemed so freeing, so very unlike Derring, to surrender to something so frivolous as turning in a circle around a room. Derring's inner life only revealed itself in the things he bought.

"Sorry. Oh, sorry," Dot was muttering as Delacorte steered her past. He jerked his trod-upon feet from under hers with swift grace for one so sturdy. It almost resembled a jig.

When Captain Hardy sailed competently by with Miss Bevan-Clark, through some graceful magic, he somehow smoothly transferred Miss Bevan-Clark into the arms of Mr. Farraday.

While he absconded with Delilah.

Her breath was quite lost for a second.

They took a wordless few moments to adjust to the feel and rhythm of each other.

It was an uncommonly sweet feeling, her hand in his, his hand at her waist, rotating about in a circle in this pleasant homely room surrounded by a cheerful lot of near misfits. He wanted to be kissing her. He wanted to feel his body against hers.

But holding her hand like this seemed nearly as intimate, and in some ways more so.

And as it turned out, it was as much a sport as a dance, because it involved the additional challenge of avoiding collision with other dancers.

They'd rotated once around when he cleared his throat. "I was born in St. Giles."

She didn't fling her arm up to ward off the terrible shock of his slum birth. Her body didn't stiffen beneath his hand. Her pace didn't falter.

She didn't say a word.

But her eyes didn't leave his face. They were warm as a hearth. And soft as that damn comfortable bed in his room.

He ought not continue. Every word he said felt like a hole punctured in his armor; every word he said planed away a bit of mystery and brought her closer to his rawest self. It felt unnatural and new, as awkward as using his left hand instead of his right, though he could, of course, fight with both. But he could not stop himself from giving her what she wanted. To ease, if he could, whatever shame or discomfort she felt.

"I never knew my father. I'm not certain my mother

was ever given his real name. And I didn't know my mother for long, either. She died when I was eight. I became a captain's assistant at ten."

Her ribs rose and fell beneath his hand when she drew in a long breath.

But there was no gushing. No questions. And no pity.

She watched him, not her feet, and somehow they remained in perfect time and managed to avoid colliding with the other dancers. Then again, he'd had a good deal of experience with navigation.

And she trusted him.

The honor of her trust, and the shame of his deception, made a wishbone of him.

"I suspect you are an exceptional man for many reasons, Captain Hardy," she finally said. "Not the least of which is risking the eternal ardor and devotion of Miss Bevan-Clark in order to get the two of them to see sense."

He smiled.

How had she gone her entire life not knowing a man's smile could cut her in two, Delilah thought. In the sweetest way.

"They are twits. But it's often easier to know how much you value something when it's about to be taken from you. Child's play compared to some of the conflicts I've dispensed with in my career."

"It was a kindness. I know the extraordinary sacrifice you made in instigating a musical evening."

"It was a kindness to myself, mostly. They were a distraction and I would never be able to read at least three more pages of my book."

A year ago, she would not have described happiness as dancing a waltz amidst shabby furniture with someone who patently wasn't a gentleman in a room that included her husband's former mistress, the worst lady's maid she'd ever had, a loud gassy salesman, two runaway twits from the country, and two meek, astonishingly homely women of whom she felt quite protective.

If it wasn't happiness, she wasn't quite sure what to call it. But it was a fine thing, and it felt wonderful, and bore so little resemblance to her previous days with Derring that they scarcely seemed part of the same life.

All at once something else had captured her dancing partner's attention, however. She could immediately feel a sudden, alert tension in his body.

She followed his gaze.

"Isn't that funny?" she said. "Both Miss Gardners are trying to lead and they are getting nowhere."

Tristan said idly, "It looks a little bit like vertical, drunken wrestling."

It seemed he could not, in fact, take his eyes from it.

"Perhaps no one has ever before danced with them," she said wistfully. "Don't frown so at them, you'll frighten them."

Chapter Twenty-One

LATER THAT night Tristan lay on his blue counterpane listening to Delacorte snoring on the floor below.

For some reason he was almost glad to hear it.

Gordon was running up and down the hallway.

He suspected Gordon of playing as much as he was hunting.

He was glad to hear that, too.

And as he listened to a veritable roll call of creaks and sighs as the house settled down for the night, he realized he hadn't heard that strange, loud thunk again. The one that made it seem as though the house was struggling to digest something.

Not since the night he'd seen Miss Margaret Gardner on the stairs.

When he'd insisted upon the Gardner sisters joining the dancing this evening, it was not for the charitable reasons Delilah likely suspected. It was because a suspicion, begun as unease the first time he'd laid eyes on them, was now germinating. He would tell Massey about it tomorrow.

Massey was probably lying awake dreaming about his sweetheart.

Suddenly Tristan realized he'd closed his hand around a fistful of his counterpane, as if it were Delilah's hand and they were waltzing again. He released it at once. Abashed.

"Sweetheart," he said aloud. Sardonically.

How on earth did Massey say that word so easily? It was such a gentle word, one that evoked blue skies and lambs and meadows filled with flowers.

Like daisies, perhaps.

None of Tristan's feelings—not the desire that kept him rigidly staring at his ceiling right now; not his ever-deepening admiration for her, or his yearning toward her kindness; not the desperate tenderness he'd felt when she sat there, trembling, his coat over her shoulders; not even the weakness that overcame him when he touched her, or even so much as looked into her eyes—were soft or gentle. They were deep as an ocean trench. They were spiky and stormy and unmanageable. Perhaps from disuse. He apparently possessed them, but they'd been left to run amuck, grow wild and leggy.

He'd once courted a superior officer's daughter, a pretty, fluttery flirt of a girl who had sought and lapped up his attentions like a kitten, and he'd been flattered and smitten. But she'd been genuinely astonished to learn he might have matrimony in mind.

"But . . . you're not a gentleman! I mean . . . I couldn't possibly!"

It was all for the best. They would have made each other miserable, and he'd only courted her because it was the done thing for a man his age. Still, his pride had taken a glancing blow, and it had left him wiser and warier.

He frankly could not imagine being anyone's "sweetheart."

"Spikeheart," perhaps.

This was simply who he was, perhaps in part due to the forces that shaped him.

He had, in fact, made a career and a life out of not being helpless, out of always knowing what to do. Which was why it was so unsettling to know that he couldn't glare emotions into silence with a look, the way he could an insubordinate soldier.

But he didn't shake his fist at the sun because he couldn't control it, did he? He lived with the fact of it.

Still. He needed to let this thing be, for her sake and for his. He needed to leave these emotions untended and unacknowledged and he needed to avoid courting temptation. There: now that he knew what he needed to do, he felt some small measure of control returning. There was some small comfort in knowing that once she learned who he was and what he was doing here—which was inevitable, if his mission was a success—he'd sail away in his ship, and he wouldn't have to witness her shattered betrayal for long.

But suddenly, as if she was already a memory, he found himself mining the moments he'd spent with her for new dimensions of pleasure. The satin of her throat. The beat of her heart against his. The glow of her skin in the dark. The rhythm of her breath against his throat as he moved in her. And her laugh.

Bloody hell. It was like hurling bits of straw onto a bonfire.

He rolled over and sat up on the edge of the bed

and tipped his face into his hands. He breathed like that, motionless. As though he were in pain.

He *was* in pain.

Just not the sort he'd ever experienced before. No tourniquet, no amount of whiskey, nothing in Delacorte's upsettingly exotic collection of herbs and medicines, could ease it.

He perhaps had one recourse.

He stood and staggered wearily over to the little writing desk and yanked out the chair.

He lit the candle and pulled a sheet of foolscap toward him.

Stared at it, as if willing it to yield its secrets, the way he'd stared at the ocean the other night.

Dipped the quill in ink.

But it was torture.

He managed eleven words. Every word was like a drop of blood squeezed from a wound.

And though he tried very, very hard, not one of them rhymed.

"LOVER," DELILAH SAID aloud. The word felt odd, very louche, and cosmopolitan in her mouth. "I have taken a lover. He was born in *St. Giles*."

She imagined saying it to the Duchess of Brexford just for the pleasure of seeing her collapse in a rustle of bombazine and a crunch of stays.

That delightful fantasy notwithstanding, she still wasn't entirely comfortable with the word.

She watched her ceiling during that hazy, lovely netherworld between wakefulness and dreaming, and reviewed the unqualified triumph of the evening. Everyone had taken a turn at singing. They were dangerously close to having a genuine musicale! Could all of her dreams be coming true in such an unlikely fashion?

Even dusty old dreams of romance she'd locked away in a keepsake box so many years ago?

She thought about Mr. Farraday and Miss Bevan-Clark, who by the end of the evening were sitting quietly together on the settee murmuring and smiling as if they'd only just met and were shyly getting to know one another. They'd certainly found the romance and adventure they'd been seeking, rather indirectly.

No. What Delilah had was a lover, not a romance. A lover who had said to her, *I was born in St. Giles,* in a quiet, diffident baritone, which seemed infinitely more thrilling and more dangerous than anything Farraday and Miss Bevan-Clark could get up to. Because she was beginning to suspect that taking a lover was not like taking a meal or taking the air—it was more like taking a beautiful drug, the sort people in opium dens apparently found surcease in. The appetite only grew with the taking of it.

And one knew what happened to people who indulged too much in opium.

I was born in St. Giles was like a thread thrown over a loom. For these kinds of revelations were the things that bound people together. She cherished the words, yearned toward them, and wanted to hear more and still more. All of this frightened her.

Because she truly did never again want to be at another man's mercy.

When jealousy had jabbed briefly and sickeningly tonight, it was alarming—and edifying—to realize how easily a man could tweak her emotional weather. It called to mind the silent, inner contortions she'd performed to ensure Derring remained happy. She'd regained so much of her *self* since he'd left her penniless.

Then again, she'd only shown her true self to Captain Hardy. Which made it even more perilous.

There was the other thing about the word *take*: it often implied that whatever was taken didn't actually *belong* to the taker. That the day would come when they would be made to give it up.

And he would be leaving soon enough, after all.

Here was where she could put Angelique's experience to use: now that she was enlightened as to the extraordinary physical pleasures, she could and should make a truly sensible decision, and not partake of Tristan Hardy again.

Surely she could manage this? It wasn't as though a stiff wind would howl down the chimney, blow her clothes off, and push her into his arms. It was simply a matter of *not doing it*. She'd managed to help create this boardinghouse, currently feeding and sheltering the most disparate people imaginable, and it seemed as though their little enterprise was well on the road to thriving. If that didn't make her a miracle worker she didn't know what did.

She sighed heavily, surrendering a little more to the beckoning arms of sleep. Relieved to have removed the serrated anticipation of sex by simply deciding not to do it. She was pleased and proud of herself in a faintly martyred way. She said a little prayer of thanks for having known the pleasure.

Nevertheless, all in all, it was probably a very good thing that Captain Hardy would be sailing away for good very soon.

TRISTAN WAS SHAVING himself ruthlessly, as if scraping off barnacles of a hull. Making himself shiny and sleek to face a new day of learning probably absolutely nothing useful about those damned cigars.

"I am shaving my face, la la la la," he tried, in the mirror.

It didn't make it any more pleasurable, really.

"I am catching a smuggler, la la la la," he tried instead. Mordantly.

He splashed water from the pretty blue-flowered basin on his face, patted himself with a towel.

He turned and looked at his comfortable room. The wilting flower in his vase had been replaced sometime yesterday, he realized. He was suddenly, unaccountably moved. And appalled to realize that he quite liked having a fresh flower in a vase in his room.

Then he remembered the sheet of foolscap on the writing desk. He lunged for his shameful travesty and stashed it away in his satchel, lest it ever see the light of day.

Satisfied with what he saw in the mirror—resolute, hard, handsome, a little weary from staying up all night and writing a terrible poem—he shoved his arms into his coat and left the room.

He had just turned the key in the lock when he froze.

His heart gave a nearly painful bounce.

Delilah was poised to enter the room next to his,

wielding a duster and looking, much like he did, cheerfully resolute.

She froze when she saw him.

She had faintly purple shadows beneath her eyes, too. Perhaps she'd spent the entire night watching her ceiling, debating with herself the wisdom of undressing and wrapping her legs around his waist again, and concluding it would be very unwise, indeed. Which was all to the best.

The trouble was, he understood at once as he stood there, eyes fixed on the soft swoop of her lower lip, that wildfires left unattended overnight tend to grow bigger and hotter.

They regarded each other somberly, making internal adjustments to accommodate the mere glorious fact of each other.

"Good morning, Lady Derring," he said finally. "Are you going to narrate the dusting of the room today?"

"Good morning, Captain Hardy. Why? Did you find my singing tolerable last night?"

"Survivable," he said pleasantly, as though correcting her with a more precise word.

She smiled at that and it really just undid him.

"You ought to hurry down, Captain Hardy. There are still some eggs left and Helga says you're a very good eater."

"While that's very flattering indeed, alas, I promised to have breakfast with a colleague."

Neither one of them moved.

So how had the space between them disappeared, and how was it that his arms were going around her waist as her face tilted up to meet his coming down?

He staggered forward with her in his arms until she was pressed hard against the alcove wall.

"Delilah." He delivered her name in a desperate whisper in her ear. It was a sigh, nearly an accusation. As though she'd enchanted him against his will.

She filled her hands with fistfuls of his shirt and pulled him up against her. Then slid them up to loop around his neck.

The kisses were frantic, savagely deep. Their lips met and parted, caressed, feasted, dueled. They drugged him. He slid his hands down and filled them with her breasts; he slipped his fingers inside her bodice and dragged the tips of them across her ruched nipples.

She arched with a cry that he covered with the next kiss.

When her head went back in pleasure, he kissed her throat.

Her lips found his ear, and her tongue traced it. He turned his head into it. It maddened him, deliciously. She moved her hips against his hard cock. Vixen. Anyone could come upon them any minute.

"Come to me." His voice was a rasp, a whisper, a command, a plea, against her lips, her throat, her ear. "Come to my room. Please. When you can. Today. I need you."

This was madness. Surely he was possessed. The sound of his own voice, hoarse and urgent, half command, half beseeching, all raw hunger—he didn't recognize it. He had never asked for a thing in life, let alone begged. He had fought for everything. He was ashamed of how all the tortured conviction of the previous night had gone right out the window at the first glimpse of her. But not too ashamed to get down on his knees if he had to.

"I will. I promise. I will. I need you, too. Oh God help me, I want you, too," she moaned against his mouth, his ear, his throat.

He let her go abruptly then, as though he'd extracted a blood vow from her.

Readjusted his hat.

Shifted his trousers. A few thoughts about the Gardner sisters and missing smugglers ought to make short work of his erection.

He stared at her, her hair mussed, her breathing like a bellows. As though she was a siren in an apron who had lured him into the alcove.

She smiled at him, and it was like the heavens had broken open.

He smiled at her and bolted down the stairs.

"YOU *DANCED*?" MASSEY was almost incensed when Tristan told him about the previous evening, he was so envious.

"A sort of waltz."

Massey stared at him, in resentful wonder.

Then he sighed. "Well, you're the captain."

"That I am. We also sang."

Massey sighed, then he resettled his shoulders resignedly, manfully absorbing his wistful envy. "Well, the jewelry sales are confirmed, sir. A Mrs. Angelique Breedlove did indeed sell some nice pieces to a broker named Reeves on Bond Street. Here are the figures."

He slid a little sheet of paper over to Tristan.

"We've also spoken to some workmen who helped clean and repair the place. Weren't paid unduly, saw nothing untoward, said nothing but nice things about Lady Derring and Mrs. Breedlove. 'Right bossy,' I think one of them called Lady Derring, but he made it sound like a virtue. Here is a list of the work they did and what they claimed they were paid." He slid over another sheet.

"Good work, Massey," Tristan said absently, relieved. Here was a record of Delilah and Angelique trading one sort of life for another. Two ropes of pearls. A necklace of rubies. Diamond earbobs. And more. Not a king's ransom, but certainly enough to get The Grand Palace on the Thames off the ground.

Had Delilah any jewelry left now? Then again, pearls against her skin would be redundant.

"I actually had a reason for instigating the waltz, Massey."

"*You* . . . instigated it?" His jaw dropped.

"Yes. And I plan to go with you today to ask a very specific question of a few vendors. A new approach."

"No one around here wants to tell us from whom they purchased the cigars, sir. They're getting used to our faces and they're bound to get suspicious."

"They will talk to me," he said simply.

This was likely true. He had his ways.

"What is this question?"

"I would like to ask them . . ." Tristan paused. He almost didn't dare say it aloud. ". . . if they've purchased cigars from a large man, built like a bear. Scar beneath his ear. Or a small man, with a pointed face."

"Sounds like the Miss Gardners' brothers, sir."

Tristan regarded him grimly.

Realization dawned on Massey's face. "You don't mean . . ."

"A suspicion. It's been growing for some time. The larger one doesn't speak in company. Perhaps because it's a struggle to disguise his voice. Always looking down, ostensibly shyly but likely because they don't want anyone to look very closely at their faces. And they both tried to *lead* a waltz last night. It was disastrous."

Massey's face twitched, picturing this.

"They hadn't a notion about what to do. They retired for the evening the moment the music stopped. I wonder if they know who I am."

"They must be getting desperate about now, if so, Captain Hardy."

"That's my concern as well. And furthermore . . . think about it, Massey. People come and go from the stables all the time with carts and carriages. Perfect way to distribute contraband. No one would give it a thought. Do you remember the gang in Kent?"

"Tunnels?" Massey said, after a moment of mulling.

"Tunnels," Tristan confirmed.

Massey gave a low whistle. "You don't think . . ."

"I don't know. But I want every man to ask around, save the ones watching The Grand Palace. Visit again the merchants we spoke to. Any locals you see smoking."

"Done, sir," Massey said.

"Something still troubles me about that room on the low floor, however. I think Margaret Gardner was trying to get into it the night I saw her in the hallway. But she—or he—has failed all this time, too."

They sat in silence apart from chewing and the noise of the pub around them, men, smoking and spilling and sweating. Tristan yearned for a bath. He felt like the detritus of this hunt for smugglers—the smoking, the spilling, the sweating of all the men in pubs like this one—was beginning to settle on his skin.

Come to me, he'd begged. Would she? The very thought of his hands against her skin made his entire being contract with a barbed longing.

A few moments later, he said, "Massey?"

"Yes, sir?"

"How did you, er, know?"

Massey's brow furrowed. "Know, sir?"

Tristan considered saying "never mind," but it would be unlike him to back down from something he'd started. "About . . . Emily."

Massey stared at him, wonderingly, eyebrows diving.

And then something in Tristan's expression, in his demeanor, made it clear.

"Ah! *Know.* Well. That I loved her?"

Tristan held very still. Didn't Massey know the word *love* belonged in a class with words like *grenade* or *typhoon*? It was not to be bandied about lightly.

"I knew straight away, somehow," he said. "She was always on my mind, like. At first. And then one day we were at a house party and after dinner she had a little sauce on her cheek and she didn't know it and . . . I just knew that I loved her. Takes you that way sometimes, doesn't it?" Massey said mistily.

Tristan didn't know.

The "straight away" part. He wasn't certain whether he was relieved or more unnerved than before.

DELILAH HAD SPENT the morning in a fever of sensual indecision. She'd finished chores and gone over the books with Angelique and was grateful for the ceaseless activity.

Given that they now had six (six!) guests to feed, as well as themselves, all hands were needed in the kitchen. Delilah reported to the kitchen late in the afternoon to do her share of potato peeling. Helga had gotten some good fresh fish and some shaffling and she was planning to make a hearty chowder, with bread and cheese and a tart for dessert. Delilah's stomach quite rumbled thinking of it.

She took up a potato and was just about to shave a curl off it when a scullery maid crashed into her with a bucket, running toward Dot, who appeared to be directing this enterprise. She tipped boiling water into it.

"Begging your pardon, Lady Derring! So sorry!" the maid yelped.

"No worries, my dear. Dot, what's going on? Why all the scurrying about?"

"We're preparing a bath, Lady Derring!" Dot made it sound like a gleeful celebration, not the hard work it indeed was. They were fortunate enough to have their own well, a miracle indeed, but heating enough water for even a hip bath was no small undertaking.

But this was the first time any guest had called for such a thing. Oddly, it felt a bit like a baptism for The Grand Palace on the Thames.

"How lovely! Who rang for the bath?"

"Captain Hardy. Paid us in good coin for it, too."

Delilah hoped no one noticed when she abruptly stopped peeling her potato.

And then merely stared at it, dreamily, for a few moments.

Then, much more slowly, a little languidly, resumed peeling it, as though the air had become softly molten, a little thicker, like a blancmange, perhaps.

She got that potato done.

And then the next.

And then she chopped them. Slowly. Very carefully.

And then the next.

And when she was certain the bath had gotten up the stairs to Captain Hardy, she laid down the knife and breathed a moment.

The words were out of her mouth before she knew she'd made the decision.

"I'll just be a few minutes," she said.

Chapter Twenty-Two

HER HEART was pounding so fiercely the blood was ringing in her ears by the time she reached his room. She tapped, just twice, with her fingertip. "Captain Hardy," she said, mouth nearly pressed to the door.

She nearly toppled in when he opened it. He tugged her gently inside, closed the door and locked it.

An enormous towel was knotted about his waist. Water sheened his thighs and chest. It clung in beads to the slopes and angles and gullies of him, the smooth mountains of his shoulders, the ditch created by muscles along his spine.

The blood left her head and headed straight for her groin.

"I only have a few minutes." Her voice was a shred.

Doubtless he noted that her expression was probably somewhere between Mr. Delacorte's at the dinner table and an appraiser of antiquities who'd been handed the Grail.

He unfastened the towel and dropped it.

She'd unlaced her dress on the way there and now pulled it over her head and dropped it. Then divested herself of the rest of her clothes.

His expression in response to her sudden swift nudity suggested he'd taken a mallet to the head, and she exulted while she feasted unabashedly with her eyes. He was like a slightly nicked and dented idol unearthed from a chamber of a pharaoh's tomb, perhaps, beautiful, carved from good sturdy metal rather than precious: from the cut of his calves, the hard curve of his thighs, the pale taut buttocks with convenient little scoops where her hands fit when she was gripping them. The flare of his torso from them.

The white slashes and dents of old scars made her stomach contract with an odd sort of desperation: How dare they shoot at him as though he were expendable?

It seemed impossible that anyone had ever gotten the better of him.

Nothing about him appeared soft or vulnerable, apart, perhaps, from his eyelashes.

She crouched to seize the towel he'd dropped, and followed the terrain of his body, first with the towel, then her lips, then her hands. She slid her fingers down the trench of his spine. She lightly scored her nails across his chest. She made him tell his story.

"This scar . . ."

"Pirate . . . boarded our ship . . ." His voice was an enthralled rasp.

"Did you kill him?"

"It was that . . . or . . . be killed." His answer, swift, staccato, riding out on a ragged breath.

So she kissed him there, on that scar. "I'm glad you killed him."

"Delilah . . ." he half choked, half laughed.

"And this one?" She'd dropped to her knees to drag her fingers along his hip, where she could guess at how he'd come to sport that puckered scar.

"Shot. I was ill for weeks."

"And you lived through sheer cussedness."

"Because I had a fever dream of you on your knees before me, literally licking my wounds. It kept me alive."

She did lick that scar. Then she dragged her tongue from his hip to where curly hair surrounded his swelling cock and kissed him coyly, near and yet so far.

"Delilah," he groaned, as surely as if he'd been shot again. "Your mouth. Please. Take my cock in your mouth."

"Not yet, Captain," she said.

He called her a string of muttered oaths. She merely smiled, drunk on power, and arousal.

"And this . . ." She'd found a scar across his arm.

". . . was a child . . . stole an apple . . . from a costermonger." He was sweating now.

She didn't ask for details. She understood that the only reason Captain Hardy was invincible now, was standing here before her, complicated and passionate and desirable, was because he'd been caught a time or two. So she kissed that scar.

And when she took his cock into her mouth, his head fell back, and his hands dropped upon her hair as a long, low animal moan was followed by a string of curses and deities he clearly felt the need to call upon to support him in this time of untenable pleasure.

Now this. *This* was wicked. She allowed her tongue to play over the smooth dome of it. His hands laced into her hair. "Oh God. Whatever you do . . . don't stop . . ."

She paused. "This is apparently called the Vicar's Hobby."

He gave a short half laugh, half moan. "Your hands . . . your hands, too . . . use your hands, too . . ."

She obeyed. The taut cords of his neck, the tension in his jaw, how his head dropped back as he took in and savored the pleasure she gave him, his sighs of near desperation—it was so unbearably erotic that when she stood suddenly, she swayed as though drunk.

He seized her hips, spun her about so swiftly she toppled forward, bracing her palms against his blue coverlet. His palms skated down her spine as he urged her thighs apart with his knee. And then he brought his hand around to where she was aching and wet and stroked a rhythm that wrought from her moans of astounded, ramping pleasure that she muffled with her forearm. "Tristan . . ." she whimpered. "Please . . ."

She came apart into a million cinders when he thrust into her. The counterpane took her raw scream. Her fingers clenched and unclenched in it as he drummed into her swiftly, his breathing gusting. "Delilah . . . dear God . . ." His voice was shredded. "I'm . . ."

He went rigid, his own raw cry stifled and wave after wave of bliss wracked him.

Before she slid like a melted thing down off the bed, he scooped her up into his arms and pulled her up onto the bed. She reclined in his arms as his chest rose like a choppy sea beneath her head.

Her hair was a mess, so he unpinned it, one pin at a time.

Laid them all on his night table.

"You can pin it again before you leave," he said

drowsily. Never had pleasure so owned him. So fully consumed him. Never had it so thoroughly relieved him, if momentarily, of the burden of being himself, the man who held up the world.

"I must leave soon," she murmured. She gave a somnolent, stunned laugh. "Never in my wildest fantasies did I think I'd need to repin my hair in the afternoon after having been ravished."

"And after *having* ravished."

"Fair enough."

He smiled. He threaded his hands through her hair. As soft as he'd dreamed it would be, full of hidden mahogany lights. "Have you wild fantasies?" He was tremendously interested in these.

She hesitated. "Promise you won't laugh?"

"I'm too sated to laugh."

"Angelique and I once talked about what we would do if the king came to The Grand Palace on the Thames."

"The *king*? Because now that you've conquered me, he's the only challenge left?"

"Because it would *madden* the Duchess of Brexford, who can never get him to come to one of her dinners. She is terribly rude to me and tried to steal my cook more than once. She thinks I'm quite beneath her."

"I think we've time," Tristan said thoughtfully, "for you to be beneath *me* once again."

She smiled and shifted to throw a leg over his thigh. Her hands were idly roaming over his chest, following the trenches made by his muscle. He shifted, restlessly. Mad hunger was an echo, but already ramping again. "Why were you stealing an apple?" she asked.

"I was hungry."

"Tristan," she said. She stopped the caresses and propped herself up on her elbows. Her hair fell down over his chest, across her face. He parted it like a curtain onto his favorite musicale. Her face was an ache.

"The difference between me and the drunk man at the entrance of your boardinghouse is pigheadedness and fortitude."

"Yes. I'm certain that's all. Had naught to do with courage, or intelligence, or skill."

"Flatterer. You must be trying to seduce me again," he said hopefully.

She was quiet, however. "You must have been so frightened." It was a near whisper.

She was worried, that was clear. She was hurting for him now, and the boy he was. And somehow he didn't mind. He had never realized these untold stories possessed any encumbering weight, any *ballast*, until he began to tell them to someone who thought they mattered.

"I *was* afraid. But I think when fear becomes a part of your everyday experience that you cease to think of it as fear. You either harness it, and turn it into a source of strength, or it harnesses you, and destroys your soul. I've seen examples of both."

"I think it's a question of character, too. And while I'm glad you're here *now*, I'm sorry you endured that."

"It doesn't matter now."

This wasn't entirely true.

The arc of his life didn't allow it. It mattered that he caught the smugglers. It mattered to him, to his men, to the king, to the loved ones of the family killed.

Dozens, hundreds, fanning out from there, people depended upon his wisdom and judgment and experience to bring them to justice.

And the questions he yet needed to ask her mattered. Who had taken that room on the first floor, for instance?

But he kissed her again, because he could not lie next to her and not kiss her, and apparently he was Achilles and she was the heel.

It began slowly, slowly as they dared knowing they had very little time, their hands moving over each other's bodies, finding the hollows and knobs and angles and silky hidden places that made each other breathe swiftly, to ripple and beg for more. But in moments it was a frenzy of tangled limbs and little bites and deep kisses and urgency rather than finesse. She clung to him as he dove in her again and again; he buried his cry of release against her throat as she shook and shook beneath him, saying his name as if he'd wrought a miracle.

Side by side again, her head against his shoulder, his heart pounding harder than it had when that pirate had shot at him, Delilah sniffed.

She was weeping! He stiffened with alarm.

She smiled a little and said, "I'm sorry."

"For biting me? I rather liked it."

She laid her forearm across her eyes and gave a laugh which contained a little sniffle.

The reflexive ease with which he pulled her closer to his body unnerved him. The ease with which she came to him and burrowed her head into the hollow of his shoulder for comfort was unnerving, too. The realization that there was very little difference between comforting her and soothing himself was the most troubling thing of all.

"It's that we're given such a limited repertoire of ways to express emotions, and I'm feeling a number of complicated things all at once," she said.

Never in his wildest dreams did Tristan think he would ask a woman the next question, or genuinely want to hear the answer.

"What are the things you're feeling, Delilah?" He dragged his hand slowly down the luxurious satiny skin of her back.

He would never again call her Lady Derring. Knowing that she'd once belonged to someone who had not seen, appreciated, or loved her.

"I was just thinking that . . . if Derring had lived . . . I might have gone my entire life and not known what this . . . lovemaking . . . what you and I are like together. And though every day of running this boardinghouse is a veritable walk on a cliff edge of uncertainty, I can't regret it. And yet Derring had to die for me to know it. I suppose I feel regret at what could never be with Derring, and also a sort of terrible fear, knowing that I might be nearly losing something. Isn't that silly?"

"No," he said shortly. He wished he had more words. "Not in the least."

He lay there tracing the little pearls of her spine, thinking about the pearls she had sold to open this boardinghouse.

"Do you miss him?" he asked gruffly.

"No."

He quietly, ungraciously, exulted.

"Sometimes . . . I feel like I can sense his presence here. Every now and again I think I catch a hint of his terrible cigars. Mostly in the kitchen, near the scullery, where I can't imagine Derring spent any time whilst he was alive."

Near the scullery.

The scullery, if he recalled correctly, was more or less beneath that mysterious suite of rooms.

And what was under the scullery?

Hell's teeth.

All that glorious, hazy aftermath of release was burned off by reason.

He should not ask the question now. When she was vulnerable and tender in his arms. When she saw him as comfort, strength, and pleasure. She trusted him, this lovely woman who had vowed never again to trust a man, and who had been a means to an end for people her entire life.

But her vulnerability was also the reason he needed to ask the question now.

There would be no undoing it if he asked it. But he knew it was already too late, and that he was destined.

"To whom did you let that suite on the first floor, Delilah? I'm concerned, you see. More importantly, does he or she play Whist, or the pianoforte?"

"The suite on the first floor?" She smiled drowsily. "Do you know, it's the oddest thing. A prim, supercilious, well-dressed man paid us two entire sovereigns to keep it for his mysterious employer."

It wasn't quite at all what he'd expected to hear. "That

is odd. Did he ask for that room in particular?" His grip tightened on her. He forced himself to loosen it.

"No, he just wanted our, and I quote, 'largest suite of rooms,' and so we gave him that one. We were uneasy and a bit resentful about accepting the money but ultimately we did, because we had to do it, and could see no reason on the face of things to say no. He wasn't the least threatening. Just arrogant. Two sovereigns. And we didn't even have to feed him."

"Hard to say no to two sovereigns," he said, absently. His mind was working furiously now.

"Absolutely. We can keep paying our staff. And heating the house."

"And you've never met this person? The person for whom you're keeping the room? Just his representative?"

"We've never met him. Isn't that odd? He said his employer likes to keep suites available all over the city, and this is another direct quote, 'just in case.'" She stretched and pointed her toes. "I imagine a debauched lord of some sort, staggering to the nearest hidey hole after a drunken evening, but I honestly don't know. The man—called himself Mr. X, if you can believe it—actually gave us half a *token*, and he said that we'd know the lord when he presented the other half. Angelique and I felt ridiculous, but so far it seems more absurd than sinister. As we promised, we clean it every day. He has yet to show himself."

Tristan took this in. It sounded absolutely mad, but he also didn't doubt her, because frankly mad people were rife among the aristocracy. And it was too outlandish a story to invent.

But was this Mr. X involved in smuggling, somehow?

Perhaps it was just a coincidence that he took that room.

Or . . . perhaps Tristan was on the entirely wrong track.

The very idea formed a small, icy knot in the pit of his stomach.

All today he'd gone into cheese shops, tailors, pubs, confectioners and asked, "Big bloke with a scar promised me more cigars, has he been in? Has a friend, smaller, looks a bit like a fox." That sort of thing. Variations on that approach.

Not one of them he'd spoken to today had seen or spoken to men who looked like that.

But he'd told his men to keep asking anyway. And to send word to him straight away if they got even a single viable response. "Use another language, Massey, if you send a message. Portuguese. I can read that, if you can write it." Both he and Massey had acquired the rudiments of a number of languages throughout their careers.

He refused to surrender to that tight feeling in his chest of encroaching doubt.

"What does the token look like?" He realized he'd pulled his arm out from beneath her. As if touching her while he did what amounted to abusing her trust was dishonorable.

"Like maybe a crest of some kind. A half of a crest. A lion's leg, a unicorn leg, perhaps? It's not fancy and it's impossible to know what it is, really."

He frowned. Neither a crest nor a token struck any bells at all.

Bloody hell. He still needed to get into that room.

She shifted away from him a little. He'd gone tense as a board, and likely she'd noticed. She was watching him worriedly now.

It got even more tense when there was a knock at the door.

They both froze.

She pulled the coverlet over her head.

"Yes, may I help you?" he called.

"Captain Hardy?" It was Dot.

"Yes, Dot. I'm afraid I can't come to the door just yet."

There was a silence. He hoped Dot was too naive to reason out why, apart from the fact that he'd had a bath, which involved a state of total undress. "A man came to the door with an urgent message for you, Captain Hardy. It's all sealed up."

His heart stopped.

Good man, Massey, to seal it. "Slide it under my door if you would, Dot, thank you. And if you would please wait."

There was a little rustle as she shoved it into the room.

He all but dove out of bed to retrieve it. Massey had sealed it with a blob of wax.

In Portuguese, he read:

> *Halligan spoke with a tobacconist four streets over who was angry because huge man with scar didn't bring in anticipated cigars. Waiting outside for orders.*
>
> *M.*

Feelings and impressions rushed at him like leaves in a storm: Triumph. Vindication. Exultation. Hope.

Regret.

Injustice.

Dread.

The last three were directed at life and the destiny that required him to leave this woman now.

But when they all blew away, duty remained.

Tristan didn't know how long he'd held still, but he could feel Delilah's eyes on him.

He turned and found her expression worried. And wary, and he instantly wanted to make it light again.

He realized he'd basked in her trust and optimism even as he'd taken advantage of it. He was accustomed to those eyes glowing when they saw him.

He strode to the little writing desk, lately the scene of a torturously written poem, and scrawled, in Portuguese:

> *Gather men. Meet me at Cox's Livery Stables in fifteen minutes.*

Massey would know why.

He blew on the ink, willing it to dry. Behind him, he heard Delilah gathering her dress, her slippers, her hairpins.

He still hadn't looked at her.

He slid the message back beneath the door. "Dot, if you would be so kind as to hand this to the gentleman waiting outside."

"Of course, Captain Hardy!" she said cheerily.

He heard her thundering down the stairs.

He finally dared a look at Delilah.

Her eyes were fixed on him unblinkingly. Worried, but still trusting.

"Delilah, I apologize, but I'm afraid I must go out straight away."

"Is aught amiss? Can I help?"

He watched her pin her hair. He thought how fortunate the man would be to watch her pin it up and take it down every day.

He didn't want to tell her a placatory lie.

"Yes. Something is amiss. But it will be put to rights."

They held each other's eyes.

Her posture was rigid. Her expression was searching, and then it went subtly guarded. And perhaps even a little cynical.

He moved to her swiftly, laid his hand against her cheek. And perhaps he hadn't the right, but he kissed her again. So she would close her eyes and he wouldn't have to see that guarded expression, so that he could instead feel her body softening in surrender. Because this might be the last time, and this was how he wanted to remember her.

Chapter Twenty-Three

Mr. Cox, the current foreman of the livery stables, was weathered and so strapping no one would be surprised if he regularly lifted horses up and out of his way to get to where he needed to go.

He couldn't lift a group of soldiers up and out of the way, however.

The only one currently in well-tailored street clothes was obviously in command.

"Cox, have you ever let a horse to or stabled a horse for a Miss Margaret or Jane Gardner?" Tristan asked.

"Nay, sir. I swear on it. Ladies do not often come in here on their own, you see, for obvious reasons. Especially not in this part of London. Though it isn't entirely out of the question."

"Are you quite certain?"

He drew himself up to his full height. "Sometimes it gets busy, like, sir, and I cannot always see every person who enters or leaves. You may feel free to speak to the stable boys." Tristan gestured with his chin, which sent three soldiers off to question the staff. "But I can tell you for certain I did not see a woman arriving or leaving."

"Did the Earl of Derring keep a horse or a team here?"

"The Earl of Derring, sir, rest his soul, kept a team

here. Well, two teams, in truth. Fine animals. Sold some time ago."

"They're better off," Tristan said grimly.

Mr. Cox was left to wonder what that meant as Tristan and his men convened upon the now-empty set of stalls.

"My next question, Mr. Cox. Have you seen a man in here, burly, flat nose, small eyes, scar beneath his—"

"—ear? Oh, but of course. That be Mr. Garr. Worked for the Earl of Derring. Drove a cart in and out from Sussex. Changed their spent team and went out again. Helped transport his statues, like. Derring was a collector."

Triumph and vindication was like a sunburst in Tristan's chest.

"His *statues*?"

"Great lot of naked people made of stone. I ask you! Who would want such a thing in their house? They delivered them to that building round the corner. Thought it had summat to do with the whorehouse. Who knows what the quality get up to."

And like another burst of sunlight, Tristan recalled what the drunk man leaning against the building had said. *Brought 'is friends, now and again so 'e did, in a cart. They was half-naked and couldna walk on their own, I s'pose, and he had to drag them in.*

Statues. Bloody stone statues.

Tristan knew, somehow, that the insides of all of those statues had reeked of cigars. Or perhaps the cigars had been stored in the bases.

"It's a boardinghouse," he said absently. "Not a whorehouse. The Grand Palace on the Thames."

"If you say so, guv. All I know is that you oughtn't go in there."

Tristan's men scoured the stables with their eyes, dragged their gloved fingers along the joins in the wood floor of the stalls where the earl had kept his team.

They nearly missed the handle. It was clever and unobtrusive; it was of carved, sanded wood, flush with the wood floor nearest the wall of the stable.

Once they found it, they could see the seams of what was likely a hatch of about three feet by three feet.

Tristan curled his fingers beneath it and pulled so that he could hook his fingers around the handle.

And then he yanked.

The hatch came up easily.

Exclamations and oaths from his men greeted this.

Cox was white. "I swear, sir, I'd no idea, sir . . ."

Tristan wasn't sure whether he believed him, but they would certainly find out whether or not he was innocent.

"Lantern," he called grimly.

One was passed to him.

He seized it and peered down.

It was about a ten-foot drop, if he had to estimate; a narrow ladder was affixed to the wall with bolts and stretched all the way to the bottom; he could see a dirt floor, packed smooth. He reached down and gave the ladder a testing tug. It seemed securely affixed to the wall.

And if Miss Margaret Gardner—Mr. Garr—had climbed down this ladder—and something told him that she had—it ought to hold him.

"I'm going down. Lower that lantern down along after me, will you?"

He handed the lantern back to Massey, who hooked it to a rope.

Tristan transferred his pistol into his hand and rapidly descended, landing on the dirt floor. He caught hold of the lamp they'd dangled in after him and inspected his surroundings.

He gave a stunned laugh.

Ah, yes. Smugglers took to England's crevices, baseboards, crannies, caves.

And tunnels.

It was actually, more specifically, a segment of a longer tunnel. Very old, well-constructed, supported with ceiling crossbeams above, narrow, tall enough for a man of six feet to travel comfortably, wide enough for contraband to be ferried through.

It was impossible to know if this had been its original purpose. England was crisscrossed with tunnels used for various purposes. He thought of the tunnel in Brighton alleged to connect the king to his favorite pub and secret rooms where he kept a mistress. And if The Grand Palace on the Thames had once been a whorehouse, well, then. One could begin to draw conclusions.

He pivoted.

About five feet in from the hatch was a studded oak door, heavy as a drawbridge.

Behind, he was certain he'd find all those cigars that various merchants, aristocrats, and the occasional adventurer like Delacorte had been waiting for in vain. Because all around him was the faint, vile scent of those cigars, and there was no sign of them where he stood.

Outside of the door, tucked against a wall, was a small trunk, blackened with age. Spilling from it looked like old dresses, costumes, perhaps, that had been rifled through and tossed about.

He was no expert on fashion, but the dresses certainly looked like the sort that Jane and Margaret Gardner favored. It must have been a challenge finding ones they could actually fit into.

How had he not known immediately they were men? And yet, he believed some part of him had. Some part of him had always known something was amiss. He had never seen them through a filter of trust, the way Delilah had, because he saw virtually nothing through the eyes of trust. Unless it was her.

He dropped to a crouch and aimed the light through the keyhole, and peered.

It didn't reveal much other than more darkness. But stacked within that darkness were little dark boxes. He'd wager everything he owned on what those boxes contained.

He stood again and grasped the door handle and twisted. It was, unsurprisingly, locked.

He pulled hard on the knob. The door shifted forward, bowing a very little inward in its frame. But it remained closed.

He released the knob and the door sank back into place with a dull, reverberating thud.

AND UPSTAIRS IN the drawing room of The Grand Palace on the Thames, the heads of the three ladies shot up from mending—Mr. Farraday had a rent in one of his shirts, Mr. Delacorte had lost another button, and they were setting about making them feel whole again.

"There's our thud again. I haven't heard it in quite some time," Angelique said.

"We've never heard it at this time of night before, either," Dot said.

"Maybe the rats have just awakened from hibernating," Angelique suggested.

Dot stifled a whimper.

Delilah shot both of them a quelling look.

"Angelique. *Really.* And we've books about animals, Dot, so you can discover that rats don't hibernate. The more you know about things, the less frightening they become."

Both Angelique and Delilah knew this wasn't precisely true—sometimes the very opposite was true—but there was some comfort in comforting Dot.

TRISTAN KNEW THAT were he stretched out on his blue counterpane right now instead of in a livery stables, the thud would sound like something the house couldn't quite digest.

Bloody hell. He wondered if the Gardner "sisters" recognized the sound.

Tristan looked up from the tunnel. The faces of his men looked down at him. Eyes tense and alert. They knew better than to shout down at this point. They'd all begun to draw the same conclusions, and who knew how voices would reverberate in the tunnel.

He fished into his pocket and gestured up at them with his lock picks.

So Tristan set to it. Within a few minutes, he got the handle of the door to turn.

He exulted as it rotated in his hand.

But the door didn't open.

He gently leaned his shoulder against it, holding the knob so that the door wouldn't spring back abruptly and thud again.

Damn. It was clearly barred or blocked from behind.

Tristan stood motionless for a moment in that dark pit. If they attempted to break this door down, it would most certainly be heard in the boardinghouse.

He knew what to do next.

"THIS IS WHAT I think happened," he told his men and Mr. Cox when he surfaced. "Derring was either blackmailed into or volunteered to smuggle cigars from Sussex—the contraband was probably stuffed into the bases of the statues. I suspect he volunteered, since he was in debt and he knew he could make a tidy profit. Stone, not marble, statues ordered straight from Sussex for an earl? Innocent as can be. Sounds like just the daft thing he'd buy, anyway, since he was a spendthrift. He may have financed the whole endeavor—paying for the cigars to be brought over and letting the smugglers do the dirty work—or he may have just played a role, seeing it as his way to solvency. I'm willing to wager that someone here at these stables, Mr. Cox, knew about the tunnels—someone who knew precisely where they led—and that's how Derring managed to meet Mr. Garr and his foxy-faced friend."

All the color had fled Cox's face. "Wasn't me, guv, swear on my life."

"We shall see," Tristan said evenly. "I think Derring had the statues brought to The Grand Palace on the Thames, where he could in privacy unload cigars into the tunnels through the entrance in a particular room on a low floor. He then departed again with the statues for his townhouse. The Gardner sisters, if you will, then entered the tunnels through the stables, fetched the cigars, and drove out with them, looking innocent and pretty as you please, or as innocent as those two could ever look. Just a couple of men with a horse and cart filled with hay or some such to hide the boxes, no doubt. They were able to deliver the cigars to merchants who had paid for them and were expecting them. Then the merchants sold them at an exorbitant profit."

"But then Derring died," Massey contributed. "Leaving the Gardner sisters in the lurch, because they couldn't get into the boardinghouse or the tunnels."

"Yes. Leaving the tunnel door barred and locked and cigars still in the tunnel. And they couldn't get into the place during all the renovations, since the place was filled with activity. Perhaps not wanting to call attention to their operation, and perhaps not being particularly murderous by nature, they concocted a plan to get into the place—they spread it around that it was a terrible place to go, and they devised a plan to get the cigars and get out . . . not reckoning that they wouldn't be able to get into that room. At all. And not reckoning that I would be there."

"That's almost funny, sir. Your being there."

"Massey."

"Sorry, sir. They're probably desperate by now," Massey said.

"Yes," Tristan said tersely.

He rifled through scenarios, but they couldn't just go and rip the Gardner sisters from their beds without proof of a crime.

"None of what I've just said has any merit at all unless we catch them in the tunnel. So we need to catch them in the tunnel. And we need to act now."

Chapter Twenty-Four

"Lady Derring Lady Derring Lady Derring . . ."

"Wha . . . *Dot*?"

Delilah had been dreaming. And Dot was whispering. Two inches from her face.

"Shhhh. Captain Hardy is downstairs and he needs to speak to you at once. He told me to fetch you and Mrs. Breedlove, and to be very, very quiet about it."

Delilah absurdly put her hand out and patted Dot's face to ascertain that she was real and that this wasn't part of the dream she'd been having.

Dot's nose was cold, like a little pet's, and it squashed a little.

She glanced at the clock on her mantel. It was half past twelve.

Delilah shot straight up in bed.

"Is he all right?"

That sick terror and ferocity were instant. If he was not all right, she would *make* it so.

If he was not, she thought that she would die.

It was not an epiphany she found welcome at this hour of the morning.

She reeled with it. And then Dot said, "I think so, Lady Derring. He certainly looks quite fine. And he's with about a half-dozen soldiers and he's the one in charge, so I would say so." She paused. "I am less certain about us."

AND AT FIRST she didn't see the soldiers at all, despite the red coats. They were motionless, blending into shadows. And then it was their very alert tension that disturbed the softness of the room. Everything else in it was frayed, or soft, or worn. The soldiers were rigid, spotless, and grim.

Tristan, she saw. Standing like the needle on a compass in the dead center of the room.

"Ladies, please sit down," Tristan said at once. Quietly.

Delilah froze.

"Delilah," Angelique urged, and touched her arm.

They sank onto the settee.

Their hands touched between them. Angelique's were as icy as hers.

"This is Lieutenant Massey." Tristan's voice was scarcely above a whisper. He gestured to a tall, sturdy, dark-haired man. Angelique and Delilah nodded to the lieutenant.

"We apologize for the dramatic nature of this request and the necessity for subterfuge. But Mrs. Breedlove, Lady Derring, we'd like you to inform the Gardner sisters that the room they originally wanted has become available to let, and then to move them into it straight away. First thing tomorrow morning. One simple sentence from you. Then hand them the key."

Delilah stared at him. Surely she was dreaming.

"I . . . don't understand." Angelique was able to speak. In a whisper.

Delilah began. "But . . . I'm afraid we've let that room to . . . but we promised . . . we can't . . ."

"Lady Derring." It felt wrong, suddenly, to hear him call her that. Delilah: he'd claimed her name. Lady Derring was a name that belonged to another woman in another lifetime. "I am the Captain of the King's Blockade and I'm afraid I must insist that you do as I say."

She reared back a little as if he'd thrust a torch into her face.

"For your safety and the safety of your guests, Lady Derring. The Gardner sisters are neither sisters nor women."

There was a silence. Her heart battered at her like it was trying to break free.

"Tristan . . ." Delilah curled her hand into the settee. She felt as though she was falling and falling.

Lieutenant Massey's eyes went wide when he heard the "Tristan."

His head swiveled between Captain Hardy and Delilah.

Tristan's face was unreadable and his eyes were cold as bullets in the shadowy room. All he was in this moment was a commander.

What had Angelique said? Like a rock or a trebuchet.

"Captain Hardy." Angelique was frightened, too, Delilah knew. But her tone was all that was placatory and dulcet. Angelique was a survivor. "You can understand that this building belongs to us, so naturally we are concerned . . . what on earth is happening? Are we under suspicion of a crime?"

Angelique had asked that terrifying question with gracious rationality. And a hint of good humor.

Then again, she hadn't kissed this man's scars a day ago. Or risen sated from his arms, reluctant to let him go, a few hours earlier. She hadn't heard him beg her with her name. She hadn't cracked open his guarded heart, cherished what she found there, never realizing in the process that she'd also cracked open her own and now—well, what had Angelique said? That it rattled around in there like dropped china? That's how it felt.

Waves of emotion swooped through Delilah like attacking birds: fury and helplessness and nauseating betrayal and scorched pride.

She was a *fool*.

Tristan was carefully considering how to answer, which was also terrifying.

"We have ascertained that you and Lady Derring are innocent of involvement in this matter."

"You've . . . *ascertained*?" Delilah repeated. Her voice was raw with incredulity.

Her lips were numb.

There was a little silence.

"Yes." His voice was hoarse. It contained the faintest apology. But only a little.

Her head went back in shock.

His purpose was Duty, after all.

"And I'm afraid I'm not at liberty to tell you the details of our presence here. Not yet. Not until we've completed what we set out to do."

"Because we might still be suspects." She said that with a certain bitter wonder.

"For your own safety. We believe the two of you and all other guests save the Gardners to be guiltless. Your husband was not, Lady Derring."

Her hands began to rise to her face, desperately. No. She would not shield herself from this, and if what she felt showed on her face, she wanted Tristan to see it, too. If anything truly moved him at all.

She gave a soft, ironic laugh. It hurt, terribly, the laugh, as if every one of her vital organs was bruised.

"Oh, now I see. You're *that* Captain Hardy."

She heard him take a sharp breath.

"Always gets his man," Lieutenant Massey whispered proudly.

"Or woman, too, I suppose," Delilah said lightly, slowly. "Is that not so, Captain Hardy?"

She couldn't read his expression. But she could feel tension in him, and in all the soldiers. Drawn back and back, like a trebuchet prepared to launch its ordnance. This was what they were born for.

"We're under orders from the crown, Lady Derring, and as such I am the crown's representative and responsible for all of these men here," Tristan said. "And it is not hyperbole to say that it's a matter of life and death."

"So you *are* aware of the uses of the word *hyperbole*. And just listen to how many words you're using now, Captain Hardy. How many of the ones you said meant a thing?"

"All of them." He said that evenly. As though it were an unadulterated truth, a commandment etched in stone.

She turned away.

She couldn't bear to look at his hard, enigmatic soldier face.

He leaned forward a little.

"I will protect you with my life."

He laid those words down slowly. As though he'd been asked to swear a vow.

She knew it was true. He'd already done it once, hadn't he? Because she'd been just that foolish before: they'd let a strange man into the house at the wrong hour, and he'd attacked her.

That Captain Hardy. That's what that particular man had said. An odd numbness spread through her limbs.

"Will you give me the key to that room, please, Lady Derring?" he asked patiently.

His hand was extended.

Her hands were trembling as she unhooked the keys from her belt and found the right one. It seemed to go on forever, the frantic jingling.

He waited patiently. All those soldiers watched.

She dropped the key into his hand, very careful not to touch his skin.

"Thank you. We shall have soldiers in every empty room of the house," he said. "We will explain the situation to your other guests now and temporarily remove them from the premises for their own safety. Please instruct your staff to avoid that floor tomorrow. For now . . ." he added, standing, "try to sleep."

This last might have been the most ridiculous suggestion she ever heard.

And he turned back to his men abruptly and they clustered in the corner of the room to listen to him, and she wondered if she was already forgotten. She'd been a means to an end, after all.

What else could they do but go back up the stairs, taking care to not make a sound?

"Fox," Angelique muttered, dazed. "Henhouse," as they went up the stairs.

"At least my instincts are good," she muttered a few steps later.

But Delilah said not a word.

"YOU'VE ALWAYS BEEN so kind, Lady Derring," Jane Gardner said to her, the following morning, after breakfast, when she gave the Gardner sisters the good news that they'd be moving into the larger suite. One of Tristan's men had returned the key to her last night after they'd prepared the room for today.

"Yes," Delilah said numbly. "Haven't I?"

She dropped the key into Jane Gardner's hand.

"Thank you," Jane said in that tiny, fluting voice. Delilah suppressed a shudder.

Margaret glanced up from between her lashes. Then glanced down again. "And the food here is *wonderful*," she said almost wistfully.

WHILE HELGA SILENTLY served breakfast to only the Gardner sisters, who were told that everyone else was out, a half-dozen soldiers waited in the livery stables.

Another half dozen were waiting in rooms on the first floor, waiting to pour into Suite Three.

Delilah and Angelique and Dot remained at the top of the stairs, the door closed.

And at eleven o'clock in the morning, a well-fed

Jane Gardner opened up the wardrobe in the room on the first floor, lifted the hatch in its floor, climbed down the ladder, and moments later retrieved one small box from the tunnel.

Massey, down the hatch in the livery stables, watched this retrieval through the keyhole of the door.

And then the person formerly known as Jane Gardner hesitated. Eyed the barred door.

And decided that of course she ought to go back the way she'd come.

When she was lost from view to the shadows, Massey pulled on the doorknob hard and released it.

The thud was a signal.

When she struggled up out of the wardrobe, cap and wig askew, arm triumphantly extending a box of cigars to her "sister" Margaret, she discovered Margaret couldn't quite take it from her.

She was already bound at the wrists and being held fast by two men.

Two soldiers helped her all the way out of the wardrobe, instead, by yanking her up by the armpits.

"I'll just take those," Tristan said.

And reached for the disgusting cigars.

WITHIN A FEW hours Tristan's crew had searched the Gardner "sisters'" rooms and confiscated their belongings (which included an interesting variety of knives and pistols), removed all the cigars from the tunnel through the stables, and arrested a few of the stable workers after some rigorous questioning—seemed a stable boy's grandfather had once worked at the whorehouse and knew of the tunnel. When they'd learned Derring was the owner of the former Palace of Rogues, they'd made him a business proposition he was in no position to refuse. If he hadn't keeled over in White's, he might have actually paid his debts in a few years.

Tristan coerced from their captives a few more names of the gang in Sussex. Officers were already on the road heading to Sussex to nab them.

It seemed the "Gardners" had been under a variety of threats to deliver the cigars to the merchants who'd ordered them, which was part of the reason for the feminine disguises.

And as for the statues, they'd all been unpaid for and returned to the stonemason, who was also arrested.

And thus the Blue Rock gang was decimated.

The soldiers allowed everyone at the boarding-house a very quick peek down the wardrobe.

"Where else does it go?" Delacorte pondered. "I suppose one of us will need to be brave enough to find out."

"I nominate Dot," Angelique said.

Dot looked uncertain. Then forgot her concern instantly in the pleasure of looking at the soldiers.

Delilah didn't want to look down into that tunnel, but she did.

Vertigo struck.

It seemed the Gardner sisters' plan had hinged on Delilah and Angelique being stupid enough—or, more charitably speaking, naive enough, or desperate enough—to let them stay, and to not question their disguises. If they'd been a trifle more murderously inclined or less certain of themselves, they might not be alive to stare down a tunnel.

Men. For God's sake. Was there no end to their perfidy?

What an astonishingly venal thing for Derring to have done at all. And all the while she had smiled at him dutifully across their dining table and asked about his day. But if he'd been in a panic about his debt, if he'd felt any guilt, it hadn't shown. Surely she would have sensed it? Then again, she'd lodged two men wearing dresses.

She couldn't imagine the Gardner sisters had slept a wink when they found out the captain of the blockade was under the same roof. Surely, being smugglers, they'd realized he was *that* Captain Hardy.

He'd been on their trail even before then, however. She supposed it wasn't so much arrogance as accurate reporting when he'd said he was indomitable.

She and Angelique had handed over to Captain Hardy for inspection the token left with them by Mr. X. But as it was the very thing that prevented the smugglers from getting into the room, it was deemed irrelevant to the investigation at hand, until they learned otherwise. Angelique kept it in her night table drawer.

One day all of this would probably seem blackly funny. Probably. After a fashion.

Apart from where Tristan had essentially used her to get the information he needed.

"It seems we're going to need to refine our interview process," Angelique said. "Perhaps include a discussion of current sleeve designs."

She was surprisingly sanguine about it all. Then again, Angelique's life had already been quite eventful.

The admiring eyes of the soldiers had mellowed her

mood somewhat, too. One's heart might rattle about like broken china, but Delilah's hope was like that one ember remaining in a fireplace . . .

The one that could fly up the chimney and set the roof on fire and burn the whole thing down.

Hope, like love, like romance, was a lie, Delilah had decided.

WHILE HIS MEN ferried out cigars and searched the Gardner sisters' room, Tristan dashed off a message to the king, sealed it, and carried it downstairs. He would have one of his men deliver it straight there.

He paused a moment in the foyer and remembered the moment he'd first stood there, looking up at a singing woman. The day was stubbornly gray, but the light through the windows managed to pick out a rainbow or two from the crystals.

"Thank you, Captain Hardy."

He gave a start.

Delilah was alone in the little reception room. He understood clearly now that he'd always been able to feel her when she was in a room. That something in him had lightened when she was near.

But now she seemed nearly crumpled in on herself. She was so still, so lightless, she might as well have been a puppet tossed there.

Her eyes were bitter. Two dark bruises in her face.

And any illusions he might have had about it all being all right in the end dissolved.

He drew in a breath that burned, and a chill raced down his arms. This, then, was what doom felt like. He realized all at once that he was, in truth, frightened, in a way he hadn't been since he was perhaps ten years old. It was an entirely new sensation. Here, at the end of his career, at the moment of one of his greatest triumphs, he sensed he was losing something.

How had he, in the process of being who he was, of doing his duty, never anticipated he might murder himself somehow?

It seemed he did not, in fact, know everything.

He walked toward her slowly.

He sat down across from her on the settee.

Neither said a word for a moment.

"Congratulations, Captain Hardy," she said finally.

"Thank you."

That made her quirk her mouth bitterly.

Neither spoke for a moment.

"I imagine you think I'm ridiculous. Two men in dresses. Smugglers. And I didn't . . . even . . . suspect. You must think I'm the veriest fool."

"Never." His voice was quiet. Hoarse. "You're just naturally kind, Delilah. You want to see the best in people. It's . . . one of the loveliest things about you. You couldn't have predicted potentially murderous smugglers wearing dresses would move in. Nobody could."

He could not now see how it might have been different, unless he'd never touched her at all. That would have been the honorable thing. And yet even now it seemed as though it would be easier to lasso the moon and pull it down from the sky than to do that.

But if she wanted the moon, he would certainly try to get it for her.

"Well." She stirred herself and sat bolt upright

and with a sort of macabre, artificial brightness, and brought her hands together in a little clasp. "Even so, *I* feel a right fool. I thought I was doing so well, you see, here at The Grand Palace on the Thames. That our guests might become a little family. That they were precisely what they said they were despite appearances. I see now that it's a ridiculous dream."

"It's not ridiculous," he said shortly.

"But you knew what they were? The Gardners?"

"I knew fairly quickly something was a bit off. But I could not say precisely what."

She gave a soft laugh again. "Imagine me not knowing what you were after this entire time, Captain Hardy. I suppose it was always right there for me to see. But I was blinded by the glory of you"—she waved a hand—"and flattered, and then of course, seduced. How fortunate that you should find a naive fool like me here at The Grand Palace on the Thames, because you were able to use it to your advantage."

Bloody hell.

"I see now, when I think about it, how cleverly you asked your questions. Well done. Did you laugh at me?"

He was suffering. "Delilah . . . no. I would nev—"

"You thought perhaps I might be a smuggler, didn't you?"

He was silent. There was no safety here. Not in the truth, and not in attempting to skirt the truth. She would know.

"Delilah. I could not be sure," he said as evenly as he could. "Surely you can see that. I cannot afford to make assumptions in the work that I do. If I do, people could die. An entire *family* died because of the Blue

Rock gang. And if they continued to fail to get into that room, I'm fairly certain they would have, of desperation, resorted to violence. They didn't count on how dedicated you were to your guests, whether or not they were actually present. Or the captain of the blockade moving into the boardinghouse and staying."

He could not apologize, and he *would* not apologize, for doing what he'd needed to do. He should not feel shame. But he did; there it was. He couldn't order it away. He could not have known that here, in this boardinghouse near the docks, that the best things about him—his strength and sense of duty and his courage and his belief in justice, the only things he'd known to be true in life, the very things that had given his life meaning—could be the things that broke his own heart.

And the heart of a woman he loved.

A woman who had been a means to an end for people her entire life.

"My work . . . is necessary and difficult and dangerous. It saves lives and I'll get justice for the ones lost."

Surely she was intelligent enough to realize this.

She gave a short, bitter, wondering laugh. Then covered her mouth with her hand. And shook her head dazedly.

"By any means necessary, right, Captain Hardy?"

She continued the inspection of his face, as though she ought to have seen him as not a hero, but an agent of hurt and destruction, just as she ought to have seen the Gardner sisters for what they were.

He could very nearly taste her pain. It was in the air, metallic, like a storm. Or like blood in his mouth.

And now he had gone and done away with the last of her innocence and trust.

"I cannot adequately convey how sorry I am that you are hurt," he said carefully, his voice low, hoarse now. "It was never my intent, and if I could have saved you from that, I would have."

This just won him a look of scorn.

He felt he earned the right not to be afraid. Nothing had prepared him for the fact that love could be stealthier, and more treacherous, than a smuggler.

"I did enjoy our moments together, Captain Hardy, and for that I thank you. And you are indeed a hero, for which I also thank you. I suppose you rather saved me and Angelique from ourselves. I consider this a valuable lesson learned. But . . ."

She stood abruptly. She looked down into his eyes.

". . . it's just as well that I don't love you."

His lungs stopped. As surely as if she'd driven a knife in.

His heart ceased to beat.

She watched him for one second longer, perhaps to make certain that blow had indeed killed, for she would read it in his eyes.

She walked past him and made her way up the stairs.

TRISTAN WAS MOTIONLESS. He wasn't certain he was yet breathing. But his eyes never left her, as if he could will her back with the sheer force of his personality.

She didn't return, of course. Her will was as strong as his.

After some time—he was uncertain how much—he

stood, slowly. Disoriented, as if he'd awakened from a dream to find himself alone in a room that now was precisely the same and yet entirely different. He'd forgotten he was holding, in his hand, a letter to the king.

Finally he moved, slowly, out of the reception room, and paused to stand in the middle of that black-and-white-checked foyer.

Which was when he saw that his belongings were neatly packed and sitting next to the door.

Chapter Twenty-Five

DELILAH MADE it all the way to the top of the stairs, to their little drawing room, where Angelique was mending a pillow that Mr. Delacorte had somehow managed to tear.

If snores could rend fabric, then Mr. Delacorte's room would soon be in tatters.

Delilah paused in the doorway.

Angelique looked up into her face, then laid her mending aside immediately.

Delilah took two steps, sank to the floor, and laid her head against Angelique's knees.

She didn't think she could cry. There was a huge hot, raw place in the center of her being that hurt savagely each time she took a breath. As though Tristan had been crudely excised from her soul. All of her tears had been scorched away.

Angelique, to her credit, did not say *I told you so.* Everything she knew about Delilah and Captain Hardy was only surmise, anyway. But Delilah was hardly an enigma, bless her heart, and unfortunately, to Angelique, men weren't enigmas, either.

But Angelique had seen Captain Hardy's face as he went downstairs.

It wasn't the face of a man whose heart was filled

only with triumph and pride and plans to set sail. He'd understood what he'd done to Delilah. Even if he would not have done anything differently.

And he'd known the cost.

And Angelique's heart ached for the fools who break their own hearts because they simply can't help themselves.

And for herself, who still had a heart to break, apparently, because it ached right now for Delilah, who had learned a terrible lesson. It was so very difficult to save people from themselves. Delilah might not have tears at the moment, but Angelique did. Her eyes burned with them now.

She said not a word.

She hesitated.

Then she stroked Delilah's hair, awkwardly, gently, as though Delilah were Gordon, the cat.

"I ought to have listened to you," Delilah said after a moment. Her voice muffled, as though speaking through layers and layers of misery.

"Oh, now. How dull would things be if you ever listened to me?"

But Delilah felt too stunned and scoured to smile. She understood now that the numbness she'd felt in the wake of Derring's death was merely shock.

This felt more like a death.

And she had just lied to Captain Hardy because she'd wanted to hurt him, and oh, she knew she had. In the heart or the pride, she would never be certain. But she had.

That delicious moment of anesthetizing revenge was fleeting, however.

And now she loathed herself for hurting him as much as she had fiercely loved him.

Loved. She would need to get accustomed to speaking of him in the past tense.

And then she thought of Angelique, who'd had her heart broken and abused more than once. She understood now and ached terribly for her.

"How could you bear it?" she asked Angelique.

Angelique thought about this. "I think there is a difference between a good man who has inadvertently done harm, and a man who seems good, but who takes what he wants because he can, and cares not for the consequences."

But Delilah wasn't ready to hear this, either.

AND SO DELILAH and Angelique and Dot and Helga and Gordon and the maids were left alone with a disconsolate Mr. Delacorte, who saw no reason to ever leave such a comforting, welcoming place as The Grand Palace on the Thames. He missed Captain Hardy. He'd grown quite fond of him, perhaps the way one does of a grumpy old pet.

But he still sat in the drawing room at night, because those indeed were the rules. He'd begun to teach Dot how to play chess, which was perhaps the challenge of a lifetime, for anyone.

Mr. Farraday and Miss Bevan-Clark, having had the adventure of a lifetime and having seen themselves and each other in an entirely different light, left a letter saying they'd eloped to Gretna Green and had taken Miss Wright with them. But that they would be back to visit soon.

Delilah had been badly knocked off her bearings. It was as though she needed to relearn how to do ordinary things, like walking and breathing and speaking. She hadn't known how much joy and hope had altered gravity, the texture of the air, the flavor of foods, her very skin, the things she craved—like his touch. She half wished she could grow a cocoon and retire in there for a bit, not feel her feelings at all while she was transformed into something new and beautiful with no memory of the earlier pain. Everyone understood she was walking wounded, and were very solicitous. But they needed her, too. They counted on her.

And in the wake of scandal, no one knocked at the door of The Grand Palace on the Thames. Certainly no one with roguish tendencies would be tempted to show up at a boardinghouse which had recently, publicly, disgorged a dozen some odd, grim-faced, triumphant soldiers hauling two struggling men wearing dresses.

Nor would any law-abiding citizens knock on the door, for that matter, knowing that smugglers had just been extricated from such a place. If a place was comfortable for smugglers, who else might it be harboring, no matter how shiny the new sign, or how kind the proprietresses?

They'd turned away a few hopefuls looking for the Vicar's Hobby, however.

And not even the mysterious tenant of the room on the first floor with the tunnel appeared. Delilah couldn't decide if he was a hero or villain. If not for him, the Gardner sisters (a John Garr and a Lee Rufkin, they were told) might have gotten away so easily. Then again, perhaps she would have let Captain Hardy into the room sooner, and perhaps he would have found that tunnel, and . . . perhaps they would never have made love at all.

Perhaps perhaps perhaps.

They could survive such a lull in business for a fortnight or so. They could make their usual adjustments: No fires in the downstairs rooms. No beef for dinner. Tallow candles in the sconces.

Perhaps they could survive it even a bit longer than a fortnight.

But when she was out doing the marketing with Helga, Delilah could have sworn she'd seen the Duchess of Brexford's crest on a carriage, out of the corner of her eye.

Here at the *docks*.

Three different times.

Like a vulture circling, she wanted to steal Helga away again from The Grand Palace on the Thames.

And vultures only circle things that are dead or about to die.

"WELL, THAT WAS work well done, sir. It's right proud I am to be part of it, and to serve under you."

They sat across from each other at the Stevens Hotel, breakfast devoured in front of Massey, untouched in front of Tristan.

Massey had found it futile, over the past week, to talk to Captain Hardy.

It was as though the captain couldn't hear a thing.

Massey was worried. They were due to go in person to speak to the king very shortly, something he couldn't wait to tell his grandchildren about, once he and Emily had a slew of children who then had a slew of children. And the king had asked what sort of award Captain Hardy wanted.

All Massey really wanted to do was go home and marry Emily.

"Will you come to our wedding, sir?"

"Yes, Massey. I would be honored." Captain Hardy pushed at the eggs with his fork.

"Will you stand up with me?"

"Certainly. Of course. I would be honored."

Massey, who'd actually been nervous about asking that question, quietly exulted and forgave himself for taking advantage of the captain's obvious distraction, or, more specifically, misery.

Another silence fell.

"Do you regret the end of the excitement, sir?"

"No."

They'd rooted out the entire Blue Rock gang. It was the triumph of his career. Of a lifetime, really.

And yet Tristan felt as hollow as a bell.

"After this, no one is going to want to let a room in the Palace of Rog—"

"It's called The Grand Palace on the Thames, Massey."

"Yes, sir."

But this was what ate at Tristan the most. He was going to leave soon, set sail across the world in his lovely new ship. After Massey's wedding, of course. But how would Delilah survive if no one came to stay at her boardinghouse? She didn't love him. He knew her to be truthful, and surely she'd meant it.

On the way to being a hero, he'd inadvertently crushed her dream.

"Sir . . ."

Tristan looked up at Massey.

"Sir, you ought to go and tell her how you feel."

A long, long silence while Tristan glared at Massey.

Then he released a sigh. He swiped his hands down his face.

"She hates me, Massey. She's stubborn. It wouldn't matter a damn what I said, even if I could get in the door."

"Then maybe you ought to *show* her instead."

Tristan went still.

And then he stared at his lieutenant, a fierce hope and inspiration dawning. "Thank you, Massey."

It was so heartfelt Massey blushed.

"No need to thank me, sir. Just go get your sweetheart."

"LADY DERRING. MRS. Breedlove."

Delilah and Angelique were in the drawing room at the top of the house, and Dot's constrained delivery made them both look up sharply.

"Dot . . . what's the matter? Dot, my dear, are you ill? Sit down at once."

"I can't . . . you must see . . ." Dot was white in the face, but she had a strange, beatific, saintly glow, as if she'd just been visited by a vision.

"She *is* going to faint. Quick, your vinaigrette, Angelique!"

"I'm not," Dot insisted, sounding a little less ethereal and more indignant. "But I can't say what I'm supposed to say because you won't believe me." And her voice took on that solemn, awestruck hush again. "You'll think me a looby, so I cannot say it. You must come down to see for yourself."

"Dot . . ." Delilah's patience was not infinite, and this particular "Dot" contained a warning.

Dot took a breath. "The king is downstairs in the reception room."

Angelique and Delilah exchanged worried glances.

"The king of . . . diamonds?" guessed Delilah gently.

One never knew with Dot.

"Or did you finally beat Mr. Delacorte at chess?" was Angelique's tolerant guess.

"That would involve a queen, Mrs. Breedlove," Dot said loftily. "And I swear upon my life, this is a king. Mr. Delacorte is in his room at present."

They stared, two pairs of eyes fixed in puzzlement, and then the truth began to dawn.

". . . of England," Dot expounded.

And Delilah thought she understood. She stood bolt upright so quickly her mending tumbled from her lap.

"A lot of soldiers, too," Dot added with relish.

Angelique stood more slowly, and straightened out her skirts.

"He said"—and Dot tipped her head back, as if attempting to recall the words verbatim—"a man he holds in high esteem told him The Grand Palace on the Thames was tolerable."

Angelique and Delilah stared at her.

"I already started the tea," Dot said matter-of-factly. "I'll bring it in."

Dot hadn't mentioned that the foyer was milling with attendants and guards, all of whom were bristling with weapons. They, in fact, lined the stairs, forming a phalanx of stern, dutiful faces so deep she couldn't see through to the front door.

They parted, however, to let the three ladies down the stairs.

And Dot all but ran downstairs to the kitchen to get the tea.

Delilah and Angelique moved, in a dreamlike state, into their reception room.

Whereupon they found more guards in more red uniforms. A full half dozen of them, to protect the king from the terrifying ladies of The Grand Palace on the Thames.

And there, on the pale pink brocade settee, surrounded by a full dozen or so armed soldiers, sat the King of England.

He was gloriously corpulent; his clothing was achingly beautiful and sorely taxed to hold him inside. The settee was groaning beneath his weight.

The *King*.

Of England!

They were awestruck. Oh, they knew how everyone spoke of him. He was someone who could not have helped the accident of his birth, much like Tristan. Who had indulged his fancies, spent and loved recklessly and profligately, who had no real hope of becoming beloved by his citizens, because once contempt settled in, it became a habit, she knew, and he made it too easy for his subjects to mock him, and oh, did they ever mock him.

His indulgences had beset his health, and he likely now had few truly comfortable moments.

But he was still the King of England. The ultimate monarch, the living symbol of the country they loved. And Delilah thought anyone anywhere would still know it. It radiated from him, his history, and his majesty. She didn't know how anyone could meet the king and ever have a joke at his expense again.

They curtsied deeply.

"Your majesty," they both breathed. At once.

"We are humbly honored," Angelique all but whispered a moment later.

"Yes," he agreed. "I would imagine you are."

He was flirting. Ever so slightly.

Polite laughter, clearly expected, rippled around the room.

Delilah and Angelique were far too nervous to laugh or even breathe.

"And you are . . ." the king prompted.

"I am Delilah Swanpoole, Lady Derring."

He didn't say a word about the late Earl of Derring. But the king's eyes flickered.

"And I am Mrs. Angelique Breedlove."

He nodded at both of them, his eyes sparkling. "I am enchanted to meet both of you."

The *King of England* was *enchanted* to meet both of them!

The radiant smile Delilah bestowed on him wasn't entirely because he was the King of England. And her eyes were shining with unshed tears, but they weren't just for him. Tristan had asked her to tell him her wildest dream. He had listened. He had made her dream come true.

Everyone went motionless when the king cleared his throat.

"I heard," the king said, in stentorian tones that could easily reach out the open windows, "that The Grand Palace on the Thames is an uncommonly comfortable, welcoming place to stay."

It could not have been more resonant if a herald had blown trumpets.

Perhaps a herald was too much to hope for?

She was certain a crowd had gathered outside, because a crowd always gathered everywhere the royal retinue appeared.

And all those soldiers would probably be only too pleased to spread the word.

They were going to be *awash* in business.

"A certain heroic captain, to whom the crown owes much, and of whom I think highly, told me as such. I find it to be true. I would be happy to stay an entire evening here at The Palace of Ro—"

A courtier leaned over and whispered in his ear.

"The Grand Palace on the Thames," he amended.

The king sounded as though he'd been handed a script.

And one wondered if the king had been here before. Perhaps a few decades earlier.

And dear God in heaven, did he plan to *stay here*?

Was he perhaps the mysterious employer of Mr. X?

Surely not. Surely that person would have more subtlety.

"But I fear I cannot stay at present."

She could not deny a little relief. But she and Angelique did smile at him, with all the radiant warmth in their hearts. After all, in his face, once handsome, now blurred and swollen from excesses, she saw someone who, like everyone else, longed to be loved. Who really hadn't a prayer of getting that sort of love from anyone else, consorting with older mistresses notwithstanding. Who had lost a beloved daughter, casting all of England into mourning, and mourning himself.

And so they did what they did best: they endeavored to make him feel at home.

"It is, most certainly, a comfortable place to stay, your majesty. Would you like a cup of tea?"

Dot had brought it in, the tray rattling and clinking in her hands.

And so it was that Delilah Swanpoole served tea to the king before the Duchess of Brexford did.

He took a sip—after a nearby courtier took a sip, nodded pleasantly, and did not fall to the carpet, writhing in death throes.

"I understand you've a list of rules for people who wish to stay," the king said. "And that you on occasion have musicales."

Thus making all of Delilah's dreams come true.

And as she was fairly certain the Duchess of Brexford was circling outside in her barouche, waiting for an opportunity to speak to Helga alone, her heart soared.

THE KING AND all the various people who'd come along with him stayed for the duration of two sips of tea.

Then he was helped to his feet by four men, and then the lot of them filed out with a good deal of orderly jangling and clomping.

All of them save one.

And so thrumming with the dreamlike thrill of the moment were Delilah and Angelique that they almost didn't notice him standing in the foyer.

Very still.

Very tall.

Hat in hand.

He wasn't in uniform. He wore a black coat that fit him as elegantly as his own skin. His buttons were silver. His boot toes glowed.

They stared at him until comprehension set in.

And then Dot's face went brilliant with delight. "Oh, look, it's Cap—*EEP*!"

Angelique had leaped to her feet, seized Dot by the arm, and tugged her up the stairs at a swift clip, herding her with little pats like a sheepdog herds a lamb.

Delilah sank back down onto the settee.

He came toward her, slowly, each pace measured, as though he feared she'd disappear or would thrust her hand out, finger pointed at the door, and shout "Begone!"

Delilah felt lit like a candle. Every cell of her body seemed to sing a soft hosanna.

"Please don't stand," he said.

She could not have if she tried. Let alone speak.

Imagine a day in which the King of England's visit was the second-best thing to happen.

"May I have permission to speak?"

Something was terribly amiss if Captain Hardy was requesting permission.

But she merely nodded, because she could not possibly speak.

He sat down gingerly across from her on the settee opposite. The one lately occupied by a monarch. The one Captain Hardy had elevated to a throne the day he'd checked into The Grand Palace on the Thames, and still did.

He drew in a breath. Released it slowly.

He leaned toward her. Hands folded on his knees.

"I am sailing out tomorrow if the weather is good. Up to Dover, to see Massey get married. Then off across the sea."

She couldn't say a word. Her heart gave a terrific jolt, as if it had suddenly sprung to life again. If this was the last time she saw him, she would hungrily memorize his face.

"Delilah, I don't know that I would have or could have done anything differently. It seemed as though I was doing the right thing all along, until I realized that I could not know what the right thing was anymore, because I have never before truly been in love, and then suddenly I was."

The brightness that burst inside her was almost unbearable. Like a new star being born. Her lips parted soundlessly. She tried to form his name. She couldn't.

"You once asked me why I wanted you. And what I told you were, in fact, the reasons I love you. The point of you, Delilah, is like the point of . . . the sun. Or a breeze on a spring day. Or a hawthorn, even complete with its thorns. You are funny. And passionate. And clever. You are perfect as you are, and you make the world better simply by being. You are so beautiful that my heart has never quite beat the same way since I saw you. There is no one else like you, of that I am certain, and you know that I am always right."

Her fingers dashed at her eyes, which were inconveniently blurring and obscuring her view of Captain Hardy. She gave a short laugh.

"It takes enormous courage to be kind in the face of so many reasons not to be," he said. "I think that the reason the world contains people like you and people like me is so that I can keep you safe should your kindness land on people who do not deserve it.

"But all of those things do not quite add up to reasons why I love you. So . . . I wrote a poem."

Her mouth dropped open.

It was very likely the last thing on earth she expected to hear. She saw the faintest hint of a smile at her raw shock.

"Somewhere, in the annals of time, these things—poems and that rot—had their purpose. You can buffer a good deal of anguish of feeling with words. It makes them easier to deliver and digest, perhaps. And so I tried. But every word was like a drop of blood squeezed from a wound. I failed. It is a terrible poem. Eleven words was the best I could do. But it is yours. I ask that you read this after I'm gone."

Astonishingly, he laid a sheet of folded foolscap on the table before her.

She stared at it, wordlessly.

Words seemed superfluous in the face of miracles.

And then he stood up slowly, and looked down at her, his eyes burning as if he were branding the image of her onto his soul.

"I will bear the loss of you, Delilah, as I have borne other things. I will bear the fact that you don't love me. But just as we are only born once and only die once, I know I will only love once. And if life is ever unkind to you, I want you to remember that you are loved, and maybe take some comfort from that, even if we are oceans apart. I know that you never again want to be at the mercy of any man. Know that I am at your mercy, now and forever."

He reached into his coat.

And, very gently, laid on the table before her a little paper-wrapped bouquet of daisies.

And while her own eyes were awash in tears, she heard his footsteps across the foyer and the door shutting behind him on its well-oiled hinges.

She couldn't move for what felt like a full minute. What need of words does the sun have?

She gathered the daisies to her and buried her face in them. They received a veritable shower of tears. And then she sniffed and tossed her head and rubbed her eyes, because she wanted to read that poem.

And with shaking hands she unfolded the sheet of foolscap and read, in writing tall and bold as ships' spires, as tall as a man who could easily reach the sconces:

Your eyes
your lips

Your heart
my heart
I am undone

"Oh." The sound escaped her. Pure wonder and pain.

She was, suffice it to say, undone. The foolscap rattled in her fingers and she laid it gently down lest her tears blur the words.

She gave a start when Dot tiptoed in and plucked up the daisies to put in a vase filled with water.

She didn't spill a drop.

Then Delilah looked up and discovered she was surrounded. Everyone had heard him leave and had crept in.

"He *loves* you, Lady Derring," Dot breathed.

"He's a good eater," Helga said.

"I miss him," Delacorte said. "He's funny."

"He can reach all the sconces and open the door at night if you go and get him," said Angelique, not succumbing to romanticism.

Apart from her damp eyes.

Delilah rose. "Dot . . . come upstairs with me. I will need my pelisse. And I need your help with something else I want to do first."

Ten minutes later Delilah was out the door.

Running. Alone.

And so buoyant she didn't even care that someone had written "The Palace of Rogues" in the dust on the window.

THE *ZEPHYR* WAS the first thing of true substance and weight Tristan had owned, and any man would be proud. It would be his home from now on, that, and the sea. Though now he knew it wasn't, of course, *Home*, with a capital *H*. *That* Home, he understood now, looked like worn settees and soft carpets and a flower in a vase on a desk; sounded like creaks and groans in the night, and the thundering of little cat feet in hallways; tasted like Helga's cooking and Delilah's lips; felt like Delilah's silken hair and arms.

He had said what needed to be said; it was now up to her. He wasn't certain whether what he felt was hope, but some terrible burden had lifted from his heart. He knew now, that no matter what she did or decided, she would be well.

He was preparing to row out when something, suddenly, made him turn.

His heart stopped.

Delilah stood on the edge of the dock, the wind lashing her skirts and hair about.

She was wearing a green dress and she was as vivid against the blue sky as a sail.

She'd cast off mourning.

Which is precisely what his heart did in that moment. And his heart felt like the sail on the fastest, sweetest cutter of all.

In case he was hallucinating—not that he'd ever dare taste any of Delacorte's wares—he walked slowly, slowly toward her, fighting the wind. If she was a vision, he wanted it to last as long as possible.

Her eyes were filled with tears, but her face was filled with light.

"I cannot bear the loss of *you*," she said. She dashed at her eyes with a knuckle.

"And I cannot bear thinking of you needing to *bear* anything. When you could be where you are wanted and loved."

He didn't dare come closer.

Not yet.

"I never told you why I wanted you, Tristan. Because the reasons that I want you are the reasons that I love you."

He scarcely dared breathe.

"I was afraid to say them aloud because I was so afraid to be hurt. Or to lose you. And then it seemed my fears came to pass. And so I lashed out. And I lied. Because I love you."

He took another step closer. Only one. His impulse was to make this easier for her, but she needed to do this for herself.

"I love you because here you are standing patiently, and you are waiting for me to speak because you *want* to hear what I have to say because what I say and think matters to you. Because you have a tender heart, whether you know it or not, and a magnificently tough hide. Because your soul is fathoms deep and you speak in poetry and you don't even know it. And you're so *sure* of yourself, which is maddening, but also such a relief because I have never known anyone so strong. I don't want to need you, but I do. I do. You make everything better. And I don't have a poem. But I love you."

Those were the words.

The ones that opened an Aladdin's cave of riches.

He was moving toward her now, as one moves toward light and air.

"I will make you happy, Tristan," she vowed. Her voice broken. She was weeping now. "If only you'll stay. Please don't leave. Please don't leave. Please don't leav—"

He took a liberty: pulled her up against his body and stopped her words with a kiss.

He wrapped her tightly so she could feel safe. So she could feel every bit of his strength and know he was hers.

She clung to him.

And then he kissed her again, because she was Home and she was his.

Slowly, as though they both had all the time in the world.

He closed his eyes and did what he'd longed to do in the hall the day he'd first kissed her: he rested his cheek on the top of her head.

Epilogue

One month later . . .

"It is exactly as you described, sir," Massey breathed, in pleasure.

He rotated in a slow circle in the drawing room at The Grand Palace on the Thames, taking in the worn settees and comfortable mismatched chairs filled with laughing people, the thick old rug that all but hugged one's feet, the fire leaping in the fine old fireplace, before he abruptly, reflexively—the way he probably would the rest of his life—stopped to admire Mrs. Emily Massey sitting beside Mrs. Lucinda Farraday on the settee. Emily was radiant in a marigold silk, one of the things he'd bought for her with his share of the Blue Rock gang reward money. Emily was grateful for such a lovely dress, she'd told him, but all she really wanted was him.

"I ask you!" he'd said, awestruck, when he told Captain Hardy what she'd said. "Is any man luckier?"

Tristan was no more comfortable with sticky sentiment than he'd ever been. Happiness had made him no more verbose or more patient with fools. He wouldn't debate the finer points of luck, given that he was certain *he* was the luckiest man alive.

"You are lucky indeed, Massey," he'd told him.

They were toasting three weddings with champagne, and singing and pianoforte music was threatened.

Or rather, imminent.

Doubtless he'd be impressed into singing. If it made Delilah's face light up with pride and pleasure, well, he supposed he'd make that sacrifice.

He stood with Massey in the window through which a rectangle of twilight shone, but he found himself shifting places in the room, subtly, almost unconsciously, like a weathervane responding to a breeze, so Mrs. Delilah Hardy would be his view anytime he turned as she moved from guest to guest.

She glowed like a jewel in garnet silk, her hair caught up high on her head, soft tendrils spilling down along the places she liked best to be kissed, her throat, her ears, the places that made her sigh in surrender. Tonight, in their room at the top of the stairs, he would make her do just that. He was confident that as the years passed they'd discover new ways to make each other sigh. Just as every day she seemed to uncover new places in his heart, and he found even more reasons to love her. Marriage, so far, wasn't far different from exploring new countries, and learning a new language.

Mrs. Hardy, who was sitting alongside Mrs. Pariseau, a new guest at The Grand Palace on the Thames, and Mrs. Breedlove, gave him a little sideways glance and a secret half smile. When she looked away again a blush spilled into her cheeks, as if she knew precisely what he was thinking.

And as for sailing to new countries, he'd hired a competent captain to make the merchant runs for him in the *Zephyr*, and he'd spent quite a few satisfying days planning and coordinating their first voyage to India. One day *he* would captain a voyage, and perhaps even take his wife. For now, he was savoring the wonder of having a permanent home, albeit one with a rotating cast of characters, a soft bed, a cat, and a future involving putting the candles into sconces and fetching things from high shelves.

Mr. Delacorte and Mr. Farraday were shouting with laughter with Mr. Cassidy over in the corner. Cassidy's crooked smile and affable, irreverent American charm had gotten him past his initial interview at The Grand Palace on the Thames, but he also had a certain subtle steeliness, a secret determination, that perhaps only Tristan had noticed. He recognized the same quality in himself. He would bear watching.

So far, of the tide of potential guests that ensued when word got out of the king's visit, the ladies had made a few interesting choices. Mrs. Pariseau, a widow by way of Ireland and Italy, could tell fortunes with cards, Delilah had whispered in confidence.

Tristan had rolled his eyes.

She was soulful and kind and dryly witty, and everyone quite liked her.

Delacorte bellowed, "Shall we have music?"

A delighted outcry from all of the females present confirmed that, yes, they most certainly would have music. And under cover of the happy squabbling that ensued over who would play first, and what they ought to play, Angelique took the opportunity to slip from the room. Ostensibly to look for Dot, who had been sent to fetch some of the little lemon seed cakes Helga had made, and hadn't yet returned. But mainly to breathe air, for a moment, that wasn't also being breathed by three couples ecstatic to be coupled—Mr. and Mrs. Farraday, who had stopped in for the celebration, Mr. and Mrs. Hardy, and Mr. and Mrs. Massey.

She'd settled astonishingly easily into this life, which wasn't precisely easy, but was filled with joy, laughter, work, and unlikely friendship. For the first time in her life her days had a rhythm and a consistency that wasn't *fraught*. She didn't at all begrudge the happiness surrounding her; it created a balmy climate of optimism. It was just that part of her was convinced that such happiness could not be sustained at such a pitch, any more than a soprano could hold a pure high note forever. And didn't a sustained high note ultimately shatter glass? She liked Captain Hardy; she believed he was a genuinely good, occasionally even amusing, person. But he was not an easy man, and Delilah was no milquetoast.

Angelique smiled and to amuse herself, she gave a little exaggerated, delicious shiver of relief. *She* was the lucky one. She was tremendously relieved to be inured to the complications of men. She'd learned her lessons early on, thankfully, and apart from enjoying the occasional admiring glance—she was human, after all—nothing could persuade her to do more than that.

And Angelique knew she was liked and would be missed should she stay away for more than a few minutes. For a brief second, she felt as though she were a ghost, looking on.

They'd had the happy burden of sorting through a dozen or more potential guests in the past eventful month, including aristocrats who had no excuse to be there other than curiosity and gossip, given that the king had graced them with a visit. Delilah and Angelique were unmoved by titles. Who would be an amusing dinner companion? Who needed comfort and a safe home? Who intrigued them? Their criteria were as shifting as the light through the windows, but they were always in agreement.

She gave a start when Dot came up behind her, eyes dancing, hands wringing urgently.

"Oh, Mrs. Breedlove, I went to fetch the cakes as you asked, but I've let a man into the drawing room. It's getting late, you see, and no one heard him knock over all the laughing and singing. Will you go and speak to him?"

Angelique stifled a sigh.

"What sort of man, Dot?"

Dot took a breath. Curiously, she hesitated. "The sort . . ." She gave up. "I think, that no matter what you and Mrs. Hardy decide, I don't think I shall ever forget seeing him."

Well, then.

It was difficult to tell whether Dot would *cherish* this memory or not. Her eyes were worried.

Angelique sighed aloud this time. "Will you bring in some tea?"

She glanced back toward the drawing room. Delilah was standing next to the pianoforte. Her mouth was wide open and she was singing happily.

Well, if she was needed, Angelique would go and

get her. She strode toward the reception room, confident she looked both stunning and every inch a lady who brooked no nonsense in her simply cut, burnished, pale gold silk.

He was facing the hearth, one knee indolently bent, hands outstretched before the fire, perhaps for the pleasure of watching the flames nick glints from a heavy signet ring. Tall. Lean. Hair a little longer than fashionable, and black. She whisked him with a glance more expert than the king's valet's and discerned that his coat was expertly cut and expertly tended. A magnificent greatcoat had been shed and was lying on the opposite settee. His cravat billowed.

"Good evening, sir. I'm Mrs. Angelique Br . . ."

The words snagged in her throat.

Surely only gypsies, or possibly wizards, possessed eyes like those. A crystalline gray-green. Amused. Perhaps a trifle jaded.

He took her in. And those eyes went smoky. His expression changed only subtly, but his conclusion was eloquent and the smolder in those eyes was all for her. Angelique, who, by her recollection, hadn't blushed in at least a decade, flushed from her head to her toes.

He stretched out his hand as if he intended to cast a spell.

His voice was smoke edged, too. "I think you have something that belongs to me."

He uncurled his fingers, and in his palm lay the other half of the token.

Acknowledgments

MY GRATITUDE to my editor, May Chen, for her insight, enthusiasm, and inimitable wit; to Avon's hardworking staff for the gorgeous cover and for everything they do to get this book into the hands of readers; to my agent, Steve Axelrod, and his brilliant staff, just because; and to all the lovely readers who wrote to tell me how much they're looking forward to the new series.

The next sparkling romance in

Julie Anne Long's

THE PALACE OF ROGUES

series is coming Fall 2019!

Angel in a Devil's Arms